THE LAST
KID LEFT

THE LAST
KID LEFT

ROSECRANS BALDWIN

MCD

FARRAR, STRAUS AND GIROUX

NEW YORK

MCD
Farrar, Straus and Giroux
18 West 18th Street, New York 10011

Library of Congress Cataloging-in-Publication Data
Names: Baldwin, Rosecrans, author.
Title: The last kid left / Rosecrans Baldwin.
Description: First edition. | New York : MCD / Farrar, Straus and Giroux, 2017.
Identifiers: LCCN 2016059403 | ISBN 9780374298562 (hardcover) |
   ISBN 9780374713010 (e-book)
Subjects: BISAC: FICTION / Literary.
Classification: LCC PS3602.A595446 L37 2017 | DDC 813/.6—dc23
LC record available at https://lccn.loc.gov/2016059403

Designed by Jonathan D. Lippincott

Our books may be purchased in bulk for promotional, educational, or business use.
Please contact your local bookseller or the Macmillan Corporate and Premium Sales
Department at 1-800-221-7945, extension 5442, or by e-mail at
MacmillanSpecialMarkets@macmillan.com.

www.fsgbooks.com
www.twitter.com/fsgbooks • www.facebook.com/fsgbooks

1   3   5   7   9   10   8   6   4   2

FOR G/C/M/C

When we are broken, to whom are we opened?

— Karen Solie, "I Let Love In"

THE COWGIRL COMES TO THE FEAST

Nick Toussaint Jr. clutches a handle of tequila by the neck. A pair of Range Rovers wing around him, playing tag in the rain.

An orange moon hangs slightly low over New Jersey.

He mashes the gas pedal. A surge of acceleration fills the hollow in his gut.

Two bodies lie still in the back.

■

Halfway up the mountain, inside a farmhouse built when New Hampshire was still agrarian, before Claymore became a beach town for motorcycle clubs, Emily Portis stares into the yellowness of her sheet, presses her ankles against each other, holds her hands balled into her abdomen, because she's ruined everything and now there's nothing she can do.

Outside, the chickens don't cackle or make their scritch-scratch sounds.

Father calls up from the kitchen about something she's done wrong, his voice enters through her skin. Her left cheek twitches. Little things she feels with vivid precision. Emily holds her eyes open bravely and turns on her side.

Two nights ago with Nick there was a bright silver bridge.

Now he's gone.

■

Eagle Mount is a secluded New Jersey community of nineteen thousand people, two yacht clubs, an osteopathic training school, a Bridgettine convent, and the award-winning roses of the Fairmont Casino Gardens. You can smell the roses nearly anywhere you stand.

Not one resident of Eagle Mount can be said to be completely unhappy. Everywhere there are vistas, tidy homes with widow's walks. Breezes untangle, rather than snarl, the little girls' hair. By nature the town is on the lookout for bad omens, hurricanes, carpetbaggers, the Norwegian cruise ships of ruin. How much fuller is happiness when it doesn't need to be observed?

Shouldn't we all live in such a way that we can say whatever's on our mind?

Saturday night, the touchiest business at the Selectmen's meeting is the news that teenagers are drag racing near the beach. The neighbors are upset, as are a colony of piping plovers safeguarded by environmental statutes. But the laws aren't clear about enforcement. People are confused as to what they can do. And so it falls to Martin Krug, chief of the Eagle Mount Police Department, to calm the room.

In his own way, Martin embodies the positive image that the Selectmen have acquired about their community during his tenure. He is their familiar: unassuming, stable, easy to sell as one of the Shore's model citizens. They listen to his plan. They'll miss him when he's gone. When Martin's finished, the agenda is reviewed, the minutes are approved, and everyone walks out to their cars untroubled, into the sort of prelude that only a community like Eagle Mount can impart.

As soon as a person asks himself or herself, *How can I live my life in the best possible way?* are not all other questions answered?

Martin climbs into his department-issued truck, a Dodge Durango, one of the few cars that fit him, and drives his aching back across town to the Eagle Mount Arts Center, new as of October.

Some of the center's windows are opaque, some are blue. During the day, they appear to be part of the sky. At night the classrooms glow white as if filled with fog.

He parks, cuts the engine, leaves the windows rolled up—he can't stand the smell of the goddamn roses—and waits for the appearance of his cheating wife.

∎

The Mexican border is thirty-eight hours going sixty, thirty if Nick goes eighty. That assumes he doesn't get stopped by the police.

He presses the accelerator and sips tequila so that his father will reappear.

When he was eight years old he cow-tipped his dad as a joke. Christmas morning, a white Christmas, Nick shoved his dad and the old man fell over backward, laughing. He windmilled his arms and landed in the kindling bucket. On his way back up, he pressed his hand on the chimney plate. He shrieked a second later, they all heard it. When he ran his hand under the tap, his palm erupted with tiny white bubbles. It made Nick sick to watch.

He drops the tequila. It's not out of vengeance, it's from fatigue. The bottle splats on the parkway. His eyelids sag like they're filled with water. He scratches a cut in the corner of his mouth and thinks agonizingly of *her*.

And how two people equal the smell of two people, the smell of two dead people.

Up ahead is a great pink something.

∎

Two nights earlier, they laid crumpled together. She touched a cut in the corner of his mouth, from where she bit him. He smiled in his sleep.

Twenty minutes later, she was still awake, by herself, darkly alone.

But she hadn't planned what came next, when Nick woke up and the secret quivered in her chest, and she'd opened her big stupid mouth.

∎

Even at fifty-nine, Martin dislikes his largeness, he wishes he were more average. To purchase sneakers is nearly impossible. Age hasn't made him any prettier, and still his great curse is vanity. He passes a mirror, he can't help but look. His face is tawny, with thick skin like an orange's. At his wife's hair salon, he picks up magazines and studies how the movie stars wear their clothes. He wishes he had such compact proportions.

Martin watches the Arts Center from a scrunched position. The front doors slide open. Out walks a pair of older ladies in navy blue, followed a few seconds later by Lillian, his wife, who looks fantastic, of course, as she pulls on her tan coat. Who does so many things to stay in

5

shape, plenty fit for those yoga pants, more than lovely enough in all cases.

But if more than enough, perhaps too much for one man.

A flimsy rain falls in the dark. The laptop in the car is equipped with a satellite connection. A quick search gets him to a website for a medical practice in Chesilhurst. His eyes jump to a status feed for @DrKimFeet.

Surgery Friday: 3 hammertoes, 1 radio frequency neuroma, 5 nails, 2 surgery centers, 1 office. & now art class. #Tired #Podiatrist

Martin looks up as the teacher exits the building. Dr. Youngsu Kim, podiatrist, part-time art instructor. Lillian smiles impassively despite the drizzle, laughs politely at something said, and it's her false laugh he hears, he knows a stage performance when he sees one. Even from a woman amply guarded, tricky for any man to predict, let alone her husband of six years.

She pauses on the walkway, in a dark patch.

The women keep going.

The doctor catches up.

She says a little something, an aside, below the breath. Slow eyes meet as they both turn in the same direction, down the sidewalk, every gesture mundane, magnetically aligned.

Martin's chest clenches, his lower back throbs.

The woman he loves.

He was married previously. A bad marriage. His ex-wife now lives outside Seattle, she manages a consignment boutique. Their daughter, Camille, is in Southern California, twenty-seven. Forever in one graduate school after another, that Martin pays for. Who else will? But he rarely sees or hears from her, he doesn't blame her. She was seventeen when he and her mother separated. In seventeen years she never had a dad who wasn't drunk, one way or another.

But ever since he quit drinking, ever since he took the job in Eagle Mount and met Lillian at a meeting two weeks after he arrived, his focus has been on the here and now. Career. Sobriety. Marriage. The present moment. The gut-burning present moment.

■

A pink neon cowgirl, at least a hundred feet tall, stands beside the parkway and waves a pistol the size of a sedan. In her other hand is a neon dinner menu, ten feet high, that reads EAT AT THE RANCHO NEXT EXIT, and underneath it, THE COWGIRL COMES TO THE FEAST.

Except she also points her big pink gun at the passing cars, so it's more like, *Hey Asshole Eat Dinner or I'll Shoot.*

Nick closes his eyes, lulled by the radio and the swish of traffic, before he remembers, *I'll kill her without a second thought.*

He snaps to attention and whips around in his seat.

■

Parkway southbound, exit 119 after the underpass, all available units, possible 11-80. Caller reports, black SUV, Ford Explorer, off the embankment. It hit the cowgirl.

When people do know Eagle Mount, outside the rose-gardening community, it's for the cowgirl. Even where Martin's parked, the stupid thing's visible through the glass. He squeezes the radio, calls himself en route, hunches even farther down, in case Lillian should notice.

Thirty-eight, update Captain Krug on EMS, ETA?

Two minutes later, Martin is first on scene. He jumps out of the car and runs down a sharp grade of sucking mud. The Ford Explorer crashed into the cowgirl's left boot. From which hangs the rib cage of the car's grille. A bulge of airbag fills the driver-side window, quickly deflating. A boy's at the wheel, nose smashed and bloody.

Just crossing Market Street.

Powder's in the air. The airbag must've deployed in the last two or three minutes.

"Hey kid, wake up!"

Ten-four, 38.

"Kid, stay with me." He reaches in, twists the key. "Listen to me! Anybody else in here? What hurts? Kid!"

He looks into the Explorer and tries the back door. Locked.

The boy mumbles something.

"What? Say it again."

The kid, drunkenly nonchalant, "They're in the *back.*"

Far away, a siren. Martin frantically presses buttons on the door panel until the locks click. He yanks open the left back door. There's a woman in the footwell, in an eggshell-colored nightgown. Underneath her, like dirty snowmelt, a gray bathrobe is dyed darkly, soaked in brown blood.

He flinches when he sees the woman's face, a smear of white. Her top lip's gone. The nose is broken, flattened by something much, much harder.

Have Memorial stand by.

Ten-four, Memorial notified.

He thinks, but the kid said "they" . . .

One twenty-five, what traffic personnel do you have?

He pops the gate. Inside is a large man splayed out. Like an animal killed on a hunting trip. Big guy, big hands. Late sixties? Khaki pants and a button-down shirt. Eyeballs rolled back, tie loosened, shirtfront paisley with blood.

Approaching the underpass now.

Martin tries for a pulse.

▪

Nick Toussaint Jr., of Claymore, New Hampshire, sleeps almost the full morning handcuffed to a hospital bed. No middle name, Caucasian, twenty years old, five-six, 137 pounds. Organ donor. Face bandaged from the banged-up nose.

It's a quiet Sunday. Leaden clouds, no rain. Martin is fresh from the station. He leaves the hospital room and gets updated by the officer posted at the door: The kid grinds his teeth in his sleep, that's it.

He departs to go find coffee number five and rides the elevator down to the cafeteria, where he spies a tower of Honey Buns. His archnemesis.

On a good day, Martin Krug can still touch his toes. He hasn't had a drink or cigarette in seven years. Ever since he had a heart attack, he's been a vegetarian, and mostly does the stuff you're supposed to do, like quit Honey Buns. He plays racquetball, he's one of those guys now, he still can't quite buy it. He refuses to give up other pleasures. The nightly ice cream. Medieval war games on his computer. Biographies in hardcover that he plans to read someday.

Especially off the job, Martin keeps to himself. At dinner parties, thanks to his profession, people are disinclined to ask him any complicated questions, but treat him, his great size a further inducement, like an enormous child. Lillian's more outgoing, hot-blooded. The mirror opposite of his first wife. By day an interior designer, at night she swings kettlebells, climbs rock-climbing walls. Also an alcoholic in recovery, but her drinking days were over before she was twenty-five, and does he begrudge her that? Does his begrudgement earn her indulgences? She thinks so.

Rarely, if ever, is Lillian in distress. Oddly, those times she is are when she's most lovable to him, more human. More like himself. They can sit on the tasseled couch in the TV room and walk through their days. But mainly she's overconfident, bossy. Attributes that intrigued him from the start. And when she projects her affirmations across dining tables that seat twelve, in the Ermenegildo Zegna jackets that she buys him, that he loves that she buys him, Martin grins and hunches his shoulders to make the others feel more comfortable, to make himself resemble a piece of furniture under a cloth.

He purchases a Honey Bun and mauls it over a trash can, crumbs flying, and instantly wants another one, wants restored all of his old vices.

His belt vibrates with a text from upstairs.

kids talking

■

The boy watches him like a shelter dog. Courage to conceal fear. Martin pinholes his lips and blows on his coffee, exhales through the same place where he used to stick a cigarette, then inhales likewise. But plain air is never nicotine.

"What are you," the kid says, "the big boss?"

In fact, his retirement is only two weeks away. Everyone asks what he'll do with his time. Finally, he figured it out: he'll resume smoking.

"I want a pen," the kid says. "I want a piece of paper."

They already did his rights. They took away his clothes. Dirty jeans, old T-shirt, a denim jacket with an air of poverty about it, a pair of suede boots with what look to be bloodstains on one toe. The kid's not ugly, Martin decides, just undersized, kind of stringy, with bloodless lips, black hair that's long enough to tuck behind his ears, peaked cheekbones like a girl. Feet and hands small and scuffed. Light blue eyes. The kind of guy the girls go crazy to rehabilitate. Though frightened about something.

Martin thinks about the dead. He waits before he says anything. Always better to let them play first, let your presence fill the room.

The kid just gnaws skin off his fingers and spits it out.

"What do you want the paper for?" Martin asks.

"I want something to eat."

"They've got Honey Buns."

"I killed those people," the kid says. "I want to write it down."

"Great. What's the rush? You need to go somewhere?"

"Shit, can I have some paper already?"

After a minute, the officer outside arrives with paper. He sends her out again, this time for a Honey Bun. He hands the paper to the kid, plus his favorite pen.

Nick writes for ten minutes before his hand cramps.

"Eat up," Martin commands, and passes the Honey Bun. "After that, we'll read."

"I'm finished. You read it."

Martin puts on his reading glasses. "To whom it may concern," he says slowly. "My name is Nick Toussaint Jr. I live in Claymore, New Hampshire. I'm the one who killed Dr. Ashburn and his wife. The reason was money. The Ashburns were supposed to keep a lot of money around the house. Dr. Ashburn used to help me with my knee. It was on Friday. I had my dad's old gun."

They'd already searched the kid's SUV. No surprises, no weapons, no drugs, only the residue of bodies. No money.

The kid licks icing off his fingers.

The door opens, a young Latina nurse tries to interrupt.

Martin scares her away, and sits down in the visitor's chair.

"But they didn't have any money in the safe," he continues, "just their passports, so I stabbed him in the hallway. So Mrs. Ashburn would tell me where they keep the money. But she said the same thing. Dr. Ashburn died. I only stabbed him because I wanted her to talk. She said she had a couple hundred bucks in their blizzard kit. So I had to kill her because I had no other choice, to say the least. I got a shovel to dig the graves and hide their identities. I couldn't find a good place so I started driving to go find one. I don't remember much after that. I probably went crazy or else I'm crazy now. I'm really really sorry. I'm really sad and I will be forever."

Martin balances the papers on his knee.

That morning, in the ash of dawn, he'd woken up from a dream about Lillian. She wore the dead woman's mouth, exaggerated like a cartoon, but without any lips, just a hole. And in the dream he'd stood there and slid his penis back and forth over the empty space.

He's repulsed by the memory. "So, you're crazy," he says, too aggressively.

"What?"

"We've got a lot to go over here."

"Whatever."

"How about we start with the gun."

"I said, it was my dad's."

"So what happened to it?"

"I threw it away. Off a bridge."

"Did you use it for anything? You say you 'stabbed' the doctor with it."

"What? Of course not. I had a knife."

"Okay. Now we're getting somewhere. So you had two weapons. Is that what you're saying?"

"That's what I wrote, isn't it?"

"Well, you wrote you had your dad's gun. So a gun *and* a knife."

"Yeah. My dad's old hunting knife. It's a Puma."

"It's a Puma. Does your dad have a lot of weapons?"

"What?"

"Where's the knife now?"

"I chucked it."

"Mr. Toussaint, are you a wrestling fan, professional wrestling?"

"No."

"It's a hoax. It's theater. Everyone knows it. But the weird thing is, no one talks about it, even though the whole thing's a sham. Where'd you get the shovel from? Also, why the money? What's the money for?"

He checks to see if there's more coffee in his cup—and without looking up he feels the kid's stare adjust. That he's registered the questions as rhetorical and doesn't know what will happen next. Smart kid.

"You were going to rob them," he says, more quietly. "So the Ashburns are known to have a lot of money around the house?"

"That's what I wrote."

"You say they've got a safe."

"They do. They're rich."

"Did," he says. "They did have a safe."

"What?"

"You murdered them. That's what you're saying."

"So, they had a safe," he continues. "They kept a lot of money around. Because he's a doctor, and doctors are rich."

"Exactly."

"So, like how much money?"

"I don't know. Like ten thousand. That's what everybody said."

"People said. How would they say it? 'Hey, everybody, the Ashburns have ten thousand bucks lying around in cash.' Come on."

"What?"

"There's no one else to rob? In a beach town? Isn't Claymore full of tourists?"

"So?"

The idea is that you want to dribble out the facts, a few at a time, so they can't know how much you know.

"Well, that means a lot of cash businesses. T-shirts. Knickknacks. Bars, restaurants. A lot of cash floating around."

"What's your point?"

He thinks of the woman's face. Her missing lip.

He says quietly, to control his anger, "Nick, are you employed?"

"I work in a tire shop. I do pizza delivery."

"I'll assume that's two different jobs. Do you like your work?"

"Man, what the hell is this about?"

"What it's about, you piece of shit, is the fact that we found two dead people in your car."

His voice booms. It echoes in the room. The kid looks terrified.

"So this is me asking you questions," he says, more quietly. "Such as, why do you need ten thousand dollars? Of all people, with two jobs?"

"I've got responsibilities," Nick says, a beat behind the fear.

"Okay. Good. Now we're getting somewhere."

The kid tries to clasp his hands together, but the left one's cuffed to the bed.

"Can you take these off, please?"

"Do me a favor," Martin says. "Look at my hand."

The boy resists.

"Look at my hand! Now, count for me out loud. How many fingers am I holding up?"

"Two."

"Two. Meaning one finger for each question you're about to answer. Now, before you say anything, I'm going to get another coffee. So I want

12

you to listen, right now, then I want you to think really hard. That way, when I come back, you can answer my questions perfectly, you understand?"

He pulls out an envelope. They found it in the kid's jacket. Addressed to one Nick Toussaint, at the same address on his driver's license, 108 Oak Hill Road, Claymore, NH. Envelope still sealed.

The kid strains forward, furious all of a sudden.

"That's mine."

"You think I care?"

The handwriting is female. No return address.

Martin taps his ear with the envelope. "So here we go. Question one, what'd you need the money for?"

"That's my letter!"

"Question two, you're going to tell me a little bit more about the doctor. Like, something simple: How does the doctor get into the back of your truck? You killed him in the house, you said. Dead on the floor. Big guy, no gun blast. You got him with the knife, the Puma, it was your dad's. Nick, look at you. You're no weightlifter. You're not even a wrestling fan. How does the doctor get into the trunk? How does his big body get into the back of your Explorer? So that's question two. I'll leave you to it."

The kid's about to say something. Martin walks out. Staircase, coffee, staircase. Ten minutes.

"I'm finished," the kid announces as soon as he returns.

"Finished with what?"

"I want a lawyer."

"Well, I should hope so."

"What does that mean?"

"You're a little guy, Nick. You need help. No offense. Most people do. Personally, I'm big enough I can muscle guys, but you're the kind who gets by on his smarts. Am I right?"

"Whatever."

"It's a math question. The medical examiner told me Dr. Ashburn weighs two-forty. I asked her again, just this morning, to confirm it. Two hundred and forty pounds. You see what I mean? Let's say you're one-forty. I'll give you one-fifty by dessert. Even then you're not lifting him. So who puts him in the truck? Mrs. Ashburn? Does the wife carry him out? On the night she's the most scared she's been in her entire life? Even if it's adrenaline, this woman—who's a hundred and eight fucking pounds—who helps you drag out her dead husband and hoist up his remains—is that what you're telling me? This woman whose face now is so badly smashed up, along with her husband's, that it looks like someone ran them over with a dump truck, and you've got the balls to tell me you did that with a shovel? And shortly after that you can't even do arithmetic? Is that what you're trying to tell me? How stupid do you think I am?"

Another nurse opens the door.

.

In the hours that follow the Cowgirl Crash, as it's called, Martin works the phone from his desk and eventually reaches the Sheriff's Department of Claymore County, New Hampshire, in the county seat, just a short ways north of Boston. But they've got no communications officer, simply a lady who says, in fact, a man *had* gone missing in Claymore recently. Two people, Dr. Nathan Ashburn and his wife.

"He's a popular physician."

"Tell me."

"He makes house calls. You don't see that a lot anymore."

By lunchtime, New Hampshire files a request for rapid extradition. Three faxes later, the sheriff will arrive Monday, to escort Nick home. Normally Martin's disinclined to a handoff, but they've established that the killings were committed elsewhere. New Hampshire will get the case no matter what. Also, his budget still aches from the cleanup for Hurricane Sandy. They're a tiny department. Twenty-six sworn officers, seven traffic agents, five civilians, eight patrol cars. They're better equipped to handle welfare checks than homicides. He'll consent to stand down.

But that doesn't mean he likes it.

Monday morning, a storm hits. At seven it's still dark out, then grows darker, as if the morning decided to run backward. Martin wakes up in his office. He'd spent the night on the couch, a piece of crap, the threshold between living and dead matter. Probably not the best thing for his lower back. Not that he sleeps much anymore. He makes coffee. The pot's not even done when the power goes out. Almost half of Eagle Mount is in the dark. The ocean waves bulge and swell while the storm does what it likes, plows the beaches, slashes trees, braids power lines around their junction boxes. Rain hammers the streets so hard the newsman insists that Sandy's back, and Martin has to deploy nearly a third of his staff on traffic duty.

At one-fifteen, the sheriff from New Hampshire arrives in civilian clothes. Blue jeans, muddy boots, a tan shirt. Can't be more than fifty, Martin thinks, with hair that thick, like brush bristles. A man who doesn't look at all unnerved by the rain.

"Granville Portis."

"Sorry about the weather," Martin says, and shakes hands. "I didn't realize you were going to drive."

"Could've been worse," the sheriff says. "I could've flown."

He shakes off his windbreaker.

"You want coffee?" Martin asks.

"Black, five sugars."

In the guy's hands is a cowboy hat dark from the rain. Martin remembers the Westerns he used to watch as a kid. *The High Chaparral. Alias Smith and Jones.* He always wanted to be a cowboy, but his father said the cowboys were long extinct, like dinosaurs.

He asks a junior officer to escort the sheriff back to the break room. He joins him ten minutes later and says quietly, "You know, we don't exactly see the kid for this."

"What's that."

"The boy. Nick. You saw the confession."

"We received it."

"You know what I mean."

"Sure."

They don't say anything for a while.

"He mentioned a girlfriend. Emily. Do you guys know this kid for anything?"

"Let's go get this done," the sheriff says flatly.

"We can do that," Martin says after a moment.

The previous afternoon, Lillian moved out. No warning. He was at the hospital with the kid. She left a note. *Please don't worry about me. I need to figure a few things out. I'll be in touch when I'm ready. I love you. Lillian.*

It wasn't the end of the world, or even completely unexpected, but what was it? What sustains a marriage, exactly? To the point: a second marriage? From the first night, they'd had an intense sexual bond. Even during rough patches, it didn't falter. Maybe she'd made that connection with someone else?

He felt like he'd been dismissed.

And the more it sank in, the worse it felt.

15

The same night, Martin bought a Snickers at midnight and went back to the holding cells. No plan in place. He found the kid staring at the ceiling. Bandaged ribs, dressing on his nose.

"I noticed you've got a limp," Martin said. "Not from the car accident. It's tough to get a limp these days. Surgeons have gotten pretty good. You must really have screwed yourself up."

After a long quiet, the kid coughed. "Snowmobile accident," he said.

"You have a snowmobile? I used to have one."

"Congrats."

"A sergeant of mine has three."

"It belonged to my dad. He was driving."

"Where is your dad?"

The kid looked up then, no expression. "No idea."

He broke the candy bar in two and passed the kid half.

The kid asked, "I still have that phone call, right?"

"You do."

"Can you make it for me?"

"Sure I can. Who do you want me to call?"

A long quiet. "Never mind."

Martin leads the sheriff down the corridor. He can't decide how far to extend himself. A pair of officers part to let them through. Four holding cells, two and two, at the moment empty except for the kid. Martin turns the corner and nods to the officer at the door.

Behind him, the sheriff from New Hampshire calls out, "Hey, Nick."

Martin rotates, watches the kid's brow flatten, his lips withdraw.

"Nick," the sheriff says, cuffs the word. As if all of this has already played out somewhere else.

Nick pushes back his hair.

In twenty-five minutes, the kid's prepped and processed, not a single additional word spoken. Portis leads the boy out the sally port like he owns the place. The rain is cold. It falls straight down. The sheriff loads the kid into a muddied white Charger and slams the door. Then he's gone.

Martin quickly returns to his office, shuts his door. Glass of water. Three ibuprofen. Out of nowhere, he pictures Lillian, her and the doctor in the rain. Two months earlier, she left for a Jimmy Buffett weekend with her sister Joan, who lived year-round in Beach Haven. Virgin margaritas, long walks, family gossip. He'd texted Joan at one point to hear how things were going: nope, no Lillian. Three weeks after that, the over-night bag was again on the front-hall table. A big design conference in Philadelphia, she said. So he tailed her. Embarrassed, angry at himself. What a lowlife. They drove across the Delaware, into rush-hour Philly, two cars among thousands as darkness fell. Logan Square. A one-way street. A posh hotel with doors of milk glass, flanked by torches. The lobby was so featureless, it could have been a prayer room in an airport. He'd stared at the flames as they sputtered, the visible fumes, and thought of a cathedral. He thought of anything except what was happening before his eyes.

They'd had him over for dinner once, the doctor. Nice guy. With maybe a little too much self-assurance, too much shine in his eyes. But pleasant, smart, a good conversationalist. Martin made him his ravioli with sage-butter sauce. And later would see his wife press her body against the guy in the lobby of a fashionable hotel.

Would feel in that moment like a corpse being covered over with dirt.

The rainstorm is only a trickle outside his office. His retirement will arrive in two weeks. Everything should fall into place, but old habits say something's wrong. He unholsters his Glock and sets it down on the table beside the keyboard like it's just another item on his desk.

He feels his loneliness. Feels himself dragged toward something against his will. Side by side, his irritation and his wretchedness. He rubs his face with both hands. Instructs himself, with doctor's instructions, *Simply breathe.*

But his nerves are all wrong. He can't put his mind at peace.

He feels in his sweat a dismantling suspicion.

■

A warm June rain taps the roof and veils shapes outside. Father is gone for work. Mother is simply gone. The days expand and still there's no Nick, no word.

She's had enough, she has to do something.

Next to the barn is the yard, the chicken coop, the snowplow blade. Below the yard is the mountainside, below the mountain is the valley and Claymore proper. The work truck lurches to a start. Emily's teeth rattle in her mouth. Soon she's in town, under the old trees of Nick's neigh-borhood, Oak Hill, where the houses once were fancy, and now are bleached.

She parks outside his house. Nick's room is on the ground floor. The shades are drawn. The living room's dark, where his mother hosts her students.

She checks her phone. No missed calls, no texts.

Her heart is a panicked horse.

She drives to Tyree's Tire Center and something's wrong there, too. No lights on whatsoever, and Mr. Tyree isn't even in his chair, Mr. Tyree who weighs almost four hundred pounds and is never not in his chair.

She gets out. A handwritten sign's on the floor, it must have slipped off the window. *CLOSED—On Vacation.*

The night that Nick disappeared, she'd driven around town for two hours. She wound up parked under the Ferris wheel. Even in the evening, it rotated cheerfully above the sand, all teal and pink. Maybe a couple people were on it. She bought a ticket. At the top, she stood up, with the idea that she'd be able to see Nick's car if it was parked near the beach. But it was hopeless, there were a million cars, she could see nearly all the way to Boston. She didn't know where he was. The next time around, the pinnacle, a hundred or so feet off the ground, she climbed up on the side. Nick was gone, she was sure of it. He hated her. She'd ruined everything. The little car swung and tipped, she felt the wind run down her shirt, felt the darkness inside her start to rise. She let go of the pole with her left hand and almost slipped, lost her balance, swung out. The whole car swung, and her body washed through with waves of fear while her sneakers folded in half over the little door. But she didn't care.

When she was back on the ground, the operator woman called her a moron and said if she ever saw her around again, she'd call the cops.

Emily laughed straight in her face.

Across the street from the tire shop is the Angry Goat. It's the restaurant where she and Nick first met, randomly, almost a year earlier. She needs to pee. Only a couple people are inside, including a man in a business suit. He watches TV at the bar, with his tongue clamped between his teeth and his chin pointed up. He turns and stares. "Come in, little girl," he says. Eyes oblique like a cow.

She angles for the bathroom, locks the door. Tremors of fear rattle in her chest.

On her way out, the cow man calls, "Hey, girl, wait."

"Leave me alone."

"I know you."

"No you don't."

"You're Nick's girl," he says. He walks over. Up close his cheeks prickle with little white hairs. "I saw Nick this morning. I see him all the time. He works right over there."

He points out the window.

"What do you mean you saw him?" she says.

"At the station," the man says.

"What station?"

"He showed me your picture once. That's what's funny about all this."

"Why is that funny?"

"Well, you know, pigs."

Emily wants to run out the door, but his words sink in and paralyze her. A strange emotion weighs heavily on her arms and pins her there, when she knows exactly what he'll say next before the words come out of his mouth.

"Your dad's the sheriff," he says.

"What are you talking about?"

The man coughs up something and wipes it on his sleeve.

"He was putting Nick in custody," he says. "That's what I'm talking about."

THE MISBEGOTTEN

Let us imagine that in the time of endless content and ceaseless optimization, the bulwark is somehow gone, she's lost the only remaining wall to preserve her sanity. Leela Mann has never failed at writing or editing to her knowledge, everything she's done is thoughtful and praised. She's even been on CNN to talk about a story. But then on Friday, in lower Manhattan, New York City, the awful thing happens: She loses her job. Again.

Two days later, Sunday, she wakes up to nothing, end of existence. Madbury, New Hampshire. Outside there's only silence, nonstop, the thick white noise of New England forest. No man-made sounds, no car alarms, no truck drivers yell in Cantonese. The sunlight's in her eyes, and it's so plainly not New York City sunlight, she pulls her leather jacket over her face.

And the moan that rises uncontrollably from her body comes from deep in her soul.

Forty-eight hours earlier, everything had been as it should be. Existence. Career. Aspirations. She was twenty-four, she loved life, she was fully employed. Spring in Manhattan! And even the bog stench of Broadway-Lafayette gave her a lift. Then her boss, Randall, the managing editor of *The Village Voice*, announced another round of layoffs. Number three in seven months. Severances would be pitiful. Regrets, threadbare. This time she got the axe—no love from Randall. So she'd skipped the farewell day-drinking to go to the Starbucks on Astor Place, email everyone she'd met in the previous forty-two months that constituted her adult working life after college—two editorial internships and two copyediting jobs: Jambands and BuzzFeed, Deloitte University Press and *The Village Voice*, respectively—never mind practically everyone else in her address book, all to say, *Hi so-and-so, I hope your morning is going well. I just got laid off, so I am sending out a shameless networking call. If you know of any job openings at all, please let me know. Thanks!*

Almost four years earlier, when Leela graduated from Rutgers, her father had offered to find her a job. At the time, he'd been the manager of human resources at Tanuja Fabrics. It was a textiles importer in Dorchester, a grimy corner of Boston that he commuted to from New Hampshire. The boss needed a personal assistant. Naturally she turned him down, mostly because it was her father who did the offering, but also because it wasn't writing or editing. Also: Boston.

At the time she'd had a clear-cut, detailed vision of what her life would become. It did not incorporate being shackled to an eighty-year-old industrialist.

But now Leela's back in New Hampshire, unemployed. Awake in gloomy wistfulness, in a friend's parents' empty house, mummified in a sleeping bag on floorboards that feel to her spine like railroad ties. No matter that every piece of clothing she owns is piled underneath her, her funeral pyre of cotton blends. And she probably *would* give her aching back for that assistant job.

So would her poor father, most likely. Around the time that she landed her first internship in New York, the boss died. A year later, his greedy children had dismantled the firm, sold the parts. Her father had been out of work ever since, and spent his days in coffee shops, reading history books to keep busy when he wasn't sending out résumés.

Just recently, her parents had put her childhood home up for sale. They didn't even tell her about it. On Friday morning—before she'd even reached the office, before she had an inkling that she was about to lose her job—Sandra, her best friend from Claymore, had texted to say that she'd seen a post online from Leela's mom, announcing the house was for sale, and was it true? She'd called her parents as she stood on the sidewalk, and had maybe demanded information a little too entitled-ly? In any case, yes, Leela, they planned to sell the house. In fact, while they were sharing, they'd also lost quite a bit of their retirement to market swings and some not-so-great stock picks. In addition, they would move soon into a rental condo in Leduc, the impoverished little New Hampshire village next door to Claymore, Leela's hometown, that was only slightly less impoverished. And no, they didn't know what would happen next.

"Please don't ask us anything more about it," her mother had said snippily.

"But I barely asked you about it."

"Leela, why don't you talk to me anymore on chat?" her father asked from the other handset.

"You know exactly what I mean," her mother said. "We don't have the patience today that's required, please try to understand."

But how did they not have more savings? What *would* happen next? Why were flaming meteors raining down on all their lives?

Every time she thinks about them, it makes her newly sad. A worse daughter than before. Her career as a journalist, though it had begun to approach the on-ramp of being a verifiable thing, had not enabled her to give them any money. In fact, she was broke, in debt. Her little brother was no help. Satnam had dropped out of college and now worked in a ski-rental shop and shared a house in Oregon with seven friends, and they lived pluralistically, they loved noncompetitively, they snowboarded when powder fell. The last time they spoke, he'd called because his new life plan was to make marijuana-laced energy bars—"no one's cornered that shit yet on a high-end level"—and he wanted to know if she had any friends who were investors. As usual, she'd lasted maybe a minute into one of her brother's speeches—"Leela, imagine: hike, eat, high; hike, eat, high"—before she felt hounded by a shame that Satnam never seemed interested in feeling for himself.

But then she lost her job. And spent Friday lunch at the coffee shop, just like her dad. Somehow, once the messages were sent, she had managed to find enough pride to not freak out and shoot up the place, instead to close her laptop and get some more coffee. Because in the case of Leela Mann, pride is her greatest talent. How she can use it to light almost any unfairness more pleasantly: by associating its positive characteristics with her own positive characteristics. The trick's not to adjust your personality, but the situation. After all, she lived in New York, and to be planless in New York, to be without a safety net, was actually both a plan *and* a net, and an age-old practice of up-and-comers. Look around! A big room full of attractive people, some with European accents, all

25

doing their striving best on laptops, *so* busy, *so* stressed, and yet all of them surely would be successful one day by force of will, and therefore Leela was not without hope.

Then it was her turn to order. She smiled at the cashier, resisted annoyance when asked to spell out her name. Really, she didn't have a right to feel so bad. When many people in the world were actually miserable. And all she had to do was find a job in America. Admittedly, in a tough economy. And pay her bills, extensive, and the money that she owed on rent, which was due. And maybe someday she'd achieve some mental rest, love, happiness, peace, though probably she'd need to go someplace else for all that to happen. Who lived in New York anymore, besides finance types? French people? Maybe she could find a job in Austin, like Sandra, or Nashville. Someplace kids her age still could afford to have fun.

•

The previous winter, early in her existence as an aspiring creative artist, on a gray, drizzly afternoon in the elite shopping mall that was Greenwich Village—long before she'd learned to scrimp, to live for a week off a pot of black beans; before she became obliged to feel singled out and ashamed anytime she saw an ad on the subway for debt relief—she fell in love with a leather jacket.

It had never happened so fast before, falling in love. With a jacket festooned with little patches and hand-razored abrasions. The kind of jacket that Solange would buy for a friend on a whim. Seriously, the jacket was amazing, and why shouldn't she have something nice, just once?

At the time she was still employed, still had only a three-figure balance on the MasterCard. But she didn't know a future yet where she woke each day with a mind full of jungle sounds. Instead, this iteration of Leela could stand before a luxury-goods store and invest in a piece of fashion's distressed shoulders way too much meaning associated with her future, so that it became not only clothing but a container, storage for anything desirable that other people possessed, that she was forced by a lack of rich-person good fortune to go without.

Two hours later, she'd ridden the subway home with a hardcover book in front of her face. The A.P.C. bag, tucked between her legs, was concealed inside a larger bag she'd deliberately obtained from Duane Reade to conceal her guilt. And Long Island City in the rain was even grimmer than usual, crustily more familiar, more depressing than even Dorchester. She jogged home from the subway, past her car, her mother's old wagon, a salted-out Subaru that still smelled of her mother's perfume—her self-sacrificing mother who'd probably never bought herself anything nice in her whole life. She *hated* herself. Eight hundred eighty-nine dollars. Plus tax. Could it be considered an investment? It was ludicrous. Someone should shoot her in the face.

But after a week, she still couldn't bring herself to return it, either. Lying there like a puppy in the rain.

It would be several more years, a decade plus, before Leela would have the mental remove to put such mixed-up feelings into a proper sequence of words, but what she felt in that moment was that to return the jacket would be the equivalent of giving up on her dreams.

Nearly every day since, she'd worn the jacket as penance. But it still took her time to learn her lesson. It sent her through a gateway, down a tapered path that lasted about eight months when it became acceptable in her life to put other things on the credit card and not think about them too hard. Meals out. A snowflake tattoo. A destination wedding for a girl she'd barely known in school.

Of course, she'd made money at the time and expected to make more, but that logic was more heady than sound, and she'd accepted it to her present regret and flaming guilt. Four figures of white-hot guilt on top of her student loans.

On the day that Randall informed her that she was laid off from the *Voice*, events spun out of control rapidly. In Starbucks, after thirty minutes, there wasn't a reply to her note. Then Sandra popped up to chat, and Leela nearly burned her fingertips typing, she told her things she'd told no one yet—that she was in debt, she could barely pay her rent, she couldn't ask her parents for anything more. She was doomed. Sandra consoled her. She suggested, offhand, if it really came to all that, couldn't she always move back to New Hampshire? Leela sighed a death rattle, but Sandra typed blithely, about how her parents had bought a house recently in Madbury, not far from where they grew up in Claymore, to rent out to college students, and it would be empty for the summer, so maybe Leela could live there for a bit, if all else failed? While she got back on her feet? But of course it would never come to that. But she could put the idea in her back pocket? It was just shelter, rent-free. If only to stave off feelings of imminent disaster? And so on.

27

That evening, eleven o'clock, her roommates in Queens staged an intervention—for their own good. She'd felt obliged to tell them she lost her job, and people proffered hugs, even beers from their name-tagged shelves, but then Carlo, head of household, gathered everyone in the kitchen, under the strings of peppers they'd dried together, where he pronounced the news firmly: she would go. Carlo pointed out that she still owed them the previous month's rent—because there'd been an un-anticipated need for car maintenance, on a vehicle that multiple room-mates had enjoyed, she could've mentioned—and she'd soon owe them the current rent, and he wouldn't be budged. The point was, she'd pay what she owed, then she would leave.

The looks around the room, from kids with whom she'd watched the entire *West Wing*, made pizzas from scratch, and discussed dreams, pretty much said the same thing.

By the next afternoon, she was gone.

To Madbury, only half an hour from where she was born, where she'd squat in an old friend's family's unfurnished cabin, rent-free. It was beyond humiliating. Had "live free or die" ever been so literal? The morn-ing she left New York it was fittingly muggy. She'd wrestled her futon into an open dumpster. The rest of her possessions fit in her car. Her life in a car! It was spine-tingling, sickeningly, to feel so reduced. But why *not* take a couple months up north to rethink her plans? When summer weather in New York was so awful anyway? She still had her 917 pre-fix. Between her security deposit and her prepaid last month, her room-mates were covered. Plus she had severance due from the *Voice* that would cover her expenses for two months, if she could live off beef jerky. And she'd pick up a waitressing job. She didn't *have* to tell her parents she was back in New Hampshire. In fact, it was probably more responsible not to trouble them. So what if she told no one she'd left New York? She was "summering" in New England. Who'd miss her for a couple months, anyway? People would just think she was busy.

And possibly Sandra was a little freaked out when she called to take her up on her offer—but of course her offer still stood. And she loved Sandra. What a great friend. Life was good.

But it's really not, not in Madbury, when she wakes up in the empty living room, in the empty house. Birds squeal outside. She urgently checks her email from the darkness of her sleeping bag: no new messages. She turns on her side and stares at the wall. And if she could see through it, the twenty or so miles from that room to Claymore, she'd see kids she grew up with, old haunts where they hung out, everything she once thought she'd left behind for good.

It's the worst.

Except she does have a shard of hope. One glistening shard.

Leela ducks back inside her sleeping bag and dares to dream.

CAN'T GET THERE FROM HERE

The hallway door opens with its sucking noise, and Nick's blood runs cold. It's been almost a week since the crash. They've hauled him back to New Hampshire, Claymore, the county detention center, a locked floor above the courthouse on the old town square. He's got a steel toilet, a blue plastic mattress, a tiny dresser with a single drawer. Not even a Bible. And all night long, his blood beats in his ears. He walks in circles, no matter how tired he is. The truth is he's afraid to go to sleep. His brain is full of memories, images, poison gas, the kind that spoils every new thought.

Nobody else is in custody. He's got the floor all to himself. The only other person around is a guard who sits in a room, plays on his phone, some kid his age he should probably know from school.

The sheriff enters the corridor softly despite his boots. He peels an orange. He wears his large hat indoors.

"Mr. Toussaint."

"What do you want?"

The sheriff doesn't answer.

"Leave me alone."

He stands and moves to the corner.

"Is this being recorded? I can see the cameras."

The sheriff chews on a piece of fruit.

"I swear," Nick says, "if you go anywhere near her."

"You don't have to yell," the sheriff says. "I turned off the cameras."

After the encounter at the tavern, Emily rushed over to the courthouse, prepared to run up and bang on the doors and demand to see Nick, but somehow Father came down the stairs at the moment she parked, closed distance quickly before she could get around him, and said forcefully that, first of all, Emily would *not* visit the boy, and under no circumstances would she attempt to see him or contact him in any manner. Two, no more piano lessons with the kid's mom. Three, she would cease, going forward, all recent disobedient behavior, and further would quit helling around behind his back. And would rejoin the cross-country team. And would know, no matter what, from that point on, her father planned to watch her every minute, every second.

She'd been mute in response, a hunk of stone.

"He's a murderer," Father said. "You can read it. I've got it right here."

At home afterward, she locks herself in the downstairs bathroom. She remembers Nick beside her in bed the previous week. She rinses her face and dries it on the shower curtain. For dinner, she warms a frozen casserole and puts a basket of rolls on the dining table, next to the dish of ranch dressing that Father likes. She won't eat herself, she stopped eating in front of him more than two years ago. Like any other night, she asks at the beginning of the meal to be excused.

Father refuses, though he doesn't say anything. While he eats, he reads aloud from a catalog that came in the mail. Once he's done, he fixes a glass of syrup milk.

Emily stands abruptly and shoves in her chair.

"What happens to Nick?"

She feels sick.

"Sit down. Don't be dramatic."

"He didn't do it. It's my fault."

"Emily."

"He didn't do anything."

"What did I just say?" he says softly.

"I love him," she shouts. The strands in Father's neck bulge. He doesn't look her in the eye. She stands and waits for something to happen, hopes for time to run past them, but it barely passes at all and she feels primal, she can't be stopped, she's on the verge of doing something awful.

Father says even more quietly, "Emily, sit."

"No."

"Why don't you have some dessert?" He picks up his glass and goes on in a drowsy tone, as if he hasn't explained it a hundred times before. "It's like a milk shake, but without the ice cream. Just real maple syrup mixed with a little milk. It's what my father used to drink after dinner. It's really delicious."

She runs from the room.

•

On Martin Krug's last day as a police officer, a lawyer shows up. They sit in his office. The guy launches into a speech, a five-minute motorcade of thoughtfulness. "So it's not a demand," the lawyer says, with a slightly repulsive humility, "it's a good suggestion," "a path for best outcomes," something "for uncharted ground." "Like a bridge," the man adds while he stares at his phone and taps out a message. "If that makes sense."

The room's hot. The ceiling fan makes it hotter. Martin would have continued to say nothing but the idiot seems unstoppable, all his reckless metaphors.

And he's about to interrupt when his computer dings: a reminder to send his daughter her monthly check.

The lawyer's voice intrudes, says that Martin should think of this moment as free therapy, "or more like a business relationship if that's easier. Some husbands find that easier."

"My wife wants a divorce," he pronounces.

"I didn't say that. You did not hear me say that."

"Please give me some credit."

The words come out weightless, no impact. The lawyer goes back to chattering, to lull his guard. Martin knows the type. Dislikes the type. And yet he senses, underneath all of the bullshit, who *he* is in this conversation. The cuckold. The pitiful one.

"I want to see her," Martin says.

"That's not possible."

"Of course it is."

The lawyer coughs. "Chief."

"I want to see my wife."

The lawyer sits upright and puts away his phone. "From this moment forward, everything goes through me. At her request. Lillian needs some space. She asks you to honor that need."

"I don't buy it," Martin says. He adjusts his position, but his back hurts no matter which way he sits.

"Understand me, Mr. Krug." The lawyer purses his lips, as if prevented from smiling by his own good sense. "She doesn't want to see you. That's a fact."

■

Middle of the night, almost three o'clock, madness hits her like a collapsing wall and Emily gets out of bed and goes into the closet to find the old shoe box, but the box is gone. She flinches. She digs, like a dog in a hole. She should have kept it safe, she should have put it somewhere for an emergency. She's furious with herself.

But after only a minute it's found again, fallen behind a jacket, and inside is the old baggie, two caps. She swallows both and opens the window to the dry night air.

The mushrooms envelop her in five minutes.

And in the darkest dark she sees but doesn't touch the old feelings, while the cracked chime of the living room clock rings three.

■

In the early Saturday dark, a bad dream wrenches Martin awake. He had been seduced by the woman from the car accident, except it was Lillian's face again, mapped to the dead woman's skull, missing lip included.

The clock reads four. In less than twenty-four hours the department will throw him a retirement party. Going by previous nights out, everyone will get drunk, sing his praises, wake up the next morning, and hop in a radio car and resume routine. Everyone except him.

He showers and shaves. The chin is deeply notched, tricky to get right. He hears himself breathing more loudly than normal. He goes to the kitchen. In the blue glow of the oven clock, the Urge appears. The Urge, the Thirst, Seductress of a Thousand Faces. He realizes he hasn't been to a meeting in two days. He eats half a tube of cookie dough with fork and knife.

And for some reason the first name that comes to mind, if he were to call someone up to chat, a name that floats up out of the ether in his brain, is Walter Dennis. A man he hardly knows.

They'd met at a dinner, a banquet in Atlantic City, about a month earlier. A glass-walled ballroom filled with police, politicians, the hired hands who bind them. He hadn't planned to attend. He'd been on his way home from his Tuesday meeting. The speaker had focused on step four: *Make a searching and fearless moral inventory of ourselves.* The speech was mind-numbingly dull. But it had made him consider that being around people, the physical act of it, to put himself out there, talk to people in a social setting—which was a lot harder than in a police setting, *and not at all his preferred method of existing in the world*, especially without the help of a double scotch—was something he'd really only learned how to do in his sobriety.

So maybe it was something he should practice.

So he went to the event.

The room had been full of small talk, a thousand gold balloons. By the time he found his seat, he'd already decided that to spend time around strangers was actually a pretty stupid idea, and what he really needed was his bed, some ice cream, the new Doris Goodwin. The dinner was sushi rolls slathered with mayonnaise. Ten minutes in, he was about to get his car, the guy next to him nudged his elbow. "What's the matter, you don't like food poisoning?"

Walter Dennis, Bergen County prosecutor. Maybe a couple years older than him. Buzzed gray hair, silver mustache. Nice blue suit, gray tie with a pattern of tiny flowers. In the front of the room, a short guy started to make a noisy speech, a rap he'd written for the occasion, and Walter suggested they grab a drink at the bar. He said fine, but he didn't drink. The guy winked. "I kind of figured that out."

They both ordered herbal tea. Learned they were in the program, in suits of similar cuts. They traded war stories, crazy cases. Twenty minutes in, no time had passed. He remembered that he smiled uncomfortably. What was happening? He hadn't made a new friend in at least a decade. Then again he hadn't needed to, he'd had two great friends, his racquetball partners. In the last year, both were gone. Jonah, his first sponsor. Chris, his cardiologist. Somehow he told Walter all about it. How Jonah had gotten him sober with his sarcasm, his street smarts. He'd worked for the Federal Highway Administration and hated ninety-nine percent of the world. And Chris had put a stent in his chest. Quiet guy, do-gooder, who took other people's pains to heart, literally. Why had he decided to tell all of this to a stranger? But it felt good, to describe his friends. Both cut down by cancer in the spring. He wore the same suit to both funerals, he didn't realize it until later.

Walter laughed to cut the silence. "See, I prefer squash. Over racquetball."

"Squash is too aggressive," Martin said.

"And that's why I love it."

There were murmurs of a new speaker, the grand finale.

"I lost somebody," Walter said confidentially. "Two years ago last week. My partner, Mark."

"Oh you mean," Martin said, because he'd thought of work, the guy you rode around with in a car, "he was your husband."

"That was a little late for us."

"I'm sorry for your loss. How did he die?"

"Also cancer. Lung cancer. Never smoked. I got him for twenty-one years."

"What was his name?"

"Mark. Mark Calmes. Best last name a man could get. He was the sweetest guy. First time we met, he was the most beautiful person I'd ever seen."

His friend Chris also had been gay, but rarely partnered, perpetually single, he complained about his loneliness.

"Martin, it's okay to mourn your friends."

"I know," he'd said, and grinned tightly, ready to break it off, then felt his tongue go cold. A number of things rushed up his throat. Now he was going to cry? Walter rubbed his shoulder. He got himself under control. Walter said, "Tell me some more about them."

Two minutes later, the applause inside in the other room had built to a crescendo. Walter clenched his arm. "That's my cue." Martin watched him walk away, hand-clasp his way to the podium. The speech was sincere, self-deprecating, people were laughing, Martin was laughing.

In his wife's kitchen of Italian affectation, against the quiet creak of an empty house, he makes a pot of coffee in the dark and remembers that Walter Dennis's business card is in his wallet. And out of thin air he thinks about the kid in New Hampshire, Nick Toussaint. A boy he can't believe is guilty. Who any day now would be arraigned. The defense would start its own investigation. Maybe Walter Dennis had some advice he could pass along, the star attorney.

.

38

Nick scrapes his fingernails against a concrete patch. He grinds his knuckles where the overhead lights create octagonal shapes on the ground. The night's orange, his life's finished, his body cramps with knowledge and fear.

Emily is all he thinks about. She must know by now what happened. She must despise him, she'll never talk to him again.

A year and a half earlier, they met by accident. His plan that night had been to get drunk with Typically, his best friend. They'd been friends since the sixth grade. His full name was Jacob Guthrie Beliveau-Boggs, but only his girlfriend still called him Jacob. By eleventh grade, he'd referred to himself in the third person too many times while drunk, when so many sentences would start, "Typically Jacob doesn't vomit," or, "Typically Jacob doesn't break into cars."

After high school, they drank even more. Nick wasn't always up for all the alcohol, and was scared to do coke, but he liked the fact that someone had an even darker temperament than him. Typically worked as a line cook at the Angry Goat, a bar-grill in Claymore. The night Nick met Emily, he'd gone over to the Goat after work. The bartenders all knew him, served him. The guy on duty had said the kitchen was slammed, two separate birthday parties; Typically wouldn't be done for at least an hour. Nick ordered a beer and said he'd wait.

Twenty minutes later, a girl appeared, asked for a pair of Long Island Iced Teas. She didn't wait to get ID'd, she slid a license across the bar. From where Nick sat it was obviously a fake. Was she even eighteen? Who orders Long Island Iced Teas except high school chicks? She was interesting to look at, though. Black hair with dyed white streaks. A great body, a nine for Claymore. The face probably knocked her down to a six, it was so long, and with a red-purple birthmark along the jaw. Big nose, too. Then again, he wasn't more than a six himself, given his height and the limp.

"Who's drinking the second one?" the bartender said, flipped back the ID.

"They're for me," the girl said, flirting. "Want me to prove it?"

The bartender laughed. Nick laughed. They watched her slink back to a booth. A girl probably used to turning defense into offense.

But then before he turned away, her exact opposite stepped out of the booth. She wore a wrinkled blue dress that stopped at the knee, with jeans underneath. Tallish. Long brown hair parted in the center, hippie-style. Broad shoulders, small eyes, a face that was strong-boned. Pretty cute, overall, in a crunchy kind of way. She crossed the dining room, she smiled at something, caught herself in a moment of self-consciousness and tried to hide it. Then she saw Nick and smiled again. He smiled back. She held eye contact. He broke away. She turned the corner toward the restrooms, she still had a smile on her face.

What the hell?

For what felt like half an hour he played a game on his phone, wondering where the girl had gone. Then suddenly both girls exited. When did she come back from the bathroom? He hurried after them. The night was prickly cold. Wood smoke, dried leaves, a recent rain. The girl with the skunk hair checked her phone by the bumper of a beat-up Toyota 4Runner. The streetlights made the white streaks in her hair shine blue.

The girl who'd smiled at him was in shotgun.

"Hey," he said. "What's up?"

"Who are you?" said the skunk.

"Nick."

"What's your last name?"

"Toussaint."

"You just walk up to girls in a parking lot, Nick Toussaint?"

"Are you guys doing something?"

"Do you have a limp?"

He glanced at the other girl.

She saw him. She smiled again!

The skunk said, "Hey, you have any beer? We were thinking about going up to Whitehall."

"Sure." He made himself look at her and not the other one. He couldn't look at the other one or else he'd smile like an idiot. "What do you want?"

"Whatever works."

Weekend nights, it was Claymore tradition that Whitehall quarry would be mobbed, at least in the summer. Swimming, drinking, getting high. But this was mid-October. Snow was coming. Thirty minutes later, he parked at the trailhead. The mountain air was silent, which meant the quarry was dead. Nick trudged the half mile up the trail. Fitful darkness, a half-moon's light. The cold imposed a sense of . . . fear? Something was off, but he couldn't place it. Were the chicks pranking him? How old were they anyway? Something had to be wrong. Why had that one girl smiled at him? When he got to the opening, he saw the girls on the Penthouse, the highest outcropping, a granite ledge. He headed up. Twenty feet below, the water was black and flat like a trampoline. He prayed they wouldn't want to swim. His left leg was thatched with scars, he hated to wear shorts. But some girls were like that, they tested you.

"Beer guy."

"It's Nick."

"Nick Toussaint, hurry up."

When he reached them, he was out of breath. He laughed uneasily. The girls had an air of belonging there.

"You guys want a fire?" he asked.

"I'll do it," the smiling girl said. Then she was gone before he could protest. Had she smiled again? It seemed important to know, but it was too dark. He pressed his left hand hard on the back of his neck. Totally confused. Totally out of his comfort zone.

The skunk asked for a beer. He opened three of them off his teeth. Typically had taught him how. The skunk was unimpressed.

In the moonlight her face looked like an upside-down egg.

"So what's up with your leg?"

"It's nothing."

"Liar."

They clinked bottles. He felt at ease around her—probably because of the birthmark. Normally he didn't like to tell the story, but what else did he have? A minute later, he was still in the beginning when the other girl returned with kindling, she scampered down the rocks.

"Here, let me," he said, starting to get up.

"It's fine," she said, and crouched by the fire pit. She looked up at him. "I want to listen."

So, three years earlier, he was sixteen. Late January. They'd gotten two feet of snow in two days. Very early morning, Saturday, ice-cold, his dad woke him up at seven in the morning with his bullshit reveille—*Drop your cock and grab your socks*—and told him to warm up the truck and load the sled. They were going out to collect a debt near Manock Lake, from some guy who lived in a bunkhouse. His dad drove, sipped schnapps from a bottle he kept in the glove compartment. Nick guessed he hadn't slept, had stayed up drinking again. Thirty minutes later, they were on the snowmobile together. They flew up a trail with woods on either side, side-by-side doubling, churning forward like two guys on the prow of a fast ship.

On a flat straightaway, his dad had passed him the bottle. Nick looked back, stared down the disappearing trail, the clouds of snow. He lifted the bottle to his lips.

A second later they'd launched into the air. A tree had fallen across the trail at a corner. His dad must not have seen it, or reacted too late.

"Holy crap," the skunk said.

"That's horrible," the other girl said, looked at him across the fire she'd built.

"Yeah, it was bad," he said, encouraged to play it up a little. Not that the story needed it. "I woke up twenty minutes later. It smelled like gas. My whole body was numb. I was trapped, I was pinned under the sled. Honestly I don't remember much, I didn't have a clue what was going on. I kept passing out."

His dad ran a mile through the woods to find help. The pain came and went like fire, like he was under a sheet of flame. He passed in and out of consciousness. They said later his dad returned in the truck of the man they'd gone to see. They pulled the sled off him with a winch, hurried him to the emergency room. In the end, he lost two toes. Left knee shattered, eleven pieces, a transverse fracture of the left tibia, plus a displaced transverse fracture of the left fibula. Basically the snowmobile had pulverized his leg. Multiple second-degree burns on both legs. All things said and done, there would be several operations, full immobilization for three months, near-full immobilization for six months, and four months partial after that.

"You didn't go back to school?"

"I had a tutor. I got my GED."

"Can I see your toes?" the skunk said.

"What about your dad?" said the other.

"Haven't seen him," he answered, surprised to be asked. Then again most people would be too polite to ask, right? What did that say about her? "Not since the hospital. He basically walked out on me and my mom."

"I'm Alex," said the skunk a moment later. "This is Emily."

A phone beeped. The skunk walked off into the dark. The fire crackled.

"I hate my dad, too," Emily said.

He was about to say he didn't hate his dad, but of course he did. "Why?"

She looked him in the eyes, unblinking.

"Can I hold your hand?" she said.

He almost laughed, but she was serious. She sat next to him and they held hands. The fire popped. The sky filled with clouds. The evening ended quickly after that, something to do with the phone call and a chance of rain. They all walked down the trail. He tried to keep the conversation going, he talked about a movie he'd seen on TV. Had the girl slowed down to compensate for his leg? He didn't want her pity. The last two minutes, they didn't talk at all.

The hippie girl, Emily, got in the truck. The skunk told him to drive home safe.

"Sure," said Nick. He felt both sick and happy, completely confused. "You guys, too." Shouldn't he ask to see them again? He didn't even know the Emily girl's last name. She stared out the windshield, she didn't notice him. It was like she'd forgotten about him entirely.

At home he'd sat in the driveway for twenty minutes. A rainstorm pounded the windshield. He turned on the radio. A lot of nights he did that, if only to avoid his mother. But this was different, on account of the girl. Who'd managed to write him off within fifteen minutes.

What had he done wrong? Something stupid, no doubt.

That night, by the time Nick fell asleep in his bed, the only thing he'd identified that he felt sure about, aside from his own idiocy, was a feeling in his gut that he needed to see the girl again as soon as possible.

A feeling that's a thousand times stronger now that he's in jail.

■

Suzanne Toussaint is long-bodied and thin-skinned and always cold. She takes on the temperature of her surroundings like a lizard. Saturday morning, six o'clock, she wakes up and drinks a shot of vodka, her father's shot. He always kept a little glass on the nightstand in case he couldn't sleep, a trick he learned from W. H. Auden, he said. He used to quote Auden at parties, he'd quote him when he tucked her in at night. *Saying alas to less and less.* There's even still a ring in the varnish.

Suzanne Toussaint is nearly fifty and feels seventy. She has a business she resents—and a case of hypochondria caused by the internet—and a certain amount of physical beauty that men used to find arresting, which seems to have vanished—and a longstanding thing for Lou Reed—and a house she inherited from her parents that is, by this point, three times liened against at the bank—and a surname that once meant something in Claymore, was public property in a way, but not anymore.

At all times she has a sense of all the lives she hasn't lived, all her screw-ups and mistakes, an awareness she resuscitates when it's dormant with self-absorption, and the overidentification with doomed heroines in shows on HBO.

She has a king-sized mattress that she once shared with a husband who looks more and more, in the rearview mirror, like a long-term houseguest.

And now she has a son in the custody of the law.

And all of it, except the last bit, was what she'd written at command on her first day of therapy, at her former therapist's request—written on flimsy printer paper that had already been used on one side for an online travel reservation—*with the liberty to construct your own personal history,* Dr. Margaret Gould had emphasized.

She'd lasted five weeks with Dr. Gould—and in that time had plenty of holes pricked into the dam that held back her miseries. But then the sessions weren't affordable anymore.

The day before, lunchtime, Friday, she'd tried to see her son, but had been refused. Too soon, even for family, said the uniformed officer behind the desk—all pimpled, no sympathy, a little shithead hamburger—she'd wanted to carve the boredom off his storm trooper face.

She left the courthouse. It was farcical. Everyone was going about their normal days. She drove to . . . nowhere. Where was she supposed to go?

When what she'd wanted to do was go back to the courthouse and plant a couple kicks into the guard's eyes.

So she smoked a cigarette, her lifelong friend. Then reapplied lipstick, and decided to run an errand across town at Aubuchon's, the one on East Toussaint—where she bumped into, who else, Dr. Gould, in the paint-can aisle.

Dr. Gould, who greeted her with an unconscious, wincing wave, until *very perceptibly,* as Dr. Gould would have said, did the doctor herself experience a profound shock of revelation—while she stared in disguised wonderment at her own shoes—as she connected the Suzanne Toussaint before her to the piping-hot, unspeakable story that had raced around town about a double murder.

But thus, as she looked up into Suzanne's face, did observant fucking Dr. Gould *quite visibly* resist flinging herself into an interaction to learn more. Instead stood squared, total hard-core marine shrew, called to attention by the micromoment's significance—frankly, she was the most subdued that Suzanne had ever seen her, even overwhelmed, and still nakedly expectant, as she waited hopefully, as her nerve endings thrummed with ready sympathy in case Suzanne should avail herself in the quiet sanctity of Benjamin Moore—"Oh, Suzanne," said Dr. Gould. "I'm *so* sorry."

And even then Suzanne didn't frown or blink. Didn't say, "Maggie, thank you." Didn't say, "Maggie, mind your own business." Didn't say or do shit except turn around and get back in her car. Drive home rigid in her seat. High humidity. Scattered clouds. The muscle above her left eye spasmed—a blood clot that raced toward her heart, probably.

And in the garage she parked, rolled down the door, and had a beer from the back-up fridge and then another.

Saturday morning, the next day, a new day, Suzanne Toussaint decides that Suzanne Toussaint will never sleep again.

The bedroom is her parents' bedroom, the wet bar was her father's idea. He'd built it one Labor Day, she remembers the weekend exactly, down to the straw basket full of her mother's prized tomatoes that sat on the porch. Did her parents love her? Does it matter? They certainly loved each other. To quote her ex-therapist, "We can simply be exactly who we think we are."

It starts to rain. So just one more shot, a half to get going, a sip and she'll dress, do her makeup, hop in the car, return to the courthouse and burn down the gate. The window drips. Why are there so many trees? So many lawns full of grass, why is everything so green? As if every element in life is humid.

She stares in the mirror. Her arms are corpse-blue from sweat. Does grief ever become abstract? She ignores the longing to hide beneath the covers.

Then she thinks of Nicky again, and the chaos sinks all the way down.

Suzanne Toussaint is daughter of two, mother to one, sister to an idiotic older brother she hasn't spoken to in at least five years, who lives in Thailand for pennies and chases girls, girls who actually are girls—she hates him. Her family once helped to settle Claymore, her great-grandfather was a New Hampshire state senator—but anyone of notoriety in their family is in the ground. Except now—her son. She can't explain anything. Murder? *Murder?* It must be her failure somehow, yet more failure, she'll get the blame and deserve it.

She stares wretchedly out the rain-beaded glass at all that guzzling green.

Her son has been taken from her.

Pain is pain.

To be a mother is a never-ending attempt at repossession.

■

Over the last two decades, an idea has grown durable in a corner of Martin Krug's mind that the world is graspable, the world of criminals. And what he knows of that world is quite a lot. For example, bad guys almost always do what he expects. Criminals as a species are mostly uneducated and inebriated. Inclined toward self-harm, self-pity, self-prosecution. With wits that have the staying power of a bruise.

Even in the strangest crimes are the same motifs. Bad parents. Lust for vengeance. Men with mommy problems. Women with daddy problems. Women with baby-daddy problems.

Any color of motive can turn more or less fluorescent, but the palette doesn't change. Though some colors are more vibrant. The summer of '93, he consulted for a sheriff's department in rural Pennsylvania. A call came through on his second day. Violence against children. The address was miles into overgrown woods. Rolling hills. Yard posts and fields. A Greyhound bus appeared without wheels or windows. He reached a pair of cabins on a three-acre lot thick with garbage and machinery parts. Out front was an aboveground pool. The surface teemed with children. Kids clung to the side, faces and arms green for some reason, like swamp creatures. One of the boys had bubbling warts on his lower eyelids.

Martin got out of the car and said hello. No response. The wart boy ducked under the water and swam away.

Up close, the surface was a half inch thick with green algae.

The front door on the first cabin was open. Three half-clothed

46

adults were passed out in a heap, like a pile of bodies set aside to be buried. There was evidence of a long high. In the second house he found an old woman, dead drunk, plus four more children, one of them probably twelve years old. The kids had half assembled a jigsaw puzzle of Mount Rushmore. The oldest one had a Ruger Single-Six stuck in his pants.

He put nine children into protective custody that day.

But no matter the case, no matter how ugly it gets, it's never the Martin Krug Show, it's never about him. More often, he's just confused.

Saturday morning he goes to a meeting. The theme is *Let's be friendly with our friends*. He jogs afterward on the beach. The funny thing about meetings, they always seem to correspond with his own problems. Or maybe that's the addict's narcissism. He takes a shower. Looks up Walter Dennis on the internet. The web's full of tributes, quotes in *The Wall Street Journal*, one of those little dot portraits.

"Walter Dennis speaking."

"Walter, hey. This is Martin Krug."

What the hell does he say next?

"Martin?"

"We met a month ago. Atlantic City. You received an award."

"That's right."

"We were at the same table. I told you about my friends."

"Martin. Of course. You'll have to excuse my memory. Every day, I lose a little bit more." They both laugh. "What can I do for you? You doing okay?"

"Thank you. I was just wondering."

"Sure."

"I've been going through some stuff."

"You're in the program."

"I'm fine, thanks. But I was wondering. I don't know how to say this."

"Blurt it out."

"Maybe, I thought, you'd want to do something together."

"Sure."

"What I mean is, the way we got along. This is new for me. I'm just saying, if you're free sometime."

"I got it. Look, Martin."

"Yeah, you know, forget it."

"Your friend, the one who died. He was your doctor."

"Exactly. Chris."

"Martin, I should have told you. You're wonderful. But I'm seeing someone."

"Oh. No."

"I'm going to stop you."

"Walter."

"Now I don't know if there's something about the office, or me and law enforcement, or it's my profile in the community."

"Walter."

"Listen. Just listen. This is not rejection. Because I'm touched, sincerely. The closer you get to figuring this out, there are going to be a lot of lucky guys. I say this, too, that your friend, if he were here right now, and he is, of course, but he would be saying the exact same thing as me. You are not alone. Do you understand what I'm saying, Martin? Say it with me. *I am not alone.*"

■

Saturday afternoon, he arrives in New Hampshire. Claymore County, population 81,000. The county seat constitutes about a fifth of that number. Ocean and mountain country, thriving apple orchards, with a coastline that hugs a ragged edge. Once there was a prosperous shipyard in town, now it makes roofing panels. Wild strawberries for sale. Family gun shops next to delis. A good view of the Isles of Shoals, with excursion-boat companies that offer cruises. Outskirts of town enclosed by unsold developments. In the center, old townhouses, Georgian and Federal, blue and red, some with their coal chutes preserved.

The valley floor runs east to the sea, west to mountains that rise gently, gain height, and become an alpine belt that shoots north.

Acres of antique shops, pawnshops, tattoo parlors.

Down by the ocean, mists rise to unveil even more trees.

At dusk, when Martin arrives, the town is windless. From a distance, the village downtown is a small grid, parts of it refurbished, crisscrossed with blackish stone walls and lit by wintry lamps. It's Edinburgh as much as Portsmouth, tarnished and elegiac, stripped and polished by years of salt and snow. A big church sits on the square. Teenagers cruise around on mountain bikes. The boardwalk bars are lined with motorcycles. Streets are named after foreign countries, Catholic saints. He follows a sidewalk down to the water. Compared to New Jersey, the sand on the Claymore beach is a little darker, the glow of the sunset paler, houses on the bluffs more heavily curtained. But it's still a beach town. A girl glides to shore on a body board. A Ferris wheel is lit up like an episode of *Miami Vice*.

He gets a room two blocks in from the ocean. The inn adjoins a tavern that looks like it dates back to the Revolutionary War. The manager shows him his room. It's not big in the first place, and smaller for being stuffed with throw pillows. The guy opens the windows. Visible in the ocean is a gray streak of current. Time passes. Martin turns to his host. Bodybuilder type, silver crew cut. He bears a strong resemblance to a certain Bergen County prosecutor.

"It looks fine."

"You're in town for the bike rally?" the guy asks.

"The what?"

"The Weirs Beach Motorcycle Rally."

"Just work," says Martin, probably too curtly.

"You'll notice a slight odor; our basement flooded. Chalk it up to global warming. If you need anything, my wife and I are the owners, one of us is usually on the premises. You'll probably see our son around, too."

The ceiling has a sag to it, it creates a claustrophobic feel. The man leaves. The room is shadowy. Martin sits in front of the dark TV. He forcibly shifts his thoughts to the kid, Toussaint. The fact that somewhere nearby is a courthouse, attorneys, all the cogs of the machine, and a young man accused of home invasion and double homicide. Who must be terrified, Martin wonders, as the system whirrs around him. A kid he can't imagine to be guilty.

His back hurts from the drive. Martin picks up the phone. The front desk tells him to call the restaurant next door for room service. He orders a pair of veggie burgers, a bowl of ice cream. Thirty minutes later a teenager shows up in baggy shorts and a tank top. Tall, black, with short dreads and a ring through his nose. Name tag, DEMEKE.

Martin spontaneously tips him twenty bucks. He feels a need to be nice to somebody.

The boy smiles and gives a little nod.

He eats, unpacks, gets on the internet, and finds a meeting that's at a church downtown. In the morning he'll confirm Monday's lunch with the Toussaint kid's attorney. From New Jersey, he'd called on a whim and spoken to an answering machine, extended an offer to help with the investigation.

Every public defender's office he'd seen before was overbooked, under-staffed, underfunded. They'd need to hire an investigator anyway, and here he was, pro bono.

The lawyer called him back ten minutes later.

After dinner, he watches TV. His eyes start to shut. He skips brushing his teeth and pulls the covers up over his head. New Jersey is far away. Let it stay there for a little while.

The last thing he does on his first night in Claymore is leave the framed photograph of Lillian inside his suitcase. But he has to get out of bed in the dark and crouch over his luggage to do so.

■

Saturday afternoon, Nick's mom turns up in a ragged cardigan, loose jeans, hair disheveled, a wool scarf wrapped around her neck, like she's a fisherman on shore leave in December. But the guard still gives her the eye.

Men always look at his mom. She gives a glance to the walls. Nick can tell she hasn't slept. He knows to recognize that her face is all marble, the telltale sign of a binge.

"I said I wouldn't cry," she says hurriedly.

He laughs darkly. "It can be tough when you're drunk."

"There's been some kind of mistake," she insists, "a huge mistake."

"Mom, listen to me."

The situation is irreversible, impossible. Nothing changes.

"Nicky, what happened?"

"Mom."

"Oh, darling."

"Suzanne."

"What?"

He swallows. His mind is lost. He's losing chances by the minute. She sways in her seat.

"Has anyone been bothering you?" he says, as softly as possible.

"What does that mean?"

"Please."

"If you're trying to scare me, you're doing a great job."

"I need you to get ahold of Emily."

"Nicky, stop."

Her voice drops, on puppet strings, her "sober" voice, heavy emphasis. "For god's sake, darling." She secures one hand with the other. "Now tell me what happened. I have to know. I'm your *mother*."

"Will you listen to me?" he says. "You need to contact Emily for me."

She leans across the table, fixes the glasses back on her nose. "Here's what I've done. I contacted a lawyer. He's a friend, he was a friend, of your grandfather's. He doesn't do this sort of thing, but he found out the name. The woman you've been assigned. She's supposed to be good, so that's good. I'm supposed to go fill out an affidavit after this, I'll see if I can meet with her. Nicky, you need to tell me right now what's going on. Anything."

She leans forward, and for a glimpse he sees her, her fear. It guts him. He drags the words out, "I just need you to get in touch with Emily."

Her face hardens again. She sits back and adjusts her scarf. She stares out the windows, boxed with mesh.

"You don't want her to see you like this."

He ignores her. "I'm asking you for a favor."

"You can't just *want* things."

"Can you please do this one thing for me?"

She sobs. So loud and instantaneous it should be fake. He knows it's not. He can't stand it when she cries. She thrusts out her bony white hands in fists. He takes them from instinct. When he does, one slightly opens.

She cries even louder.

"That's enough," the guard says over the intercom. "No contact."

He takes the folded paper from her hand and drops it down his undershirt. His mother rocks back in her seat, sheds tears. Not for one second does he believe it's an act.

■

The week that Nick met Emily, nine months earlier, it took him two days after the quarry to find her again. It nearly didn't happen.

He'd stressed about it every minute. He'd never had feelings like this before! Luckily, he ran into the skunk girl at the hardware store.

Three nights a week, he delivered pizza for Coney Island Pies, an

Italian restaurant near the beach. Tips were good, they comped him for gas, he ate free, he liked to drive. It was a good gig.

That afternoon, someone ordered a personal-sized Hawaiian pizza to Mitchell's Hardware, and there she was, sitting on the counter next to the register while she took pictures of her shoes. If she was surprised, she didn't show it.

"Look, it's Nick Toussaint."

"You're Alex."

He held out the box. She took a slice and started to eat.

"Hey, can I ask you a question?"

"Let me guess. About my friend?"

"Yeah."

"You don't remember her name."

"Of course I do. It's Emily. So will you give me her number?"

"Not unless you want to call her dad."

"Why?"

"His number's easy. It's three digits."

She laughed at her joke. He didn't get it.

"Look, forget it," he said.

"How about this, be a gentleman. Write her a letter."

"A letter. Like on paper."

"She doesn't have a phone. I'm not joking. How much do I owe you?"

"Twelve bucks."

She handed him a twenty. "She's only sixteen, you know that, right? Give me three bucks back."

He nodded automatically in recognition of a good tip. He peeled the change off a roll in his pocket. Sixteen years old. Did that change anything? Should it change things?

He asked the skunk if she'd still be at the store at seven, he'd drop off the letter when he got off work.

▪

Dear Nick,

I don't know what happened or where you went but now you're locked up and Father won't let me see you and I can't get around him. I'm so sorry for everything. Please forgive me. I feel so guilty. It's all my fault, I know it, and everything's just so awful and miserable that I can't put it into words.

Everything I told you, I take it back a million times. I feel so horrible about what I did. I miss you so badly it's like my whole body's broken.

I hope this letter reaches you, but I don't even know if it will. Your mother's being really nice by the way. I went to look for you that night. I wanted to fix things, I drove everywhere, I couldn't find you. I ended up at the Sundial, I wanted to see if I could spot your car from the top. I know it sounds crazy, but I was completely freaked out. I couldn't figure where you'd gone. It kills me that I still don't know what happened!

I've been staying with Alex, she and Meg are really worried about you, too. Meg called the police station. They said you're not allowed anything for now besides visits from family or your lawyer. I swear I'd be there every second if I could, I'll do anything I can to help you.

Anyway so we came up with a plan, that I'll write letters and give them to your mother and see if she can sneak them in. And if this one doesn't reach you I'll just write another one, I'll write a hundred, whatever it takes.

Do you remember when you wrote me that letter after we met? I thought about it this morning. I woke up so happy. I had dreamed you were here with me, we woke up in bed like we used to. We both got dressed and ate breakfast. It was so so nice. Then I woke up.

I'm so worried about you, I'm engulfed. I don't care what happened. Not that you can't handle anything, I know you can but don't forget how truly special you are. You're a man, the best one I've ever met, and I'm here for you, even if you don't need me to be. I want to be with you so badly. I think about you every second.

I feel so alone. I probably shouldn't write things like that to you, I should only send you positive things, but I have no one else I can tell, I really don't. I still don't even think you'll get this letter but who knows. I think not withholding from you is the most important thing right now.

Don't worry, I'll be strong for you, I just want the emptiness to end. I don't have any idea what you're going through, and I don't know what part my father has in all of this, but I am so, so sorry for anything he's done, anything I did. I know whatever you did, you did for me, for us and our future. That makes it so much worse. But I love you to the point that it's really overwhelming me right now!

Being with you is the best feeling in the world. Being without you is the worst feeling in the world.

God I am really depressing in this letter.

If you can send any kind of message to me please do it but don't feel obligated. I love you. You're in all my thoughts.
Love,
Emily

∎

The work begins: Monday afternoon, Martin rides shotgun on the face-to-face. The kid recognizes him, naturally, and is spooked off the bat. But doesn't say anything until the attorney finishes with how a discovery phase works.

"I don't get why he's here," Nick interrupts. "I thought you're supposed to be on my side."

"I am. We're both on your side," the lawyer says. "As weird as that seems."

"I retired," Martin says. "I'm here in an unofficial capacity. I care about your case."

Which is true, actually. Two hours earlier, he'd said as much to the lawyer. They met for lunch. Maria Brenner. Small frame, big hair, cheap suit, pricey glasses. With a pebbly veneer of acne beneath her makeup.

She ordered for both of them. He hadn't even opened the menu yet. "Tuna melts with chips," she told the waiter. She turned to Martin. "You're not a vegetarian, are you? Gluten-free?"

"Fish is fine."

"Oh boy. So do I call you Marty?"

"It's Martin."

"Thin skin, I love it." She laughed. "I'm going to call you New Jersey. Honestly, there's nothing else in this place worth eating. Call me Brenner."

Parents from Mexico, Monterrey, who currently reside outside Boston, retired, in panting expectation of grandchildren. Dad had been an engineer. Mom was a pharmacist. Brenner and her little sister were first-generation, so her sister was the lucky one who got to be the screwup, whereas Brenner, firstborn, needed to please. For career, one of her grandfathers had been a judicial clerk, he'd sent her books all her life, a box every couple months, with a sheet of reading instructions. Philosophy. Poetry. Law. It wasn't until ninth grade she figured out he was dismantling his personal library, to transmit his education to hers.

"Of course I don't remember ten percent of it."

"Maria, tell me—"

"It's Brenner, please. Even the fiancé doesn't call me Maria."

"Got it. And congratulations."

"Yeah, I never get that. People want to congratulate me, they should wait and see if I go through with it."

He'd laughed. "Is there a problem?"

She smirked. "Are you kidding me? He runs a Honda dealership, he doesn't hate my cats. I'm not stupid. What were you going to say?"

"The point is," Martin said, "am I the only one who thinks there's something seriously wrong with this kid's story?"

"No, New Jersey, you're not."

At that point, she only knew what she'd heard and read, she said, so she wanted to know his impression. He told her he thought the confession was a crock. She said she was still waiting to get ahold of it from the sheriff's office. Which was when Martin pulled out a thumb drive from his pocket.

She spun it around with a finger. Then tucked it away.

"Remind me again what you're doing up here."

"I'm on vacation," he said.

"You're retired. Retirement's not vacation."

"I'm sentimental. Come find me at Christmas. The kid's not your guy."

"Yeah, and shit happens. So why him? Why now?"

He'd had enough of the inquiry. "Here's the thing. You're going to do your investigation no matter what. Which means you need someone to dig around. Ideally pull noses without local relationships getting in the way."

Not to mention that maybe he needed a couple weeks away from home.

Brenner shrugged. She could tell there was more. "It's appealing, obviously. The chief who took the kid's confession now says the kid's innocent, that's pretty solid jury appeal. You are willing to say that in court."

"Of course."

"Small town, all the tourist dollars, the prosecution wants a conviction fast and clean. Trust me, they think they've got a slam dunk. The woman who runs point, we're friends, we get dinner. But she'll come down on this hard."

"Here's what I want," Brenner added. "You work for me. On my orders. I don't need you riding around wild."

"I get it," he said. "One-way street."

Then she stared at him. A long stare. Few normal police officers dismantle homicides. Definitely not ones with captain bars. She bit off a chunk of sandwich and nodded at her plate a couple times and swallowed.

"First thing they'll try is to get you removed, conflict of interest. I'll take care of that. The only thing that took place in New Jersey was the car crash, we should be fine. After that, who knows?"

"They're going to hate you," she said after a second.

Later, in the room, he hunches his shoulders while Brenner walks the kid through all the jargon. Introductions. Arraignment. How the next couple weeks play out. The kid can't sit still. He interrupts with specific demands: he wants pen and paper, he wants his mother to be granted twice-daily visits. He looks even skinnier if that's possible. Neck so transparent it could be a flower petal.

"Like I said, Mr. Krug is going to be assisting with the investigation," Brenner says. "We're allowed to reinvestigate everything the police looked at, to see what they got wrong."

"But why's a cop doing it?"

"Not a cop," Martin says. "I don't even have a badge anymore."

Not true, in fact.

"Whatever."

"Nick," he says, "I believe you're innocent."

But the kid won't even look him in the eye.

When they leave, he gets an uneasy feeling, an old feeling. The kid's got too much fear. Of the wrong kind. To the point that it's unwarranted in some way, given what Martin knows. Which means there must be things he doesn't know. Big things.

Ten minutes later, he and Brenner stand on the sidewalk, chatting, about to go their separate ways, when a Dodge Charger slows to a stop. The window rolls down. The sheriff stares at them a moment, lips in a single straight line.

"Chief Krug. What are you doing here?"

"Retired, actually. It's just Martin now."

"Well, that was quick."

"You're telling me."

"So, what brings you to Claymore?"

"Same as anybody," he says. "I needed a vacation."

"That's what he told me," says Brenner.

The sheriff's mouth stays fixed.

"Ms. Brenner," he says. "I take it you two are working together."

"Mr. Krug's helping with our investigation."

"Well that sounds like perhaps a conflict," the sheriff says.

"Your colleagues agree with you. We think they'll change their minds."

Martin asks, "You don't play racquetball, do you, Sheriff?"

"Try the Parks Department. Building over there on the corner," the sheriff says after a moment. Then stares through them both before he drives away.

•

First, how do you scare a middle-aged woman who's already panicky by default, inclined to paranoia, self-mistrust—and probably too smart for her own good—*or quite singularly stupid*—also prepared by life thus far to counter the littlest problems with exaggerated primal reactions, sharpened tooth and yellow nail, despite the high manner she'd been raised to uphold—how do you scare a woman like that witless?

Stick her only child in jail for murder.

Second, it's not funny, nothing's funny. Each night is a contest of nightmares. All day long the landline rings. She feels trapped in her old house—she wants it sold. Anywhere she goes, people glare. Her feet cramp, her breasts ache that week, the discomfort carries her mind at bewildering moments to her life's other slow-motion abandonments— her deceased parents, the husband who vanished.

But this is all so much worse for being . . . how much worse? She can't begin to comprehend.

The doorbell screeches. It can't be a student. She canceled all her lessons that week. Suzanne peers out the window—it's the girl, Emily. She forgot completely. Coincidentally arriving at the exact same hour that the girl used to take her piano lesson.

She pulls her in with no words, a hug, tells her to make herself comfortable. The girl sits on the couch. A cotton dress over jeans. Composed, but impatient.

Suzanne offers iced tea, coffee, herbal tea, LaCroix—wouldn't Scotch be more appropriate?—and at the same time can't help but wonder what the girl knows that she does not.

"Tea, please," says Emily.

"Sugar or milk?"

"No, thanks."

"I'll be right back."

"Thanks, Mrs. Toussaint."

Kitchen, kettle, stove. And a quick twist for her nerves. And one for the road. The kettle dings. She doesn't hate the girl, in reality she admires her—to have such presence at sixteen. It's obvious her feelings for Nicky are real. The age difference notwithstanding, she even likes them together. But the girl's not her concern—except as a source of information.

She holds out the mug. Her own glass clacks with ice.

"We need to be strong for him. I know it's hard."

"It's not," the girl says emphatically. "I mean, I know. I'm being strong."

"Of course," says Suzanne. To soothe both of them. "And I know how it sounds. But I do think it's worth saying out loud. Right now, we're all he's got."

"I know that," the girl says forcefully, and takes the mug.

Suzanne lowers herself to the settee and smokes. The poor girl's trapped in the emergency, she doesn't know how yet to put on a brave face—and to figure this out actually pushes Suzanne into a calmer, more empathetic state, because it makes sense when the girl's so young. And she needs at least a few things in her life right now to make sense. You can't just yell all day. Don't they have things in common? Both of them conscripted by the situation in which they find themselves. Suzanne half smiles. This poor girl. Why love a boy when he can vanish?

"Let's start over," she says quietly. "You're the one who's closest to him. Strange as it is for me to say it, Nicky's going to look to you first. Can you do that, can you support him?"

"Mrs. Toussaint, I just said—"

"I know you're struggling, Emily, we're all struggling. But you can do that, right? Please, call me Suzanne. May I ask you a favor?"

"What is it?"

"So now, when you write to him," she says, "I want you to remind him that he has us, all of us, for anything. He needs to know there's a community out here, all right? He doesn't listen to me."

The girl stands. Putters around.

"How long is this going to take?"

"What. Right now?"

"All of this."

"I don't know. How would I know?" She adds, less defensively, "We don't know what happened, do we?"

"No."

"Because if you did know anything . . ."

"What?"

Suzanne leans forward, arms on knees, one woman to another—but the girl's halfway across the room, staring into the kitchen.

"Emily, you have to be honest with me. If you know anything, about what happened that night between the two of you."

"I told you, I don't know."

"But maybe Nick said something. He must've told you something."

"He didn't," the girl says darkly.

"We don't have to talk about it. Just walk me through it again. For my own peace of mind."

"We were hanging out."

"At your house. It's okay, I'm not a prude."

The girl flinches. "He walked out. He just got up and left."

"But why?"

"He had something to do. That's all."

"And then came everything else," Suzanne says.

"Yeah."

"But before that, you're at the house, you're hanging out. You're sure nothing unusual happened."

"That's what I just said."

"Of course. I'm sorry. We're all adults here," she adds, then realizes that's not true at all. Why must she cede ground to a sixteen-year-old? "But I don't understand, Emily. There must have been something. To make him run out like that."

"He didn't 'run out.'"

"But something must have made him leave."

"There wasn't."

"There has to be!"

The room's silent in the aftermath. The girl puts down her tea, too hot to drink.

"I'm going to go now."

"Have you had lunch?"

"I need to go."

"Well, if you say so." Suzanne rolls up her sleeves. She wants to laugh. She wants to claw her own ears off. "This was good," she says woodenly, and automatically walks the girl to the front door, like she's a student who just finished her lesson. "So the plan is just stick to what we're doing. No matter what anyone says. Nicky did nothing wrong. We need to trust. Trust in the law, and the truth. It'll be hard. It'll be really hard. But then this will all be over."

But the girl doesn't respond and doesn't move a muscle when Suzanne embraces her. So she's the one who's trembling.

∎

Dear Nick,

Please write me if you can but I understand if you can't. Your mother says you're doing okay. It makes me feel better. I worry about you but honestly I'm really happy that you're able to receive these letters, it makes a huge difference to my own state of mind. Love and love 4EAE.

I don't know what you hear in there but they say you killed two people and drove them to New Jersey. We know that's insane, your mom and I talk about it all the time. You have a ton of people out here who support you and know that's all lies. We love you so much. We are your champions and we're sure you did the right thing no matter what happened, <u>we can't wait for everyone to know the truth</u>.

I think about that night a lot. It drives me crazy when I hear people talk. I tell myself, you need to be strong and not stupid, imagine how hard it is for Nick.

I don't really share my feelings with other people, I don't want to know what they think. I just walk around like a rock. Alex and I watched TV last night. They didn't have anything new, they just talked about all the stuff that's bullshit. We turned it off and promised not to watch again or listen or look into anything online. It just makes me so mad. What happened to innocent before guilty? Meg had a good point, she said that a small town like ours is full of idiots, but to expect people who are idiots to behave not like idiots is being just as stupid.

I never wanted to get you in any trouble. I'm so sorry. <u>No matter what don't lose hope</u>, and please don't worry about me. I've moved full-time to

Alex's. Father hasn't said anything about it but I'm not surprised. What-
ever you do, please don't think badly about me, all I do is think about you.
I love you so much. Soon this will all be over and we will do exactly as we
planned.

Love, love, love,
Emily

■

By the time she met Nick, Emily had known Alex Rosenthal for a little
over a year and a half. When they first became friends, Alex was a junior,
a popular-unpopular who floated between groups. Emily was a freshman. To adjust from middle school wasn't easy. Classes were much more
difficult. The schedule confused her. She got tongue-tied and flustered.
Girls were snobbier. Boys were more unpredictable, also more predict-
able. Eleven hundred kids total, and she felt like everyone was staring
at her, like she was an exotic animal, to be viewed behind protective
glass. Even her backpack was wrong.

But at the beginning of ninth grade her biggest problem was that
she got dumped. Come September, Hazel and Leila wouldn't talk to
her. In middle school, the three of them were inseparable, they called
themselves the Sand Dollars, they wore matching sweatshirts. Leila,
leader, petite and cute. Hazel, the funny one, second-in-command. Emily,
tagalong, emotional backstop. Three halves of a whole, which meant
the math was probably wrong from the start.

She found a note in her locker on the second day of school. She read
it over until she couldn't make out the letters anymore. The Sand Dollars needed to split up. Three would become two, and they weren't even
Sand Dollars anymore, that was too embarrassing. Leila and Hazel
reached their decision that summer when they shared a cabin at Keuka
Lake Empowerment Camp for Girls. Basically, they'd moved on, sorry
(not sorry?), because camp had taught them to want more out of life,
leave behind outdated versions of themselves and quit apologizing, start
actualizing, and they'd realized that Emily all along had obstructed
their progress as young women, what with Emily's uncoolness, her
weirdo home life, her rando clothes—the girls didn't cite those things
specifically in the letter, but had hinted as much before. So it was im-
plicit that she'd been a charity case until that point—and charity, seem-
ingly, was not an actualizable idea. Anyway, they didn't expect her to

understand, but all was good, though please don't talk to them about it because that would be too Very Very, and remember that SCHOOL IS COOL, keep in touch, lol, L&H.

The loss was too big. They'd been inseparable for years, always at one another's houses. Now, nothing? She couldn't comprehend it.

For weeks Emily drifted in and out of classrooms and dazed fogs. Tormented herself with second-guessing, to understand how her best friends had become her enemies. Actually, it was worse, she didn't even have enemies, she had nothing. And she'd so looked forward to high school, if only a new locker. September became a month of desert days. She ate lunch by herself, meat and cheese roll-ups, and slept a lot, and asked herself questions she couldn't answer, and was angry, Very Very, but in a way she didn't know how to actualize.

She became obsessively concerned for Leila's and Hazel's social progress and carefully tracked them around school, prayed they'd be accepted into one of the better cliques.

For the first time ever, Emily Portis got a C on a test. She was punished by Father with two weeks of chores. She feared worse and focused harder on homework, but there was piles of it, she could hardly breathe. Then, a few weeks later, it wasn't so bad. Tryouts for cross-country weren't difficult, they just needed girls. The team had a big sister–little sister program. She got matched with a senior girl who gave her a cookie at practice that said *Emily!* on the top in white icing. She was so touched, she didn't eat it, she took it home.

By October, Emily could see Leila and Hazel in the cafeteria and not be destroyed. Her new comfort didn't last long. The same month, another freshman, Jessie Baker, picked Emily as her subject for an assignment in torture.

Jessie was in her algebra class, ash blond and moanful. She'd recently transferred from a Boston magnet school and had quickly figured out the social tiers at CHS and applied, as much as a girl could apply, to be a Zeta, clique of the populars.

Zetas were by and large older girls and rich. Occasionally they took in first-years, even from the not so rich, like Jessie, but then they'd make those girls hustle a little bit harder for membership. All of this Emily would learn later on. At that point, she knew only that on a Thursday a new note appeared in her locker. She unfolded it, felt her blood stop. *Nobody likes you.* After that it was math class, murmured teases, a trick note that she thankfully figured out before she embarrassed herself, though within a week the ordeals had progressed to the halls. No bathroom was safe. If Jessie found her alone, especially if she was with another aspirant or even a full-fledged Zeta, a best-case scenario would go:

"Hi, Emily."

"Hey."

"I like your sneakers."

"Thanks."

"They're boy sneakers."

"No they're not."

"Do you know why you don't have any friends?"

"I have friends."

"Then I won't tell you."

"Tell me what?"

"Nothing. You can ask them yourself."

"Tell me what?"

"Never mind."

How did they always get under her skin? She wanted to ask her big sister on the cross-country team but was too embarrassed. She wouldn't go to the bathroom, she didn't drink water until afternoon. She found satisfaction, in fact, in not going to the bathroom. Though for the rest of the month her stomach hurt.

By November, the trees' leaves were down, cross-country practice was cold and dark. The big attack came on the Monday before Thanksgiving. Later, Alex informed her that it had been Jessie's initiation test for membership, that Jessie needed to demonstrate initiative, do more than throw together an anonymous hate page. So Jessie upped the ante. She narrated a slide show, complete with scribbles, that spread from phone to phone, about how Jessie had loaned Emily her North Face at a Zeta party over the weekend, the rum-slushie party at Piper Samavai's family's camp that everyone still talked about, where, behind the wood pile, up in the trees, Emily had jerked off some boy from Leduc and sprayed his junk on the sleeve, and returned Jessie's jacket just like that, all comed on, like it was no big deal.

In the pics it did look real enough, sleeve+slime.

By the next morning, half of the school had seen it. The other half saw it at lunch. Buildings quivered with a visceral thrill, no matter that

Emily Portis would be the last person invited to a Zeta party, definitely one girl Jessie never would consent to lend her treasured puffy to.

After lunch, Ezra Mullan, a senior, let it be known online that the fluids in question were *his* fluids in the photos, but it was just phlegm, no sperm, no homo, and definitely no "Emily Portis" involved, whoever that was. Poop emoji, thumbs-up emoji, crying-while-laughing emoji. And thus was the severity of events so adequately counterbalanced that everyone could laugh off any icky awkwardness about what took place, because they knew that no one would be called into the principal's office, because Ezra was cool like that, one of the school's top-tier African-Americans, aka the Blacks, the popular boys' equivalent of the Zetas, that consisted almost exclusively of white soccer and lacrosse players who made honor roll while enjoying hip-hop, Genesee Cream Ale, and the materialization of sluttishness.

CHS did have a handful of black students, but only one of them, the captain of the lacrosse team, belonged to the group. There was also an actual African kid, a senior who'd been adopted from Ethiopia when he was nine, but he was Dark Side, the goth clique, and hardly black at all.

The point was that, by fourth period, once the rumors had had enough time to flow and travel, practically everyone in school knew a number of new things for fact. That Ezra Mullan got blow jobs from Briana Bittner before soccer games. That Briana was a Zeta chieftain and Jessie's sponsor for her pledge campaign. That Briana had loaned out Ezra and his loogie-hawking for her newbie's initiation campaign. And that some freshman girl named Emily Portis was a total slut.

But all of this was only known to Emily herself after Alex explained it much later. Because the one person who knew nothing, besides the teachers, was Emily. Barely online in the first place, she had no phone, she didn't text, she never stressed about data usage. No boys begged her for pics, because how could she take them? She might have been homeless, as far as anyone knew. So Emily wasn't aware that she'd decorated Jessie's coat. Or that, on occasion, Emily Portis paid twenty dollars for boys to munch out her fuckhole. And qualified for asshole-eater welfare payments, and liked sex best on her period, and once got fingered by Mr. Becker to improve her grade in Algebra. And did bestow discount blow jobs, just five dollars, on any African-Americans who knew that week's password, which was "yoohoo," which became #yoohoo, which trended that afternoon within the cacophonous jungle that was life at CHS, online and off.

Understand that Emily was clueless and embarrassed during a break, and didn't know why exactly, when she walked past the senior cafeteria and a tableful of boys sang out "Yoohoo!" and the whole room laughed.

Finally, sixth period, Biology, Mike Komorowski showed her his phone under their bench. Mike was almost more oblivious than she, he just wanted to confirm that his lab partner was, in fact, the Emily Portis whom everyone talked about. She asked to go to the nurse. She ran past half of the school's classroom doors' tiny windows, then stayed home the next two days. She thought about ending it all with her mother's pills. She curled up on the bathroom rug and chewed on her fingertips. She was utterly miserable and wholly confused. Then on Friday came the one and only Alexandra Rosenthal.

Alex was also on cross-country, but she didn't really talk to the other girls. Emily knew her as the black-and-white ponytail that bobbed ahead of her in the distance. She'd heard what teammates whispered, that Alex was a girl with no parents, with an older sister who wore an Indian headdress to the mall. That Alex would probably be valedictorian when she graduated, but was also well-known as a pothead. And still somehow routinely placed second or third for their team. So a total weirdo, but kind of untouchable.

Friday morning, Emily was between classes when Alex yanked her aside in the hall and dragged her outside, to a secluded quadrant by the library.

She demanded, "Do you have any idea what's happened in the last couple days?"

"Sort of," Emily said. Aggravated to be put on the spot.

"I didn't think so. Just listen for a second."

So Alex explained what had occurred Monday night, Tuesday day, and also what had taken place since then. Like the night before, when much of the senior and junior classes had showed up at Scotty Metz's house, whose parents were out of town. Jessie had been there, too, with a flock of aspiring Zetas. Alex spotted them in the TV room while they filmed each other doing lap dances on each other, on view for the enjoyment of upperclassmen.

"They'll send a hundred tit pics before they graduate. They're a joke."

Alex knew about the yoohoo incident, of course, and found it beyond grotesque. At the party she'd gone upstairs, and there it was, the infamous North Face, on top of other jackets, pink with fake fur around the hood. She'd stuffed it inside her bag. Found Ezra outside, the same Ezra from the original prank, and asked for his help. The previous year, they'd both done *The King and I*, nonspeaking roles for extra credit in English class. They used to sneak away from rehearsal together and get stoned. Naturally, she explained, it was simple to talk Ezra into her idea, because as a rule Ezra was up for anything, the stupider the better, which included "ejaculating" on a jacket more than once.

The two of them took a picture with Jessie's jacket, re-seminated.

"Whatever, it wasn't really come," Alex said. "The kid got in early to Dartmouth, he's not an idiot. The point is, as of today, now everyone laughs at *her*. It's become its own thing: take a photo with spit on your arm, tag Jessie. She'll never make Zeta. I almost feel bad."

Alex took out her phone, a video. Older boys whom Emily didn't recognize pointed to white splotches on their clothes, captioned in a scribble, "jessieyoohoo."

"But you don't even know me," Emily said.

"I just hate freshmen. With overplucked brows."

Then Alex laughed, a laugh that glittered, and lay down in the grass. Her hair made a black-and-white blanket. She grabbed Emily's wrist, yanked her down like a child. The air smelled of snow. They lay side by side for half a minute, both of them looked at the gray sky, then a hand appeared and rubbed Emily's ring finger between the bones. She shuddered.

Alex didn't let go.

"I would kill somebody for hands like yours. Also, I love your dress."

"I made it," said Emily. It just came out.

"Wait, seriously?"

"Yeah."

"But that's so ghetto. Can you make me one?"

•

Much later, decades later, after the name of Emily Portis sifts to the bottom of the American public consciousness, she will still remember the Night of Speed Metal as the moment when her second life began. October, freshman year, the same month Alex commissioned a boy to spit on a jacket, still a year before she'd met Nick, from that point forward Emily had decided she would forever yield charge of her life to her new best friend, Alex, her magical friend.

Who insisted Emily read this, watch that, make up for lost time. Sneak out, steal a candy bar, introduce herself to the world of teenagers. Get over the feeling that she was in the wilderness and all alone. It got to a point that Emily wished she could pin their friendship to her sweatshirt. Bewilderingly, she discovered that with Alex she was happy, maybe for the first time yet. She admired her to a point where she began to think about herself not as an "I" but a "we" in her mind, as in *We're so lucky she likes us*, and *We're so in love with her*, and *What does she even see in us?* As if her "I" wasn't big enough to fit all her new experiences, or big enough to justify Alex's attention.

But mostly she was happy. Alex had decided to undo her new friend's sad existence in a hundred ways. Half of her plans were terrifying. Like the chimney game.

Behind the Claymore town dump was a wood-chip trail, a two-mile hike that led down to an unused service road in the woods that ran next to a burned-out furrow filled with trash, and after another mile there was a creepy old cement tower, three stories tall, that was stained with smoke. Once upon a time, the Claymore Fire Department had used it for training exercises. Now homeless people lived there, people said.

"And Satanists," Alex said. "They're the worst."

"You're joking."

"No, Satanists are the worst."

"You are joking."

"Still no."

Alex had on a yellow maxiskirt. She picked up the hem and walked down into the culvert like someone entering a lake. Emily followed her, she'd follow her anywhere. They'd known each other by that point for three weeks, but it may as well have been three years.

The inside of the tower was covered in graffiti. Garbage everywhere, ivy vines. The floor was littered with leaves and a ripped sleeping bag. She wanted to run.

Against one wall was a concrete fireplace, a dark hole thick with cobwebs. Alex bent down, took a deep breath, and shoved her hand straight up the hole.

Emily shrieked, "What are you doing?"

Alex stared back, eyes wide, her arm stuck up all the way to the elbow. "One, two, three, four." By nine, she couldn't stand it anymore and yanked out her arm.

"But what if there was a raccoon up there?"

"That's the whole point, you wimp."

The game was her sister's invention. Emily lasted three seconds her first time, her hand writhed in the dark. It was horrible. Next time, seven seconds. Afterward they climbed upstairs. Alex pulled out a small pipe and got high. They walked home along the train tracks, went to CVS, ate King Cones while they sat cross-legged on the handicapped ramp.

They began to spend all their time together. At school, cross-country, weekends whether or not there was a race, they walked together on the beach, down to the docks, and got cappuccinos to go and told each other everything. Alex hitchhiked one time, scored them a ride to Leduc. Hitchhiked! Father would have killed her. But her grades actually improved as a result of all their time together. Alex was determined to be valedictorian, and a lot of times they just did homework side by side, or made rally posters for cross-country meets. They'd watch one of Alex's favorite horror movies, or some TV show she loved, or just watch You-Tube, or read together, or walk around town. And Emily did anything, everything that Alex suggested, despite that she often worried and had to hide it, or felt young in a bad way, afraid that her new friend might see something to make her walk.

But gradually it seemed unlikely. With Alex, life was to be approached passionately, not too sensitively, not sensitively at all, in fact, seeing how she was stoned so much of the time. Whereas Emily felt so weighed down by her feelings that she was also a touch removed. She vowed to keep her new friend in the dark, from her total dullness, her family, her food rituals. She was already skilled at concealment, it wouldn't be too hard. She especially made sure she didn't mention a single thing about home.

During her first sleepover at Alex's house, afraid she might say something in her sleep, she zipped her sleeping bag completely around her head and nearly suffocated.

But in the course of that first afternoon, after the fire tower, outside CVS, on a crazy impulse she showed Alex her sketchbook. It was in her backpack. Only her art teachers had seen it before. Her heart raced, she handed it over. It was like she'd fallen under some powerful spell. Alex didn't say a word, just leafed through the pages of all her drawings. Dresses, figures, girls in plaid shirts ten times too large.

Alex pointed to a drawing of a basic sundress, asked if she'd actually made it before. She said yes. Alex asked if she'd make her one.

She was almost too embarrassed and overjoyed.

The dress took two weeks, a hundred adjustments. The previous summer she'd started a part-time job at a fabric shop, and Alex would visit when she was closing, they did fittings in the back room. In the end, it came together terribly. It draped like a flag in the rain. She wanted to throw it in the garbage, she was so angry. Naturally she feared, before the inescapable final try-on, that Alex would be disappointed, upset, and then she'd burst into tears, because Alex was the single most authoritative person in the world who'd have the right to say, *You have no talent.*

She couldn't stand the idea of Alex teasing her a little, if only for the discomfort she knew Alex would feel.

But Alex loved the dress, complimented her endlessly.

And Emily discovered how much she liked to be praised.

The dress articulated something she'd wanted to say for a long time.

In the months that followed, she made her friend a dozen better things. A yellow dress for Homecoming. A yellow bumblebee skirt (Alex's favorite color was yellow) with black and white stripes to match her hair, that was so short it got Alex in trouble with dress code after it distracted nearly every boy in school.

When Alex quit smoking pot on New Year's Eve, she cited Emily's good influence. And also quit Diet Vanilla Coke because that shit was gross.

They were best friends, they wrote it down, they couldn't picture their lives without the other.

So when Alex insisted in late March, beginning of spring—later to be known as the Night of Speed Metal—that Emily sneak out at two a.m., of course she'd found the guts, despite white-hot fear, to crawl awkwardly across the roof, hitch down the tree, and sprint across the field toward the headlights on the road. Half-thrilled, mostly terrified, all because she couldn't risk to tell her brilliant friend no.

Twenty minutes later, they'd pulled into a parking space across from a diner by the beach. The boardwalk was dark, windy, and cold. The ocean was flat and silent. There was muddy snow all around. Not even the Ferris wheel ran at that hour. And yet the sidewalk was full of kids she knew by face, at least a dozen kids who lingered by a dumpster, smoked cigarettes, only wore T-shirts and flannels as if it wasn't still winter. She spotted a knot of Zetas, they listened to music off somebody's phone. Did everyone normally sneak out? Was it typical to be out so late, and she'd been clueless once again?

Alex led them inside the restaurant. The manager said loudly, "We're closing in five minutes." Her voice made a tableful of dudes turn to stare.

They took a booth. Alex whispered, "I'm such a bad bitch."

"I guess."

"My therapist says I want to think I'm 'of interest' to somebody."

"She said that?"

Two minutes later, the manager kicked them out. Alex perked up again, ignited by the outrage. The boys came out and lit cigarettes. Alex asked for one. They were all twenty or twenty-one, they were in a band, they'd moved to Claymore from Laconia to work tourist jobs while they practiced and played shows. The plan was to move to Brooklyn once enough money was saved.

They played speed metal, the shortest one said, with influences of power ambient.

Alex said, "I hate everything you just said."

"What's your band's name?" Emily asked.

"The Power of Elephants," said the short one.

Alex said, "So what does that mean?"

The tallest one said, after a brief moment of silence, "Do you ever think how, like, if kittens breathed fire, they'd only breathe a really small amount of fire?"

"Why would I think that?"

"Why wouldn't you?"

"You're such dudes. I bet you don't even play your own instruments."

"Yeah, well," he said, "who the hell are you?"

"I'm Miss America."

"I'm Emily."

The tall one had the head of an elephant tattooed on the back of each hand. He had a tiny dog next to him, a pit bull puppy on a leash. Emily kept an eye on how Alex watched the boy, how the boy watched Alex. She'd never seen Alex interested in a guy before, she was fascinated. Did it always happen so fast?

The short boy said they lived around the corner. Everyone left together. On the walk, she pleaded to Alex again, through her teeth, "Can we go now, please?"

"If you're in trouble, you're in trouble."

"But I'm scared."

"Don't be a pussy."

The house looked haunted. The tall boy locked his dog in a cage under the stairs. Inside, the kitchen floor was uneven, it tilted to a hole through which she could see the plumbing. Alex and the tall one were quickly alone in a corner. Emily went into a den and sat on a dirty couch. The room was gross. The boys filed in. Someone lit a joint and passed it around. She would leave any second, she told herself. After all, she had enough money for a cab. The joint came to her, Emily accepted it awkwardly. She'd never smoked anything before in her life. *Don't be a pussy.* She sucked on the end and burst out coughing.

"You have to inhale," one said.

"Leave her alone," said the short one. He handed her a water bottle.

She drank almost the whole thing, then glanced up, worried. Did he want to share it? Had everyone stared at her? But they were occupied, they watched TV, a nature show, whales who flew through the ocean on wings. She got up and looked around the kitchen. Alex and the tall one had disappeared.

"I love whales," announced the short one.

"I do, too," she said from the doorway.

She sat down again. Was she stoned? She didn't feel stoned. The whales were nice to look at. The short boy leaned toward her across the couch. His hair was curly, it smelled like pineapples.

"Do you want to come hear us play?"

"I guess."

"You guys, let's go."

Suddenly everyone was moving, like athletes summoned by a coach. They banged down a flight of stairs to the basement. Emily stayed seated, she felt light-headed and nervous, maybe she *was* stoned.

The short one stood up. He had his eye on her. "Come on," he said, and pulled her up by the hand. "You probably won't get it but that's cool."

She stood up but he didn't budge. Suddenly she was right in front of him. She was at least three inches taller. She wondered what would happen if she touched his hair. Her throat went cold. What if he wanted to kiss her? Was this how it happened? Where was Alex to offer advice? She wanted him to kiss her, she realized. It thrilled her. So, what then? What if she kissed him? She ran the image through her mind. She liked his dimples, she liked the divot in his chin. Her arms got goose bumps.

But then he pulled out a paper envelope and shook out what looked like potpourri.

"Here." Offering. "It'll help you take it in."

"What are they?"

"They're mushrooms."

She swallowed them and finished off the water bottle. The taste was gross. They went downstairs, to murky darkness, a tool bench. Five or six mattresses leaned against the walls. The boys plugged in their instruments. Emily sat in a folding beach chair on the ground, closed her eyes, and thought about how the sun would be up soon, she had a track meet later that afternoon, she was in serious trouble.

Then she felt weirdly light.

The walls were expanding, or something like that?

The boys started playing. It sounded like a single note, so thick it droned. She sat back in the dark, the crazy sound, and it was amazing. Though when she opened her eyes she didn't like the boys' faces at all, she couldn't look at them for some reason, their geometry had become alien, so she stared at the plumbing in the ceiling instead, and that was *so amazing*.

And the music was actually really subtle, while the indoors became outdoors, and her skull wasn't a barrier anymore, and her memories were let loose to run.

For the first time that she could remember in her life, Emily Portis disappeared.

After forty-five minutes, Alex clomped downstairs. She found Emily smiling at the ceiling. In the neighborhood's silence, four a.m. dark, Emily couldn't look her friend in the face because Alex's face was scary the way the boys' faces had been scary, something about the angles were incorrect, so she focused on getting into the truck. Soon they chugged out of town. Emily rolled down her window. Alex talked. She herself couldn't speak. Time had folded in on itself, so had Emily Portis. And every house they passed was densely unlit. Parked cars seethed with malicious parked car–ness. Trees bled tree-ness into the ground. In the distance the mountaintop was even blacker than the sky. Somewhere on its side was her family's old house. The mountain's darkest outcropping sucked her home.

"Hey, weirdo," said Alex. "Why are you being so quiet?"

She needed to open the door. Air rushed into the car. She undid her seat belt.

"Shit! Emily, stop!"

Alex braked so hard, the tires squealed. The car fishtailed in the road. Around them were thick woods full of sticky oil three feet deep, oil that slowly oozed toward them.

She had to close her eyes against the horribleness that encroached.

"What the hell? You think that's funny? Are you nuts?"

"It's cool," she said quietly.

"What'd you just say?"

"Don't look at me."

"Why?"

"They took away your face."

"What?"

"I'm sorry!"

"Oh, shit. Holy shit. You're high."

"He said mushrooms," Emily said slowly. "He said they were mushrooms."

That was the night that Alex almost peed in her pants from laughing.

And it became a founding story in their mythology, the Night of Speed Metal. Emily actually didn't mind, she could see beyond the storm. To be teased by Alex turned out to be okay. Bigger than that, she liked to feel a little dangerous, she enjoyed it. She didn't even get busted for sneaking out.

By January, she tripped two or three times a month, by herself, sometimes in her room but mostly outdoors, in the woods. She'd hike up the mountain while Father was at work, she loved it. And the experience was always so agreeable, full of woolly branches and crunchy meadows, that each time in a rush of self-loathing and guilt and rebellious pleasure, she would justify the mushrooms as an act of obliteration, that she was a girl who needed to disappear, for her own sake and the world's, and also because that's how it truly felt when she'd blend into nature, the softness of the world, and all her dark thoughts ran away and left her unaccompanied. Blissfully, at least for a couple hours, she was no one.

∎

Alex and her older sister, Meg, who went by Headdress, lived in a rickety, messy apartment nicknamed the Sisterhood, four blocks in from the beach, the second floor of an old brick building, above a bakery, with a rusted outdoor staircase spiked to the wall.

Every time Emily visited, the apartment was a glum Mardi Gras: stuffed trash bags, empty soda cans, magazines, old pizza boxes, moisturizer bottles, Meg's bikinis, Meg's surfboard, Meg's laundry, and all the smells of feminine musk. And in a corner would tower a neat pile of Alex's books from school, her posters from Diversity Club, her stuffed backpack.

The apartment was nicknamed the Sisterhood because it was just the two of them. They were on their own. Their parents, Fred and Kiki, were artists in New York City, though this fact of life, their being artists, their being feverish, hand-wringing, serious painters, who needed to live and work in New York and only New York, had not materialized until Alex was in seventh grade, back when she still went by Alexandra, and Meg at the time was seventeen.

It happened over a long weekend, Alex had told her. Their parents presented them with a bold new family plan. That the girls would be provided with all the essentials and more, clothing allowances, eating-out money, vehicles, spending cash, college educations if so desired, extra money for Meg as compensation for guardian duties, extra allowance for Alexandra for putting up with Meg—plus, as a family, they'd come together one weekend every month, for longer vacations twice a year, with locations of democratic choosing, within reason—all so that they, Fred and Kiki, could pursue their art careers in New York City, without children, while the girls remained back home.

"But why don't we all just move?" Meg had asked.

"I want to live in New York City," Alex said.

But this wasn't the plan their parents had in mind.

Meg became Headdress shortly after high school. She lasted one semester at UNH-Manchester, in the pursuit of a women's studies degree. For which a class required anthropological work at a local strip club. Meg had never been to one. She befriended some of the dancers. For the sake of research, she started performing herself. Back in the day she'd done ballet and jazz, now she liked the freedom, the attention, the music, making money for herself. Her academic excuse quickly faded. Soon she danced full-time.

Her nickname referred to the costume she wore, a Native American headdress with glass beads, wrapped feathers, strands of bells. She'd bought it off eBay. It didn't stay in the club for long. Meg wore it to the grocery store, the mall, the beach, because it was good for her brand. To be seen around town, to remind those who'd seen her dance that it was perhaps time to see her again, and entice those who'd only heard word of her dancing—a clever brand needed to work on several levels of customer-activation. (Over time, Meg would explain marketing to Emily on multiple occasions.)

From what Alex told her, her sister, Meg, aka Headdress, was alternately hopeful, morose, smart, and shortsighted, which depended on the lunar cycle and/or meds, and/or current boyfriends. Sexually greedy. Diagnosed depressed. Alex explained that, despite what Emily might generously think, Meg didn't strip for school, wasn't a dancer with a heart of gold. Was simply an exhibitionist with a rocking body who loved to make money and not have to face real-life decisions.

As the younger sister, Alex had learned absolutely nothing good about life from Headdress, and not much more from Meg.

The summer before her sophomore year, Emily spent many nights at the Sisterhood. Father tolerated sleepovers, as long as she kept up her GPA. One night in July, late, hot and humid outside, Meg ran up the stairs in a loose tank top and short cutoffs. A man shouted something. She went straight for the broom closet, came back with a shotgun, flew out the door just as the guy tromped up the stairs.

He backpedaled into the night and said unpleasant things about women.

"What the hell was that?" Alex snapped.

"Chill out. It was nothing." Meg read Emily's look instantly. "He followed me home because penis. The only thing to see here is the need for the two of you to get your concealed-carry permits."

"That is such bullshit," Alex spluttered, and went to her room.

Emily didn't budge, she was too scared, frozen by awe. Meg opened the window, poured herself a glass of wine, then remembered something, dug around in her bag, and tossed Emily a Ziploc baggie of mushrooms without a word.

Emily and Meg didn't hang out much because Meg scared her. Headdress frightened her even more. Both personas were twenty-seven but sometimes thirteen. It was hard to predict. Headdress, in particular, would invite you into weird little corners of her world. Her mysterious insomnia. Her bumpy relationship with Adderall. Her troubles at the club like when construction workers came in, and after a dozen dances her thighs would be scratched raw because the guys couldn't be bothered to change out of their Carhartts. However, Meg liked to do mushrooms, too, and she had a connection at one of the clubs where she worked.

After Alex stomped away, Meg ordered Emily to sit down. Given what had just happened, it was yet another opportunity to counsel Emily's off-grid ignorant self on the ways of males. This didn't happen infrequently, that Meg would assume a yoga pose and play mother, as though she believed Emily to be a lost creature who needed instruction. For example, she should never leave guys fully satisfied. Also never send naked selfies from her phone. "Your generation should just skip online dating. Or say in your bio you want to have a baby." Because some dudes wanted romance, Meg explained, but others wanted you to be their mothers. Some guys you met, you texted, but should you ignore them for a little while, they flipped out. And some guys just wanted to smoke a girl out in exchange for a hand job. She should avoid those guys.

Meg picked up a catalog. "Do you ever look at Victoria's Secret? Honestly, it's like my diet porn."

Alex came out, crashed into Emily on the sofa, cuddled into her side. The three of them could smell the ocean, low tide, the sourness on the breeze.

"Of course," Meg resumed, stood up, removed her bra under her tank top, "if you're in love, like, love-love? It's totally different. You're his slave. It's the same for guys, they'll do whatever you want at that stage. Alex will tell you, I had this one guy Darren."

"Mr. Salt Life. He was gross."

"No he wasn't."

"You were, like, borderline assaulting each other on a nightly basis. Do you remember how drunk he got?"

"Ew, you were listening?"

"No I wasn't."

They stared each other down. For her part, Emily couldn't help but look at Meg's breasts through her shirt, so unlike her own breasts.

Meg said to Emily, "He was really hot."

"The only way Darren was hot," Alex said, "is if you consider super-creepy to be really hot."

Meg pretended Alex wasn't even in the room and lowered her voice. "I was in it for the sex. It was like a drug. Darren worked for his dad's roofing company. One time, he was on a job site, I sent him a pic of me in bed. Like, hand in my underwear, ass up, and it was like, *You'll want this so bad you'll break your neck.* He told me he had to go jerk off in his truck."

"He should've broken his neck," Alex said.

"Look good, fuck ugly." Meg shrugged. "At least he knew what he wanted. It's a turn-on. Emily, most boys don't. Most are like, 'sit on my face,' you know what I mean? All talk. Also, no matter what, believe me, the reverse can be true: if you love him, you'll do anything."

"Like you were with Trevor," Alex said.

"The point is," Meg said, "the heart pimps the body out."

Trevor was Meg's only significant ex whom Emily knew of. Her big love, the one who got away, whom now she lurked online and in real life. According to Alex, he hadn't been Meg's type at all. Straight-edge, reserved, a wedding photographer who wore black leather suspenders and shirts buttoned up to the neck. They'd met because Headdress needed headshots. The months they'd been together, Alex said, were the happiest period of Meg's life thus far. But then Trevor decided he wanted her to quit dancing. He was controlling, easily jealous. He never raised his voice, just turned dismissive, ice-cold; anger, he once told Meg, was an inefficient emotion. It was eight months since they'd broken up, and Meg had done everything she could to forget him, unsuccessfully. Occasionally she'd still park outside his mother's house, in case he turned up to do laundry. Only recently had she begun to recover, she'd met a surfer dude who graduated the same year at CHS.

"Emily, if you remember nothing else, beware the drunken double-tap."

"She's not online," Alex said. "Also, she's a prude."

"I am not," Emily said, shocked, a second too late.

"I meant it as a good thing."

"I'm sure she's not a prude," Meg said. She turned to Emily, consoling. "Honey, I'm sure you're not a prude."

A garbage truck on the street started beeping. Emily got up and poured herself a glass of water. Her face was on fire. How unfair. And what did Alex mean? Her heart hammered, she was sure they could hear it. The big-sister tone of Meg's voice annoyed her, but it was Alex she was mad at. Was she a prude? Was that better or worse than being a slut? She wasn't even completely sure what a prude was.

"By the way," Meg said to Emily, "my friend said to be careful with that baggie. That batch is supposed to be superstrong."

■

The next day, her boss gave her the day off, and the first two things Emily did were to check her bag and make sure Meg's Ziploc was still there, then take the bus all the way to the beach, to see the ocean. The sunlight was crystalline, almost too much. She worried the whole way about her prudery. Swallowed two caps and two stems on the ride. She decided that even if she were the last prude on Earth, it probably made sense, it suited the narrowness of her feeble life thus far.

She sat in the last row, next to the window. A pod of motorcycles swarmed darkly around them in traffic, like sharks. A man in front of her, totally ordinary and old, stroked and pinched his girlfriend's neck in a way that made her feel uncomfortable.

Forty-five minutes later, she'd gotten as far as the public locker room at the beach and couldn't leave. The terror was real. She clamped her eyes shut. She licked her lips, so dry. Little noises sounded like explosions. It was all she could do to open her eyes, but the visions persisted, everything heaved and dripped. She wanted to kill somebody, she could honestly kill somebody.

A woman came out of one of the toilet stalls, bathing suit down, her breasts wobbled left and right. She said, "Are you okay?"

How did she know to ask?

Was this woman the person she was supposed to kill?

Emily smuggled herself outside. She'd never been so afraid. She ran. Ten minutes later, behind the Dairy Queen there was an old wooden bench under an awning that faced the woods. She sat and shivered in the darkness, she couldn't calm down. She wanted to die on the spot. A prude, Alex said—the horrible irony made her laugh. She fixated on a bush in front of her, a small fist of blackberries. She counted the berries, and sang a song the way her mother used to sing. Two hours later, the world was restored, mostly. She walked to the bus stop. Maybe this time she'd actually gone crazy. She passed a little house, painted red with vivid yellow trim, like a McDonald's, but with ornate scalloped railings and boxes stuffed with geraniums. Wasn't life the real insanity? At the bus stop, she decided she'd be fine with whatever was life's opposite. Nothingness. Death. Oblivion. Actually, it was about the only thing that she was comfortable with at that moment, the notion that right there, on the sidewalk, she could collapse in front of the crazy house and it would be of no consequence, it wouldn't matter, she was absolutely fine with that: the future without her. Die/live/ whatever.

But something was different a day later: her mood stayed the same.

And for weeks from that point, she would smile calmly at her little desk, and quite enjoyably write down list after list, stream-of-consciousness inquisitions, of pros and cons. Like little written-out versions of Truth or Dare, to see how far she could go with the question, life or death, and the ways by which they could be achieved. It brought her peace, to witness herself be so imaginative about the matter.

A comforting fog snuck in as Emily started sophomore year. After two full diaries, she couldn't decide, life or death, so indecision became decision. She'd wait a bit. In the meantime, she quit mushrooms. Continued to run, even started to place in races. But she didn't care at all about her performance. She still made A's to satisfy Father, to give him no reason to pay her any attention, but she cared about grades even less. Overall, there was less soreness in her chest. No more panic attacks. Her hands and legs didn't shake when she was in the bathroom at school. What fueled her during class, or after school, or while she ran, or at the dinner table at night while she sat, and didn't eat, and just withstood, was how it all would play out come Christmas. Death/life/ whatever.

How she'd arrange it so there'd be a sliver of a chance at the final moment to go either way, and she'd let fate decide.

For now all she had to do was settle on the method.

And it was earlier in the evening on the same night that she first met Nick, in October—the night that the three of them went up to Whitehall—that she'd sat at her desk with homework, and waited for Alex to pick her up, when she had her epiphany. She'd hang herself in the barn. Quick, simple, easy. The realization came to her out of the blue: how all she'd need was a chair to kick away, or use to climb down.

But just as she reached this happy conclusion, there was a noise downstairs. Father shouted at the phone. Something to do with the cost of Mother's treatment, the insurance for her facility up in Maine. For nearly ten years, her mother had been in and out of clinics. Not even the diagnoses remained the same. Trichotillomania. Panic disorder. Anxiety disorder with OCD. Anafranil, Abilify, Adapin. Now she was in full-time care, in a facility outside Camden, about three hours north and east. Emily still hadn't visited.

At the sound of Father's voice, she couldn't take it anymore, instantly felt shredded to raw strips. In the closet was the old baggie. She guzzled the remains.

How long had it been, six months?

Then she remembered that Alex was picking her up soon. The plan was to sneak out to a bar in town so Alex could try out her new fake ID.

High / not high / who cares.

Hours later, after the bar, after the boy, after Whitehall, during the drive home from the quarry, it started raining, a big downfall. Alex turned on the wipers and told a long story about how the boy they'd just met, Nick Toussaint Jr., the one with the limp, seemed to be totally into her, as in *her*, Emily. She'd laughed, mainly to disguise the injury. Because there wasn't much she was sure about in the world except that boys preferred Alex. Also she was still deep in the high, she couldn't even remember the boy's face. All she wanted to do was to go to bed.

"At least he's more interesting than boys at school. And older," Alex said. "Did you realize he's nineteen? And he's into you."

She'd said nothing, hopefully loudly.

"He's not tall," Alex said. "But he kind of makes himself look taller."

Still nothing.

Alex turned to stare at her. "Hey, are you tripping again, weirdo?"

She shrugged.

"You are. Seriously? Who the hell gets addicted to mushrooms?"

"Will you just leave me alone? For once?"

Five minutes later, the rain stopped. Alex dropped her off at the bottom of her road. *She'll probably never call me again*, Emily thought. The tires hissed away into the endless valley. The forest around her was drenched. She could hear it breathe. For a brief moment, she allowed herself to consider maybe Alex was right about the boy. She couldn't even remember his name. Had she told him hers? But it was too impossible. And she knew she should be embarrassed about her behavior in Alex's car, she'd allowed her self-centeredness to bully her best friend.

Of course the boy preferred Alex, that was natural law, who was she to complain?

When she looked up at the house, smoke rose from the chimney. Another fifty yards of trudging and she saw her father's police car parked nose-out to the road.

He was supposed to be at work, he'd give her hell.

She used the front door anyway, so Very Very.

"Where were you?" came the voice.

The living room was hot and dark. It smelled of citrus. He switched on the light. His lap was full of orange peels.

"Where were you?" he said quietly.

"Out."

"Out, you were out." He smirked. He said, singsong, "And how did you get 'out' exactly?"

She wanted to laugh. She had no idea what she'd say next. But for some reason, and she had no idea why, for the first time she didn't feel afraid.

"I snuck out."

"You 'snuck out,'" Father said evenly. Surprised. He placed his hands on his lap. "Do you do that? Regularly? Where did you sneak out to, once you snuck out?"

"We drove around."

"'We drove around.'"

"I said, we hung out."

"You're full of surprises. You were with that girl," Father added a moment later. "Who happens to be such a wastoid even her parents don't want anything to do with her."

"I don't think people say 'wastoid' anymore."

"What did you say?"

"I said, no one says 'wastoid' anymore."

He would expect her to explain herself in detail. To possess enough discernment to identify what she'd done wrong, but not to understand why or what it meant. How many times, since she was little, had she stood before the stove and recanted? Anytime she was in trouble. Always measured enough for him to savor. *Begin at the beginning. What was your first thought, before you did anything? A problem always starts somewhere. If we don't know how this started, how will we know where to begin and what to fix?*

Father stood up awkwardly, he pretended he hadn't heard, he lifted the stove lid and the room jumped with color. He dumped in the peels.

His voice was so light it was weightless. "You think I don't know her situation. You think the entire town doesn't know her situation. That someone in my position isn't privy to the details."

She said nothing.

"Do you really think I don't see the pattern here."

She said nothing.

"Emily, are you listening?"

"Fine. I'm sorry."

Life/death, basically it was a math problem.

"Oh, don't worry about apologizing." He sat down calmly, and fixed his shirt. "You don't need to worry about that. You're in control. Don't tell me you're not in control. You're sixteen. You'll be driving soon. I'll even let you use the work truck. Did you see that coming? Well, you're practically an adult. Coach Hopper contacted me, did you know that? She said you skipped a meet last weekend. You have anything you want to say?"

She said nothing.

"You don't eat, as far as I can see."

She said nothing.

He laughed scornfully. "You're on a bad path, Emily, you don't need to speak to see that. Anyone who's got eyeballs in her head can see that."

"I broke the rules. I disobeyed," she said.

"Well that's an understatement," he said, and folded his legs.

"I put myself in harm's way."

"Take a seat, Emily."

All of a sudden there was a fire inside.

"I was really stupid, I'm so sorry," she said flippantly, with the voice of a little girl.

"Slow down," he said.

"It was stupid. I'm sorry, I'm sorry, I'm sorry I was so bad."

"Do not use that voice."

"It'll be the only time, I promise, I'm just a stupid little bad girl."

"Emily, quit it right now."

He coughed and slammed back in his chair. Eyes furious.

She bit her hand to stop from talking. She'd be held responsible anyway.

After half a minute he said, "I would like you to sit down. Start at the beginning and tell me." He coughed again and clenched his fists. "Tell me exactly when you had the first idea. That you wanted to break our rules."

She couldn't win, only withstand. But she *could* withstand, and not take him at all seriously anymore. He was Very Very insignificant.

And in a math problem only one answer is ever possible.

That night, Father kept her in the room for forty-five minutes while she went through her mistakes, so that in the gaps in their relationships she might find space to process her transgressions, note how one led to another, and realize how much the entire chain dragged her down, grasp not only what such a thing meant for her own reputation, but also Father's reputation as her guardian, as county guardian, and also the reputation of their family, a name that rang long in the valley.

But none of that was on her mind. Instead, the whole time, what she thought about, what really bothered her, beneath even her fantasies, was what Alex had said about the boy. Was it Nick? Because as she slowly recovered her mind, she couldn't figure out any reason why Alex would have lied about Nick, why she'd say the boy liked her, her as in Emily.

■

From beat to chief, among other truths that appeared inevitably over a long career of policing, Martin had seen enough guys tell themselves they were doing the right thing when really they were just doing the lazy thing.

Always, when cadets start their careers, they expect the public to be better. They learn that, on the whole, most people do worse.

He said this all the time, to kids who already eyed their twenty years—who forever looked, to Martin's eye, like so many popsicles in uniform—that in policing, everything goes to shit, always.

Always, people lie to you for no good reason.

Always, you get thug boyfriends, pregnant baby mamas, grandmothers with an axe to grind.

Always, people hate you, especially when their iPhone's missing.

Always, you buy the next round.

Always, you'll be threatened, spat upon, called names that are nastier than anything you could've come up with. In this respect, your imagination will improve.

Always, if a fellow officer dies, if a kid's shot in the street, each time a shithead on the news takes cops for granted, you feel everything intensely for a moment, then overall you feel things a little less.

Or you feel things more, and the chip on the shoulder grows.

Always, you have people whose value to the species weighs less than toilet paper, and they're the ones who hold power over your career.

Always, between a good fuck and a nap, you take the nap.

What's the difference between a beat cop and an extra large pizza? An extra large pizza can feed a family of four.

People choose their poison, though frequently it chooses you. Weight gain. Insomnia. Heart disease. In his case it was caffeine, nicotine, alcohol, repeat.

Always, the facts aren't worth much, emotions even less, especially when the everyday truth that eventually all police officers must stomach—and no one takes it well, because it tastes like shit, so naturally you need a drink to wash the shit out of your mouth—is that the bad guys do their thing and you help them. *You help them.* You exhaust every option, you go past your limits—your limits are just the start of what you'll do—but then it comes time to put some tweaker back on the street, who goes on to steal and rape again—rape and kill, kill and steal.

Sometimes it's thanks to some bleeding-heart defense attorney. But sometimes it's thanks to you.

You who are almost never the good guy.

You're so rarely the good guy, not even your chiropractor likes you, and that guy you're buying a beach house, with the rate you pay.

When everything goes south, and it does, always, you say to yourself, *This is it. This is me.* Naturally your spouse worries about you, gets upset about the time away. Naturally she turns jealous over the hot probie. She resents you, fears you, definitely fears you unconsciously. You're a nonfeeling monster who runs on sugar and saturated fat.

Your daughter is afraid of you, and that truth is the one that dogs you all day. That the look in her eyes when she sees you come home is no longer just simple love.

And even the kids you buy ice cream for, as a reward for wearing their helmets to skateboard, to them you're just some fucking cop.

Then pension time rolls around; you made it. And if you're at all like the majority, you get divorced and collect boat catalogs. You screw around with a thirty-six-year-old who knows the score, who's also divorced, who likes cops, who has friends who are cops and friends who date cops and everybody goes to Vieques together. And if you're lucky you make your first boat payment six months later off that shiny new security gig that bores you to death. And you still die in five years, you piece of shit.

But one thing Martin won't tell recruits, because most recruits are good kids and they figure it out on their own, because their dads were cops or their aunts were cops or a granddad was in the FBI, and these kids worshipped their dads and aunts and granddads, and had strong minds like their sisters, stout hearts like their mothers, nasty funny streaks like their motormouth brothers, and still for some boneheaded reason they wanted to live and die in service to others—they wanted to be cops—since he loves those kids, he never tells them the truth, that the job is a prison.

Where, no matter who you are, any rank, you need help, but you don't ask for it. Because you're an asshole. Even at the Toy Drive you bitch in the car. You were born dumb and now look at you. Your back's a wreck. Teeth are brown. Eyes are cold and flat. And every bad scene haunts you for the rest of your life.

But how do you ask for what you don't know you need?

So your tolerance for stinking crap grows. And tolerance has a cousin named indulgence. Because once you figure out that some people are habitually at their worst, not biologically above disproportionate nastiness, then it's much easier for your own standards to drop. And in the heat of the job, two a.m., three nights in a row, after two weeks of such crap amid a four-month backbreaker, the fact that the bad guys don't play by the rules makes the rules seem less important.

They say police officers have the longest memories of all. The trouble is they can forget to use them, after years of work alongside so much pain. Especially when it becomes logical, deeply felt, to think or even say out loud, *If he didn't do it, you know he sure as shit did something else.*

Which is why, after a fashion, even though he'd tell the last kid on Earth that being a cop is the best job out there, Martin will admit that sometimes he likes defense attorneys.

■

Four days into his first week at his new job, it's all red tape to cut and forms to complete. Police reports to order. Property records to check.

Dispatch calls and photographs that must be applied for and reviewed, plus diagrams and on-scene video and rap sheets. A dozen or two dozen requests to put into the field. Lab reports. DNA. Forensics. Field notes and logbooks. Ultimately, procedures upon procedures mirror the endless legalese. And all of it's five times worse since it occurs in New Hampshire.

The state's not exactly used to this sort of thing, or familiar with Martin Krug. Not just new to the beat, he's a foreigner. Witness statements turn up incomplete, barely existent. He doesn't know the pathways or even the proper nicknames to find them. Calls go straight to voicemail. Assistants lose his notes. Text messages exit the galaxy.

Then again, he hasn't been part of a double murder in more than a decade. On two hands he can count the number of homicides he saw. That used to be a good thing. Then again, what man's life ever was improved by less experience? Small-town policing had been a cruise, mostly, with a seat at the captain's table. He listened to complaints. Started winter coat programs, made Scout troop speeches. Mostly, he'd been an HR manager.

On his fourth day in Claymore, Martin visits the scene, the doctor's house. It's back to an ordinary home again, free from police gear. Set behind a windbreak of trees in a green hilly subdivision, the development overlooks downtown Claymore. As if ratcheted up the incline by money. Nice house. Recent construction, two stories with a basement and a wraparound porch. A pair of skylights above the kitchen, gray paint job, glossy black trim and brassy gutters. Storybook New England, quaint like the neighbors. Everyone nice and quaint.

A shingle hangs off the mailbox. FAMILY PRACTICE, N. ASHBURN, M.D.

But the doctor's house is a little nicer than the others, a little more polished. The medical practice is attached to the garage, a small cottage, almost a guesthouse. No toys in the yard, no basketball hoop. So no young children. Probably no young grandkids, either.

He pictures a bistro poster in the half-bath, just like the one in his own half-bath. On the porch is a cedar wine chest on steel legs. Lillian purchased the exact same one back in March for a client, same color even. It's that year's model. Eleven hundred bucks.

So maybe we know, he thinks, the doctor had money. Perhaps a recent influx of more money, for such largesse. Therefore it's not unworkable that some kid, person, or persons could dream up a couple thousand bucks stashed under a rug.

Martin gets out and walks the perimeter. A red-haired woman stares from a window next door. He waves, smiles warmly. She disappears. Perhaps too warm.

Through the garage windows are two SUVs, Lexus, one white, one goldish, sparkling clean. Along a wall is a workbench, vise grip, work gloves. The tool locker is a double-wide, gray, with horizontal shelves. A potter's wheel stands by, still in its packaging. Bags of golf clubs hang from a beam. A retired couple with money, nothing more.

He goes back to the porch. Steps are clean. Porch is clean. He sits on the stairs and tries to work through some of his questions. To start: If the kid did it, forget incentive, how'd he do it? The kid's not big. Never used violence so far as they knew.

"He's spindle-necked," Martin says out loud, to the flagstones.

Yet somehow a scrawny, hollow-chested kid overpowered or surprised the big doctor adequately to stab him multiple times. And strangled the wife?

While presumably she put up a fight, on the worst day of her life. But not enough to leave any marks on the kid.

What was she strangled with anyway? The kid says a thin rope. So he just happens to keep a garrote in his pocket, the kid with no priors.

And somehow, by his lonesome, he loads both bodies into the truck.

And cleans up the mess.

And drives off without being noticed by the neighbors.

Detectives have a low tolerance for ambiguity. You don't build the truth, you build a case. Brenner didn't have the autopsy yet, but they already knew a couple things. Multiple knife wounds to the doctor's gut. Jagged, rough cuts, which probably meant a struggle took place. And so agreed the scene report and samples, blood that had been found on the floor. Also, there was a wound on the back of the head. Bruise, old blood, presumably from when the body hit the ground.

Blood on the wife's robe was verified as the doctor's. Probably the killer transferred it, or maybe she'd embraced the body at some point, or gotten blood on her in the Explorer.

At some point the bodies may have rolled around together in the back.

According to the report, latent prints inside the house matched to the doctor, the wife, and Nick Toussaint Jr. They also got a great print for a plumber who confirmed he'd been to the house two days before the attacks took place, to replace a toilet. Otherwise clean.

The poor guy wanted to know if it was okay to cash Mrs. Ashburn's check.

Martin gets up from the stairs and telephones his new colleague.

"New Jersey," Brenner says. "This has to be quick."

"I'm at the house."

"So?"

"I thought we could do a walk-through together. If you're free."

"Martin, I have eleven pending cases. Twenty-plus briefs marked 'open.'"

"Okay, I get it."

"Do you? I have to be in court twenty minutes from now. Then I have to testify up in Ossipee because some moron reopened something we all thought was dead months ago."

"I said, I get it."

"Call me when you crack the case."

He walks in a circle, with a chest full of aggravation. If the kid did it, then there's gotta be an accomplice. Plus some motive he doesn't know about yet. Some reason the kid would jump to give a false confession, despite the setting, the handcuffs, the senior cop who shouted in hospital rooms.

But if the kid didn't do it, then he likely knows who did, or has a good guess. Either way he'd taken a fall for some reason, and won't say why because—

Because he doesn't know why.

Or, the kid knows why, and he likes why.

Somehow he is the why.

Or he wants to protect someone. For whom, out of indebtedness, he can stomach two murders.

"That's one hell of a debt," Martin says under his breath.

Or he actually did do it, with an accomplice.

Or he simply did it, solo, just like he said.

Martin retrieves his notebooks from the car. Sits on the stoop, clips his nails with his penknife. For the last couple days he'd dug through the Ashburns' public lives. Four speeding tickets in five years between them. Their credit score was fine, no obvious trails of addiction, no known wacky sex. No proof of subpoena service. No record they purchased guns, boats, exotic pets. They'd bought the house in cash after selling a previous home at profit, otherwise didn't appear to spread around much money. Donations to Republican candidates, local charities, the Sierra Club.

He'd found an adult daughter, Moira Ashburn, employed at a veterinary clinic nearby. She's next on the list.

A pair of curtains flash in the neighbor's house. A minute later, he knocks three times on the door.

The redhead opens it a foot.

"Are you with the media?"

"Police, ma'am. With the Public Defender's Office, actually. My name is Martin Krug. May I come in?"

"I've already talked to the police."

She's forty-something, exuding interest but defensive. Self-justifying in most things, with that tone, he'd guess.

A little girl says something indecipherable in the background, in conversation with a television show.

"Can I ask first," he says, "why you thought I'd be the media?"

"I'm just surprised."

"Have you had a problem with the media? Mrs. . . ."

"Not yet we haven't."

"So what I'm doing here," he says, after a moment, "is repeating the police investigation on behalf of the defense. Just in case the police missed anything."

"I don't see how they did. Not on my part at least."

"I'm sure you're right."

"I heard that the boy confessed."

"Ma'am, can I ask you a couple questions?"

"Go ahead."

"The night of June seventeenth, you were at home?"

"If you want to know where kids like him go wrong, you should start with the motorcycle rally. All the scum that washes up around here, that's where the drugs come from."

"Ma'am, you were at home on the night of the seventeenth."

"We were. Me, my husband, and my daughter."

"I have a daughter, too. How old is she?"

"She's four."

"That night, did you hear anything strange? See anyone in the neighborhood that surprised you? Any strange cars, for example."

Then the child starts to wail. Martin knows what comes next, he quickly writes down his phone number and hands it over before the door closes.

At noon, he breaks for lunch, gets a sandwich. Thirty minutes later he's back to dog it, fast and furious. But after three hours, nothing's new, nothing's different from the reports. He's about to quit when he remembers: the doctor's office. Attached to the garage. He'd forgotten about it completely. Going senile faster than he knew.

The door is locked. There's a row of tiny brass hooks in the kitchen. He snatches all the keys. One works. Inside is a cramped lobby, a small rounded desk for a receptionist, piles of file folders, two pale blue prescription pads with the doctor's name on top. And no sign of forced entry. Nothing unusual.

He moves restlessly. The one examination room's got all the usual stuff. So what's he missing? There's something right in front of him, he knows it. And there it is: No computer. No cords, no dust abnormalities.

Not only is nothing missing, there hasn't been a computer here for a while. If ever.

He picks up one of the prescription pads and taps it against his leg.

What doctor's office doesn't have a computer?

Martin goes into the garage. He looks more closely at the tool locker. It's locked. He's an idiot: the drawers are way too deep for wrenches. A little silver key unlocks it. It's all files inside. He checks the *T*s, and look at that, Nick Toussaint Jr.

■

sorry u guys . . . kinda sad update but
does anyone know anything more w/r/t
ashburn murders? im not finding much,
not much here on FB either :(

> Claymore Kid® is in custody, trademark
> mine. Judge Toffler will preside. For
> now the Kid keeps rooms at the
> courthouse.

Hi Al. How do you know all of this??

> Friend on the inside. FWIW the Kid's family used to be hoity-toity. Let's just say you'd recognize the last name. Mom gives piano lessons up on Oak Hill.
> I hired the husband to fix my roof years ago. F-ing prick took me to small-claims court for $75. He said I owed him lunch breaks. That kind of family now.

DUDE IM STILL LAUGHING

> Yeah well according to the checkout girl at Hannaford's tonight the Kid did it for revenge because Dr. Ashburn messed up some kind of medical treatment on his leg.

You guys hey, hey Al, how's things?? Thought I would chime in here with some info. So my daughter is same year as this guy's girlfriend at CHS so naturally the school is all talking about this on social media, surprise surprise. Real name of the girl I won't say because she's a minor (let's show some class howabout??) but turns out she is the daughter of let's say a prominent official, I kid you not. (Also, Al, of a family we all "know," so to speak.)

> This generation can't surprise me anymore lol

FURTHER EVIDENCE
CLAYMORE = MYRTLE BEACH OF
NEW ENGLAND.

The previous week, at a gas station in central Massachusetts, during her drive up to New Hampshire from New York City, Leela Mann checked her email on her phone and found two messages: a note from her father that she archived without reading, and an actual response to her email of employment desperation.

It was from a boy she once knew, during her internship at Jambands, Bryan James. Except the message didn't originate from Jambands.com, but a domain she couldn't recognize. Or, a domain she did recognize, as in *really* recognized, but never had received an email from and didn't quite believe was in her inbox. Never mind attached to Bryan, of all people.

How on earth had Bryan James found a job over there?

What she remembered best about Bryan was that he always wore a Yankees cap, and generally gave off a glow of someone for whom life kept going great. He was attached most strongly in her memory to an evening that had followed her last day at the website—Bryan was the same guy who once informed her, boastfully, that occasionally he liked to stream porn at work for the moral challenge of *not* pleasuring himself—when he DM'd her out of the blue to say he'd received an invitation to a cocktail party that night, at the august offices of a literary magazine, and he wanted to know if she'd be his plus-one.

For two hours, she couldn't decide what to wear. She'd finally settled on a romper from Urban Outfitters, a bright vintage print of roses that she could picture on Greta Gerwig. Romantic, quirky, austerely whimsical. *The new her.* Then, at the party, she was ravaged by nerves. She stepped through the door. Music, smoke, loud chatter. People turned, people stared—as if she'd punctured their moment. The bubble quickly resealed. Everyone was older, sophisticated, voluble in the soft light of overhead lamps. The kind of people whom Greta Gerwig probably actually hung out with. None of them in a little girl's onesie.

She'd found a beer as fast as possible. Closed her eyes slowly and, after a long time, opened them again and floated around the rooms for an hour under the gaze of so much taxidermy—stuffed birds, old men in blazers—while she listened to rapid, pitched conversation about what Truman Capote had said about Bianca Jagger (she didn't catch it), about the dogmas of Lorrie Moore (she didn't grasp them), about fields of significance to be tilled in the Benetton-hearted songbook of John Mayer (she agreed totally). And she loved it all, despite her self-consciousness, her heavy hands and feet. And so she tried, *tried*, to smile at the right moments over someone's shoulder, laugh in the proper spots behind the joke, echo people's feelings in her face as best as possible so she seemed like she, too, had something valuable to say.

Though not once did she volunteer her thoughts, or suggest that anyone should ask her anything, so no one did, which seemed painfully unfair.

For nearly another hour Leela sulked next to a piano and pretended to read a magazine. She was about to get rid of any prideful feelings with steel forceps if necessary, and simply go get pizza, when Bryan found her. There'd been an emergency at the office, a server on the fritz. He was apologetic. He coaxed her to stay. He was happy she was still there. He'd put on a bow tie, even tucked in his shirt. She smiled.

"I'm so nervous," he said. "My bowels are totally messed up."

"Mine, too," she said. "But mine are always messed up."

Four hours later, they were flat-out drunk and stupid, and it felt great, it felt like freedom. Inside a bathroom she found two porkpie hats. They crashed on a couch, talked about their favorite books, favorite old movies. Was that girl across the room Julia Stiles or a look-alike? They went to find out, but she vanished hastily, and then lo and behold, epiphany: it turned out they had a mutual vampiric thing for Mark Twain, as found photographed in a sepia-toned picture on the wall—which, for an exciting, brief moment, felt originally erotic to both of them, the idea of the three of them in a threesome. The two of them and Mark Twain! Too much.

Later, one thirty, with a dozen people in the room, Bryan leaned in and muttered, "I love your legs."

"What'd you say?"

"I love your legs. In those shorts."

"Thank you. Actually it's a romper."

"I want to fuck you on the stairs."

"What?"

"You heard me."

"No, I didn't."

"Let's go."

"You're joking."

"Leela, I want to fuck the shit out of you."

And she couldn't help but laugh. The "shit" out of her? Wouldn't that be a little unerotic? She looked at him. He was bothered, seriously all worked up.

His hand slid up her leg.

At which point she'd excused herself, fled outside, hailed a taxi. Embarrassed for him, swiftly even more embarrassed for herself: did she seriously just run away?

And so it wasn't a big surprise that she didn't hear from Bryan James again—not until the email she received at a gas station in central Massachusetts, from bryan_james@newyorker.com: *Hey what's good. Your timing's great actually, a kid got booted yesterday. It's a big mess but there's going to be an opening soon for a junior web producer. Like asap. It's grunt stuff but sometimes you write for the site. They move fast so let me know, we'll see what happens. Maybe you could be my work wife ;)*

Leela said loudly, "Holy shit."

A woman at one of the other gas pumps turned to stare, but she didn't care, she really did not care this one time.

∎

Leela's roommate for her first two years in college, Rebecca Dinovelli, took an English class their second spring called "Introduction to Creative Nonfiction." In Leela's mind, it didn't even make sense on a grammatical level. Also, Rebecca was Biology, not English. Who was she kidding?

At that point Leela hadn't declared a major yet. She possessed a great fear about it. The decision seemed too big. For at least a year, in a recurring nightmare her father, dressed in battle fatigues, stopped her in a hallway and asked, "So what do you plan to do with your life?" Kids talked about it all the time. If pressed, she made up stuff about how she wanted to help other people; total bullshit. She was considering a double in International Relations and Computer Science. After all, she liked to travel, tech jobs were plentiful, she liked math well enough. Though what would she do then, really? Join the CIA?

Other students around her, kids like Rebecca, talked about their lives so purposefully, she often felt confused and stubbornly negative. She had no idea what the future held. How could they be so sure?

Anyway, she did so little in those years outside her schoolwork, her existence hardly qualified as life. She slept a lot. She went to a protest one time and stood in the back. For a month she'd volunteered at a soup kitchen, then the manager blamed her for someone else's mistake and she hadn't returned. Basically, she went to class, did her homework, struggled to go to the gym twice a week. Often she was homesick. She knew the late-night guys at Dunkin' Donuts, it felt like the one back home. On campus she recognized the creative types, the extroverts; she wasn't them. In comparison she dressed like a roll of beige carpet. But she badly wanted to be doing something, something with intent and purpose. Something to warrant all the longing to *be* somebody that she carried around.

So far she'd only known desire as a vacuum, pointless.

Then she got bored. Or more bored than usual. She'd done her homework, gone to the gym, microwaved a plate of frozen mozzarella sticks. Why didn't anyone text her? Everyone Leela knew was still in the library. The course packet for Rebecca's English class lay there on her bed.

The first reading was photocopied from a magazine. She went through it in thirty minutes, lips parted as she turned the pages. "The Fourth State of Matter." She was genuinely stunned. The story was about physics, but also about a massacre. A horror story, then, yet also surprisingly interesting, and totally screwed-up.

She felt seized by the words. She looked up the author's picture online. She went back and reread the story more slowly, to figure out what she'd just read. It made her cry.

The last time she'd cried while reading had been at the death of Sirius Black.

But she felt something else this time, she felt less dumb. She lay down in bed. Her body was flush with tingling. She stared at the speckled ceiling and closed her eyes. She tried to convince herself that her body *wasn't* tingling, but there it was again, a buzz on her skin. As if she had levitated a quarter inch off the mattress.

She opened her eyes.

For the first time in her life, there was a sense that, while she'd read the article—and this had never happened before, not once—she wanted to be the person who'd written it. But what was that bullshit? Was she insane? In high school she worked on the newspaper as part of a computer class. For one assignment she created a blog to review ice-cream shops. Big deal. She'd certainly never thought about writing anything besides papers. It wasn't like anyone had ever told her she was good at it.

Leela looked up the magazine's website. She hadn't heard of it before. There were a thousand links, she couldn't choose. She clicked a subscription ad, a discount for college students, ten dollars for a year of issues, plus a tote bag. The bag looked cute.

Five minutes later Rebecca texted, inviting her to a party.

The tote arrived two weeks later. She'd forgotten about it. Then the magazine first arrived, rolled up in her mailbox. She took it to a coffee shop, bought an almond croissant, read almost the entire thing in one sitting.

And between the tote bag and the magazine's arrival, and a couple woozy days afterward, within the span of only a couple weeks Leela Mann had incarnated a quite ridiculous, crazily unlikely ambition that would *not* be voiced out loud anytime in the near future—from fear of extreme embarrassment—to become a writer. It *was* insane. So she didn't do anything about it for a while. Then, fall semester, she took Rebecca's class for herself. Loved it. It changed her life. Without delay she decided on majors, Computer Science and Journalism, and she really only chose the former to keep her father from implosion.

Her mom didn't care, but her dad was furious. Journalism? Was Leela crazy and stupid, or just stupid? Why not study telegraph design? At least then she'd please him, show an interest in history for once.

Ultimately, though, he did nothing more than complain. And from that point forward she started to talk about the magazine as if it were something more. It was the Magazine, proper-named, properly capitalized. Something to take to bed at night. As though the two of them were hooking up, Rebecca pointed out one time. So ridiculous, but true, she was in love.

But her love for the Magazine, plus a brief tenure as a reader for the university literary journal, was bigger than a hookup. The Magazine found her friends, through the lit mag and elsewhere, people who knew about and also liked the Magazine, and other magazines, and liked her tote. Kids enrolled in short-fiction workshops that she also took, who drank beer afterward, went into New York City afterward, to seek out readings, bookstores, taco shops that were talked about. And eventually they even worked up the courage to read things out loud to one another that they'd written. Things that they weren't too crippled by self-loathing to share, or definitely were too crippled, but hey, *beer*.

By the winter of junior year, she had all new friends. One, Matteo, was editor of the school newspaper. Four inches taller, one and a half times smarter, he carried around the same tote bag, he even convinced her to start pitching him ideas and published some of them, her first legit clips. Furthermore, he introduced her to the novels of Penelope Fitzgerald, the nonfiction of Mary Karr, and got rid of her darned virginity—in all three cases, wonderful developments—and somehow, four months later, Matteo was still good for board games night the week after she broke off their relationship.

Because Leela knows from real commitment. She's never missed an issue of the Magazine, not one. The writers are her faraway gods. At night, all seasons, while New York City was muffled by snow or heavy heat, she'd stalked them through the web, the women, mostly to see how they wore their hair. Chimamanda Adichie. Emily Nussbaum. Larissa MacFarquhar. The one and only Lahiri, of course, her mother's bedside reading, her copy of *The Namesake* stained by watermarks.

Even today, Leela prefers to pretend Jhumpa Lahiri does not exist. Hadn't she moved to Capri by that point, switched to writing only in Italian? (That's so Jhumpa.) Though why Leela imagines Jhumpa Lahiri to be her competition in any form, she prefers not to contemplate, just merely dislikes her and her writing in a way she does not want analyzed.

She still totes the tote. But is aged enough in her affection, by this point, to keep her fondness to herself. In only her second month in New York, she'd terrorized Zadie Smith on a 6 train. They were sitting across from each other, seven a.m., when Leela, through a tired morning haze, realized who she was sitting across from and involuntarily yelled, "AHH! AHHHH!" As if stabbed twice. Everyone on the train turned to witness her humiliation. Including, of course, Zadie Smith, radiant, petrified Zadie Smith, not even in her customary head scarf but box braids, and pulling them off so well, what with in addition the totally reasonable fear for her life—Zadie who'd looked up from her phone and quickly dropped her eyes, as though this happened to her occasionally, price of fame, being recognized in public by a gibbering wreck.

So what exactly Bryan James meant, from an email address at the Magazine, about a job opening at the Magazine, she had needed to know immediately. She took almost twenty minutes to reply, sitting at a picnic table near her car. Then drove away, toward Claymore, on a total body high, which had dissipated in about five miles, going up the sun-flattened highway, as she'd remembered, once more, that she was un-employed, on her way to New Hampshire, away from New York. Stuck for the immediate future in a single, crushing story line, about the pit-falls of available credit, where nothing good would ever come to pass. Least of all her dream employment scenario.

And if only every passing car's muffler would bellow nicotine.

When she'd finally arrived in Madbury, she found the house, Sandra's parents' house, exactly as described, a tiny blue saltbox with a gravel drive and flaking paint, set back from an isolated country road, surrounded by thick forest. Front-door key inside an old metal watering can. Not a neighbor in sight, and no furniture inside. The house was completely empty. It smelled like Pine-Sol.

But at least it was clean. She'd propelled herself into motion, piled all her belongings in the middle of the living room, made a bed from her clothes, then proceeded to get drunk on cheap wine she'd bought at the gas station. And with her mind quickly crimped by headache, all she could think about was Bryan's email. She refreshed her inbox every fifteen minutes. The job had likely been filled, probably while she was driving through Connecticut, while it had waited in her inbox to be checked. Game over. Life over.

She got up to go to the bathroom and stepped on her goodbye sou-venir from *The Village Voice*, a small box that contained roughly 497 business cards with her name on them. Cards she'd never handed out to anybody.

She kicked the box into a corner.

An hour later, her first evening in the state of her birth, she'd pulled on her leather jacket and gone for a walk to try to wipe away her drunk. About a mile up the road she discovered a convenience store / auto repair / state inspection center. The guy behind the counter gave her a look like she was the first brown person he'd ever seen. She brought a bag of groceries home in the dark. Squatted on the floor next to a pile of books to check her phone: still nothing. So she ate peanut butter with a spoon and posted two hilarious screen grabs on social media that had nothing to do with her actual situation or emotional galaxy—but that's what social media was for, your ideal self.

Because ideally Leela Mann was a young woman of leisure, wit, and advanced emotions. A young woman of contemplation and dry humor, not dread. A young woman who was sure of what she wanted her life to become, if only it would become.

．

And it is not until four days later, muggy Thursday morning, right after a run, right after Leela walks in through the front door of her borrowed home, that Bryan James acknowledges her email, via text, to suggest drinks that evening, in the East Village.

For days she'd waited apprehensively. And worried: What if her message was stuck in a spam filter? What if he'd switched his email system? But she couldn't write again, she didn't want to seem desperate. So pretty much all she'd done ever since was some good old freaking out, winging around the house like Spider-Man at the gym. While she got used to the fact that the life she'd known was pretty much done, and she needed to find employment, needed to apply for New Hampshire unemployment. And probably should put her sexual organs up for sale on Craigslist. Though only hands, mouth, and butthole. A baby was the last thing she needed.

But then her phone dings as she claps mud off her running shoes.

Hey I've got news how abt 7 TMS

Hey what's up! Cool. Details? TMS?

The Masticated Stoat. Haven't been?

Of course

I'll tell u more tonight. It's a surprise ;)

Mysterious . . .

And now, in the nuclear fallout of this correspondence, she will shower immediately, dress as fast as possible, and haul her ass back to New York Shitty to whatever bar / coffee shop / restaurant she just lied about.

The drive is normally five hours. Leela gives herself six. It takes nearly seven thanks to traffic, not to mention a wrong turn she makes in an attempt to wedge herself into the FDR's hell on Earth. What is wrong with her brain? Finally, Manhattan, Lower East Side, golden-green dusk, she finds a spot four blocks from the address. She'd already texted Bryan from a red light, she claimed a subway delay. On an island of phonies: the *phoniest*. Still, she made it. She locks the car with a serrated sigh and jogs across Houston Street in her worn-down flats.

Her phone vibrates.

Where r u

One sec

She pants as she arrives at the bar. She'd lied about knowing it. Behind the front door is a dark hallway of flocked purple wallpaper, lined by oval portraits of weasels being eaten by other animals. Leela rushes through, she feels her pits begin to stain. The main room, even darker, is morbid, cramped, and cold, like a speakeasy for the unwell. Though depressurized by all the deliberate laid-backness of so many dudes and their cool-girl counterparts scrolling through their phones.

"This place is so pretentious," Bryan says when she finds him at the bar.

"I'm sorry I'm late. Do you want to leave?"

"I sort of used to like it? Now I'm like, let's go drink boilermakers, you know?"

"I'm up for that."

She's not joking. But he barely hears her, he has his eyes on his phone.

"No, forget it."

"Bryan, it's great to see you."

"You too."

He finally looks at her and smiles. Her heart beats hard from the run, she tries to hide it. Does she smell? He looks better than she remembered. The stubble is new, even his glasses look fashionable, or maybe he's just dressing better, all the boys are dressing better.

"Hey, so yo," he says, and extends a fist. "Congratulations."

"About what?"

"The *Voice*. The layoffs?"

"It's bad, actually."

"No doubt, no doubt."

The crowd, beautiful and loud, squeezes them against the railing. Everyone knows she doesn't belong there. Does she tell him about New Hampshire? It could ruin everything.

Bryan rattles his head and slurps his drink, garnished with the world's smallest pine tree.

"Look, screw those guys at the *Voice*. The point is, you should be psyched."

"Should I? What about?"

He laughs resignedly. As if they're in the middle of some type of game. "I'm sure I know what you've heard, but Condé's actually pretty sweet."

Her heart skips a beat.

"Bryan, what are we talking about?"

"Like, brass tacks?"

"Sure?"

He checks his phone again then sighs. "Who knows what HR's got up their sleeve, they're in Connecticut. But if it's Lian's decision, that's my boss, as far as I know it's down to you and some dude. In which case you're probably the underdog. But that's a good thing. Seriously, look at what's on paper. Are you a chick? Yes. Are you a colored chick? Yes."

"I'll let that slide."

"Oh, don't be stupid," he says.

Leela stares at the bartender, in his fedora, but he won't meet her eye.

"Seriously, the only thing lacking, at this point, between you and this guy is longreads. You don't have a ton of longreads, right?"

"What do you mean?"

"We practically invented the whole thing, obviously, but now it's everyone's thing. I'm not saying you should go and, like, file ten thousand words this weekend, but it also wouldn't be the worst idea."

"Bryan, I'm not sure I understand," she says flatly, wiggling on her stool. "Can we just start at the beginning? What are you talking about?"

Because she is seriously confused. And she can picture her stupid forlorn face, she hates the nerves in her voice.

But Bryan's already back on his phone, not listening. He looks up. Coughs. "So here's the deal," he says. "My boss runs the website. She's one of the original Gawker girls. She was the big digital hire a couple years ago, to overhaul all things digital, get the apps launched, et cetera. I came in to help with podcasts. Anyway, Lian came over, she brought along this database guy. Who was a black belt, for real. But then they go to outsource, and our dude's shifted into editorial, at which he blows. Anyway, a month ago, he got caught hacking emails. Like, all the way up the business side. Anyway, he's gone, and now it's down to you and this other dude, somebody's old roommate at Wesleyan."

"And you're not joking," Leela says, she sounds truly amazed, she doesn't care. "You think I have a chance."

"You're the underdog, like I said. I think the interview's a lock. I forwarded your stuff, Lian likes it. She told me she's going to email you at some point soon. I think she's going on vacation for a couple weeks. Plus HR has to post the job opening for a while. Normally they handle everything, like, 'We'll put your stuff on file, there's a chance we'll have an opening at *Modern Bride* in seven years.' But if an editor wants to bring in someone specifically? So, yeah, at some point I think you'll meet Lian. If things go well, she'll want you to meet a bunch of other people. If *that* goes well, you'll meet David."

"David."

"I know. Anyway, I'm not clear on how strong our guy's hookup is, or what Lian thinks of him, so this'll take some time to play out."

"That's amazing. Bryan, thank you."

"Hey, I owed you one."

"What?"

He looks at her meaningfully, he cringes slightly.

She clutches her legs with both hands, while her body fills with horror.

"Anyway, the dude," he says. "I saw his shit. You're about the same on programming. He coded his own Wordpress plug-in, but who cares. He's not as experienced as you as an editor, which is good, because they'll want you assigned to some blogs. The thing is, he's published a lot."

"So have I."

"You know what I mean."

A thought catches her, not in a good way.

"I don't, honestly," she says slowly.

"Don't make me say it. He's published more significantly."

"What does that even mean?"

The cringe is back, but more defensive. He finishes his drink.

"Political essays. Stuff in translation. He used to intern at the *London Review*."

She says, "So my work is less significant for being personal."

"It's unfair, totally. Believe me, your pieces are way more fun."

"You did not just say that."

"What I mean is that it's less likely, okay," Bryan says quickly over the noise of guitar rock, though now with exhaustion, more than a little male impatience, to have to explain something so basic, "it's less probable to be the kind of stuff that Lian or Remnick, fair or unfair, will be predisposed, you know, to identify as high-end shit.

"They'll think you're a blogger," he adds.

"And he's the 'writer.'"

"Exactly."

"Oh, great."

"He tutored kids with Dave in San Francisco. That's really good optics right now. I mean, they want the best."

"But so," Leela says, dazed, "'the best' could still be me, potentially."

"Absolutely. Potentially." Bryan signals the bartender for the check. He says loudly, "Dude, what do I know? They like go-getters. What if you found a story out there and reported it out? Didn't you do that piece a year ago that blew up?"

It was true. She'd even been on CNN.

"And that was what, three thousand words? Call up some people, knock it out, then stick it in your pocket. What's the worst that happens? You really want to impress Lian, go find something new. It doesn't need to run anywhere. Better yet, it doesn't, then maybe she wants it. Seriously, you've got time. I mean, how amazing would that shit be?"

He smiles generously, signing the bill on the bar. The bar itself is a long, crooked elbow of light, it up-lights everyone, even Bryan, and now she only feels guilty. She wishes she were a better candidate for the job.

"I mean, imagine you show up at Lian's door," he says, "hand over a story during the interview, and you're like, 'Hire me and you also get this.' Suddenly dude bro is dead in the water, right?"

"Absolutely," she says. And does actually contemplate the idea.

"Trust me, the last thing we need is another white boy who loves Gaddis." He stands, his eyes fall to her hand. "Wait, did you get a drink?"

"I'm fine," she says, in fact dying for alcohol. "I've got this thing."

"Was that my bad?"

"It's no problem."

"Shit, it was."

"It wasn't."

"I'm so wiped. They've put me on this special issue, I haven't slept in a week."

"Bryan, really, thank you."

"Anyway, this place sucked."

"It was great."

The air outside glows liquidly. There's no name above the bar, just a hanging sign, a metal weasel looking roughly chewed. Bryan stops on the corner and lights a cigarette. Leela steels herself against desire for nicotine, fixates instead on the twilight street vivacity, the couples, the shop curtains, the facades. There's an old man in a diner having dinner in the window, alone with his radiant tablet. Normally he would make her sad, but she's got something new, in the New York night: a sense of hope.

And in about a minute, after Bryan leaves, she'll need to find two gallons of bodega coffee to get her back to New Hampshire.

"You know this is my dream," she says quietly.

"I know. You told me."

She frowns and laughs. "I didn't."

"At that party. You even had the tote bag. You're, like, the core fan."

He blows a plume of smoke over his shoulder.

"I need to say something," he says.

Oh, shit.

"About that night."

"What night?"

"The party. What I said."

"I don't remember."

"Yes, you do."

"Please," she implores, "it's fine."

He shakes his head. "I was wasted. Which is not an excuse. But I want to say I'm sorry. For coming on to you like I did. It wasn't consensual at all."

"Please don't apologize," she says sharply.

He doesn't hear her. "The other day, I got your note, I was so psyched. I'd been thinking about this moment for a while."

A pair of women walk by, walking a dachshund.

Leela tries desperately to swap souls with the dachshund.

"Anyway, I've got a thing for brown chicks, fine, at least I know my hang-ups. Just, seriously, congratulations. Lian's going to love you. I'm happy I can be the messenger."

"My messenger, yes. Thank you."

But she means it, she does. Enough so that when Bryan hugs her with feeling, she can will herself to mirror his emotional state, if only to leave a good impression. It's something she once read, attributed to Maya Angelou, though maybe it was a greeting card: That people inevitably will forget what you say, what you do, but they'll always remember how you made them feel.

"Just think, we might work together again," he whispers in her ear. "And not for Phish fans."

■

Thursday, Martin interviews the Ashburns' daughter at home. They talk first on the phone, she says she's happy to meet. Perhaps too happy? An old bell rings in his mind, a piece of advice from his first captain: Beware the agreeable, for they will fuck you over twice.

The address is in the small town of Leduc, twenty minutes northwest of Claymore. He drives past subdivisions, signs for the shore, into the woods for seven miles and eventually over a bridge laced with green oxidation.

Downtown Leduc is sad, deadbeat, a tiny mill town with no mill. A tattoo parlor's front window is papered with skulls and crossbones. The daughter's condo is two blocks adjacent to the main street, in a pair of squat, yellow, three-story condos that look out of place, with a FOR SALE sign in the yard.

A dog barks when he knocks. Footsteps. A moment later a woman's in the doorframe, a Dalmatian between her legs. Moira Ashburn, with a long stare. High cheekbones as a feature of a too-slender frame. Caucasian, brown ponytail, glazed eyes. Corduroy pants, tight tank top. Confidently poised in the doorway, but nervous, the way her eyes don't stay still.

"I'm Martin," he says. "We spoke on the phone."

"Come in," she says tersely, "we're having juice."

She holds an e-cigarette so loosely, it's as if she's performing a magic trick. Behind him he hears a sound rising audibly, a whine. He looks up as a drone launches into the sky.

"Are you selling?" he says, referring to the sign.

"That's the neighbors. That's their drone."

"I'm sorry for your loss," he says, following her back into the house. The dog barks happily. He wonders if the "we" she mentioned meant the dog.

In the hallway a red mountain bike is perched against a wall, spattered with mud. Through the hall is a kitchen covered in green vegetables. Another woman, maybe five feet tall, washes her hands in the sink. With legs that bulge in cycling shorts, mud on her calves and socks, a long scar on her right leg. Black hair, pixie haircut, fine features. Sports bra in pink fluorescent, no other top.

"This is Jennifer," Moira says.

"I'm the girlfriend," she says, extending her hand. "Nice to meet you."

"Nice to meet you."

The daughter sits on the couch. The girlfriend sits at the other end. He takes a chair. He asks, "So what do you do, Jennifer?"

"I'm in retail. In Claymore. At the New Balance store."

"Moira, you work in Claymore, is that right?" He looks around the room to ease up on the eye contact. "But live out here."

"Is that a question?"

"How tall are you?" asks the girlfriend.

He says to the daughter, "It must get aggravating, having to commute all that way."

"Otherwise I'd have to live in Claymore."

"People do. There must be something nice about it."

The girlfriend juts forward at an angle, one hand on the back of the couch, like a painter stretching away from her ladder. "So if you're a police officer, how come you're not in uniform?"

"I used to be," Martin says. "I retired recently. It's a long story."

Moira Ashburn draws in smoke and stares.

"So, no longer," says the girlfriend.

"No longer."

"Now you're a lawyer or something."

She takes Moira's hand and starts to massage it.

Moira takes her hand back, tucks it under her leg.

"I'm a consultant," he says briskly, to indicate that he's not really watching, also to show that he's irritated by the girlfriend's presence. "A consultant in police matters. Now, Ms. Ashburn—"

The daughter sneezes, jumps up to blow her nose.

"Ms. Ashburn, I am sorry to have to do this," he says, and follows her with his voice. "It's probably best if we get straight to it, then I won't take up any more of your time."

"Fine."

"Where were you on the night your parents were killed?"

"Hanging out. Watching TV." She sits down again. "I was probably stoned."

"Ms. Ashburn, can you—"

"It's Moira," she says flatly.

He notices she's got a slight spasm in her leg. The girlfriend picks up on something, jumps into the gulf: "Let's start over." She takes her girlfriend's hand again, no resistance. "We were watching TV. Both of us. You can check the Netflix queue. We went to bed after, that's it." She pauses. "We heard your client confessed."

"Do you guys know him? Seen him around?"

"Who?" says Moira.

"Nick Toussaint Jr."

"Why would I know him?"

"I don't know. Small town."

"You're asking if I'm friends with the kid who killed my parents?"

"I'm asking—"

"She just said," Moira says, "he *confessed*."

He holds back. He can tell she feels trapped. After a moment he says softly, "There are different types of confessions."

The girlfriend laughs. "Now you sound like a lawyer."

"Ms. Ashburn, do you or do you not know Mr. Toussaint in any way?"

"Jesus. No."

"Okay. I'm sorry." He takes a deep breath deliberately. "I understand this is a difficult time. I've been through it before. Not from your perspective. But I've talked to a lot of people who've lost family. I am truly sorry for your loss. And I will be out of your hair as soon as possible, but the more you tell me, the better it is for everyone. Including you."

She sneers. "If you say so."

"All I want to do today," he continues wearily, "is review what you told the police. People you met, things people said. For example, what you were doing that day, can you remind me?"

"I don't remember."

"You don't remember."

Jennifer coughs. She fixes the waistband of her shorts and taps her fingers on the edge of the couch. Something in her face changes. Not quite a correction in atmosphere, but almost.

She says, "Moira had a certification exam."

"You don't have to tell him that."

"We were here, at the house, like she said," the girlfriend continues. "Moira did well on her test. We were celebrating."

"You don't have to tell him that!"

"Ms. Ashburn," he says, "you're currently employed as a vet tech?"

"You obviously know that."

"Ms. Ashburn."

"It's *Moira*."

"She's getting her real estate license," Jennifer says calmly. "That's what the exam was about. She's looking to change jobs."

"There's no money in medicine, that's what my dad always said."

Then the daughter stiffens unconsciously, stares out the window again, releases a soft cry. It catches them all by surprise.

"Your parents," Martin says, "seemed to have been doing well financially."

"They inherited," Jennifer explains. "Both of them."

"Which suggests that Moira now stands to inherit, is that correct?"

Both women stare at him. A dumb move. He tries to recover. "How close were you to your parents?" But he screwed up, and the daughter knows it. She stands up and goes into the tiny kitchen, trailing vapor. She begins to put away dishes.

Jennifer says quietly, beneath the noise, "Is our relationship a problem for you?"

"Was it a problem for the Ashburns?"

"I'm asking you."

"I don't see what your relationship has to do with any of this."

"That wasn't the question."

"No," he says grimly, "it's not a problem."

She smiles, adds quietly, "Then, yeah, it was a problem for them."

"How much of a problem?"

The daughter shouts from the kitchen, "Not enough to fucking kill them." She slaps a plate into the dish drainer and hurries down the hall. The dog runs at her heels. The air trembles.

For a moment, he has no idea what to say next. There's always a point when an interview starts to drift away, crumble at the edges into the sea. The girlfriend gets up. Her cycling shoes make loud clicking sounds on the floor. The room gets smaller the more she moves. She turns and comes back, stands in front of him, uncertain, as if weighing some type of decision in her mind.

He notices the scar again on her leg.

"That scar looks bad," he says.

"You should see the other guy."

"You're protective of her."

"I love her. I love her a lot."

"How long have you known each other?"

"Almost a year."

"How close would you say they were as a family?"

She laughs darkly. "Yeah, not close."

"Why?"

"Because they're family. Don't you have a family?"

"This is my job," he says. He stands. "Like it or not, my job is to ask a bunch of stupid questions and see what my stupid brain comes up with. The thing we do know, that kid in there is innocent. Somebody else is walking around free."

"Well, that's not my job," Jennifer says. "My job is to take care of my girlfriend."

She moves to fold laundry from a pile. He wonders where to go next, if he screwed this one up. Something's off. The girlfriend's waiting. What is it? For the other shoe to fall? There's a nervousness in the air. Something's wrong, and he missed it, he's missing it. He's been played in some way.

"I'll see myself out," he says.

"They were assholes, you know that," the girlfriend says when Martin walks out through the front door.

A little brown-haired girl in the yard stares up at the sky, with a remote control in her hands.

"Her dad especially," Jennifer continues. "Complete asshole. They wanted a princess, you know what I mean? A country-club queen. She should've turned out just like all the other rich kids, but instead they got a really wonderful, special daughter. But they didn't see that for shit. They didn't see *her.*"

He listens partially. Wondering at the same time: What if the girl-friend had something to do with it? If she's this worked up? Maybe the girlfriend's got the profile for something like that?

She doesn't notice his absent-mindedness. "All her life they had two reactions. They were uninterested, didn't pay attention, or they judged her and put her down. Total assholes."

"They don't sound nice."

"I don't know anything about your client," she says. "But Moira's been through some shit. Now she's going through even more."

"When was the last time she spoke to her parents?"

"I told you, they didn't speak," the girlfriend says conclusively, spell-ing it out. Inviting him to leave with her permission. "I mean, maybe they talked at Christmas."

He says, unconsciously, "But they only lived down the road."

There's a scuffle in the street, a crash. The drone is in two pieces. The little girl stares at her toy, then turns around and stomps angrily back inside.

He thinks: she didn't even make a sound.

The girlfriend moves in closer. The top of her head barely reaches his nose.

She says quietly, "Moira had nothing to do with it."

•

By the time he met Emily, Nick had been off girls for a while. They were too much of a hassle. First of all, chicks loved all that online stuff, texting, messaging every second, but it went without saying, it was so stupid. Like all other fakery, social media, religion, reality TV. Anything that involved people crapping from their mouths just to rationalize their bullshit behavior. As if confessing and telling the truth were the same thing.

Admittedly, during his convalescence, in the rented hospital bed, he'd spent a lot of time online with the curtains closed. Jerked off about six thousand times. Occasionally he begged chicks for sympathy nudes. He'd tried to think about anything except the accident, which meant a lot of time mainlining the web. But school came through the com-puter, too: he was tutored online one-on-one so he could get his GED. And he did well, actually, if only to please Suzanne, allow him to get back to his self-prescribed cure of vape pen and Call of Duty. Which

Suzanne didn't approve of, but she also filled ashtrays in every room. He just needed her credit card for level upgrades.

Months later, once he was on crutches—standing was excruciating—he wanted out as fast as possible, even away from the screen. To do something with his days. Dr. Ashburn wanted him to apply to college, but Nick knew Suzanne didn't have that kind of cash, not after his medical bills. What was college but more bullshit?

When the last cast was finally off, Suzanne came through in a different way: she got him the job at Tyree's. Turned out she and Tyree's little brother had dated in high school, back in the day, so Nick got paid pretty decently to patch flats and do oil changes. He wasn't even acting a part, he enjoyed the job. He liked making money even more. Tyree sent him on a Honda course, gave him a pay bump. Like he said, cars weren't going anywhere, they definitely weren't getting any better.

The pizza gig he took on for more cash, to help with his mother's bills and put a little aside. And because he had the time. But it also made him wonder what else he could do with his life. He talked about starting a T-shirt business. He talked about going to culinary school. He cut down on the weed, spent more time reading books. He bought a dumbbell set that he was really, really into for about a month.

By his eighteenth birthday, after a year-plus entrapment in fiberglass casts, after most of his friends didn't swing around the house anymore and most had left town, Nick Toussaint Jr. began to display a moody inattentiveness and touchiness that hadn't been there before the crash.

One thing he discovered about himself: he liked to go for long walks. The park, the beach. Some nights he'd put in a dip, just walk alongside the ocean. Stare at the pier lit up like a racetrack, the untroubled faces of so many kids that rolled through his vision, kids he'd known his whole life, who'd gotten so much ladled into their laps. Lives ahead of them like highways, wide open, to do anything.

The immobilization was what had done it, split the world between himself and *them*.

And he felt inside his soul a painful loneliness.

By the time he met Emily, he hadn't kissed a girl in a long time.

Following the skunk's instructions, he wrote the letter. It took him an hour, at the tool bench in the back of the garage. High shadows fell.

He rewrote it three times. He wasn't used to handwriting, his fingers cramped. His penmanship looked like a kid writing a note to Santa Claus. Who the hell wrote letters anymore? What would she think? Anyway, how was he supposed to sign it at the end, "love Nick"?

He laughed. Did he really just ask himself that question?

Equally out of nowhere, he wondered what his dad would have done.

His dad had been a drifter, self-described. Nick Toussaint Sr.: story-teller, entertainer, proudly Catholic with gold around his neck. "Never let anybody put a tattoo on your arm," his dad used to say, meaning it as a metaphor for something—his dad who had multiple tattoos, including "Suzanne" on his hip. His father who, for Nick's thirteenth birthday, had taken him out drinking, a late night in a bar on the boardwalk called the Harbor. The excitement quickly faded. He threw up in a gross-out bathroom. All he'd wanted was to go home, he didn't know any of his dad's loser friends. Near midnight, his dad shouted, "We're lovers, Nick, not fighters." Then he walked up to a woman Nick had never seen before and put a huge kiss on her lips, and everybody laughed.

The father who left him in the woods.

Nick got an envelope from Mr. Tyree with the shop's logo, a smiling tire. He drove the half mile back to the hardware store.

"That's for her to open," he said to the skunk. "Not you."

"You're cute," she said.

He walked out, jingling his keys. Couldn't even remember what the hell he'd written! Everything inside him was tuned to a single note. Probably the wrong note. Sometimes at home Suzanne was afraid of him, he saw it in her eyes. He'd try to shrug it off, but the truth was there. And what was sort of fucked-up, he liked it. He grew out his hair. Bought a pair of boots that looked like ones he'd seen in a movie. Living up to a stereotype he saw flash in people's eyes, the way customers at Tyree's took him for a punk, because of the limp, the coveralls, the attitude. So he cultivated it. But girls didn't like that stuff unless you could also be tender, he knew that much.

On a whim he blew off work, drove up the mountain above town. He parked in a lookout. The view took in the apron of the county, the ocean, the horizon. The day was breezy and bright. He went to the scenic marker and stared over the valley.

And without thinking ahead of time he made himself a promise, in words that weren't words, that this would be the last time he'd ever think about his dad.

Because the truth was Nick didn't mind his life, his new life. He was fearless, because what worse could happen? He felt so small, still the clouds seemed close enough to touch.

It would become his new duty, as of that moment, to think forward, quit living in the past. Imagine a new life built from scratch. He just needed something to start with.

■

To Emily Portis:

Your friend said this is the right way to reach you. Sorry if it's bad. I don't write a lot of letters.

We met the other night. I don't know if you remember me. My name is Nick Toussaint Jr. My father's name is Nick, that's why the junior. People ask me that all the time, you'd think they'd figure it out on their own.

I liked meeting you. You're really pretty and cool. I'm sure guys tell you that all the time. I'd like to hang out sometime if you want. We can go somewhere, whatever you like. Here's my number: 603-627-4949. Text me or return something through your friend. Do you like movies?

By the way if you don't want to see me that's cool, just tell your friend to let me know. I'll be honest I'm not the type to play games if you know what I mean.

I would like to see you again. I think you're really special.
Thanks,
Nick

■

Emily finished reading the letter for a third time, then a fourth time, and her heart was racing even worse. Her thoughts dissolved. She didn't know what to think, she was suffocating, she was on fire.

Alex ripped the paper out of her hands and started to laugh two seconds later.

"I think he's illiterate."

"Shut up."

"He calls you special."

"I can't believe it."

Even after the fourth time, the words spun tornadoes through her body that flashed with electricity. To continue to exist, to keep herself from a delirious spin out past the reach of gravity, she made herself quit smiling.

You're really pretty and cool.

No one had ever said anything like that to her before.

"I'm calling him Junior from now on," Alex said.

Emily snatched the letter back. She read through it a fifth time. "What do I do?" she whispered.

"What do you mean? What do you want to do?"

"How should I know?"

"Jeff Goldblum, bitch. Life finds a way."

It was the most intense moment of her life.

"I know what I'd do," Alex said. "I'd tell him to stick to texting."

But she didn't listen, she looked frantically for a pen.

Her body and soul were more primordial than words, thousands of miles out of reach—and that was a serious problem in this situation.

"I need to write him back," she said. "Seriously, what do I say?"

·

Dear Nick,

Hi Nick,

Nick,

Hi Nick. This is Emily. Thank you very much for your letter. You're so cute. I think you're special too. I love movies and I would love to see one with you and talk about it afterward.

Hello Nick. It's Emily. Thank you for your note. It's in my pocket. It's been there every moment since I got it. It's so embarrassing how wrinkled it is. I already ripped one of the corners this afternoon and I nearly started crying about it. That's not the most embarrassing part, I think I'm going to sleep with it tonight under my pillow.

Hi Nick. I got your letter. It was so nice. Let's meet this weekend and kiss for sixteen hours straight

Dear Nick, Thank you for the note. You're pretty cool, too. What are you up to tomorrow or anytime you're not busy for the rest of your life

Dear Nick, I can't stop thinking about you I'm boiling over I'm worried this is all a joke I don't even really remember what you look like except I think I remember you were cute and I liked your hair and eyebrows I'm thinking right now about kissing you and it is driving me crazy it's crazy I'm crazy

Dear Nick

Friday morning, Martin returns to the Ashburns' cul-de-sac to knock on doors. But nobody he talks to saw anything, heard anything, and the redhead isn't home.

He restores Nick's file to its rightful place. It didn't reveal much except notes about the kid's injuries from the snowmobile crash, otherwise he received a clean bill of health. The file establishes a professional relationship between Nick and Dr. Ashburn, nothing more.

The previous night, Martin had gone through the rolls of local knuckleheads. Guys on parole. Ladies with records. Anyone recently charged with armed assault. Brenner's assistant had been through once already, he'd found two men who robbed an emergency-care clinic with a shotgun nine years earlier. But both had an alibi for the night the Ashburns died, and they worked at the same steel warehouse now, verified and on video. After them, no magical names.

Martin grabs the register off the desk in the doctor's office, plunks down on the Ashburns' back porch, into the stiff embrace of a wooden chaise, and proceeds to call the last ten patients the doctor saw.

Six people answer their phones.

Of them, five report the doctor in a normal state, with normal rapport. One says he'd seemed distracted, but no idea why.

End of the day, orange dusk, Martin decides to visit the doctor's golf club. According to Brenner, it's the preferred roost for the Claymore wealthy who hadn't yet flaked off for richer towns.

He immediately finds much to annoy him. Upper-crust shrubbery. Mercedes, new and old. Stars and stripes next to the New Hampshire state flag, next to the club's flag, white with green insignia: a pair of American Indians nobly posed straight-backed and mum, courtesy of smallpox.

He hates country clubs, golf clubs, old-money crap.

Martin interviews the manager first. And doesn't exactly care if his condescension fills the room. It's a windowless, low-ceiling office. Horse paintings. Dog paintings. The man lives up to expectations. Fearful, pudgy, he wears a visor indoors and idly plays with a pocketknife, flicks it open and closed with his thumb while he talks about nothing.

Martin wants to stick the knife into the son of a bitch's leg. But he probably still wouldn't learn much.

The halls are striped red and green. More paintings of animals, fox-hunts, as if it's not New Hampshire outside but Yorkshire. Who are we when we hate the world we inhabit? At the bar, everything's old, the plants, the men. A semicircle of windows overlook a course fenced by trees. The golf greens are striped by long shadows. Night will fall soon: another day of no gains. He needs to do something. He barges into the conversation of a trio, three older golfers with cocktails and shaky hands. The nervous manager appears in the doorway to vainly listen for trouble. But no one has a word to say against the good doctor, or the wife, none of them would call him an asshole, no one knows of any enemies or threats or knocks against the family name, except the daughter, conceivably? A disappointment. But every family has its black sheep.

And what does Martin expect, anyway? A self-selecting pack, self-satisfied elites believing only the superlative best of their dead. As they hoped to be remembered one day.

He purposely takes his time to find his car in the shaded parking lot. Old habits die hard, and sometimes they still pay out: a forty-something guy jogs down the front stairs. The prep-school letterman who never grew up, eyes down, no handshake. There'd been a certain matter, the guy says under his breath, involving a receptionist the previous year. Basically, doctor balled the secretary. Everyone knew, they didn't want to speak ill. But something must've come out? Because either the chick took off or got fired, and suddenly Mrs. Ashburn had quit all her charity work and ducked back behind the doctor's desk.

"The wife used to be his secretary?"

"That's what people say."

"What else do they say?"

"No, that's it."

"Pretend I'm dumber than you think."

The guy looks uncomfortable. "Well, she's the second Mrs. Ashburn. But you guys already know that."

In fact, they didn't. At least he didn't.

"Keep going."

"The daughter comes from the first wife. But that was, like, twenty years ago. I think she died. Violet was Nathan's secretary, back when. If you see what I'm saying."

"So he's a repeat offender," Martin says. "With secretaries."

"Yeah. So it seems."

The guy continues vaguely, losing enthusiasm. How Dr. Ashburn had gone into crisis mode, one to pour his own drinks at the bar. No one knew how Mrs. Ashburn had figured it out. But recently, things had seemed better. The doctor and the Mrs. were happy again, they sat together at bingo nights.

"What's this woman's name? The previous receptionist."

The guy hesitates. "Look, Nathan was a friend."

"You're the one who came to me."

"I just don't like . . ." The guy stares away. He refocuses. "The story about that kid doesn't add up."

"I agree with you."

"I saw her last month."

"The receptionist?"

"I never knew her name. I had to get some tennis shoes. She must've gotten a new job. You won't miss her, believe me."

"She sells shoes?" He has an idea. "Is this at the New Balance store?"

"You've been there?"

"I think I'm going to."

The man starts away smoothly, conscience clear. But something's wrong. Martin pinches his windbreaker. He says quietly, whispering across the distance between them, "Hey, if Dr. Ashburn didn't tell you the woman's name, how'd you recognize her?"

The guy smiles. Like they're both in on a joke. "From the office. Nathan was my GP. He played doctor to the whole town. The guy knew everything."

"Everybody."

"Sure. That, too."

▪

And that night he telephones on an impulse. And he has no idea what to say, staring at the room-service tray, the empty soda glass, the dirty plates, with a half-formed chart in his head of possible outcomes.

And, as though the cosmos endorses his plan, Lillian answers. And announces immediately, before he can say anything, that she doesn't want to talk to him, not for a couple more weeks will she be ready, in which respect she appreciates that he left town and gave her space.

And from there she has quite a few big words to use to describe her current emotional state until Martin interrupts, "What are you talking about?"

"What?"

"This was a mistake."

He's temporarily lost in contemplation of what he's done simply by calling her, when she hadn't called him first: so cliché, so pathetic.

"Martin, I want you to know something. That I'm truly, truly sorry. About what's happened. This is not *on* you."

"Well, you are the one cheating."

"I just want you to know that I know it. How hard this is for you."

He should hang up. He feels so heavy. Is it over? Is it all over now?

"Lillian."

"I've been alone," she says, "for a long time."

"Oh, so it's my fault."

"I didn't say that."

"You just said it."

Her patsy. Her stooge. He needs to think about something else.

"I'm on a path, Martin. A path that I've been on since I was a little girl. That's what I am trying to explain. I don't know where it's going. I've been in pain. But for the pain that's been added, I totally own the fact that I'm the one responsible."

He feels like he's been under sedation for months. And everything's been out of control without his notice.

"You have some balls," he says, "you know that?"

"Can you please not talk like that?"

"How about what I need?"

"Of course," she says gratefully, almost reverently. He's speaking her language, the loftiest of superficial platitudes. "Martin, what do you need?"

"You're really asking that."

"What I'm hearing," she says, "deep down, is bitterness. Which we both know is only an amplifier for self-pity."

"Sure."

"But in this scenario that is totally normal."

He lies down on the ground, to elongate his spine. Displays on his face a calm and easy sympathy that is different in five hundred ways from his thoughts, which grind and gnash.

"I really am sorry," she says, after a long silence.

"Here's what I need," he says. He trails off. But what does he need? Where is he going with this? What does he want? He realizes, he *knows*, he is deeply, deeply angry.

"I want to know something," he snaps.

"Of course. What is it?"

It comes out of nowhere, full speed ahead: "Did you fuck him in our bed?"

"What?"

"Did you?"

"Oh god. Martin."

"I want to know. Did you fuck this guy in my bed?"

"Are you listening to yourself? You really want to know that?"

"Goddammit yes. Lillian—"

"I'm sorry, but I need to go, I just can't."

■

A little man in wraparound sunglasses and a black baseball cap sits parked on the street outside her family's house—the same man from the day before, the day before that, now he's filming her again, or why else hold his phone in such a way, aimed at her porch?

Suzanne throws the door open and says loudly, "I'm going to call the cops."

No reaction. Sunglasses, sweatshirt, not a twitch.

She slams the door. And wishes the force of repercussion would strike the little prick at the base of his skull. She makes a fresh show in the window of picking up the phone, and feels in the moment an outpouring of righteous persecution that's so strong she drops the handset—fervor like her body's just a talisman for magic, a voodoo doll—finally, she has literally become the Red Woman—but the rush becomes instant fatigue a moment later, from the world looking in, a world against her, and her complete lack of sleep over the past week.

She crumples into the couch face-first.

She becomes more like her mother by the minute.

What does he see, anyway, of interest? Is it the house? Wood siding scored to look like stone blocks. A mansard roof. Can he see all the way inside, the grisaille wallpaper that her father had preserved? None of that explains the phone.

Among her students, even the littlest ones have phones. They yank them out as soon as the lesson ends—when it used to be the rectangle you'd grab after class was a pack of cigarettes.

She hates at least half of her students, their reeking expertise. The previous week a ten-year-old, thoroughly overparented, threatened to quit because there was nothing, she'd said, that Mrs. Toussaint could teach her about the piano that wasn't on the internet. So that night Suzanne went to the web, and the girl was right—and if only the little twat would disconnect her umbilical cord from Mommy and plug it into her computer, maybe she'd finally learn the Mahler theme.

She crushes the drapes. A second later the doorbell rings. The nerve of this man! She shouts, "What do you want?" and flings open the door.

Dr. Margaret Gould, with a foil-wrapped pie dish.

Behind her the man in the car adjusts his camera.

"Maggie," Suzanne says, out of breath. "I'm so sorry. I thought you were someone else."

"It's fine. You must be under so much stress."

"Thank you. It's an off day."

"So that's sort of why I'm here. The other day. In the store." Her eyes crinkle. "I want to apologize. I wasn't myself. I just feel so badly for you, and your family."

"It's fine. It's really nothing."

"No, it's much bigger than that, we both know that."

Her tone makes Suzanne pause, open her eyes just a little bit wider. The doctor's black jeans are pressed. Dirt-free tennis shoes. The pie was likely purchased, rewrapped to appear homemade. But the eyes shine, a most minuscule glimmer.

The fact that Suzanne is only a little buzzed makes her judgments order themselves with a certain predetermination toward aesthetics. Where refined suggests calculated, and calculated becomes cold.

But cold is Suzanne Toussaint's starting place.

"Maggie, can I help you with something?"

"That's why I'm here," says the doctor. "I just feel awful."

"You said that."

When has she ever not lived almost completely inside her head?

"I want to help," the doctor says. "Help you. If you'll let me."

"You want to help me."

"I'm sorry, but I thought," the doctor says, a little breathlessly, "considering recent events, what's happened, Suzanne, if you want to resume our sessions—I would be so happy. Sliding scale. Let's not worry about that right now. I want to be here for you." Breathing quietly, Suzanne thinks, like a cat. "There's going to be a lot of hurt. In what your family's going through. But, if I can: Let it happen. Let it take you places. That's what I want to help you do."

There are a million ways to hate a woman, but how many to dislike your former therapist?

Dr. Gould had been wild for two things: Zen breathing and confessional truth. The first was easier to explain, regarding benefits. Truth turned out to be more complicated. In Dr. Gould's office, truth was the raw stuff that provided pages for "Personally True," which was the title of her work in progress, also a chapter title in the book proposal she'd shown Suzanne during what would become their final session—a technique of her own devising, she'd claimed, of redrafting one's story, how to reconstruct one's life so far to become whatever shape that one preferred, around so-called personal truths, numbers one through infinity. So Daddy wasn't the Ferrari of assholes, he was conceited. Those libidinal feelings toward Mother weren't real, they were symptomatic of a person type with too much love to give. And so on. Whether something was "true" in the frightful real world mattered less than if it was subjectively appealing, "personally true," the way one preferred one's history—leave alone other schools of analysis, leave alone the carefree child you must once have been, leave alone the parents who used the child for their own social purposes.

And Suzanne figured it all for so much certain horseshit right away, the kind that kept a billion therapists in business—people's never-ending thirst to be comforted, to be the center of a universe, neon-lit against the great black wall of outer space, or even just a small office in a shopping complex—and maybe she'd said as much, even insultingly? Because, come on: the idea that repression might become the basis for a healthy life? Was her wheelhouse. But therefore end session, end treatment, commence goodbye.

The air is thickly humid. Suzanne says quietly to the doctor, "Did you know I grew up with Stephanie Condren?" She closes the front door behind her and steps forward into the doctor's space. "You know Stephanie, right?"

"Stephanie Condren?"

"Our parents were friends. We hang out online these days, if at all, if you know what I mean."

"I know Stephanie, of course," says Maggie.

"Stephanie is a bitch." Emphasis on "bitch." "Last night, she put up a post for anyone to see—I don't think Stephanie understands privacy settings very well—and there was a link to that story in the *Globe*. Regarding Nicky. Commenting, Stephanie, that she is stunned that such a thing could happen around here. Not just that, but by a young man she knows personally. Or thought she knew, she writes, considering 'the things he's done.' Not 'accused of doing.' 'Things he's done.'"

"That's not fair."

"But then, much later in the thread, which had, I think, somewhere like three or four dozen comments and likes and whatever, then you, Maggie, you chimed in. You said you, too, were surprised. To see him accused. And yet, do we ever really, truly know who our neighbors are? You said. Quoting some shit to that effect. I mean, you couldn't even say something original."

Dr. Gould says nothing for a moment. Both hands grip pie. "You're angry," she says. "I don't blame you. No one blames you for that. With everything that's going on. Suzanne, you can count on me. If not before, then starting here, right now."

Suzanne Toussaint does not slam the door, she merely closes it. Turns around, lowers herself into the couch again, turns the phone off again, and tucks in Suzanne's extremities, closes Suzanne's eyes and tries to breathe without rattling Suzanne's ribs—and can't help but remember Dr. Gould's primary instruction, from back in their first days, on how to breathe properly, from the stomach, one breath at a time, to let the body relax, the mind be free.

•

In their few sessions, before the book proposal was revealed, they'd come up with a list of a dozen truths that in Suzanne's case *were* true, verifiably, and not fantasy, and had definitely messed up her life.

1. It's true that Suzanne Toussaint was fundamentally ignored by her beloved daddy, generally cultivated by her mother in her own image, to be an adult as soon as possible—and so, in a way, from birth, she was buried alive in images, examples, rich impressions, and left to find her way out. And thus was she tolerated to smoke cigarettes around the house at age eleven. Pale Mommy in men's golf shirts, men's shoes, the

same shirts and shoes Suzanne wore, side by side digging in magnificent gardens—her private, unpredictable mother, who used to say things to her like she'd never met a child she actually enjoyed, daughter included.

2. True also that Suzanne loved her piano early. She didn't have superhuman powers, she couldn't memorize by ear, but she had dexterity, speed—she was always almost too good for her age. Dr. Gould said music possibly had been an attempt to find something to match her parents' passion for each other?

3. Her parents had been a pair so reclusive, so tightly wound, she'd been the odd one out.

4. True as well that Suzanne's parents formed her, ultimately, by dying in her last year at school. So she quit. Goodbye piano, goodbye practice, goodbye formulaic artistic ambitions, hello Manhattan, Lou Reed, and the Palladium, hello Black Beauties. And goodbye, dreams! Goodbye, the moody little girl who wowed the Marlboro Festival with her physical technique. She got legal voices imposed on her, enough money for a good half decade of meager living—the old family money was long gone, vacuumed by poor decisions, bad investments, Daddy's pills. She got the house in Claymore, took some smart advice not to sell, and stayed in her crappy, delightfully ramshackle East Village walk-up. So therefore, for a time, she got good in high heels, knew the bouncers and club dealers by name, discovered the pleasure of being lost while feeling found. A class in Semiotics in the afternoon to have something to do, a different path to consider, but mostly it was a life of nighttime smiling, goose bumps, tobacco smoke, red eyes and a million friends, everyone bright and burning, nights that became mornings that became nights.

5. And along the way she acquired the will to fuck. And found it true that men do get better with age. At pretty much everything, but sex especially. Men from the bar, men smiling in the street, *Hey, what's your name?* She craved transgression, craved distance from her feelings, craved for craving's sake. At least sex in those days still *was* something.

6. Fact: She once fucked a divorce lawyer on the floor of a steak-house coatroom, he'd said his topcoat was alpaca.

7. And maybe it's also true that she'd gotten to be a bit of a master, then and still to this day, of telling herself stories that serve her needs.

8. True that Suzanne Toussaint returned to Claymore at twenty-six, restored to the old family name and its floun-dered quarries, to the lumber liquidators and tombstone dealers who'd done plenty of Toussaint business in the past. Late in May, lush mountain greens, ocean waves in grayish navy blue with white epaulets—and it was true that she was full of yearning in that period, even back in New Hamp-shire, but empty otherwise. She unlocked the mothballed house. She saw the end of existence around every corner. Opened closets of old coats and robes—mere ideas of coats and robes. Cats had moved in and multiplied, the stairs were black with cat shit, the gardens were dead. She was home.

9. Truth: One of the first things she remembered, going in through the front door, was how she used to listen to her parents having sex. Through the crack under the door, she'd eavesdrop, lie down on the floor, press the side of her head against the crack so it folded back her upper ear. She loved the chaotic sounds, even if she didn't know what they meant—only that she wasn't supposed to enjoy them.

10. And it remains true that Suzanne Toussaint counts her misfortunes daily. They give her direction, they are what is certain. And for solid hours those first two weeks back in Claymore she'd been feverishly angry, acutely sad, dressed like a bale of gray wool. She ran into classmates around town, she couldn't connect. Boys bought her drinks, they wanted to sleep with the girl who'd returned. But she slept with no one—and *fuck them*. Then, two months later, a large tree branch fell during a thunderstorm, ripped down half of her gutters. She hired a handyman. He came recommended by a neighbor as effective, cheap, and nice to be around, not bad looking. With a cross around his neck and a knack for conversation. Nicholas something.

11. It is true that to be left behind is an act requiring more than one party.
12. Her least favorite truth, to be viewed from behind a veil, is the reason that she'd finally gone to see a professional—that a woman abandoned, at least "a woman" like her, becomes a fanatic. Arms encircling an absent neck. That when a woman marries a man, and the man bucks convention and takes *her* name, then leaves one day and takes her name with him—she'll think of him every time her name is pronounced. And will become a woman to pick up the phone and press no buttons. To carry around the remains of her marriage in her hands, and see ghosts in the street, and say the wrong thing to liquor store cashiers—she'll say he's dead, Nick's dead, he was killed in Boston, murdered in the street, shot in the gut.

Is it possible, ever in this life, to pull back fired bullets? She puts up her long hair and lights a cigarette. "I said go away," she yells out the window, to the man in the car. Who's probably a therapy victim, too. She struggles to find her drink, she drinks crookedly. If the whole world's in therapy, maybe the cameraman also sees an analyst. Then again, if everyone's in therapy, don't everyone's issues become everyone else's issues? She smiles and bites an ice cube. Her eyes close. Ever since she was a little girl, whenever she smiles, her eyes close automatically. Her husband once asked, "Did you know you do that?" Implying on the nose—he only knew one way—that she's afraid of happiness, she doesn't like to see it.

On the side table is a photograph of little Nicky. Even fixed in time, he shivers, after a swim in the ocean. She wants to dive into the picture and rub warmth into his skinny little arms.

There's a noise outside. A car parks. She looks out the window. Whoever it is, the cameraman is compelled to drive away. And from the new car comes a child, her next student, strutting up the walk as her father jumps out of the car. The girl forgot her lesson book. The father hugs her tightly.

Suzanne struggles up to answer the door.

She wants her strength back.

She wants her son back.

·

Three days after he'd met the girl up at Whitehall, a cold rain fell on Claymore and Nick was pissed. Usually people loved ordering pizza in bad weather. It was good for tips: customers felt bad for dragging you out in the rain. But for some reason he was getting shafted left and right. On top of that, for three days, he hadn't had anything to do except worry. He'd never participated in anything so weird. He didn't know what was happening with the girl, the stupid letter he'd written. All his frustration came right to the skin. He snarled at a customer who didn't even tip a dollar.

Then the skunk sent a reply. Not actual correspondence, but a directive via text, that "Junior" should meet them, if man enough, that evening around eleven down at Little Horse, and bring beer, or Smirnoff and Snapples, Diet Peach, no Red Bull, they weren't sluts.

He raced home, parked, grabbed a six-pack from the garage, crossed the house on his way out through the living room, and found his mom drunk in one of the window seats, wrapped in a wool blanket, peering at him steadily from under black, heavy eyelids, with a grimacing face.

Suzanne had never been like other kids' moms. He was old enough to begin to see her for what she was. First of all, she wasn't like anybody else he'd ever met. More stuck-up, for one thing. Opinionated, spontaneous. She liked to light a fire in the fireplace in July. On multiple occasions she'd slept in until three in the afternoon, stayed up until sunrise playing piano. Addicted to television, and also probably the smartest person he knew, and among the weirdest. Which was odd to say about your own mom. One day in a silk gown, the next in jean cutoffs. She was beautiful, he knew that. She had a closet full of party clothes she never wore, short dresses and high-heeled shoes. His friend Typically used to stop by just to flirt. One time she made him explain what a MILF was, while Nick stood by gagging. But she was also weirdly childish sometimes for an adult. There'd be an onslaught of neediness, of persistent questioning, clawing desperation. When his dad walked out, it didn't help.

More than once someone asked him if his mom had a brain injury, due to the stuff that came out of her mouth. Of course he loved her. Typically was in a similar boat. His dad had remarried and took off for Alaska, he'd explained the psychology of mama's boys several times.

But that autumn Nick honestly couldn't stand to be in the same room as Suzanne anymore. Her drinking was over-the-top. He'd tried to get her to quit, but she refused, she made excuses, she was always her best co-conspirator. Twice in a six-week period, he found her passed out with a cigarette burning between her fingers. Once it singed a hole through her sweater, like a volcano in the middle of her chest.

Nick didn't pay rent, but he paid rent.

That night, he announced, "I'm going out." He was halfway across the room when she said, "That's my beer."

"I'll get more."

"We drink and drive. We never surprise."

"I'm going out."

"You make it sound like a job."

"Okay, thanks, Mom."

"Where's my goodbye?" he heard from the porch.

Little Horse was a blank inlet where the cove met the ocean. People called it Little Horse because the inlet was shaped like a horse's head. But there really wasn't anything there, no reason to go. The beach was normally deserted, that's why kids liked it. From the house he drove up Jefferson, past the courthouse, the red mulberry trees, the Victorians, then out to the beach, the boardwalk. Personally he liked it better over there, the town's other cheek, the seedier streets, all the acne of amusement parks, the Sundial, the pulsating go-kart track, the dive bars wrapped in Budweiser banners, the bars that his dad used to love.

Another minute and he turned off, where in a bend was a sandy parking area. The ocean glittered. Someone had left the pier light on, otherwise the beach was dark. His car smelled of sausage pizza. He rolled down the windows to let the breeze clean it out. Five to eleven. Too early. His nerves were on high fizz.

He thought about the girl, Emily Portis. All day, he'd tried to remember her accurately. What if he exaggerated her? Maybe she's dumb as bricks. Or maybe she didn't like him, not a loser like him. The dropout. The burnout. Probably she didn't remember him at all. Or she pitied him for the limp, that's why she'd asked to hold his hand, the way you console a kid in the hospital.

He rolled up the windows and got out. Spat on the ground between his feet. Walked twenty feet down the sand. No sign of anybody. He waited angrily, optimistically, pessimistically. Maybe it was all just a stupid joke. Why did he think she'd like him anyway? The cold reality of the situation sank in fast. He humped, shivering, back to the Explorer and sent a text to Typically.

U wont believe this

Typically wrote back instantly.

Wassup

The girl I told u abt

Continue

Total no show

Ahhh
F that
Good reason to get wasted tho

Headlights. The 4Runner. The lights didn't extinguish. Two girls hopped out, one stepped forward. Her front was black due to the lights behind.
"You're Nick."
"Hey."
He couldn't tell which one it was.
"It's Emily."
"Cool."
Cool? Shit.
"I mean, hey," he said.
Shit!
The girl fidgeted with her dress, she wore it over jeans.
"How's it going?" he tried. She didn't answer. "Where's your friend?"
"Do you want to take a walk?" she asked.
They marched out into the darkness, away from the parking lot. Fifty yards across the sand, dead silence. He had to do something. What if he held her hand? Then he took it, just like that, almost unconsciously. It

was smooth and small, cool to the touch, like a shell. He couldn't help but smile.

She let go a second later and walked away toward the water, arms crossed, legs stepping slightly left and right, off balance. He could hear the sound of a stereo somewhere. Okay, so she hadn't liked the hand thing. *Shit.* He caught up.

He said, "The other night was so cold."

"Can I ask you a question?"

"Sure."

"Do you go up there a lot?"

"What, the quarry?"

"I'd never been up there before."

He wondered if it was some type of trick question. "I mean, not much." Total lie. He and Typically went up to Whitehall all the time. Why was he lying? What difference did it make? Did it mean something bad, to go to the quarry a lot? Why's he so wrapped up in what she thought?

"I thought it was beautiful," she said quietly.

He shook his head in agreement. With zero confidence this could end well. He was doing it wrong, whatever "it" was.

They walked down the beach, toward the boardwalk lights. A minute later, he saw the hand dangling again. This time she let him hold it a minute longer.

"I was delivering pizza last night," he said. "It's pretty good, for a job. You set your own schedule. So this guy answered the door. He's going to pay me, he's getting out his wallet. Then his wife, I mean I think it's his wife, she shows up, she's got a baby strapped to her chest in a sling. You know what I mean? And in the other hand she's carrying a bong. I was like, holy crap. With smoke coming out of the top. I mean, that can't be good for the baby. The guy's like, 'I don't have money for a tip. Do you want a hit?' Like, instead of a tip, he grabs the bong and holds it out to me. And the whole time I'm thinking, *Hey, how about not in front of your genetic offspring?*"

The girl laughed. Thank god. The story was so much more stupid than he'd realized. But she had a nice laugh, smooth and easy. He felt a tight feeling in his chest. This girl just got him.

She asked what he liked to watch, in terms of movies, after all he'd mentioned movies in his letter. The letter! He'd watched something like two hundred movies when his leg was banged up. So he talked a little about that, listing favorites. Was he showing off? What if she hated *Inception?*

He asked, did she like movies?

She liked movies.

But all he could think about was how much he wanted to kiss her. Her hair was swept backward by a strong gust of wind. If only there was some way to let her know how he felt. To know how *she* felt. Maybe she wanted him to kiss her? God, he was a coward. The desire was so strong.

She said, "How old are you?"

They stopped near a lifeguard chair. His heart raced. Up the beach, the Sundial spun slowly, a spinning pink and green rose.

"Nineteen," he said.

"I'm sixteen."

Her eyes were closed for some reason. Deliberately? Was it a sign? Should he kiss her now? Kiss her lips, then her neck? At least she wasn't looking at him, he probably looked desperate and girls hated that, they wanted you to act decisively. *Quit stalling.* But his impulses refused to connect to his thoughts, his cascading thoughts. He should kiss her, he knew that. That's why she'd closed her eyes! So what held him back? They were standing two feet apart. He remembered something he'd read in a book, that you can't combine being afraid with being sure.

She said a second later, eyes open, "Are you too old for me?"

His heart pounded grumpily.

"I don't know."

"I don't really care," she said formally. She sighed, adultlike. Her voice was matter-of-fact. "I was just asking, in case it mattered to you."

Then she sat down on the sand, like he wasn't even there.

He was totally confused. He stood there grimly, gripping the lifeguard chair. He was out of his depths. He should go home. She was more intelligent than he was, probably a lot more intelligent. Maybe he was missing out on an entire level of communication.

"I remembered everything you said the other night," she said, after a long silence. "After I got your letter. I wrote it all down."

He snorted quietly. "Why would you do that?"

She didn't say anything. He was amazed. He really didn't understand this girl. He looked for eye contact, but she wouldn't look up. He stared at his boots, coated with sand. A long thirty seconds. Did she want him to sit down?

"I liked the story about your leg."

"It wasn't a story." He sat, clumsily adjusting his knee. "It's just something that happened. I don't know."

Emily stared at her feet and picked at her jeans.

"I was on mushrooms. The other night. In case I acted weird."

He laughed into his fist. This girl!

"No shit?"

"Yeah," she said, and laughed. He laughed, too.

"I mean, that's cool. Do you do that a lot?"

"I stopped."

"I stopped drinking. I mean, I cut back. Not like I was alcoholic or anything."

"That's good."

It was true, he'd gotten tired of Typically's adventures. Tired of trying to re-create episodes of *It's Only Sunny*. Tired of Typically, to be honest.

The breeze off the water got intense. He noticed the girl had pockets sewn into her dress. Her hands were grasping the fabric inside, but not from cold. She leaned against him. It was awesome. They bullshitted for a while. He felt better, he put an arm around her. She didn't seem to mind.

"What do you want?" she said softly. "Like, from life."

"You mean now?"

"Forever."

He wanted to kiss her so badly. She was different from any other girl he'd ever met. Definitely stranger. But in a good way. Wind swept down the beach. The dark was frigid. Nick didn't say anything for a moment, he needed to say the exact right thing, but what was that?

Then she got up and walked away.

"Hey. Hey!"

"I'm sorry," Emily said roughly. "We should go back."

"What happened?"

"Never mind," she called back, "I'm stupid. I don't know what I was talking about."

"Wait, hold on," he said, and stumbled to catch up. What was up with this girl? "Let me at least answer." She paused. He didn't have anything. What a loser. No wonder she'd run away.

"I want to be remembered," he said, above the wind. Really? But it was true. He felt it in his gut. Then, of course, the wind stopped. His words hung in the air.

"What about you?" he said. "You can't leave me hanging like that."

She stared over his shoulder at the Ferris wheel. It was tough to feel like he'd done anything right in the last half an hour. Maybe she hadn't heard him. *I want to be remembered.* What a creep.

She said formally, "What do your parents do?"

"My mom gives piano lessons. I don't know about my dad."

"Maybe I could take lessons. I always wanted to play an instrument."

"With my mom?"

"Could I?"

"I guess so," he said, laughing. "Why not?"

He wanted to say how much he liked her. How much he liked her little eyes. He should make his move, he knew it, yet he was frozen again.

She said, "Do you want to kiss me?"

Her hair was dark. As if her hair was outer space, her face the moon.

He put his lips on hers.

Her lips parted and pulled him in.

It was *amazing.*

■

Dear Nick,

I've got to tell you something and it's so weird but please don't worry, I'm totally fine and nothing's wrong. I just want you to hear about it from me before anyone else tells you, even your mom. Hopefully she gives you this letter but doesn't read it. I trust her not to.

I closed up the shop last night (Sunday) and went over to Denny's. I wasn't hungry but I didn't want to go home. I had that Willa Cather book in my bag so I just planned to get some tea and read. And then this guy in a black baseball hat stops by my booth, sort of floats up like a ghost and asks me if I'm Emily Portis. I was like, "Who are you???"

And then he started asking me questions, like what I thought about you, what really happened, if I was involved in whatever happened, if I felt embarrassed. I honestly had no idea who he was, I was just scared. But then it was so awful because I started answering him, I knew I shouldn't but I couldn't help it, I felt like such an idiot but I was afraid. He was really creepy, standing there, and I didn't know what else to do.

And then I noticed he had a bag on his arm, like a computer bag. One of his hands was sort of hiding it. I totally figured it out because I saw a camera, he was filming me. I was so mad! I asked what he was doing. He got red in the face, totally weird, shouting stuff, and then he called me the c-word. What a sicko! I told him to leave me alone. A manager came over and kicked him out.

Anyway, I wanted you to know, but please don't go thinking anything about it. I'm a lot happier today, or at least I'm not as scared as I was. The world's full of jerks, that's what Alex said at breakfast this morning. It all just makes me miss you that much more.

Nick, I love you with every single part of my body. You'll get out soon and this will all go away, <u>and then we'll be gone</u>. Do not let anything change the way you think about me.

Do you remember the day you took me shopping at the mall? You never knew how happy it made me feel. It's dumb but you were so cute, you tried to be awkward about it, but I could tell you knew exactly how you wanted me to look. To look for you. I liked that. All I wanted was for you to say what you wanted, I would have done it. I would have done anything. I still will. <u>Anything</u>. I will always be a hundred percent honest with you.

I think what makes us different from other people is that we say and do exactly as we please, no matter what people think. "It's never too late to be what you might have been." I read that today. God my feelings are so raw. But I'll dream about you tonight and we'll be together.

Nick, please forget everything I told you that night. None of it's real, it doesn't exist. All that matters is us, right now, and what comes next.

And never doubt and never forget how much I love you, forever and ever.

All my love, Emily

·

Monday afternoon, a little over a week into Martin's time in New Hampshire, the day is more fall than summer, the sky is grainy, a churning wind shakes down branches from rickety old trees. And back to the doctor's house he's pulled by magnetic yearnings, a rippling dissatisfaction in his gut that makes him drive through Dunkin' Donuts along the way and order a cruller.

In the parking lot afterward he pauses to brush his hair, brush the crumbs off his chin, see if anyone's paying him attention.

It's not just vanity. Lately he's gotten the feeling he's being watched.

The night before, the boy from the restaurant brought him dinner again, the black kid with blond hair, Demeke. He'd stood in the doorway, stared for a moment. On a whim Martin asked him to stay for *Jeopardy!* The boy gave him a funny look but sat down.

Martin asked where he was from.

"Here," the kid said. "Claymore."

"Sorry," he said, "I mean originally."

The kid's tone twisted. "What's that supposed to mean?"

He nearly said that the kid as sure as hell wasn't from Claymore originally. Unless the New Hampshire accent included French and/or West African influences. But it had been a long day. He apologized and held his tongue. They watched TV.

"My parents own this place. I live upstairs."

"I didn't know that."

"Aren't you supposed to be a detective?"

He laughed.

"So where are you from?" Demeke said. "Originally."

"Nowhere," he said. "Absolutely nowhere."

The kid laughed. "You are seriously weird."

The next morning, Martin parks in front of the doctor's house. He stayed up the whole night worrying about his marriage. No husband in the world wants to imagine what he imagined. But the kid's laugh makes him smile. Time to go play detective.

He unlocks the front door. Spends a minute in study of the walls. Traces the wallpaper with a fingernail, over apple bushels, bouquets of yellow flowers. The furniture, the table, the jar of potpourri, he studies it all. For the first time in Claymore he feels strangely calm.

Something right's going to happen. Not something wrong.

A phone rings, the house phone. From upstairs and somewhere else. The kitchen. Once. Twice. After the fourth time, it goes to voicemail. Then his own phone rings, on his belt. Brenner, the boy's attorney.

"I was planning on visiting Nick today," she says. "But something's come up."

"You want me to go?"

"Yes. But I need you to have a soft touch, New Jersey."

"What does that mean?"

"We're not connecting. Me and the kid. Something's in the way. It could be I'm a woman. Anyway, so it goes."

"You want me to connect with him."

"We know his father ran away."

"You're saying you want me to go play Dad."

"Soft touch, Martin. I'm serious."

In crime, secrets are always plain. You just have to look in the right spots—even in New Hampshire. The previous week, Brenner had explained that, in the southern half of the state, they basically only saw assault, property, and fraud. Plus the opioid epidemic: heroin, fentanyl, overdoses in public. With copper stripping on the rise as a result, and synthetic weed, spice, K2. Prostitution was tolerated, assuming narcotics didn't also get a hand job. But her bread and butter, Brenner said, was repeat customers passing bad checks *and* robbing places. Husbands and wives who beat up on their husbands and wives after a binge on something cheap and powerful. Making her clients mostly two-swallow types: they did something stupid, then they did something else that was stupid.

And meanwhile her office was underfunded, overworked, taken for granted. The boss had checked out. Her assistant was a burgeoning alcoholic. They got by.

Martin leaves the scene to go see Nick. At the courthouse, he's escorted by the same guard as last time, max age of nineteen. Did he graduate high school? The room's all concrete, vinyl, and plastic. Two heavy tables, four old chairs, the small cutout window. Not a single happy color.

Three minutes later, Nick strides in eagerly, and Martin feels strongly emotional for no good reason. Then the kid's eyes go dark. He isn't the expected.

"Where's Brenner?"

"She couldn't make it, sorry."

"I told my mom, I want my lawyer."

Martin feels hot. His lower back has been threatening to spasm. He shoves up backward and props himself against the wall.

The kid says, "Are you okay?"

"Let me tell you where I want to start." *Be paternal.* "Why don't you tell me what really happened that night."

"You know what happened."

"Let's pretend I don't have a clue."

"I wrote it down."

"Nick. We both know it's bullshit."

"It's what happened."

"No, it's crap," he says. He breathes through his mouth while the queasy feeling in his stomach seeps upward. "But for some reason you're sticking to it. When in fact you're being an idiot, you realize that."

"This is awesome. Anything else?"

"Do you know where you're going? Because this only goes one way. The state attorney, she doesn't screw around with double homicide. Prosecutors I know back in New Jersey, they'd kill for this woman's conviction rate. Stalin didn't have her conviction rate. You've heard of Stalin?"

A buzzer goes off somewhere—the cold breath of jail. Nick doesn't notice, he's so accustomed.

"This state has capital punishment," Martin says quietly. "It's on the books. Now, they don't use it often, it's sort of fallen out of favor—"

"Like Stalin."

He laughs, caught by surprise.

"Why don't you go get us something to eat?" Nick says flatly.

"We'll do a trade. I'll pick up lunch, but first you give me something."

The kid's leg beats up and down.

"What are you hiding from us, Nick?"

The kid looks around everywhere. Innocent as can be. Which may mean Martin's on the right trail. "Nick, please," he implores. But nothing more. He leaves, goes out, lies down in the backseat of his car. Chomps Motrin like they're heroin breath mints. His thoughts slosh around, to no avail. Fifteen minutes later he buys a bag of cheeseburgers at Wendy's, baked potato for himself, returns and feeds the kid. But even then the kid still doesn't talk.

He remembers, *soft touch*.

"I'm staying at an inn in town," he says, while the kid chews his sandwich. "The Crow's Nest. Did I tell you that? It's not bad. A little too antiquey for my taste." No response. "They do a good breakfast. There's a kid who works there, African kid, he goes to your high school. De-meke. Smart kid. You know him? Skater type." No response. "When I was your age, you didn't have diversity in the schools. You had Catholics and Jews, that was about it. We thought about adoption, me and my wife. For about a minute. I guess we decided we're too old. I mean, she

136

also didn't want them. I probably could have gone again. I have a daughter, from a previous marriage. Camille. Her mother wanted something French; it would 'help her value herself.' I'm not even joking." No response. "My wife's cheating on me. The current wife. It took me a while to figure it out. Not sure what that says about my investigative skills. It is what it is. To be honest, it's probably one of the reasons I'm up here. In addition to your case. My daughter's in California. We're not in touch these days. Which is my fault, I'm sure."

The kid says, "Hey, you want to do something for me?"

"Sure. Name it."

"Go check on Emily. Do whatever she needs."

Then Nick summons the guard and walks out.

∎

There'd been a night, two months into hanging out, when he and Emily did a double date with Typically and his girlfriend, Cindy, at Bowl Haven, a bowling alley in Hampstead.

Typically and Cindy had been going together since middle school. He'd promised her an engagement ring, but it was still unseen. Bowling was their thing, candlepin bowling, totally stupid looking—but the purpose of the night wasn't bowling. At that point, Typically still hadn't met Emily. Over time, he'd gotten bitchy about it, called Nick pussy-whipped and other things. Not that he cared. But Emily began to wonder why she'd heard all these things about his best friend and they'd never met.

The place smelled of French fries and old carpet. By the time they arrived, Typically had nearly drunk a pitcher of beer by himself. He had on a Bruins jersey, gray sweatpants. He looked like a shorter version of the Michelin Man. With a Canadian flag bandanna wrapped around his head.

Typically got up and grabbed him in a headlock and made chimpanzee noises while Cindy escorted Emily to the bar to order food.

"So what's it like," Typically said, releasing him, "doing bang-bang on the sheriff's daughter."

"Screw you."

"Hey, just doing my job."

"What job?"

"Taking care of my little buddy."

It seemed to Nick in that moment that he'd spent his whole life putting up with people who claimed to have his best interests at heart.

"Though honestly? I don't know anymore," said Typically, not sarcastically. "You dumped me, basically. I mean, what happened to us?"

"You're such a turd."

"You're absolutely right."

The girls came back with nachos. The four of them bowled as teams. Nick watched Cindy ask Emily questions. She complimented her on her clothes. When she found out about Emily's dream of designing clothes, she said she was a clotheshorse herself, she loved to shop online.

"That is the truth," Typically said loudly. "She's got all kinds of shit she doesn't wear. It's straight up *Sex and the City*, have you guys seen that show? I had my wisdom teeth out, I watched, like, three seasons in two days. It was informative."

Nick watched him say to Emily, "I'm what they call a plastic gangster. I'm a sweet-nothing nothing. There's nothing to fear here, I swear."

After half an hour, the bowling was actually fun. They were in the lead. Emily was the best out of the four of them, she said she must be a natural. After an hour, Typically was permanently seated next to her, whispering, arm around her shoulder, while Nick and Cindy were up and down to bowl.

"I don't want you to get the wrong impression," he said at one point to Emily. He poured himself more beer. "I'm not in love with you, okay?"

"Okay."

"I mean, look at that girl. Cindy," he shouted. "How hard do I love you?"

"You love me so hard."

"I am so hard in love."

"He really is."

"She makes me want to be a better man."

"Because he's pathetic," Cindy said.

"Yeah but someday I am going to lay down some offspring in that uterus, you know that, right?"

Even Nick had to laugh. "That's gross," he said under his breath. No one heard him. It was probably the best night they'd had all week. Fifteen minutes later, he was about to say they should do it all again soon, then Typically grabbed one of Emily's hands to study it up close, like a palm reader.

"What I see is you've got an old soul. I tell that to you honestly and for free." He sat back and stared square at Nick, which made Nick uncomfortable. Wondering what came next. Something always came next.

"The thing is, in real life," Typically said loudly to Emily, to the group, "where the government's concerned, souls aside, you are a little young for my friend."

"Jacob," Cindy cautioned. She was the only person who used his real name.

"Don't get me wrong," Typically said. "I'm blue state to my balls. If there's grass on the field, et cetera."

"You're a piece of shit," said Nick. He pulled Emily up by the hand.

"Oh, calm down. Don't be a bitch."

"We're going, actually," he said, and grabbed their shoes.

"What's happening?" said Emily.

"We're leaving."

They heard Cindy say angrily, "You're such an asshole."

Only a few seconds later, by the video games, Typically ran up behind them and tackled Nick. They went down hard. Nick twisted away and scrambled to his feet. His knee burned. Then Typically was on top of him again, at least fifty pounds heavier. He got him in a wrestling hold with his left hand over his face, then crashed them down to the ground with his thick legs wrapped around Nick's middle.

"Get off of me."

"You're making me do this."

"Fuck you."

"Jacob, stop," shouted Cindy. "The manager's coming."

"He can quit anytime."

Nick elbowed his best friend in the belly, but it made no difference. As soon as he'd had a drink, Typically became oblivious to pain, and he always completed the mission. He leaned in, pressed his lips against Nick's ear, and his voice was like a missile blasting into his skull: "Fucking stop, you prick, and listen: that chick is quality. But when you get caught, not if, what happens, huh? Because that's my job, asshole. To tell you shit you don't want to hear. So think what her dad's going to do, the fucking sheriff, on the night he finds you knee-deep in his sixteen-year-old."

∎

139

Outside the courthouse, in the emptiness of his SUV, Martin looks up a number on his phone and presses call. He glances at a crow on a wire, self-righteously perched, watching over all of them, lord of the wire.

"Dad? What happened? Are you okay?"

He laughs uncomfortably. "Why do you think something happened?"

"Because you're calling me."

"Maybe I just want to hear your voice."

"Am I on speaker?"

"Camille, I just wanted to touch base. How are you?"

"Well, I'm driving, I'm not really supposed to use a phone."

"Just talk for a second."

"Yeah, okay. So what's up?"

"Where are you off to?"

"It's a lunch. For the department. You sound weird, you know that? You are still going to meetings, right?"

He chuffs, "What do you mean I sound weird?"

She laughs lightly. "Just forget it."

He hears what sounds like talk radio. Or is someone else in the car?

"So what's the lunch for?"

"It's an award thing. It's nothing. For one of my papers. It doesn't matter."

"You won an award? But that's wonderful. What was the paper about?"

"You're not interested, trust me. Even Roger can't take it."

"What?"

"Let's catch up next week or something. I really should go."

"Wait, who's Roger? Do I know him?"

She laughs again, but more knowingly. "Now you sound like yourself. I'm going to let you go, we'll catch up soon. If you need anything, just text next time."

"Camille."

"The check hasn't arrived, by the way. I'm guessing it's in the mail?"

"What do you mean?"

"The check?"

He remembers: the reminder on his computer back in New Jersey, that popped up during the visit with Lillian's lawyer. He sees the check on the kitchen counter, signed and sealed.

"Darn it, it's at home. I'm out of town for work. I'm in New Hampshire."

"I thought you retired."

"I'll have my bank send you it tonight."

She hangs up a few seconds later. In the distance, there's lightning behind the mountains. The thunder booms on a count of eight. It echoes in his chest. Up ahead, a stoplight turns yellow. Thunder, rainstorm, sunbeams. History's full of little guys hauling their millstones. What comes after yellow? His mind can't help but race in a hundred directions. What the hell is he doing? The light's newly red when Martin plows through it, and almost cracks into a blue sedan pulling out into the intersection.

The driver screeches, stops, lays into his horn.

And Martin slams down the accelerator.

But the blue sedan follows him, tails him, hits the horn with staccato blurts, *blat ba blat blat blat.*

This can't go on much further. He parks at a laundromat half a mile down the road. His lower back throbs in his throat. The sedan slashes to a diagonal stop to his left. Right away the driver's out, hot and fuming, a fat white guy in an oversized T-shirt rolling toward him with three hundred pounds of momentum and a neck tattoo.

He slams his hand on the windowpane. "What the fuck, man? Roll down the window, get the fuck out of the car."

"I'm sorry."

"You almost killed me, you know that? Get out of the fucking car."

Martin rolls down his window, trying to keep his training under control. The truth is he caused this situation. What the hell did he get himself into?

"Sir, I'm sorry," he says slowly. "Please. Get back in your vehicle."

"Who are you, the fucking cops? You could've gotten us killed, you realize that?" He stabs at Martin's eye with his finger. "Did you think about that, you dumb piece of shit?"

"I won't do it again."

"You think I give a shit?"

"No, of course not. I'm sorry."

There's so much anger, the man's quivering, he doesn't know what to do next. Martin genuinely feels regretful, he feels remorse for this man. But his primary concern is if the guy's got a gun under his seat.

The man tells the sky "Shit" and slams his palm on the roof of his own car.

"I'm supposed to be at my girl's house right now. She had our baby yesterday. You hear me? Yesterday, my baby girl. So what happens, I wind up dead because some dipshit ran a red light, huh? Who the fuck's going to be the father then? You asshole."

The man gets back in his car, gives him the finger, and drives away. It starts to rain. Martin rolls up the window and exhales deeply. He gets out, lies down in the backseat. His nerves sizzle in the aftermath of the situation. Lightning lights up the sky. One Mississippi, two Mississippi. Thunder booms on six. It's getting closer. He closes his eyes and vows to never run a red light again. What if he'd killed them both? Memories stubbornly crowd around his thoughts to torment him. He pushes them away, he counts the girls he never kissed, the sights he never saw. Thoughts such as these, thoughts even older and stupider, suddenly stop when he remembers Camille, the phone call. All he wants to do is help her. And how does she see him? A naive old man who writes checks. Who can't be trusted to drive a car, who's piss-poor at texting. Is that what family is these days, just exchanges? Is their connection cellular like blood, or cellular like phones? Are humans capable anymore of the old ways?

Probably the worst part of old age is the fact that all the stuff you wanted to forget when you were younger is now all you remember. Martin dozes off. When he wakes, he feels bloated and lonely. His regret slowly boils down to dry salt, to a single, crystallized realization: that in the course of the phone call he'd neglected to ask Camille a single question bigger than the conversation itself. For once raise the goddamn periscope.

•

Eventually, months into hanging out, they'd talked about running away together. It quickly became a plan. California. Los Angeles. They searched for images of the beaches on Nick's laptop. They watched *Singin' in the Rain*, her favorite movie. And none of it was a game, they didn't play games. For his part Nick refused to be drawn in by anyone. He was nobody's sucker, and he didn't care what other people thought. He told her, he'd never lied to her and never would. And the truth was, he pointed out, they needed to go as soon as possible, before they got stuck in a little town where nothing ever happened except death by nearness to idiots.

Compromise, conformity, Claymore. Nothing for nobody except the shithead rich. Where the only thing kids could do, to get any forward momentum going in their lives, was to leave.

Of course, Emily would miss Alex, she didn't like that. But Alex soon would attend college, she couldn't just follow her around forever.

And if they sat around and waited for the right moment to come along, for everything to be absolutely ready and perfect and safe, for the solar system to give them a thumbs-up, they'd never start.

By that point it was March. Most weeks, they managed around track practice and school and jobs to see each other four or five times a week. Father didn't know anything, as far as Emily could tell—or, if he knew, he didn't stop them, he was too busy at work as it was. At the end of the month Nick bought her a phone. A flip phone, prepaid, nothing fancy. A thousand texts for thirty bucks a month.

She was dumbfounded, she didn't know such a thing existed. Alex was there the afternoon he gave it to her after school and even she was taken aback, that she hadn't thought of it, either.

That first night, Nick had just fallen asleep when his phone lit up on the other side of the room.

Are you awake?

> Barely

I love my phone. I can't even explain.
I could type all night.

> Cool but I have to be at the garage rly
> early so just a little longer

Let me tell you 5 reasons I love you

> I won't stop u

One of their favorite meeting spots was a basement room at the Leduc Public Library. The first week in April, a big snow fell outside. The windows were filled with white. Nick sat in a stuffed armchair. He pulled her onto his lap. She could tell he had something on his mind.

He drew a breath and said he'd been thinking again about the plan. She nodded and tried to make her face as grave as his. He turned her phone over in his fingers. *Why would she ever go along with it?* he wondered. *I love him so much*, she thought. She kissed him spontaneously, and he kissed her back, wetly, a long kiss on her neck, until she laughed and pushed him away.

"We should just do it," he said. "Leave. Just go for it."

Though he was feeling, in fact, that the plan was probably impossible, for a number of reasons. He looked at her casually. She didn't speak. In fact she liked to hear about his ambitions, his devotion to their future together. She couldn't picture what would become of her life in years ahead, but at least now it would be something. And she hadn't had that before, she hadn't had a *something* before. She reminded herself to tell him this sometime, to make sure he understood what a gift he was.

"So let's do it," she said. "Really do it."

She pulled away from him, but remained in his arms. He looked stunned. He was stunned. She wasn't.

"Really?" he said.

"Let's set a date."

"When?"

She thought about it for a moment. "It can't be before this summer."

"But you think you could do that?"

Actually, she'd been thinking about it for weeks, delighted to consider such adult steps ahead of them. Even if they were only fantasy steps, what was certain to her was that the calculations could get figured out, laws be circumvented if necessary. It hadn't occurred to Nick that she'd have such thoughts. That his intentions would be taken for more than just talk. Suddenly everything in the room, the books, the snow, took on a singular significance.

She nodded. "This summer."

"This summer," he said, considering. "Okay, this summer."

"This summer," she said.

Then they grinned at each other, sinking into a type of brief trance that's only achievable when two minds meet in fantasy. At the same time, their smiles dropped a bit. Because it was a fantasy, really, the whole idea, as long as she wasn't eighteen. Or so it seemed to Nick. Maybe there were legal back roads he didn't know about? He watched the snow pile up in the window. After all, their joint excitement was too high to be restricted for long, and hadn't they already beaten pretty serious obstacles? Emily calmly looked around the room, curved mouth smiling, and her gaze didn't rest. Going west had unexpectedly become the only thing she'd ever wanted to do. And this step was a part of it. The first part. Which meant there were so many parts still to come.

They looked at each other again. To hell with it. They'd go. They kissed.

"I knew you'd say yes," he said. "I knew it the first time we met."

Emily laughed. "Don't be such a goof. How could you?"

"See? You still don't know how serious I am."

■

It really all started with *On the Road*. Kerouac had changed everything for Nick. Suzanne brought the book home from the library during his recuperation, she said it had been one of his grandfather's favorites. At first it was too weird, too old-fashioned. He just couldn't get into this guy, what was happening. The story was hard to follow, he didn't know what type of book it was. Then, a day later, he'd finished it and started over, and that was something he'd never done with a book before. He wanted more of it. Not just the book, but the life, the way Kerouac seemed to live, the way his characters joked around and did cool stuff. All the guns, fishing, mountain climbing, the cars. New York City, New Orleans, Cheyenne. All the girls.

Laid up in bed for those months, he was constantly wide awake, always in some kind of discomfort. And was angry, bitter, and gradually tired of streaming crap on his laptop. His eyes hurt, so he switched to books. They also made more sense in a way, at least to him. Because the guys in Kerouac books, they struck Nick as like him. Sort of introverted. Guys with reserve. But look at the stuff they did anyway.

He read every Kerouac Suzanne could find. Then one of the librarians in town sent her home with *The Monkey Wrench Gang*, and he loved that, then *Brave New World*, and some Chuck Palahniuk and *The Hunger Games*—none of those really clicked. But then came *Fear and Loathing in Las Vegas*. And he met the end-all, be-all of his new existence.

Who the hell was this guy?

Hunter Thompson intercepted his life from a trajectory of total bullshit and ignorance, basically. One night, with *Fear and Loathing*, he actually felt his brain enlarge. It used a muscle that had never been activated before. Like he'd seen through something that previously had been opaque. He lay back stunned by the realization. He stared at the blue shaded lamp, the dusty window blinds. It was like his mind had gotten smarter by a full leap.

And that was just the beginning. He also got into some Buddhist stuff his mom had on the shelf, thanks to Thompson, but the real draw was that Hunter was himself a Kerouac character, but in real life. Like Nick himself could become one day, became the idea. Because he might not be much, he was nine-tenths sure about that, but at least he wasn't completely stupid.

The books confirmed it for him, that he liked books. Or, he liked books like *these* books, serious books that didn't take themselves too seriously. How come they never gave you this kind of shit in school? Which was exactly how he began to think about himself: an outsider, but with some kind of brain. And he decided he liked his mind, doing things with his mind. He'd never felt that way before. Maybe even took a small amount of pleasure in feeling smarter than all the jerks around town. Claymore surely had more idiots per acre than most places.

But the point, Hunter Thompson seemed to say, in all the stuff that Nick read—and Kerouac was after pretty much the same thing, and Nick totally agreed with this idea, so he was ready when it hit him, but still stunned, scrunched up in bed, when he saw the lines written out, things he felt like he already knew at some level, but had never seen put into simple sentences—was that in life *there is no point*. It's all bullshit. Everything. A person lives, dies, it doesn't matter. The president of the United States doesn't matter. To help, to hurt, to get screwed over, to screw someone over, do good, do bad, yell, tell people how to live their lives—none of it mattered. It just wasn't real, it was shit people did to kill time, to conform, to avoid feeling afraid, to make themselves more comfortable with impending death.

But so many people freaked out along the way and made themselves victims of something. Or lied about their lives. So F that shit. He hated liars. His dad used to lie about stuff all the time. It was Shithead Survival School lesson number one. Hunter Thompson kind of said this made sense, that to expect otherwise is silly. Because the whole thing is a lie and made liars of folks. But if you could face up to the truth in that, then you'd tell the truth all the time. Most people simply can't. And therefore society is a joke. It's the Matrix. The Matrix wasn't Keanu Reeves and D batteries, it's young people who thought they should go to college, join the country club, mow the lawn. It's the shit people post online. Everyone who stared at their phones while they walked around.

Obviously most religions were scams. The steeple clock was basically the only thing his dad's church was good for.

Nick didn't know yet about a lot, but he could smell bullshit. And Hunter Thompson seemed to say, at least between the lines, that in such a world, the best a guy or girl can hope for is to try to live honestly. To be the one who doesn't cave. Be a freak. Have fun. Laugh, read books, and get laid. Do dumb shit but learn from it, and get less dumb. And get stoned once in a while, perhaps, and maybe get rich, though money only seemed to make things worse.

But then there was love. Not just sex. Love. Kerouac and Thompson both ceded a unique significance to love that they didn't assign to anything else. As though nothing else mattered as much.

■

In early April, with his plans focused on the summer, Nick went to one of Emily's track meets. Snow had melted. It dropped off the roof. He took a seat inside the gray gymnasium. He was adjusting his knee when he noticed the sheriff nearby, watching from the stands. With a hand pinning a dark cowboy hat to his knee.

Emily ran the sixteen hundred. It said CLAYMORE in crimson across her racing top. Nick ducked down and watched her legs blur. She placed third and beamed, and he wanted to stand up and clap, but remembered her father. He snuck a peek. The sheriff had disappeared. He looked everywhere and found him by the scorers' table, greeting someone. At the same time, the sheriff watched Emily as she came out of the team huddle, pulled on her sweatshirt. But she was looking for Nick, and she found him. At which moment the sheriff followed her line of sight.

Nick texted her from the car. Half an hour later, Emily jogged out, hair wet from a shower, face flushed. She jumped into the car and kissed him sloppily, grinned, then pulled away.

"What is it?"

"Nothing."

"No, it's something."

He let out a deep breath. "I was thinking you should come over to dinner tonight."

"Wait, really?"

"Sure."

"But won't your mom be there?"

"That's the point."

"Have you even told her about us?"

"You know I have," he said.

"Wow." She took a deep breath. "So what do I call her? Mrs. Toussaint?"

She looked at him, excited eyes, and hugged him swiftly above the shifter. So maybe it wasn't a completely crazy idea.

At dusk, they arrived with two pizzas. He unlocked and opened the old front door slowly. Now that they were at the house, he started to freak, scratch compulsively at his scars. His precise worry, based on the one time he'd brought a girlfriend home before, was that his mother would find Emily stupid, or boring, or unappealing in some way that would provoke an outburst. And/or that she'd be drunk.

"Mom? I brought pizza."

"Good god, I'm starving," his mother announced, from somewhere in the back.

He reminded himself: summer, California, escape.

"Emily's here," he said offhandedly.

Suzanne appeared in the kitchen door. Hair wound up, several strands falling out.

"Emily," she said slowly. "Remind me of your last name."

"Portis."

"That's right." She stepped back into the kitchen and called out a second later, "Nicky, if you're having a beer, get Emily something."

"She's pretty," she said loudly a moment later.

Emily nudged him through the door.

Suzanne appeared again. She looked Emily up and down.

"Do you know who Courtney Love is?"

"I don't think so."

"Kim Gordon?"

"No?"

"I like your dress."

"I made it last week."

"I wouldn't have guessed. Nicky, set the table."

"Mrs. Toussaint," Emily said, "can I do anything to help?"

Suzanne smiled, took her hand, and led her back into the kitchen with a slight wobble. Of course she'd been drinking, he thought morosely. And who the hell was Kim Gordon? He had set down the pizza boxes and started to set out plates when his mom strutted in and told him in a heavy whisper to put them away. Then he heard her escort Emily to the butler's pantry behind the kitchen, the wooden shelves behind dusty old glass panes.

They returned with a water-stained leather chest.

"Are you kidding me?"

"Nicky, how often do we have company?"

A breeze lifted the curtain in the window. His mom was practically giddy, taking out the old china and silver, laying it out in rows. She reminded him of herself at an earlier age, a memory he couldn't place. When she was happy. She angled herself toward Emily, away from Nick, and got into the story, which he'd heard three thousand times—the night his grandmother tossed the case overboard after his grandfather insisted on taking her out in a rowboat for dinner, and brought along the silver for propriety's sake, only he also forgot an anchor, so they'd attached a line—

"Jesus, Mom."

"I like it," Emily said. "I think it's funny."

His mother smirked and grabbed her cigarettes from the sill.

"Nicky's embarrassed. Look, he's blushing."

They sat down to dinner. In ten minutes he'd eaten an entire pizza by himself. He couldn't say he was surprised that his mother barely touched her food. Emily scarfed down three slices.

"Mom, try eating."

"Emily, how old are you?"

"Sixteen," she said. "Seventeen in September."

"We'll have to pick up some sparklers."

"What?"

"For her birthday. Nicky, don't be a jerk."

He cringed to demonstrate that he was wounded. In fact, he'd merely suffered a conventional pleasure, watching the two of them bond, but didn't want to show it, or have something turn up to reshape his feelings. Time passed quickly and he felt good. *It* felt good. When he met Emily, he felt like he'd met the first person who really understood him. Maybe Suzanne would find some way to see that, to not be jealous about that.

The front-door knocker clanged. His mother barely lifted her eyes. Just like her to forget she'd booked a lesson. He got up to answer.

The sheriff stood off the deck, hat in hand.

"Is my daughter here?"

Eyes cold, inquiring.

"I'm sorry?" Nick said nervously.

"If you could please send my daughter out. Her name is Emily."

His mother and Emily appeared behind him.

"Why, Sheriff," Suzanne said. "What's the trouble?" Her tone was as matter-of-fact as a turn signal.

"Mrs. Toussaint."

"Mr. Portis."

"If I may—"

"We're having pizza. Do you want some?"

"Emily, get in the car."

His mom crossed her arms, stepping forward slightly, and obstructed the door.

"You know, I was so pleased that Emily stopped by. She is going to make a great student."

"Excuse me?"

Suzanne gestured to a sign in the window, yellowed from years in the sunlight. *Suzanne Toussaint, Piano Instruction.*

"She stopped by to ask about lessons," she said. "My son Nicky and I were just eating. My schedule is pretty booked right now, but with Emily's interest, well, you don't see a lot of kids who really want to study."

Emily descended the porch stairs.

Nick's whole body clenched.

The sheriff said to her, "This is true?"

"Yes."

"You signed up for piano lessons."

"So what? I'll pay for it myself."

Suzanne laughed. "One minute they hate tomatoes, the next day it's

all they eat. You know what I mean." She took Nick's arm. "Emily, I'll
see you Sunday at three. Good night, Sheriff."

■

Your mom is amazing.

She's ok r u in trouble

I'm fine. I miss you. I love you forever
and ever.

I love you too

Say it, forever and ever.

4EAE

What?

4=for e=ever a=and

Oh well I didn't know that.

Lol sorry

4EAE

4EAE

■

In jail, Nick's anticipation of the scheduled phone call gets him so
keyed up that he does 120 push-ups in bursts of eight and ten. He
pauses between sets, standing atop a steep couloir of dread, and beats
his legs with his fists. He reminds himself to stay hopeful. He resumes
his push-ups.

And even the guard remembers the proper time of the call, and
brings Nick to the pay phone with its flexible metal cable, the coiled
garden snake.

Emily picks up halfway through the second ring.

"Nick?"

"It's me."

"Oh god," she says.

"We only have a little time."

"I can't believe it. I miss you so much!"

"I miss you, too. I've got a lot I need to say." He pauses to catch his breath, to say exactly what he practiced. His heart jumps in his chest. "I've thought it all through, so please just hear me out."

Loud buzz and ratchet. The door in the next room opens from the stairs.

"Hold on a second."

"What is it?"

He sees through the window the sheriff's hat.

"Nick?"

"Shit. Shit!"

"What is it?"

"Your dad's here."

"What? What is he doing?"

The door between the two rooms is half glass, chicken-wired. He watches the sheriff quickly turn the handle. He doesn't know what to do. He doesn't know what he's supposed to do.

"Listen—"

"Nick, don't—"

"I have to go."

"Wait!"

"I love you," he says, and hangs up the phone.

The door opens. The sheriff takes a seat at the table. He tenderly removes his hat. He says quietly, "It's none of my business who that was, Mr. Toussaint."

"What are you talking about?"

"I can look it up later, if I want. The number you called."

"It was my mom."

"I'm glad to hear it."

"Screw you."

"What I mean is," the sheriff says, "it's nice to see a child take a parent into consideration. She must be at her wit's end. Mr. Toussaint, let's face facts."

"Stop calling me that."

His hands are bone-dry, but his mind is a fireball, his emotions are all hate.

"Everybody knows how this is going to play out. It's about the truth. That's all. You do a little time and get out on good behavior. So, naturally, we're all counting on you to reassure your mother that she's got nothing to be afraid of."

"I'm always available to pass along a message," he adds. "You do know that."

■

Hey there friends, check out the video
I just posted. I was at Denny's the other
night and in walks who else but the
GF to our Claymore Kid®. Dear heck!
Now, as someone interested in citizen
media, I do think you may enjoy seeing
what she's really all about, at least in
this humble recording. Basically I asked
her about her meal and taped the whole
thing. Caveat: There is a little editing
toward the end because GF gets kind of
salty, but feel free to share. It seems
pretty clear the girl's hiding something,
or am I nuts? Anyone care to guess
regarding what? (I am nuts, of course,
but anyway . . .)

■

Martin leans on his elbows on the table, getting to the end of his report for Brenner. Unsaid is how imagination failed him, experience failed him. Out loud, final point, there's the daughter, Moira, the juice maker, the depressive. With essentially no motive besides animosity, and no priors whatsoever.

"But also no real alibi, I thought you said," says Brenner. "Except the girlfriend."

"Right."

"Who works at New Balance. We'll call her Sneakers."

"Except Sneakers. And the TV queue."

"For what it's worth, we do know Sneakers has been in trouble before."

Five years ago, a possession charge, a small bag of cocaine, party size. Then again, not larceny, not assault, not murder.

Brenner cups her hands around her mug.

"So let's say the daughter finds out somehow that Sneakers used to bang her dad."

"She doesn't know that."

"And that's confirmed?"

"She doesn't know."

"Tell me why not."

"From the reaction on Sneakers' part."

He elaborates, when she gives him a queer glance. Basically that a telephone call the previous afternoon with Sneakers had not gone well, but was telling. In which he'd laid out what he suspected, hints of it. Enough that she got what he was going for and played instant defense, angrily. Suggesting, to Martin's ear, that the guy at the golf club was right about things, or close enough. Further cemented when she became resistant and sufficiently contentious, in her self-protection, after he started asking about her relationship with Dr. Ashburn, that she threatened to call a lawyer. Which probably meant very little on the face of things. And then meant a little more when she hung up on him.

He'd driven to the store. She was helping a customer choose a pair of running tights. Petite, professional, big smile. She stared away for a moment, past the window display, and caught him watching. Recognition. Anger. Fear.

Though, in fact, the fear was in her eyes first. The look of someone with something to hide.

Brenner said impatiently, "So you're saying you didn't actually ask the daughter, Moira Ashburn, if she knew."

"About what?" Martin asked.

"About what? About her girlfriend, aka Sneakers, aka slag, who fucked Daddy dearest prior to commencement of fucking her."

"Why would I do that? You'd honestly want me to?"

Brenner gripped her head with two hands and stared at the table. "New Jersey, let me play this back to you. The daughter of our murder victims doesn't know that Sneakers and her father used to have a thing, we believe. Yet we haven't confirmed that. When, in fact, maybe she does know, so how about that, could that lead to something? How are you not seeing this? How about maybe she found it all out recently. Couple weeks ago, I don't know, something tipped her off. She confronts Sneakers. 'You fucked my dad, then came for my ass?' And maybe Sneakers says she'd do anything to stay together. A plan hatches. Revenge. After all those years of homo-bashing."

"We know exactly where she was on the night. The TV queue."

"Please. Based on what? An IP address? I can get you an IP address by three o'clock this afternoon. How about an eyewitness, Martin? How about some corroboration?"

"But you really think—"

Then Brenner laughs, and coughs hard, which makes her laugh harder. She stares him down, hand over mouth. The coughs go away. He doesn't know which way to turn.

"So you're saying—"

"Martin—"

"Hold on," he says gruffly. "You honestly wanted me to barge in on her life, ruin her relationship with this woman"—can't he at least get points for sensitivity?—"all because the girlfriend, reportedly, once upon a time—"

"Her name is Sneakers," Brenner says, and laughs all over again.

He's about to start up when she interrupts, "Jersey, quit. I'm busting your balls. I'm sorry, this is how I let off steam. Look, the daughter, the girlfriend—I mean, I wish there was something there, but frankly, without a smoking gun . . . It's not like murder is even a solid revenge tactic in this scenario, right? For two chicks with no form? And then what about the double play? I.e., why kill the mom? No, it's a dead end. I'm just messing with you because we've got nothing else."

She says a second later, now seriously, "Let's face facts. We're no further than when we started. I'm not holding that against you. The little piece of shit confessed. End of story."

Martin chomps a pickle and stares at his plate.

"The biggest single fact in this case," Brenner says, "is that we're screwed."

She calls for the check. Whether or not Martin likes it, she's right, faultlessly. Reading between the lines had led him to a couple interesting suspicions, but nothing more. Nothing to call a solid lead. When no other evidence turned out to be more than circumstantial? Questions like, how'd Nick move the Ashburns? Why kill them in the first place? He'd talked to Nick's coworkers, employers, got zilch to build context. Not that it would've mattered much anyway, with a confession on the table. Nothing matters without additional witnesses, tests, anything close to hard evidence. Something to prove that the kid's story, that he'd stuck to thus far, was a lie.

"Look, you're nice," Brenner says. "You're unusually dedicated for a cop."

"What a compliment."

"But I have plenty of cases where the conviction's not handed over on a silver platter." She looks angry for a moment, utterly recognizable to Martin as someone who's also frustrated and upset and disappointed and perplexed, then she swallows it down. She adds, "No matter how many holes I poke through his story, believe me, the DA's going to eat exactly what's on the plate."

"That boy's innocent," he says. "We know that."

Brenner laughs. "Who cares? What are you, twelve?"

He says vehemently, "He shouldn't have to deal."

"Oh, give me a break. Have you lost your mind? Who is this about, really?" This time Brenner doesn't laugh. She leans in angrily. "You put him on trial, he gets life. Or maybe worse. Jesus. Maybe you really still are a cop." She adds a moment later, "Let's say Nick changes his story tomorrow. Retracts the whole thing. What does that say? She'll burn him to the ground. Why did he wait so long to retract? What's he lying about this time? Even in our best-case scenario, we're still screwed."

Two hours later, after a long nap at the hotel, his alarm wakes him from a dreamless snooze. He splashes water on his face, drives to the doctor's house. He's mechanically functioning, and the thought cheers him up, that at least he's still functioning. But he needs to be, he needs to straighten himself out. The rest of the day's schedule is nearly full. An hour later, he'll see the girl, Emily, like he'd promised. Also, that morning he'd received a call from the mom, Mrs. Suzanne Toussaint. A request that he stop by that evening. Until now, she'd been dealing exclusively with Brenner. But she heard about him, wants to meet him. For some reason she asked him not to tell Brenner that she called.

The Ashburns' house is creepily silent. He climbs the doctor's stairs to the second floor. Quickly aggravated, struck again by the lack of family photographs on the walls. Knowing the daughter now, it newly offends him and gets the best of his emotions. *Focus on the job.* The afternoon light shines through the windows, heavy and brown. Around the corner is the master bedroom. There's a shelf on one wall of lopsided clay pots. The comforter's still imprinted. The wife had lay there reading, prior to attack. A paperback's undisturbed on the comforter, cover-side up. He wonders about the couple's love life. Could the doctor still seduce his wife? What kind of sex did they like? He stares at the clay pots, recalls the potter's wheel out in the garage.

A year before, Lillian bugged him to take a pottery class with her, at the new Arts Center in Eagle Mount. He'd refused once, twice. So she turned to painting.

He pokes through the dressers. This time he finds a vibrator, he missed it last time. Does it mean anything? It wobbles diminutively when he flicks the switch. Purpose lacking: he knows what purpose lacking feels like. Then a phone rings from the bedside table. It yanks him out of his imagination. He's about to pick up the telephone and answer when something stops him.

On the third ring, he notes a distant sound. The kitchen phone.

Which is to say, none closer.

He bangs heavily down the stairs.

A telephone base station rests on a side table in the hall, stationed below a round mirror. The light on the charging base glows green. It's plugged in. The screen lights up when he presses the speaker button. But there's no dial tone.

Martin crouches down and peers beneath the table.

■

"So tell me again, what you used to strangle the wife."

"Leave me alone."

"Nick, please."

"No. I'm sick of this shit."

"Really? What are you sick of?"

"This!"

"You wrote in your confession you used a rope."

"It was a rope."

"And you're sure about that."

"Yeah."

"Except it wasn't. It was something else."

"Like what?"

"First, I'm asking you, is that a possibility?"

"Dude, what are you even talking about?"

"Just the option that it wasn't a rope. And if it wasn't, what might it have been?"

"It was a rope!"

"You go around with a rope in your pocket."

"No, I tie it around my nutsack."

"Where'd the rope come from, Nick?"

"I thought you were on my side of things. You're supposed to be helping me."

"That's what I'm doing. But you need to tell me the truth."

"Bullshit. No one's helping me."

"Nick, listen to me, we are doing everything possible."

"Yeah, whatever."

"So this rope," Martin wheezes. "It was something else, wasn't it?"

"Screw you. I'm done."

"You know, I saw Emily. Like you asked."

"What? You did?"

"Just now. Before I came over."

"How is she? How's she doing?"

"So the rope, Nick. What if it was a telephone cord?"

"Tell me about Emily."

"Say it was a phone cord. Maybe you didn't have it on you. Maybe it came from the phone in the hall. The cord's missing from that telephone. It looked to me like someone yanked it out."

"I want to know about Emily."

"You rip out the cord. Or someone else does, I don't know. To use it like a rope. Except it's more expedient, a phone cord, more impulsive, to use what's at hand. We're talking about a crime of spontaneity. A sudden compulsion. Not something planned. And for some reason nothing to involve a knife, for example. Which we believe is on hand."

"Either tell me what Emily said or shut up."

"Fine, Nick. We'll do a trade. You level with me, I'll tell you about Emily.

"Nick, Jesus, give me a break. Work with me here.

"Nick, look at me, I get it. You're scared. You don't know who to trust. You're all by yourself, your girlfriend's out there. My point is, tell me this one thing, I'll work with you.

"Okay, here's what's up, Nick. I'll help you, okay? But you have to help me first. Because I want to help you. But I'm locked in place. I'm in jail so to speak. I can't do anything until someone else does something. See what I mean? Here's what I know. You're innocent. Of this whole mess. And you're in big trouble. But right now you've got the next move. You hold the key.

"Talk to me, Nick, and I'll tell you what Emily said.

"Nick, please, enough.

"Fine. Emily's doing okay, she's fine. You know, sad, frightened. What do you expect? I went to the store, I introduced myself. She had a couple questions. I would've stayed longer but she had to get back to her customers. Mostly she just wanted me to pass you a letter. You hear that, Nick? I've got something for you. So what do you have for me?

"Nick, please.

"Nick, you have to stop this.

"So you're just going to sit there. Then tell you what, I give up. At least say you're happy about that, you stupid kid. Just keep screwing yourself, Nick, screw over everybody you care about. Here's the letter. You happy? Honestly, that's all you'll have from now on, from her, once you're in jail. And that's assuming she doesn't get sick of you, the boyfriend in prison. The way you're going, you're going to rot behind bars the rest of your life. Or be killed.

"Look, we've got a shot. Nick, I believe that, honestly, or I wouldn't be here. But I need your help. Help me help you.

"Nick, please, help me."

•

The first piano lesson was an instant failure. Emily didn't actually care about piano. But she tried to pretend. Nick's mom was solicitous. She ushered her in, put a lesson book on the stand. They sat together on the bench while Suzanne explained about the keyboard's layout and the instrument's anatomy. She demonstrated some simple fingerings, played a minute of something pretty. Her fingers lifted off the keys like they were riding breaths of air.

She stopped a moment later.

"You don't really want to learn piano."

"Yes, I do."

"No, you don't."

Nick's mother lit a cigarette, got up and walked slowly around the room. Emily watched. Every movement was an unfolding, hair swept to the side. Beautiful, majestic, she was probably the strangest adult she'd ever met. Emily felt herself intimidated by the little things. The decisive command of her voice. The considered pauses between gestures. Suzanne wore a long dress that day that swept the floor, more like a man's robe, dark gray, stitched with flowers along the hem. But she wasn't a hippie, she was too angry for that, with an air of disgrace, or simple sadness that Emily recognized even if she couldn't put it into words, that she also felt. She was in awe.

"Believe it or not, I teach piano to connect people to the joy of it. The music. At least I try," Suzanne said knowingly, and laughed. But nothing was funny from the look on her face. "You know, our families go back a long way in this town, yours and mine," she added a moment later. "Not on the best terms."

"I didn't know that."

"I doubt that. Your father's quite aware. I'm honestly surprised . . ." Suzanne didn't finish her sentence, turned to the hallway instead. "Nicky? Come in here. We're going to listen to some music."

He walked in with an agitated look and sat next to her on the piano bench.

"How's it going?" he whispered.

"I don't know," she said.

His mom was hunched over in a corner. She pulled out a CD from a wooden crate on the floor. "We have forty-five minutes until the lesson's over. I'm going to lie down here, and the only rule is that until the music stops, neither of you can leave this room. Emily, will you close the curtain, please?"

And so began her weekly education in classical music.

Afterward, Suzanne would disappear for about an hour, leave them free to be in Nick's room. But for that forty-five minutes, once a week, she'd sit with her boyfriend in the smoky, brown indoor darkness. Where she learned little, academically, and many times she fell asleep. But sometimes her whole body would shiver from the music. She felt things she'd never felt before. How lucky was Nick to have Suzanne for a parent? And she, to be inducted into this family? It made her even more angry at her own life. She'd glance at Suzanne occasionally when she thought she wasn't noticed. Nick's mom seemed to always be staring at the ceiling, eyes wide open, except for when she'd turn her head to the side and blow smoke and stare at her with an open question in her eyes.

■

Barely a mile out of town, the main street goes up and up, starts to climb through dark switchbacks, faithfully going west and north into the mountains, toward something, though Martin has no idea what that something might be. It's late. The streetlights stopped a while ago. At first, down low, he'd passed farms, cemeteries, shuttered gas stations, and small shops, then came cabins and trailers set back from the road, driveways, fenced fields. After a couple more miles, it was nothing but darkness and trees, a damp atmosphere from the rain. His tires hiss on the road. He drives forward on trust, the trust he's placed in the possibility that the kid's mom is right, that her story makes sense, and that something useful awaits him in the woods.

Trust that Suzanne Toussaint, who gave him two names earlier that evening, was right when she said she knew exactly where he should look next for clues in the case: Ben Barrett and the Purple Panther. So he must trust that a rural titty bar, supposedly located out in the middle of desolate nowhere, will adhere to the case in some magnetic fashion.

He almost blows past it. The address he found matches a personal storage facility around a bend, on a hillside plateau. He backs up, points his headlights at a field. Self-storage units, premises ringed by barbed-wire fencing, a faded metal sign, BARRETT'S EXTRA STORAGE SPACE.

An artificial haze of yellow light hovers above the facility. There must be at least a hundred lockers. A parking lot with two vehicles. Nearly a dozen variations on BEWARE OF DOG and NO TRESPASSING signs.

He parks on the road. The office looks closed. Six long strides get him through an open metal fence. He assertively walks up a wide gravel lane, past rolled-down garage doors numbered with stenciled paint. No dogs so far. He turns right at the end of the path, left after the next one. And then, around a corner, there's another parking lot, set half a mile back into the woods, surrounded by tall trees. But this one's full of motorcycles and pickup trucks. A semicircle group of trailers is lit up by strings of lights and a neon sign, the outline of a panther that glows with a dull purple glare.

"Who are you?" Nick's mom had asked when he'd shown up on her porch.

"Martin Krug."

"And so?"

He'd laughed.

"Well," he said, "you called me."

"And why would I do that?"

Her lipstick was brightly red, almost a fiery orange. Her eyes were slightly wet. Nerves overstrained, hair unkempt. Barefoot and distressed. The mother of a boy locked in jail.

"I don't know, to be honest," he'd said softly. "Mrs. Toussaint, may I come in, please?"

She led him into the living room. It was the size of three rooms, with dark curtains, oil paintings. It was like a mausoleum. There was a houseplant so big it belonged outdoors. In one corner was a grand piano. Oriental rugs overlapped, picture frames were hung densely. A bar cart was full of nearly empty bottles, two filled ashtrays. And through the kitchen door, he spied cereal bowls on the floor, more ashtrays overflowing, towers of pots and pans in the sink.

She sat on a window seat and stretched out two long legs in dark denim. She was tall. Attractive. Bone-dry in an aristocratic way. He couldn't tell if she was thirty-five or fifty-five. Her hair was in a bun. She moved unhurriedly to light a cigarette. The smoke made her look even older. She'd definitely had a couple drinks. Was she a drunk? He could see where the kid got his cheekbones, and the beaten dog's disposition.

"Mrs. Toussaint."

"Suzanne. Do you want something?"

"I'm fine. Listen, almost anything you can tell me could be useful."

"Why don't you give me an example."

He'd already decided he wouldn't mention his visit with Nick.

"You said you wanted to talk to me without Ms. Brenner around. Why is that?"

"People never really know what they know, don't you think?"

"How about you tell me something I should know."

"My son's innocent. That appears to be news to some people. Including Ms. Brenner, if you ask me."

A telephone thrummed somewhere. She glanced at the bar cart.

"Do you want me to fix you something?" he said.

"Thank you. Vodka rocks. The ice is in the bucket."

He made the drink, staring at all the photos on the walls. Ancestors back to wagon days. While he was stirring, he asked about her family, pre-crime. "Just give me an idea of what your and Nick's lives were like." She seemed to think about it, but said nothing. He tried to picture the boy there, in the smoke. What painstaking routes he'd need to use to navigate such a woman. Then she coughed and it all came rolling out, the missing husband, current existence, lack of funds. Then even more: miserable town, miserable existence. Miserable parents who, prior to dying, had burned through whatever remained of the old family cash. Miserable husband who'd left, who'd gone awol, who wasn't kicking in for shit. He'd been the drifter type, she said, who finally got sick of a settled life, ergo a bum. By the time he'd ditched completely, she and the boy weren't surprised, she said, just sad.

"Do you have kids?" she asked.

"A daughter."

"Children misunderstand love. They think a parent's love is a normal emotion."

"That's a good point."

"Children take your existence from you. They don't even say thanks."

A sudden rain hit the roof. It smacked the windows and struck the shutters.

"I'm a terrible teacher, you should know."

"It looks like you make a living," he'd said, and rubbed his eyes. By that point he was getting weary of such crap.

She looked at him inquiringly. "I teach piano," she said. "It's not investment banking."

"Yeah, I get it."

"Do you?" She stood up suddenly. Angry about something, coldly inflamed, no longer playing princess. "Do you know when it all started, what's happening to my son?" So she started to tell him about the accident and the surgeries, the recoveries, the limp, the vast monies spent on medical bills. But he knew it already so he asked, to end things more quickly, "So what were they doing out there, at the lake?"

She paused. "My husband was owed money. By a quote-unquote friend of his."

"Who?"

"Ben Barrett. Now there's a guy you should be looking into. I don't know why the police don't lock him up out of habit."

"Why's that?"

"He's an asshole. He's the worst person in town. That's what Nick always said."

"Worst how?"

"They were drinking buddies. Nick used to tell stories about Ben's 'business ventures.' He ran a strip club in the woods. A sex club, if you'll believe it. I assume it's still there. It's popular with your local ex-cons."

"Do you have a name?"

"I made Nick take me once. The Purple Panther. A total shithole. But I said, if he was going to be the sort of guy who went to places like that, he'd better get used to having the type of wife who came along."

"And you think Mr. Barrett could be connected to your son's case somehow."

She came to a halt. As if she hadn't thought of it before. She frowned. Shaken. With so much noticeable need to keep her world together, he quickly felt bad for pointing it out.

She looked him dead in the eye, and he couldn't look away.

"My son has a hard time staying out of trouble. That's the truth. Especially when it's not his fault. But he's innocent." Then a full ten seconds' hiatus. She looked around the room. Her breathing was light and fast. "I've been searching online. For news. You won't believe the things people say."

"You should stay off the internet."

"Women I've known my whole life. Bragging how their kids would never be involved in this kind of thing." Her voice cracked. "I can't take it."

"Mrs. Toussaint, this Barrett guy. Is that why you wanted me to visit? Because if you have any idea how he's connected—"

"I don't know! I don't know."

"I am sorry about Nick," he said a couple seconds later.

But she didn't hear him, she was done, recomposed, regal again. "Give me one reason," she said with an icy tone of detachment, facing away, "why my son would do any of the things he's accused of."

"I understand, believe me. The trouble is he confessed."

"And you're the idiot who helped him write it down. *Without* a lawyer in the room. I'll take you to court when this is done. You want to do something? Try fixing the mess you're responsible for, how about that?"

And so, two hours later, in the sodden woods, in the darkness, he watches men go in and out of a door cut into the side of a double-wide trailer. Less like men, more like goblins. The whole thing wasn't so much a club as a case study in contemporary redneck architecture, four trailers soldered together in an arc. The design school of Circle the Wagons.

And when the door opens, out comes a booming soundtrack. Bumpers gleam in the purple light from the neon sign. There's a kid's BMX bike under the stairs leading up to the trailer door. A bouncer looks him up and down, from behind sunglasses. He smiles.

At first it's too dark. Once his eyes adjust, the interior's just as makeshift as the outdoors, but more modified: a portable nightclub. Beer signs. Strings of patio lights. How many people can they fit in there, forty? A young woman gyrates against a pole at one end. A couple of twenty-something guys, with subelectrical twitches, sit at a plywood railing and watch.

A bar, two feet wide, built into a corner near the bathroom, is staffed by a weathered young woman, with a homemade haircut and an ample spare tire revealed by her shirt. Is she sixteen? Fourteen? Do her parents know she's here? She stares at something on her phone and laughs.

He says, over the music, "I'm looking for Ben Barrett."

"Who's that?"

Surprisingly her voice is sturdy. Maybe she's not as young as she looks. He pulls out a twenty-dollar bill.

"I'm in town for work."

"No shit."

"Is Mr. Barrett around?"

"I don't know who you're talking about."

The music quiets. The dancer gets down off the pole. The men withdraw from the stage, as much as there is one. Men who, to Martin's eye, aren't just dead inside, but look like they buried the bodies themselves. A new song cues, hip-hop this time. He tries a different line, memories from vice-squad PowerPoints. "A guy downtown told me I should come by here. Ask around about getting a date for the night."

"I don't know anything about that." The girl looks up at him with mistrust. "Who downtown?"

"Guy at a bar. A dive bar near the beach."

The girl returns to her phone. "So you want a beer or not?"

For ten minutes he watches the audience watching the show and ignores the pain in his back. He tries to lose himself in the raucous music. He actually likes a lot of rap, more than he likes strip clubs at least. Why can't he just enjoy the show? He was in New Orleans once for a sergeant's bachelor party, he drank five Sprites and turned down every lap dance the boys offered. Lillian would've put his balls in the microwave.

He squirms on his stool during the next break between dancers. He enviously watches the young guys drink. Then the door opens, and two guys walk in, with tattoos he remembers from training seminars. One's got on a green polo shirt from Ralph Lauren, wrinkle-free, and a shamrock tattooed on his cheek. The other guy's younger, gleaming bald, with a neck like a chicken leg.

Sometimes a shamrock's just a shamrock. But sometimes not.

"Can I help you?"

Martin turns around. "Ben Barrett?"

The guy with the shamrock. "You a cop?"

Martin laughs. "No."

"So what's funny?"

The guy doesn't want an answer. He's got a Boston accent so thick it sounds like he's playing a prank. Up close, the tattoo looks hand-done. The guy says, "So you're the type of guy who looks for a thing."

"What do you mean?"

"You tell me."

"I was looking for something a little more than this."

"What's your name?"

"Martin."

"Where you coming from, Martin?"

"New Jersey."

"That's nice. What're you doing way up here? I mean, this is the boonies, compared to New Jersey."

"I'm in town for business. We're trying to land New Balance," he announces. He deliberately shrinks his shoulders, tries to look nervous. "It's pretty boring."

"I bet it is." The guy licks his lips. His nostrils were recently pollinated. "You know, normally this isn't how this goes."

"How does it go?"

"How about this: have a good time tonight," the guy says. "But don't come back."

The man turns around without a word. His friend follows him back outside. Martin's about to leave when a pretty girl appears. Much too pretty for this dump. He'd guess she's topless, but he can't really tell. The plumage of an Indian headdress flaps around her shoulders, with several white feathers hanging down over her breasts.

"Hey, good looking. Care for a dance?"

He smiles, if only for the bare-bones appeal. The music begins again, somehow louder.

"I don't dance," he shouts.

"What?"

"I don't dance!"

"It's not that kind of dance."

He says, "I like your hat."

She leans in. "I think," she says loudly in his ear, "that you're going to buy you and me some drinks."

She returns a minute later with what looks like champagne, more likely is ginger ale with a drop of vodka, twenty bucks, from what he knows of strip-club economics. He puts his cup on the rail. She doesn't touch hers, either. They have to shout to be heard.

"What do you do?"

"Software."

"That's boring."

"You're right."

"I'm taking an internet class."

"That sounds interesting."

"I'm going to launch my own platform."

"What does that mean?"

"Dance on the internet," she says. "But for myself."

"How does that even work?"

The music gets louder.

She says loudly, "You'd be dumb not to see me dance."

"You seem confident about that."

"I'm really good."

"Are you?"

"I'll change your life."

So he accepts defeat, gets up with a sigh, a prayer, while she gives a noticeable nod and says something to the bartender. Martin orders himself to honor her persistence—and who knows, maybe he can interview her afterward about her boss, get her to say something he can use for the case.

And therefore is he lightened of money, led away, self-conscious for being twice the young woman's size, a pet Volkswagen taken for a walk.

They proceed to the trailer next door, through a curtain of beads. Pink lights, pink darkness. Three folding metal chairs. There's a candy jar full of condoms on a shelf. A narrow porch swing hangs from the ceiling on big bolts, in front of an oil painting of a dead elk. The elk glows in the cast-off glare.

When they walk in, one chair contains a good old boy in denim shorts. A young Hispanic woman, fully nude, writhes on his lap. He's got five hot dog fingers clamped on her ass, the other five mounted on a breast, like she might come apart and he's holding her together. She rubs his groin through his shorts. Then the song changes, the girl dismounts, grabs a towel from a doorknob. The man-child stumbles out after her.

The music becomes something more sinister, a male singer hissing.

The headdress woman leans into Martin's ear.

"You want something like that, you picked the wrong girl."

"I get it."

He lowers himself into the tiny chair. Worried more about the chair than anything else. She begins to dance, no hesitation. He groans, he can't help it; his lower back is clenching, on fire. How long has he possessed a failing machine? And how old is this woman anyway? Is she his daughter's age? Younger? He strains to make his face at least semi-enthusiastic. Her little nipples catch the light. She climbs up, balances herself on his thighs. *No.* His back won't take much more. While her abdomen ripples like a sheet in the wind, flesh come to life. And no matter that her body is tiny, so supple, and she's good at her job, even just her minuscule weight as she gyrates goes straight to his vertebrae, and he's about to complain about the pain when she tips them slightly backward in the chair, and the angle shoots a rocket up his spine.

He seizes out of the chair and knocks her over.

"What the hell?"

"I'm sorry."

He clutches his spine and squirms.

"Jesus Christ."

"It's my back. It really hurts."

To the point he'll soon be seeing stars.

He throws himself down on the ground. It smells horribly. He'd laugh at himself or apologize more but it's all he can do to breathe.

"You could have said something."

"Here—take the money—"

He reaches for his wallet but even that's too much. He grimaces in pain. She starts to laugh. The music rages. It's all too ridiculous. He starts to laugh, too, as little as he can manage. From a loudspeaker hanging off the ceiling the singer says he wants to fuck someone like an animal—and that's what he is, a fucked animal, a father and husband, completely unrecognizable in the current situation.

"My ex had back problems," the young woman says. "Just move over."

She drapes a clean towel on the ground. He does as he's told, shifts to the towel. She removes her shoes, then walks on his back. He yelps, but it's alternately wonderful and excruciating. She hikes up and down his spine through that song and the next one, and the result is so painful, so heavenly, he closes his eyes. Then she's gone, with fifty bucks that he pays gladly.

He must fall asleep for a minute. He looks around in a daze. The room's empty. He didn't ask the girl a single question about the case. There's a door with an exit sign, the sound of motorcycles outside. Why did he spend all those years at the chiropractor, not in redneck strip clubs? He lumbers outside, into the dark, like a bear on the loose. He stops abruptly. Two motorcycles roll away. Inside, they tell him Headdress just left. He's about to ask for her number, then realizes how that sounds. He walks back out, through the storage center, to his car. His back starts to cramp again. The desire to drink is a drip in the back of his skull. In the truck, he kicks off his shoes while Eagle Mount comes to mind, the sandwich shops, the clothing shops, the coffee joint where Lillian liked to meet for breakfast, the town he once swore to protect, where time was he had a life.

And all of a sudden the girl appears, the dancer, his mind's eye focuses on her tongue, his lizard mind pictures what such a tongue can do.

When he scrubs the image, it's replaced by the night his father grabbed him by the tongue. He hasn't thought about it in years. He was taking a bath when his dad stopped in the doorway. Often he worked nights. They didn't have much money. For once he'd gotten home early, and Martin, from his pleasure to see his father, stuck out his tongue. Just as a joke, a tease. His dad glowered, told him to pull in his tongue or he'd rip it out. So he stuck it out again, smiling. Seven years old, still dumb about the world. In a flash his father's hand whipped across his face. Grubby, big fingers entered his mouth, pinched his tongue like a pair of pliers. The pain was scalding, electric. He was yanked upright in the bathtub, he almost slipped and crashed. And still with the tongue in his grip, his father dragged him out of the tub like a dog, pulled him down the hall, dripping, dancing, running naked through fire. He tried to yell for his mother but he couldn't speak without his tongue so all he made were choking sounds. While his father laughed.

．

Al ill assume you saw that new vid on
YT it looks really bad are you ok??

        hey al hate to say i think the same thing
        rly not up to ur normal standards lol

Yeah thanks for your "concern" guys but
things are a huge mess. It's a long story
and really complicated legalistically so
I'm talking to lawyers and we have
multiple requests to get the mirror
copies down. But that course of action
is ongoing and taking for fucking ever,
so I ask everybody please understand
that this takes some time, just give me
the benefit of the doubt.

        HEY WHAT R U TALKING ABOUT?

Al so sorry for you. Hate to say it but I
saw the video on the WUNH
homepage, I think it's trending.

        Yea except that video was uploaded
        without my knowledge, not meant to be

shared ever. It's the footage from
Denny's I told you about, but I was only
interested in posting the edited video,
obviously, which I did, however the
original movie UNEDITED was
automatically posted to my YT channel
by virtue of privacy settings on my
phone that I didn't know about, that
apparently by default are set to their
MOST public levels when the app's
bundled with the OS, meaning the
phone's been uploading everything I've
filmed the whole time without me
knowing

I JUST FOUND THE GIF OF U ON
REDDIT U WENT BATSHI!!!!! WOW
LMFAO

.

Friday evening, Emily wakes up to the sound of Father's car pulling into
the driveway.

She'd gone home to pick up more clothes, lain down in bed for a quick
nap.

The car door opens and closes. Boots clomp up the yard. The front
door opens and closes, the basement door opens and closes. And from
the basement come the flowing sounds of woodworking tools. He'll
have seen the truck. He knows she's there. She double-checks that her
bedroom door is locked, opens the window and rummages in her backpack, and tells herself she's no longer afraid.

The previous week she got stoned for the first time with Meg, while
Alex was at work. Alex had quit her job at the hardware store, taken a
waitressing gig at Scones by the Sea, a teahouse for old-lady tourists.
Alex said it was because she wanted to get waitressing on her résumé
for college, plus she needed to make more money. Emily had a guess at
an additional reason: the new job meant that Alex was mostly unavail-
able to Emily and Emily's problems at pretty much all hours. She'd also
gone unusually quiet on texts, and Emily couldn't fathom why, not
completely—why, in her worst time of crisis, with her boyfriend locked

171

in jail, her best friend had basically decided to vanish—without reaching some extremely bad conclusions.

But Meg was there. On the couch, in the kitchen, giving her a ride to work. And she didn't appear to mind that Emily basically lived on their pullout couch on a permanent basis.

Then, the previous week, Meg had gotten home from another surf session with her new friend-boy, stretched out on the floor, and packed a bowl. She offered Emily some once it was lit. For once, she didn't decline. She was surprised to feel touched, even cared for. She felt like someone had noticed how awful she felt. And it did have healing properties, Meg said.

As a result, after more than a few days in a row of similar sessions, while she sat huddled in her hoodie, lifeless on the futon, she'd also inhaled Meg's visions for the future like secondhand smoke—Meg liked to talk when she was high—based on philosophical arguments around dancing the sacred body. Though she also confessed, just that afternoon, that once enough money was in savings, she planned to quit and go back to school full-time.

"It'll please my sister, if nothing else."

"But why keep going? You're so much smarter than that."

Emily knew it was weird of her to say this, offensive even.

Meg thought it over. "I think because I like the attention. Alex hates it. I'm pretty sure I embarrass her with the whole headdress thing."

"Oh, I don't think so."

Alex had said so countless times.

Meg continued, "She thinks I've squandered my potential. Well, she's right. You realize she's the reason I take those classes. Otherwise I'd have to put up with her bitching all the time."

Meg's current schooling included two courses at a nearby community college, "Women Against Empire: Politics of Protest," and "E-commerce, Me-Commerce: Today's Business Tools." The latter required a practical thesis, and she'd told Emily before, in vague terms, that she was on the verge of launching her own dance business online, of some fashion, what she called "Cam Girls 2.0."

Meg said, "Can you keep a secret?"

"Of course."

"You know that scholarship Alex got to Reed? It doesn't cover everything. Like, not at all. This is super on the DL, but I got a call from our parents. Kiki asked if I could kick in, for the college fund. Supposedly the art market's tanking; they can't sell a single thing. Seriously, you have to promise not to tell Alex."

Friday evening, at her own family's house, Emily hears a squeal from outside. Father's car speeds down the road. No more woodworking, he must've gotten a call from work. She lifts up the windowpane and lights a joint that Meg rolled for her. Existing simply in the moment, in the experience of witnessing her life become memory. Then she thinks about Nick. All she does is think about Nick. She jerks her head, rubs her arms. It's insane to contemplate the accusations, but sometimes she indulges them. What if somehow they're real? Why would he ever do something like that? If so, what part did she play? In this scenario, she can't escape a logic that pulls her toward a culmination of thoughts, a storm cloud of thoughts, that doesn't frighten so much as embolden her. That if Nick did do something wrong, it was for her. And so whatever he did, in a way she did it, too, with him. Criminals together.

She sits down at her desk and prepares to write another letter.

■

The guard announces his mother's arrival. His heart races. His whole body twitches. He can't respond differently and it shames him.

She sits down across from him. Long hair pulled back, black sweater, white jeans. Her long fingers in her lap hold what must be Emily's latest letter. She says something but Nick doesn't hear it, she barely exists, she's a vehicle only.

Then a loud voice intrudes, "Excuse me, Mrs. Toussaint?"

The guard enters the room.

"May I see what's in your lap?"

"I'm sorry?"

"The envelope in your lap."

"What are you talking about?" Nick snaps.

The door opens again. The sheriff enters. He says calmly, "Now let's not have a fuss."

"What's the problem?" his mom says. "I can bring my son a letter."

"Mrs. Toussaint, you are not allowed to pass any materials."

"That's not true. I checked online before coming here."

"Ma'am, which one of us works here? Are we going to have a problem?"

The guard reaches for the letter. At the same time the sheriff touches her shoulder. Both Toussaints lurch simultaneously, one away, one toward. The envelope falls. The guard goes for it, but Suzanne falls faster, grabs and grips it tightly, and stands up fast.

But not before the sheriff briefly grabs her wrist.

She spins, slaps him in the face. Even as he stares at her in surprise, gape-mouthed, he totters backward.

The guard doesn't know what to do, but his hand hovers over his gun.

Nick watches it all unfold. He watches like he's observed other things unfold, frozen, locked in place, about to piss himself. At the same time his mother stands her ground, gives him a look like, *It's okay.* Then she assertively leaves the room, marches out through the open door, followed by the guard.

"You thought I didn't know about this?" the sheriff says to him quietly. "How stupid do you think I am?"

■

The next day the kitchen smells like fish because Meg cooked shrimp for dinner. The air is full of little flies.

Emily undresses in the salty humidity, puts on sexy lingerie hand-picked by her stylist, and waits for the camera to be prepared.

That afternoon, Alex had finally found time to be a friend. Sort of. At first she'd asked how she was doing, how Nick was doing. But that only lasted five minutes before her own misery came pouring out behind her locked bedroom door, all liquid eyes, repressed sobs, pouting anguish during a lengthy monologue, then full-on fury about how Headdress was going to ruin Meg's life and Alex's life by proxy, assuming either of them would live to see Headdress's new business venture go live.

Alex and Meg had been bickering for days. Emily tried to stay out of it, she barely had enough energy for her own problems. Then much was revealed when Meg turned up at the Sisterhood with a carload of shopping. Boxes of drapes, two light stands, two hard drives, two pairs of blackout curtains. A new printer, a clothing stand on wheels, all sorts of other odd things, including lingerie and a bag full of sex toys.

All of which, they learned, added up to Meg's final project for her business class, Headdresslive.com, her new "platform," to debut that night. It even had been advertised around town. The clubs where she danced allowed Meg to hang special banners she'd gotten printed, to announce the great unveiling of her brand.

To Emily's confusion, Alex explained in her bedroom that all the bullshit followed a recent trend where dancing girls became cam girls, became bodies streamed for tips in virtual currencies. A couple months earlier, Meg had read a magazine article that got her thinking, hence night class, hence Walmart, hence her big plan.

However secretly intended, Emily thought of mentioning, to help with her sister's college tuition in the fall, but she kept her lips sealed.

Alex fell back on her bed and covered her eyes.

"My sister is a prostitute."

"I don't think it's that bad."

"She graduated with high honors, did you know that? She just wanted to take a gap year. Now look at her." Alex paused. A picture of the four of them, the Rosenthal sisters and their parents, was framed on her desk, taken when the girls were much younger. "Did you know Kiki went to Brown? Who later turns out to be the one who tells Meg, Meg told me this, that college is a waste for creative people like them. All of my mom's friends these days are girls in their twenties. I'm not even exaggerating. She and my dad took in two of them to pay the rent. So she's totally cool that her oldest daughter is a stripper. Unlike Fred, but he doesn't even remember the world being otherwise.

"Have I ever shown you Meg's zine? I was so obsessed with it. It was about Meg's social life during senior year, the year my parents left. There's a lot of sex. I was allowed to do the stapling. It completely freaked out all the dummies. Look: each cover had this chick wearing a headdress. It's from a drawing my mom made in college. That's where the idiocy began. She was doing it anonymously, but by issue three kids had figured out it was Meg. Not that she cared. They were buying out the stock. I mean, the stories were pretty explicit. She wrote a sex advice column. She talked about who was hooking up with who, also anonymously. So it was like an X-rated crossword puzzle. You could buy it at the comics store. Then my dad read one. He'd been kept in the dark. Of course, Meg showed my mom the layout in advance. Kiki thought it was awesome. I think she still felt bad about moving to New York. But she hadn't told my dad anything, even though Meg's mailing her a copy of every issue. So Fred finds one. He explodes. He didn't even call first, just drove all the way up from New York. Honestly I thought he was going to hit her. He's really scary when he's mad. Thinking we're going all Miley on him. Normally he's, like, this little ogre. If he gets a good review, he's really funny, he just wants to horse around. But all of a sudden, Fred's going to move back to Claymore, pull the plug, give up his art career to keep us from becoming sluts, his words. 'Which is what appears to be happening.' It was a whole weekend of that shit. As if he hadn't been the one who wanted to leave! He's so two-faced. So we voted. Three to one, just maintain. He was outnumbered. He was so pissed. My mom's cowering the whole time in the kitchen. In the end he still pulled rank. Kiki had to tell Meg the zine was over. And the last thing he said that weekend? I totally remember this. It wasn't like, 'I love you,' or, 'You guys be good.' He said, 'If you're going to be adults, you have to be responsible for your own decisions.' As if we'd wanted to be our own parents in the first place."

Alex left for work a few minutes later, with several more follow-up questions beforehand about Nick and how he was doing, how she was holding up. But Emily could tell they weren't real so much as necessary, for Alex to tell herself that she was acting the good friend.

Emily watched her good friend drive away. Probably with a huge sigh of relief.

From Meg, she'd learned that Alex had been spending a lot of nights with a kid named Jersey Mike, a senior, a total doofus, though hot. They'd met at a party. According to Meg, Jersey Mike was so-called because the hockey team was full of Mikes and he was really into sandwiches. Also into snowmobiles, and he fronted a rap band called the Potheads. "He's like the sledneck version of Jay-Z," Meg said.

Though Emily could guess what was really going on. The new job. The boyfriend. Obviously her current situation was too much to handle, and Alex needed excuses to get away from her, the girl who'd literally moved into her life.

And maybe Alex was subconsciously also preparing her for the fall, when she'd move to Oregon for college, and Emily would be forced to live without her best friend.

So maybe she needed to be more responsible herself, she wondered, as she wandered around Alex's bedroom. Take possession of her problems. Deal with them on her own. Maybe doing so was the least she owed her friend, her great friend, who'd given her so much. Before they parted. For twenty minutes Emily stewed on such thoughts, and watched a game show in the living room. Feeling Very Very frustrated, wracked with self-reproach and deep uncertainty. She still hadn't told Alex what she'd told Nick that night, her secret. Maybe she never would. Look what telling Nick had done.

Then Meg appeared and asked if Emily knew how to work a webcam.

Around eight p.m., she monitored a chat room while Meg posed before the camera in her headdress and a blue silk nightgown, while they waited for onlookers to arrive, to pay Meg to perform whatever dances or sexual acts they wished to see.

Emily felt queasy at first. Was she betraying Alex somehow? But the feeling receded while she watched Meg practice her routines, stare deeply into the camera's eye.

By eight thirty, nothing.

By nine o'clock, a handful of visitors had come and gone, paying zip, arriving to type obscenities before Emily kicked them out of the chat room.

At nine-thirty, Meg said flatly into the camera, "I can't believe I spent four hundred dollars on this crap."

She got off the bed and changed into a sweatshirt. They split a can of bean dip on the couch, while Meg caught up on one of her shows. Then Meg threw a bag of frozen shrimp into the microwave. Soon the kitchen smelled like fish. The air was full of little flies.

When Emily had her big idea.

∎

Three hours later, in the dark, she drives back to her bedroom on the mountain and locks the door. She needs space and time to herself, away from Meg, away from Alex. Because look at this girl.

The photographs burn in her hands. She doesn't know this girl. What she's doing, what she's thinking. What does she mean by the poses she assumes? Is she thinking at all?

They'd spent nearly thirty minutes on hair, the same on makeup. Even touched up a mole, Meg's idea, that was an inch below her left breast. Afterward, they inspected the results on the laptop before sending a chosen few to the new printer.

"You look so good," Meg said.

"I don't," she said. Feeling a smile creep through her lips, her prudish lips.

"You do. Superhot. Trust me, if anyone should know. But what are you going to do with these?" Meg asked, referring to the tiny pile of photos.

She hesitated an instant, then said, "I thought I'd give them to Nick."

"Holy crap, I love it. Was that the whole idea?" Meg laughed. "Jesus, you're so his moll." Then she'd laughed again, genuine and joyful, which boosted Emily's confidence, when she really had no notion of what she'd done. Only that she'd felt wild when the idea struck, and that it felt good to follow the wild.

Because in the absence of options she needed to create options.

"Meg," she'd called on her way out the door, "please don't tell Alex."

"Why not?"

"Just don't. You promise?"

"Whatever," said Meg. Then her voice rebounded. "Honestly? I didn't think you had it in you."

Back at home, the tone of her voice echoes in her head. She gets an envelope from her desk and tucks the photographs inside. She smiles. She feels untethered and free. She touches her chest under her shirt, the mole that Meg covered with foundation and concealer.

Because what is not possible is not thinkable, and what is not thinkable is not doable, so she's done nothing, nothing at all.

But look at this girl.

∎

The first fire in the valley began with a faro game in 1891. Faro was a popular game at the time, similar to poker. One afternoon each week, men from several branches of the Portis family, as well as other families working nearby, finished their work and plodded across the fields, over the stone walls they'd built themselves, to meet for a regular game. They were loggers and farmers, not fishermen. Fishermen they considered lowly. The land men prided themselves on being strong freethinkers and isolationists, for whom gathering to lay bets was not a vice but a chance to meet, relax, and share news, away from their wives and children.

It was early December. The weather that night was bad, dumping snow, adding several inches to many that had fallen. By seven o'clock, Bronson Portis was drunk. Then again most of them were drunk. But Bronson was nervous, too loud. He dealt the cards sloppily. *His face inscribed by years of routine inebriation.* The nerves could be attributed to the fact that, for the first time in his life, he felt flush. He played hand after hand, mostly losing, and it did not seem to bother him. He'd come into a large inheritance the previous month when his father died and left all of the money and Portis land to him and his three younger brothers. They were rich.

So it never would have occurred to him that his inheritance might vanish even faster than it appeared. That by night's end he would lose it all to Peter Toussaint on a single rash hand, lose not only his own land but that of his brothers, their bequest, because the deeds were still in his name, the eldest son, after he'd dragged his feet for weeks about going into town to visit the lawyer.

If he'd won the pot, Bronson would have taken an entire mountain from the Toussaints. But he lost.

The next day, word spread quickly across the valley. For the Portis families, the world flipped upside down. Days and nights were reversed while wives raged, husbands seethed, children grew sick from all the tension. Families paced on floorboards that soon would belong to people they barely knew. *Snow fell on snow and became quickly ice when an unseasonable freeze held the mountains to extremely low temperatures.* Among the Portis branches, no one knew when the Toussaints would claim their spoils, but it was certain that they would, fair was fair.

Initially, the brothers avoided Bronson. *They waited for him to lie down and give up the intake of breath.* When that didn't work, they took matters into their own hands. The night after Christmas, summoned by messenger, Bronson rode out on the public road under a half-full moon to the farm of Walter, his second-oldest brother. Starlight brightened the scattered clouds. They met in the barn, all men. Overbreathing like horses, the younger brothers and also four of their cousins who'd gathered to inform Bronson that he was banished henceforth from Claymore and was no longer their blood. If he appeared again in their presence, they'd shoot him dead.

Bronson listened mutely and didn't protest their sentence, to their surprise. The men waited for the guilty party to say something, anything. The air was cold and still. As for Bronson, he didn't look at anyone. He simply turned to leave and sheepishly rode away, head bowed beneath the moon, as though in subservient acceptance of their order. But without apology or expressed regret, it seemed to the brothers that perhaps he was mocking their decision, through nonaction. He'd always been too proud, too fast to claim credit when responsibility ought to be shared. Now it was as though he'd shouldered their unhappy fate hero-ically, despite being its maker. As if the banishment was his own idea. They were outraged.

Half an hour later, Bronson's youngest brother, Taylor, *the impulsive one*, rode up and ripped his brother off his horse by the coat and beat him nearly dead on the road with a clinch cutter.

What made matters worse, if that were possible, was that people knew that Bronson had kept some of his own land out of the pot. A parcel in Leduc of thirty acres belonged to the family of his wife, Eliza-beth O'Brien. Bronson still had a place to live and farm, he and Eliz-abeth and their young son, Ernst, and would not become destitute.

So it wasn't until months later, in the early summer, during a beauti-ful evening in June, with the fields and forests green and the mountains free of snow, that the valley got resolution as well as a first taste of jus-tice in extremity, a style that became common for a time. Bronson Por-tis died at home, burned to death during a late-afternoon nap. Elizabeth had torched the cabin first, where he and their son were sleeping. She soaked the floors with kerosene, set them aflame, then went outside and ignited the pasture. Flames reached six feet tall, people said, in red and orange walls, before Elizabeth closed herself in the barn and burned it down as well. And from their plot, the fire began to spread, until by the following morning nearly a quarter of the valley was razed.

Since she was a child, people had said Elizabeth O'Brien was pos-sessed, broad enough to contain two people, one of them a monster.

The clouds of smoke that rose that night were said to be so voluminous and tall in the moonlight, they resembled the sheets of a brigantine voyag-ing out to sea.

Late Saturday evening, early Sunday morning, Granville Portis parks the sheriff's car in front of the old family house in the dark. He knows the entire story by heart. He's known it since his own father read it to him when he was a little boy, from the book of Portis history. Their moun-tainside is where the family relocated after Bronson's shame. The house was his father's house, his grandfather's house, built by Granville's great-great-grandfather. Who was the first man to die in it, following the days of fire. When, for several years of contagious turmoil after Elizabeth O'Brien's insanity, men could be shot over nothing by their neighbors, killed for a rumor. Families spread butchered in their gardens. Years when madness was in the air, before order was enforced by law.

He shuts off the car, notes the absence of the work truck. It prompts him to boot up the department laptop, so he can launch the tracking software.

When he was a boy, in what was still called Whitehall County, at least a dozen families in the valley could trace their names back to the initial clearing. Most were gone by that point, erased by time or choice. People had sold their farms to the land trust, to New Yorkers, to rich folk from Boston. People for whom "country" meant "countryside."

Of the old names he remembered, there remained Portis, Condren, Ashburn, a few others. And Toussaint, of course.

His grandfather had been the one to record the family history in a book, published in an edition of three, bound in pebbled red leather. *The Portis Family in America*. Granville had inherited it, found it to be mostly unreadable. Though the Bronson Portis story still gives him chills to this day. He'd told the story several times to Emily when she was little, to explain lessons about responsibility and loyalty. She probably won't remember. He watches the laptop's start-up screen. Why does it take so long to load? He stares at the barn and closes his eyes, and wonders if she remembers that the Toussaints were involved, if the irony even occurs to her.

His own father, Emily's grandfather, Francis Portis, had been a roofer, tinkerer, and all-around amateur. Amateur inventor. Amateur preacher. Amateur parent. Dark glasses, wrinkles, short-tempered, and violent. He once attacked one of their horses. It happened during an attempted mount for breeding. The animal got overexcited and kicked his father in the chest, knocked him straight across the barn and broke two of his ribs. Francis had gotten up, come back on shaky legs, grabbed a pitchfork off the wall, and stabbed all four tines into the flesh behind the horse's shoulder. The animal crumpled. Its lips reared and it screamed a high-pitched sound so loud and painful that Granville had thought his ears were bleeding.

His father was a man who lived most of his life without women. Puttering from house to barn, barn to field. He was religious but didn't like church. He baptized the children himself. When Granville was seven, his mother ran away with a lumber salesman. *I have to go. I'm sorry. Forget about me.* These were the last things he remembers her saying. Occasionally she sent letters that Granville's father wouldn't let him read. But his dad didn't chase and never remarried.

Instead there was Marleen, for a brief period. Marleen was Belgian. She worked in town as a private maid. Three years after Granville's mother left, his father hired Marleen to move in with them and keep house, which she did for the next four years, starting when Granville was ten.

She'd been shaped like a small pear, slightly bruised. But with a round, pretty face, fine eyelashes, wavy red-brown hair, and a secretive smile. He disliked her from the start, especially for how close she and his father became and how quickly, how indispensable she presumed to seem. Marleen became devoted to his father's interests, his inventions. She kept their household running smoothly so that he could think and work. No one had ever encouraged him so, certainly not Granville's mother. And Marleen could talk about anything. Farming, horses, meteorology, the simple appeal of a well-made tool. Cheerful, bossy, the smooth skin of her cheek pinkish-red even in winter, but she was also quite stern and demanding with Granville and his little sister, especially if his father wasn't around.

Marleen had "a European manner" that his father respected, he said. "True refinement." Granville didn't see it. He disliked everything about her. She smoked little cigars when she thought no one was looking. If she broke a cup in the kitchen, she blamed the dog. He did appreciate her cookies, little Belgian cookies, thin as paper. They were probably the best Granville had ever tasted. Better than anything his mother ever made.

With Marleen's support, in 1964, Francis Portis became the inventor of a new type of machine for grinding coffee, one whose crank even the most arthritic could turn. He expected it would make them wealthy, and it nearly did, for a time. With a New York lawyer's help, he secured a patent for the Portis Grinder. Two years later, they'd sold it to a kitchen-goods manufacturer in Pennsylvania, after efforts to establish production and sales proved too difficult, and also not very interesting. Francis Portis was an inventor, not a businessman. Besides, they were rich. Instead of involving himself any further with the grinder, Francis returned to his workbench, to invent something else.

He never invented a single other item of value. But the sale of the Portis Grinder provided for their needs, on the side of the mountain, for almost ten years, while his father sought no extra income.

Soon after moving in, Marleen also showed an interest in Granville.

He resisted at first. She would reserve time for the two of them to do his homework in the evenings, in the empty upstairs study, after his father had gone to sleep. Granville did everything he could to aggravate her. If she commanded him to sit up straight, he'd hunch his back. He snarled at her questions, insulted her intelligence. Still, she seemed not to care. It gave her peace, she said once, their time together, *he* gave her peace. And so she would read, or knit, or simply hum under her breath while he did his schoolwork.

Any man's potential, especially a young man's potential, Marleen said, required firm encouragement. And he did find, despite her stiff manner, that she radiated a mysterious sort of relaxing warmth. Was it what inspired his father? Gradually he did his schoolwork more diligently. He asked questions just to solicit her. She'd respond if she knew the answer, otherwise ignore him. Occasionally, if he dared a joke and she found it funny, she let out a tittering laugh that he never heard elsewhere around the house. As though only in his presence, while his father slept, could she let down her guard.

Granville possessed, Marleen would say, so many of his father's best characteristics, so few of those that were second-rate. For example, she loved the way he thought about people without too much judgment. The way he talked about his teachers and friends, trying to figure out why they did or said different things. These were signs of a penetrating mind, she said, where his pious father instead would be clouded by prejudice.

"You're probably able to read my mind right now," she whispered one evening, giggling. Of course he didn't have the slightest idea. But he was thrilled that she thought he might. He had certainly misjudged her.

Soon he wasn't able to think about anything or anyone else.

One evening, a year into Marleen's tenure, she told Granville that he reminded her of a boy in the town where she was born, back in Belgium. Her first boyfriend, her skating partner, Julien. He'd also been her best friend, her secret friend. "You're both so inquiring," she said, and pulled out one of her little cigars and lit it with a match. "I bet you could be a doctor someday. That's what Julien became."

Instantly Granville hated Julien, he was sick with jealousy. He focused his eyes on the floor. Marleen moved to the window to smoke. He found himself staring at her pale legs beneath her skirt, what little could be seen. Then she stepped away for a moment and paused mid-step. A single turn of the rounded calf, he was in love!

"What kind of doctor?" he asked.

She laughed. "A brain doctor, of course."

Despite the sale of his grinder patent, Francis Portis was a disappointed man. Angry about the way the world rewarded cowardice, "smallness" was his word, when men like him went ignored. His success had made things worse. He had ideas, dozens, more valuable to society than a simple kitchen device. But one after another, they were spurned. The mail never rewarded him. He complained frequently, stomping around the house, about the failure of the country to honor its most productive members. Soon he blamed Marleen. There had to be a problem with the paperwork, her paperwork. They fought about it more and more. His father was a bully. Granville's soul burned from the unfairness of it all. He was recently thirteen, he'd jump into the middle of arguments to defend her, even though Marleen demanded in their night-time meetings that he keep quiet, that it wasn't smart to draw attention to how they felt about each other.

Often, if he'd been banished to his room, Marleen would sneak in late at night and bring him a snack, try to make him laugh. She'd lie in bed next to him. One night, similar to other nights, she said she needed him to see things from his father's position. Because how could such a man, a closed-off little man so out of touch from all that was changing in the world, isolated on his mountain, how could a man like that understand his special son? A man so walled-off from love, during that era of love: look how he treated her like a slave. It made her cry spontaneously, just to remember the things he'd made her do at times. But she wouldn't talk about it in detail, she was too overcome. It made Granville furious. He wanted to leap up and fight. She demanded he calm down. She told him to be quiet. She said she realized she'd brought him to that antagonism, but she was having none of it. If anything, he could blame her. Blame her? But then she got angry, panicky, she needed him to *relax*—and before he could stop it, she pressed her fingers into his chest, pushed him down against the little bed while her face contorted with pain and excitement. "Just stop it, stop it!" she'd hiss, even though he was barely doing anything. Once she even beat him around the head, she was so out of control. It was like a devil possessed her, and he hated to see her like that, when he didn't know what he'd done. But then it passed. She'd wipe away her tears, smile, apologize over and over, kiss him over and over, then slip down and swallow his semen when it came out, she did this many times. But the most important thing to do, she'd say afterward, in a tremulous voice, was nothing. Nothing more than what they were doing. She needed Granville, needed him more than ever, to preserve the status quo and be quiet, if only for her sake. Therefore their secret must be kept, she'd say, with icy seriousness. He'd answer her with a confused nod. Because a man as ignorant and spiteful as his father, Marleen said, a man so mean, would never grasp their special relationship.

She had a primitive horror of exposure, if Granville even hinted about making their love public. When his feelings were so deep and true! She made him promise to preserve their secret. To press the matter, she'd remind him, as if to embarrass him, that even *she* had needed convincing at first, to witness his erection the first time she touched him, to bear out the aptness of her touch. So he promised.

In the end, it didn't make a difference. He turned fourteen in the summer. One afternoon his father returned home early when an appointment was canceled. He found them naked in the living room, performing intercourse on the floor. Marleen left for town that evening. His father didn't lay a finger on her before she left, he saved that for his son, with the phone book. The pain passed through him like electric shocks. Only when Granville's little sister came running did he stop.

He got away from Claymore as fast as possible. It was because of Marleen that he went to college. He lasted two years, finished later through night school. Ultimately, school wasn't for him, and by that time he'd found his bride, Emily's mother. After his father died, they decided to move to the mountain, drive back to Claymore, back to the land, with a desire to be completely self-sufficient, apart from the modern messes.

But even Emily's mother never knew why he'd gone to school in the first place, to honor the debt he owed Marleen for her belief in his potential.

Finally the computer loads. He opens the program and waits for his daughter's beacon to appear, the small green dot. He'd long ago attached a GPS device to the chassis of the work truck. Only thirty bucks online. He'd even stuck one on the Toussaint boy's Explorer. And there she is, on the screen, the small blip, geo-pinpointed to the house in front of him. He laughs at his worry. She must've parked her truck behind the barn. He strains to look. All he can see is the basketball hoop.

For a period, fifth and sixth grade, Emily loved basketball. He'd coached her team. Then they quit together midseason, after she told him that playing at home was much preferable, she hated playing on a team with boys.

He halts the memory by an act of will.

And remembers again that the girl he raised was all but gone. Like a piece of paper in water, all his efforts had dissolved. The memories they shared, it almost brings him to tears. Everything he's done, volumes over the years, his life's work, essentially, to produce a reasonably smart child, a girl unlike the skanks he runs into every day on the street, his efforts had been so quickly undone by her adolescence.

Look at the boy she spends her time with, the family name she prefers to spend her time with. Look at the person she's become. Inheritor of her mother's sick blood.

He unclips his hat from the roof. Rubs his eyes, red and burning, and kicks open the door but doesn't climb out. His head pounds from headache. Chest burns from heartache. He pops the laptop out of the car mount, switches from the satellite connection to his own Wi-Fi network. The bars pop up. He launches the browser. Lingers before typing in an address.

A bird's voice floats out from the woods with urgency, like an ambulance.

He feels spied upon, he changes his mind and claps the laptop shut. And with a sigh he propels himself into motion, out of the car. He looks up at the house. Wonders what it would take to burn it down. The answer: not much. Even though keeping that household running had required every ounce of strength he had for the past sixteen years.

The truth that no one tells you is that kids destroy your life.

Granville Portis struggles to climb the drive, toward the house of his fathers.

■

The boy tells Brenner he wants to see the New Jersey cop. Brenner relays the message. Martin parks at the courthouse and bangs upstairs.

Nick says, as soon as they're alone, "I need something." Then the kid leans in, beckoning, puts his lips to Martin's ear. "Get my mom out of town. Somewhere safe. As soon as possible."

Martin leans back.

"What's going on?"

The kid looks furious.

Martin says, "Does she know about this?"

"You work for me, don't you?" His voice curls at the edges. "That's what I want."

"You want me to do what? Kidnap her?"

It feels like the last straw. What is he, the kid's puppet?

"You do this," Nick says, "and I'll tell you what you want to know."

Martin stares at him. Stares at him some more. He glances over, the guard's laughing at something on his phone.

"So it's a deal?"

"Sure." Martin stands. "Hey, I brought you the newspaper."

"So what?"

"Check out the Red Sox game. Page five."

The night at the Purple Panther, the strip club, Martin had gone straight back to his hotel room afterward, dug out his bag, picked up the picture frame with Lillian's photograph, and junked it in the garbage. He'd been emptying the trash into a larger can in the hallway when he saw a note on his door, a Post-it note. *Phone call from Emily Portis. Contact her tomorrow at Georgia's Fabrics & Sewing —Demeke.*

The next morning, he'd stood next to the cash register just after opening. Emily Portis wore a T-shirt, blue jeans, sneakers. Every inch a teenager, but with a woman's eyes, a woman's face to support her effort to appear brave, even officious.

"I have some questions about Nick's bail application," she'd said in a serious tone, hands on the counter. And it wasn't an act. She wanted to know anything he could tell her about the latest news. "Please don't leave a single thing out. Thank you." A worried forty-year-old in a teenager's body.

So he gave her what he could share. There wasn't much she didn't already know. Still, he didn't pull punches, and she stayed rock-solid throughout. He was impressed.

"Look, it's the confession," he'd said. "If you can get him to change it somehow."

"Nick doesn't lie," the girl said. "He doesn't need to lie."

"Well, it's that or we should believe he's a murderer."

Then, seeming to make some inner calculation, the girl gave him a sealed envelope, wrapped in clear packing tape, with strict verbal instructions to pass it to Nick, only Nick. She made Martin swear on his life not to open it himself, and under no circumstances should he allow it to fall into other hands.

An envelope, he'd discovered, perfectly sized to slide into a newspaper.

The midday sun warms the window, the table, the room. Nick stares at him from the other side of exhaustion.

"I hate baseball," he says.

"I doubt that," Martin says. "I sincerely doubt that in this case."

■

So it happens that on a balmy Sunday late afternoon, while the sky turns rose pink to the west, Martin Krug finds himself driving fast, north into Maine, escorting a silent middle-aged woman he doesn't know well to nowhere that he can picture accurately. What the hell is he doing? He carefully strokes his thinning hair. He needs a run, he needs a meeting. He doesn't need this.

Nick's mother lights a cigarette and holds the tip out the window. The smoke blows back into the car, whirling around their heads.

"Do you have to smoke?"

"Can we listen to some music?"

The road hugs a coastline fringed with fjords. He turns on the radio. Classic rock. Suzanne stares out the window. He watches for a moment in the rearview mirror. She'd elected to sit in the back. He is the chauffeur, he is the appointed domestic. For a second there's a conspiratorial smile on her lips as she glances out at the ocean. Then the face is drawn again, pale and serious.

She'd been weirdly compliant when he showed up. He told her that he needed to take her away, at Nick's request; that was the extent of the information he possessed. Which wasn't a problem for her, for some reason. Had they discussed it, the two of them? Was that why she seemed so unconcerned? Suzanne didn't ask questions, didn't even want to drive her own car. He smelled booze. He said they could always rent her a car later. In her brow the sea was calm, the opposite of the spirit he'd encountered last time. Here she relinquished the decision, any decision. Like someone being sent to surgery.

Finally they get there, the Boothbay Inn & Cottages. A tumbledown motel he'd found online. She pitches her cigarette butt out the window. The parking lot's half-filled. Deciduous trees on either side, and a dozen tiny cabins like identical row houses, like a showcase of two-room garden sheds. A swimming pool in the middle glows blue, ringed by a white picket fence and weeds.

She gets out of the backseat and crosses the gravel smoothly, even elegantly, while wearing heels. Something his wife had never quite pulled off.

"Are you coming or not?" she calls.

"Why would I?"

"I'll tell them you kidnapped me."

At that moment, all he really wants to do is to turn around, get back to the kid, figure out what the hell is going on. His stomach burns, his mind's doing backflips with implausible scenarios. Brenner had been equally surprised when he called her, just as confused, but she couldn't do anything, she said, she was in Boston for a family gathering. By that point it was nearly eight p.m.

Nick's mother is inside before Martin can answer. He watches through the lobby window. She smiles at an old clerk. She does have a nice figure, he can't help but notice.

Something his sponsor once told him after a meeting: to monitor yourself, to keep tabs on yourself, is like hiring unskilled labor.

She returns with two keys.

"I assume you're staying," she says, and tosses him one. He catches the key with his left hand. His right hand clenches his sobriety coin in his pocket. He walks around the car and opens the hatch.

"For future reference," she says, "I hate checking into hotels alone."

She struts away without her luggage.

■

Alex's rapping sex buddy, Jersey Mike, is the one who finds the naked pictures of Emily Portis on Meg's computer.

Alex is the one who finds Jersey Mike looking at the pictures an hour later, pictures she hasn't seen before, hadn't known about. She subsequently flips out, first at Mike, and kicks him out of the Sisterhood in a rage, then Meg, who leaves for work in a huff, and finally Emily.

Emily is the one who sits timidly on Alex's bed while being lectured, informed that she's a doofus for becoming a Headdress disciple, complete with sexual objectification and neediness and cannabis tincture, for being not much better than your typical slutbag on the Zeta princess council.

Alex is the one who says things to Emily like evidently she's too dim to understand the sickening truths that squirm between the photographs' pixels, that those photos demean her, demean women, punish women when life for women is increasingly worse these days, and doesn't Emily know, *doesn't she know*, that part and parcel with being cis female, any female today, is the certainty that trivial mistakes can produce dire, lifelong search-result consequences for anyone involved?

"I'm so lucky you're my friend," Emily says finally, sullenly.

"What'd you just say?"

She stares into Alex's bewildered look, stares back forcibly. There's a lot inside her that agrees, even sympathizes with Alex's position. But then a much greater sense of outrage takes control.

"You're such a hypocrite," Emily says quickly, to get the words out as fast as possible. "It was your boyfriend who was looking at them. *Your* boyfriend. That's disgusting. Did you even stop and think how that makes me feel?"

"I already apologized about that," Alex says. "Obviously I'm angry about that. That's not the point."

"Really? What's the point?"

"Those pictures are porn."

"No they're not."

"You crossed the line."

"He's in jail. For murder. Do you even know what that means?"

She hears herself shouting, she balls her hands into fists.

"Why does that mean you have to take pictures of your bush? That's such a slutty thing to do."

"You did not just say that."

"What were you doing with her costume anyway?"

Alex goes on, layer upon layer, regarding things that Emily can't bear to hear. After a moment she can't even hear them anymore. The tone is enough, it starts to blanket her thoughts. She feels suffocated, shoved down into places she thought she'd climbed out of permanently. But this is a totally new situation. She doesn't know how to defend herself.

"You're saying it's my fault," she says quietly. She feels trapped in the tiny room. "It's my fault that Mike saw them. I put you in this situation."

"That's not what I said. Why are you speaking like that? You're not listening."

"I think I'm going to be sick." She falters, truly nauseated. She slumps down to the floor. Alex waits, grimacing. She turns to the window again. When nothing else is said for a moment, Alex paces by the door.

"I swear to god I'll kill him. It's so gross."

"You mean I'm gross," says Emily. "How ugly I look, that's what you're saying."

"Please. You know I'm not."

Now Emily is the one to stand. She doesn't know how she manages, her whole body shakes. An emptiness fills with righteous anger, a dark tornado, because she *isn't* stupid, she *isn't* at fault. The sickness is suddenly gone, and she feels far worse in a way, to an extent that pushes her beyond her self-control: she becomes the sickness. If Alex were to touch her, she'd smack her. And in the center of the whirlwind she's still baffled and hotly ashamed. Her heart thuds in her chest. Her worst thought: what if it all gets back to Nick somehow?

"Did you ever stop and wonder," Alex says quietly, "if maybe there's a reason Nick's in jail?"

"What does that mean?"

"I love you, you know that."

"No, what do you mean? You've been totally awol."

"That's not true."

"Your new job? And that asshole?"

"I was scared, okay? God, I'm sorry."

"You were scared?" Emily laughs. "*You* were scared?"

"Fine, I'm horrible," Alex says. She squats in her chair. "I let you fall under my sister's influence. It's all my fault. Whatever."

"You're being stupid."

"Don't you think I wanted to be here for you?"

"How would I know?"

Alex pauses longer, goes inside herself. Sincerely scared about something.

"The things they say he did . . ."

"Alex, what are you saying?"

"What if you're wrong?"

"No. I'm not wrong."

"But what if he is guilty?" Alex asks flatly. "What if he's guilty. Even a little?"

"He's not."

"So you haven't even thought about it."

"Of course I haven't thought about it."

"Well, someone killed those people." Then Alex is up again, enraged all over again. "I'm going to murder my sister. Honestly, I think you should just go, I need to be by myself."

Alex opens the door. It makes everything seem even more terrible: she's being kicked out.

Emily says quietly, "Do you realize how selfish you're being?"

"Please, just go."

On her way out, she can't help but say, with her throat jammed with poison, "Why are you being like this?"

"Being like what?"

"Like such a bitch."

A moment later, totally lost, flung equally by Alex and herself into no-man's-land emotionally, she leaves and slams the bedroom door behind her. The sound's a violent clap. Her face tightens in the hallway. Alex's words sink down into her body. From prude to slut. She staggers out, down the stairs outside, a girl to be ashamed of, to be shamed, another part of the filth that is *her*.

Emily runs down the jangling staircase, gets in the truck, and turns the key. Where it occurs to her that a piece of what just sent her racing outside is the conviction that her best friend, her former best friend, is somehow right, about all of it. Which means now Alex and Nick are lost to her forever. She has no one.

JURY SELECTION

Another pastoral Sunday morning in New England, irregularly sun-rich and honeyed, and yet it offers no inspiration, no gain in yardage, while all day long, over a period of many days, between pauses only for toilet, jogging, and other forms of self-torture, does Leela Mann attempt to remain in stewing calm above her keyboard, refuse to budge from her squatter's nest in Madbury, until she may claim to have found something, anything, about which she can type ten thousand words

The web's a snail's-pace connection, tethered off her phone to a single bar of service. Still, she double-fists her motivation! In full possession of her senses. And sniffs up angles in paragraph-length attempts that seem great for forty minutes but then perish from awfulness, die quickly from vapidity, and are buried in potter's fields of cloud-based files.

Files that she spends even more time organizing, an effort she will admit is the most idiotic procrastination.

But she only leaves the house for groceries or exercise. And barely registers in the world. No social media, no news websites outside her research. Her walks to the convenience store are the extent of any connection to society, partially because she's horrified of running into her parents somehow, or a kid from back in the day.

It's only when she's safely bundled back inside her hovel does Leela relax her guard and return to the matter at hand. How not to quit. How not to give in. How to land this goddamn job.

Though by Sunday morning, all efforts seem futile. She wakes at six, half-light. Summer chill seeps through the house's cracks. She stares around the cluttered floor. She still hasn't moved her possessions into other rooms. Energy bar wrappers and her mini collection of metal water bottles are nearly the sum total of her kitchenware. Laundry she washed in the kitchen sink, underwear and T-shirts and her running shorts, hang off the staircase to dry. The floor is warped, she notices, angling toward the empty fireplace. Should she tell Sandra? She hasn't sent a single note since she arrived, except to say she got in okay, to confirm her continuing existence.

She works up the nerve to log into her bank account. She turns away just as the balance loads.

But this is her normal routine, how she writes. From the bank website Leela moves closer to actual work, by watching fifteen minutes of an old episode of *RuPaul's Drag Race* that she's already seen probably three times. Though today she doesn't even enjoy that. Because if she can't come up with this story, then what? Likely the Magazine will need to evaluate her on coding skills, against dude bro's. Skills that, she is the first one to admit, aren't much more than copy/paste. Between a good Jane Austen novel and *The Hitchhiker's Guide to Python*? In the end, does she even care about computers? Algorithms are things she uses, has been reasonably good at using since fourth-grade Mac lab, but nothing more.

And yet Leela Mann must become the perfect algorithm for this job.

By noon, she's stir-crazy, she can't sit inside any longer. She definitely can't eat another energy bar. She starts up the car and drives half an hour to Durham, the main campus of the University of New Hampshire, if only to escape for a little while her turgid mind.

Growing up in Claymore, she and Sandra always talked about sneaking out, to crash a frat party. Of course they didn't, but they'd visit campus on autumn Saturdays, drink cappuccinos, pretend they were college students. She parks outside a newish-looking coffee shop. It could just as easily belong in Brooklyn. Inside, there's even a cute little barista girl with sleeves of tattoos, for whom the line to be attended is six guys long. And look at the menu written on butcher paper, so it can be torn off and rewritten on a whim. Look at the baklava croissant! Look at the identical tea tins arranged in rows, like a conquering Bushwick army!

By the bakery case is a newspaper stand, and the only paper available is *The New York Times*, weekend edition, four inches thick.

Though if she's being honest, all of these things do give her a sprinkling of pleasure at a moment when nothing else does. To be in a slightly fashionable space, fantasizing that she still lives in New York. Is she superficial, or is she superficial *and* other things, too? Naturally she understands, of course she does, that everything in that room, including her, if it *were* back in New York, would be merely one drop in a big pool, a reservoir of a mega fortunate essence, a temporary, extremely privileged status quo—though a "quo," perhaps, that is still possibly the New as of This Now?

Wait, what?

Because, surefire, this quo will be disappearing soon, New York or not, right? What's the half-life of a quo? At that moment, at every moment, it was already slipping off the front pages of the indiest publications. The cool, the edge, the juju, the quo—veritably nothing in the bigger scheme. And yet, for its exceedingly brief existence, was it not still self-aware and competitive, therefore *alive*? Wasn't there some value in that . . . essence?

And therefore was not such a point of view, the view from inside the quo, itself a flame to light the present moment?

In which case: To be an ingredient in a juju is better than not being at all?

Wait a second, was this bullshit a story idea?

The bulb in her brain illuminates to half-dim. There was something here. About how a kid who grew up in New Hampshire, and munched on an unexpectedly delicious baklava croissant—but was still stuck in Durham while said kid did the munching—would have envied a Brooklynite's perch on the edge of newness. Would have wanted to get the hell out of town. A kid to whom something felt *due*, the same way she'd long ago desired to fly from Claymore County.

So that could be the personal-essay component, open *in medias res*. And then . . .

Then pivot to generational analysis with regard to other avant-garde eras in New York City . . .

Then pivot to a brief history of global urbanism and sex, w/r/t gentrification patterns over time matched to romantic inclinations . . . E.g., wave patterns of where to find the gentrifier types, i.e., the fashionables and the financial types they were fucking; heretofore the fashionables and the mostly white cools; heretofore the mostly white cools and mostly nonwhites they knew (and were probably fucking); heretofore the artists and the mostly nonwhites known by mostly white cools, fuck, suck, or no; heretofore the gays and the nonwhites unknown to whites; heretofore the gays and the nonwhites unknown to whites who were fucked; heretofore the nonwhites unknown to whites, gay or straight . . .

Plus possibly an interview with whichever chef invented the baklava croissant?

Finally, pivot to a conclusion, first-person POV, whereupon the *metaphorical* baklava croissant—whose doughy inner layers could mirror Leela's own inner life, never mind her experiences of the NYC hustle-struggle and those of kids her age, those overnurtured *meh*-llennials whose life/work balance was so out of whack, so unfair, so podcast-able—*whereupon* the metaphorical croissant crumbles into some rich dude's flat white, and then . . .

But all of this occurs so rapidly to Leela while she waits in line that she instantly knows it's stupid. And likely previously written. Because the idea is too easy, plus dumb. "Outer boroughs" + "expropria-tion" + "soulful inquiry by college-educated person born in 1990" equals already done, proof-positive that she is similarly if not *more* cliché than the café around her.

And it's not just her ideas that are flawed, but her native algorithm, the program that brought her to that moment: Leela Mann, broke-down semi-narcissist in expensive leather, who brews light beer intellectually and produces think pieces instead of thoughts.

Because, shit: Is she not this girl? Is she really, honestly anything more?

"Can I help you?"

"The Merguez sandwich," she says. "And a *New York Times*."

"Excuse me?" says the sexy cashier a moment later. "Your card's busted."

She holds it up. The magnetic strip cracked.

"I'm so sorry," says Leela. "Can I write you a check?"

"Uh, I guess."

"Sorry. Thanks so much."

Ten minutes later, as she drives back to Madbury in the slanting midday light, she of course is not sorry. Screw that. Overrun with emotions, yes—but remorse isn't one of them. Though it's possible that she just wrote a bad check for a fourteen-dollar sandwich.

But even the psychology behind *that* drama, in *that* school play, whose script combines all the insight of her morning's profound realizations, warrants way less than ten thousand words.

Of all the jobs and stories, everything she's done so far in journalism, the most popular and controversial thing Leela Mann ever wrote was an essay for *Salon* regarding why she had yet to take a picture of herself. A simple fact that was and remains true, no matter that she is web-savvy and tech-positive, for one easy reason, being ninety percent honest, that she's never felt so inclined.

In college, at the newspaper, she wrote about academic politics and housing practices. Sorority hazing. The sex lives of Muslim students. A series of album reviews where she interviewed her dad on the phone after she made him listen to new music. Predictably he loved Taylor Swift. Unpredictably he didn't hate Gucci Mane. "This guy is telling his stories!" Her best piece of work involved attending a state fair in Sussex County, to report on a pig scramble, which she wrote from three different points of view—the pig farmer, the public, the pig—and won herself a hundred-dollar gift card from the Journalism Department.

But after college, while she hustled her ass in the off-hours to get things published in various places around the web, none of it appeared to be much good. Also, little was for money, at least not much money. Articles on fan fic. Fan fic on fan fic. Recaps of other people's recaps of trashy shows.

She once wrote a personal essay on the Chinese New Year that occurs in a young lady's intestinal tract when the lady's trying to survive on lentil soup—but no one seemed interested in that one.

On the whole, during lunch, during the long subway rides to and from work, when she thought about her ambitions, her daydreams always dressed like nightmares. Her labor was for nothing, was how it felt. Then one day an assistant editor at a site suggested, via email, how about something on growing up as a girl *and* South-Asian-diaspora-ish in New England? So she wrote it. It ran. It was fine. But then another editor got in touch, at another site, and she asked her to do it again, just slightly different. Quickly, it became a trough. It even paid! By now a half dozen articles, at least, including her one writing foray during her internship at BuzzFeed, in the personal-essays vertical, about the time she'd made out with a guy at a loft party in Gowanus because he smelled like her mother's cooking.

It turned out that he lived in Crown Heights, his only window was right above an Indian restaurant's exhaust system. And she'd basically known she'd hook up with him for narrative's sake before they even kissed. But the kiss wasn't bad.

The reality was that editors, many editors, loved themselves some apples-on-apples. No matter that they knew, and she knew, and they knew she knew, and everyone knew that everyone knew, that it was all so much editorial racial profiling. Still, Indian ancestry was a good thing. Wasn't she only sort of miffed about the profiling thing anyway, if it came to her career? Maybe she'd start a club online: Sorta-angry Indian girls, who are basically not Indian at all, unite! Kind of!

For whatever reason—and there were many, which she'd discussed extensively with friends—a Leela Mann byline was simply perceived to be better equipped to critique whatever Aziz Ansari did next, no matter that she was from New Hampshire and liked to ski. And even though she did have a couple problems with all of that, she kept them to herself. After all, she needed to start somewhere. And the money wasn't bad.

But the *Salon* story was unusual. It had almost nothing to do with ethnicity. For a long time, posing in photographs had made her uncomfortable, profoundly. Her father was an amateur photographer. Since they were little, she and her brother had been dressed and posed at his whim. Family vacations were for touring Civil War battle sites—Gettysburg, Manassas—and they were made to wear little blue kepi caps. Even though maybe fifty South Asians fought for the North? He still loved it, made them pose by every monument, of which there were hundreds, thousands, and she hated it every time, the trapped heat, the self-consciousness, the *weirdness* of it all.

To this day she hates to stand before a camera, smartphone or otherwise. All the pressure to fake-smile, lips shiny, eyes aglisten. Everyone having such a good time. While a tiny part of her feels like they're commemorating the Union dead.

And so, also, yes, she never really loved her nose. She'll admit to having nice legs, and long fingers for someone who's barely five-four. She does hate her mother's love handles, which are her love handles, and she could do without the spots below her chin. But mostly she hates the nose. Which is shameful. Intersectionally pathetic, and without a doubt extremely vain in its own apparent ghoul-shape. She gets it, she owns it, and down the road she'll get over it. And become comfortable eating in restaurants lined with mirrors. But for the moment her deep reluctance is real, and she'd made a decent argument out of it in the article, she thought. The editor agreed. That if Leela Mann never felt the need to see her face snapped, filter or no, then there was nothing to defend; her position was only offense. Case in point: During college, her roommate Rebecca took her as her plus-one to her brother's wedding. During the reception she'd overheard Rebecca ask her mother, "Will you take a picture of me? I look so good tonight." Well, she could never imagine saying such a thing. So if the world had a problem with the global lack of portraits of Leela Mann, it was the world's problem, not hers. And she was pretty sure the world didn't have a problem. And therefore she didn't predict that so many people would be bothered by approximately two thousand words on the subject.

Within four minutes of publication, half a dozen people had left comments. How'd they find time to read it so fast? Calling her stuck-up, egotistical, self-involved. Within an hour over a hundred people had weighed in along the same lines. Stupid bitch. Sexless bitch. Self-hating, race-traitor bitch. Further variations on the theme that Leela pored over at her desk—meaning that she sat on the floor of her bedroom, her computer on top of *JavaScript for Dummies*, until she cried and needed to flop facedown on her comforter, drizzling snot, and discover that every ounce of self-doubt she'd ever experienced had been unexpectedly, completely validated.

Ten minutes later, her editor texted to warn her about some heated, "slightly personal" opinions in the comments section, and encouraged Leela to stay off the internet.

Then, a day later, *Salon* loaned the story to *The Huffington Post* to republish. Where it acquired a catchier headline: "Why One Millennial Among Millions Hasn't Taken a Selfie." From there, in the blink of an eye, came dozens of more comments, eventually hundreds. Way more full of orientalist fuck. Soon, random emails would appear. How'd they find her address? Newsfeed geyser eruptions occurred like so many natural wonders. One diss involved her and Mindy Kaling as self-satisfied dyke lovers, which was, on its own, sort of fantastic to imagine? And there was also an all-caps shout-out to HER COCKY VAG, which she took as a feminist compliment. But it got to be too much. Inside her unhappiness, she dug out a lair, but even there she couldn't keep her eyes off the web. She was the most horrible young woman to ever navel-gaze. Conceited, Narcissus-like, the black mirror to Malala Yousafzai. For such a stupid twat to pen this article? To gain license to address the masses about *not* navel-gazing, *not* taking self-portraits? The world was that much worse because of her existence.

At her roommate's suggestion, she took a day off. Put her phone in her underwear drawer and iced out everybody. She went into the city. Walked around Central Park. She bought a package of new dish towels from a cute shop on the Upper East Side. She loved buying dish towels. Normally they mopped up her nerves. Not this time. She was back on the internet in less than a minute after walking through the door, until Carlo, the boss roommate, who'd just gotten home, called her superpathetic and then showed her how to install a program to block her laptop from even being able to load *Salon* or *The Huffington Post*. So that her worst tendencies, manifest in computer use, would be controlled by the computer itself. How much of her was still human anyway?

That evening, like a summons from Valhalla, an urgent request appeared in her inbox. A CNN producer wanted Leela Mann to show up in her office immediately, midtown Manhattan, proceed to hurry up. She was about to say no, but Carlo convinced her otherwise. Thirty minutes later, in her single suit, Leela crossed the East River, and tried hard not to be afraid—that's when she really wished she'd said no. They put her through makeup. She'd never worn so much makeup. Were they trying to lighten her skin? The stuff melted off anyway. She drank three bottles of water while she waited, then a hot-chick producer stopped by with a request: the scarf that Leela had been wearing when she arrived, could she put it back on, drape it across her chest, sari-like? And lose the suit jacket? They wanted something a little more "exotic," and was that cool? Leela thought at the time, why doesn't she just say "Indian"? Do they want her to do an accent? Ninety minutes later, she rode the train home in a daze. The network squeezed her segment into a talk show late that night, which likely no one watched except her. And she wasn't at all sure whom she was watching. All sweaty, this girl, and monosyllabic, wearing three bottles of water weight like a neck brace. She hated every second of it; it was like having her photograph taken a million times in a row. But then came the internet the next day, particularly her parents, who emailed everyone they knew, all her relatives back in India, *Leela is a celebrity!! A TV star!!!!!!!!!! LEELA'S ON TV!!!!!!!!!!!!!!!!!!!!* And for a week her inbox and newsfeed were a forest of exclamation points. Total reverse of the public reaction. Her father started sending her story ideas, about himself, or some cousin in Guwahati who'd invented an umbrella for people's shoes. The following month, she even received an email from one of her favorite professors in college, a request of permission for Leela's *Salon* article to be included in a syllabus for a new course at Rutgers, "Introduction to Creative Nonfiction on the Web."

And all of it, all of it, troll garbage notwithstanding, was simply great.

But that was more than a year ago. No big articles since then, no TV requests. She's back in Claymore County, alone, ashamed, unemployed, squatting in an unfurnished rental.

After lunch she takes a long nap on her pile of clothes: ninety minutes.

Does the full maintenance routine in slo-mo: shower, shampoo, condition, shave, treat hair, tweeze eyebrows: sixty-five minutes.

A quick glance over the start to a novel, forty pages, that she wrote during a crazed, three-week period the previous year, about a girl who trades her nose for a functional tail in the center of her face: twenty-five minutes, including comma adjustments.

A jam jar of white wine: eleven minutes.

And while all of this is taking place, at least once every five minutes, she imagines what her competition is up to: Dude Bro, Real Writer, probably with an MFA from Iowa and a PhD from Stanford and who knows what else, was hard at work in his East Village studio on the final revisions to his debut novel about Orthodox Jewish/WASP intermarriage on Mars in 2216, while simultaneously he wrote the pilot script that had already been commissioned, while all the other Real Writers in town, who'd caught the buzz, who'd heard snippets at readings, eagerly anticipated passing around copies at artistic retreats. And literary agents would ejaculate six-course compliments into his ears! All for the chance for a big publisher to top off the right critic's stack of galleys and launch a name.

O ambition! O emotions! O brain!

Leela gives up and checks her email. One new message, from her dad. She can't bring herself to read it. She stares out the window. She does feel horribly about her parents. What will they do? The idea that they probably don't know the answer to that question either, that their future is also up for grabs, makes her throat close. It's beyond misguided that she hasn't told them that she's home. What a selfish, shallow girl. She stumbles on her way to the bathroom and stubs her toe. She calls her brother, he doesn't answer, he's probably too stoned. So when she can't avoid it any longer, she zips herself into her sleeping bag with her phone,

203

opens her dad's email, and reads a long-ass message about some crazy true-crime story that recently took place in Claymore, more or less.

What the hell?

She grabs *The New York Times* off the floor. Nothing about a "double murder story," as her father put it. She turns back to her phone. The link he sent goes to a short article in *The Boston Globe*. Dateline, Claymore. She's never seen her hometown in a dateline before. She grabs her laptop, reads the article. And feels like a meteor has just crashed through the ceiling.

Hours later, at ten that evening, she steps outside the house. The night is hushed. The woods are full of moonlight. Her eyes sting. Her legs are sore from sitting cross-legged. Since she read her father's email, she hadn't left the living room except to pee and fill up her water bottle. Frantic web research. Phone calls. Email inquiries. Deep-dives into social media. She left requests for information anywhere she could, even on Craigslist. *Hi. I'm a journalist looking into the story around the Ashburn murders. If you or anyone you know . . .*

As far as she can tell, the story's been ignored. Why? Local TV hasn't run anything. There isn't a town newspaper anymore. And yet a kid from one of the founding families in Claymore—even she's heard of the Toussaints—stands accused of killing two people, then goes on a drunken rampage with the bodies, and this isn't news?

She dares to smile.

She goes back inside the house, brushes her teeth, turns off the overhead light, zips herself back into her sleeping bag, to the tune of frogs quietly chirping in the trees. She closes her eyes. Smiles in the darkness. She grabs her phone, can't help but refresh her email one last time. And there's actually a new message, a response to her post for information, from a name she recognizes right away, Justin Johnson.

A name that makes her stomach plummet.

Leela Mann. You know I'd recognize that name. What's up? It's Justin. I'm over at DROP now and holy crap I'm obviously responding to your Craigslist post because guess what, I'm in Claymore. Let's get something to eat, I'll fill you in on what I've found. This story's even more messed-up than it looks.

THE
CLAYMORE KIDS

Three days after Justin Johnson's *DROP* story breaks, Claymore High School blasts an urgent email out to staff, students, and parents, instructing them to forcefully deny, please, any requests from nonstudents or non-CHS personnel in the coming days to borrow old yearbooks, school newspapers, telephone directories, photographic or video footage of school events, any digital archives of the school website or class materials, and/or any materials featuring pictures of students or any information about them.

The announcement, the first in school history, follows three confusing days of disturbances that crash over Claymore's shorefront defenses, which the town is by no means equipped to handle.

When, within thirty minutes of an early-morning run time, the *DROP* story is shared more than a hundred times. *DROP* is a new print and web magazine, Brooklyn-based, nine months old. It's a big investment by social media royalty in old-fashioned journalism, of both the high-end adversarial and gossip varieties—like *Spy* in its heyday, people say—which may or may not prove profitable but still seems cool for the present moment, even gutsy. So the story is soon prominently featured on an assortment of gatekeeper websites, whether or not their editors actually read the full thing, or even part of it.

Within three hours of publication, social shares number close to one thousand.

Testifying how broadly and mysteriously the *DROP* story will appeal in the coming weeks, it is throughout the day paraphrased, teased, wondered about, sneered at, and otherwise promoted as the read of the moment, the day, the week, for its dirty pictures and breathless pulp, and also because of that distinctively rare event in online media when someone breaks actual news, or what looks like actual news.

Before sunset on the East Coast on publication day, a summer day of above-average temperatures from Maine to Florida, the *DROP* story acquires more than three thousand likes and almost a half dozen seven-hundred-word responses, via opinion writers from different publications, who alternately praise and criticize Justin Johnson's account, even if they don't agree on a single reason to discuss it.

If anything, what appears to be the burning broad consensus is that it's too soon to know whether to embrace or rebuff the vision presented. Or just flat-out mock it. Or take the dispatch on its own merits and analyze the crimes discussed, with more expansive questions about the fourth estate and humanity in present-day America. Or use the spring-back of the account's metaphorical diving board to address other issues, like the perils of unsafe sexting. Or fourth-wave feminism and the value of consent in an age of livestreaming and "sextortion." Or the evolution of women's sex-positive expression, from de Pizan/Hesse to Rihanna feat. Lorde. Or the history of phrases like "benevolent sexism," "hegemonic masculinity," "pussy affluenza," and why they remain in quotes for public digestion. Or the tragic history, regarding both female eroticism and rape culture, that is specific to New England, sacred turf of Louisa May Alcott, Shirley Jackson, and other chroniclers of the northeastern bloc's transgressed young women. So the opinion writers have a field day and do all of these things.

By eleven p.m. Eastern, on the day that the story appears, the "ClaymoreKids" hashtag cracks the ice. That same evening, Fox News airs a short piece from its Manchester affiliate, in which an excited reporter stands on the Claymore courthouse steps and paraphrases the story known so far. For gotcha's sake, they also include a "no comment" interview from a surprised employee of the Claymore County Sheriff's Department, with a closing pledge to remain on the case.

The next day, an op-ed columnist in *The Wall Street Journal* ridicules *DROP*'s "new spin" on time-honored journalism and attacks Justin Johnson's lilac prose, then travels further, into full-out denunciation, regarding the article's inclusion of barely blurred photographs of a nude minor.

Arguing that this is not only ethically gross, but only by a hairsbreadth not criminal, not the distribution of child pornography. Which leads to the columnist's appearance that evening on an MSNBC segment, sitting opposite *DROP*'s death-faced legal counsel, while a sex-crimes expert argues that the minor in question likely has a strong case for a lucrative defamation suit.

By midnight, day two, half a dozen media people are on the ground in New Hampshire. And why not? It's August, the president is on vacation, the news is arid and self-obsessed, there's breathing room for scandal. The group includes a Fox News TV crew of two and an NPR team of one. An editor at *Vanity Fair* who's taking a couple days away from book-leave at the MacDowell Colony, plus a stringer out of Boston for *The New York Times*' New England desk. As well as the scooped-to-hell reporter from *The Boston Globe*, all blue-balled up, who wrote the first story, the original dispatch on Nick Toussaint Jr.—one of the deviant "Claymore Kids" in question, as Justin Johnson so branded them.

But despite the competition for news, when the journalists run into each other they greet each other collegially, with solidarity and all the constructedness of the first day of fall semester, as if they haven't seen each other since before summer break.

Then, day three. Seventy-two hours after the *DROP* story, the same day that the school board issues its warning, it's not the *New Hampshire Union Leader* but the *Los Angeles Times*, of all venues, that breaks news. Because the paper so happens to have a reporter on the ground, an old hand who'd been on vacation with her family in Maine, who'd been quickly rerouted to Claymore and mightily eager to do a kick-ass job, working from an electrifying sense of dread fed by rumors of more Tribune Company layoffs. As a result, the California newspaper publishes the article that provides scripture for most reporting to come—trumping even the *DROP* piece on the way to becoming a playbook to rehash, for the simple fact that it's well reported. Interviews. Researched backgrounds. Curt inventories of facts. Summaries of court records. Multiple verified names named with verified attributed quotes. All told, eight townspeople in and around Claymore offer their opinions about the case and its allegations, their measured thoughts about the crimes and the alleged killer's sixteen-year-old girlfriend, and what her racy photos say about their town, their region, their country as of now.

And so the article is shared. Discussed ravenously by Claymore parents, grandparents, and teenagers. Dissected at Denny's and The Fredericks Family Creamery and the local bars, to a point that it turns citizens subliminally feral, chomping to know what happens next. People take sides, people argue, bystanders intervene. People are surprised by how their neighbors react. At this stage they're not quite turned on so much as spotlit, like actors, even if they're not personally mentioned in the stories, as of yet.

And the eight quoted in the *LA Times* piece become marked persons, thought of differently, reconsidered in the footlights of something akin to Greek tragedy, to the point that those people, who were formerly neighbors and friends, are now a privileged sect, "the Quoted." And some of the Quoted will take back their comments in public forums, they read speeches off their phones. Some go apeshit online and call out Conspiracy and Injustice, call out by name any sticklers who judge them, who stalk the web with their moral measuring sticks.

Eventually all of the Quoted will regret allowing their names to be used, if only because they had no idea that the story would become the top result for many years should anyone search for them online.

But as all of that occurs, at the same time as the *LA Times* story's publication, another story appears—quietly at first, then much louder, by virtue of up-voting in the right internet spaces that can make a story surge. The piece emerges only after a young editor, three weeks new to a job at StankTuna, a gossip website, chooses to publish, for a hundred dollars, an article that she receives by blind submission. It's forwarded from a grad-school friend who's an intern at *Politico*, who notes in their Gchat, "This is probably more up your guys' alley than ours." In the article, the author says he resides in Claymore and knows the Claymore Kids sufficiently—which isn't without merit, especially where clickbait's concerned; and clickbait's always concerned at StankTuna. So the website runs the story to beat its rivals, in which the author, for the first time publicly, names the girl from the photos, and tells stories about her family, about an old rivalry that exists between her family and the boy's, a conflict dating back to the nineteenth century, and then relates stories about the girl and her rivals, a record of nasty behavior and cyberexhibitionism, with a gross-out anecdote involving a winter jacket. A girl for whom disgrace does not count.

At which point, shit gets real.

And despite the website's retraction the following morning, its aggressive mea culpa, contritely expressed new commitment to fact-checking, and a pledge to fire the young editor responsible, Emily Portis becomes news.

No longer a girl called Girl, but a name.

And so the Claymore Board of Selectmen summons an emergency session for the following day, day four. When, in an otherwise slow but still competitive August news cycle, a modern-day Romeo and Juliet story plus ye olde Yankee township, plus double homicide, plus porno selfies, plus accusations of pedophilia, equals so much lurid delirium.

∎

But before any of that happens, ten days preceding, ten days before the *DROP* story kicks off the madness, the first thing Leela remembers about Justin Johnson is that much is extroverted. Chunky glasses. Rubbery nose. A gently frayed, preppy look, with an obesity that seems artisanal, plus an oversensitive, defensive manner that's always vaulting him into the prow of conversations, putting himself out in front of the herd, even when the herd is a group of friendly colleagues. Also midforties, recovering Catholic, biracial, originally from Connecticut, now a Prospect Heights mortgage owner married to a social worker named Tamlyn whom he met in grad school—a social worker who resembles Amber Rose—with a pair of twin toddlers certifiably so adorable, Leela envied *them* when she saw a picture for the first time.

All of this she'd learned two years earlier, on the day she became Justin's research assistant at BuzzFeed, and he'd given her a two-minute life story while waiting in line for coffee. Favorite movie: *Hav Plenty*. Favorite band: the Buzzcocks. Favorite song: All of Drake, on repeat, forever.

He lowers himself into the booth, bulkier than she remembers. Her former mentor who is now, evidently, her competition.

"It's great to see you," Justin says, chewing gum. He strains over the booth to half hug. "Admittedly under some pretty weird circumstances."

"It's unbelievable that you're here."

"So I've got something coming out." He exhales loudly. "Day after tomorrow."

She laughs. She wants to barf.

"That's amazing."

"I haven't filed yet. I've got an interview in the morning, then I'll wrap it up on the plane. To be honest, it came together really fast."

"How long have you been in town?"

"Almost a week?"

She's angry and jealous and also mad at herself. But can't let it show.

"You know this is my hometown," she says.

"I think you said you were from up here?" He looks around for a waiter. "So you're up here visiting your folks?"

"Yeah. I mean, I can't believe it." The "it" could be a hundred different things. "My parents actually took me to this restaurant for my graduation dinner. From high school. How crazy is that?"

"Really crazy," he says, deadpan.

She knits her hands together beneath the table. They're in the Angry Goat, a Claymore institution. In high school it was the "fancy" restaurant, where kids ate before prom.

Justin looks at her questioningly.

"Leela, be honest. Did you notice I'm fatter?"

"No."

"We can talk about it. Tamlyn says I'm fat. Like, really fat."

"I think you look good."

Justin smiles. He always was self-conscious about his looks. The waiter arrives. They order.

"You do yoga?"

"Why would you think that?"

"You're Indian, you live in New York, you're in your twenties. It's ninety-five percent likely that you do yoga."

"Well, I don't."

She lets the New York comment slide.

"So," she says. "How are your daughters?"

Justin frowns and smiles at the same time.

"How about we just talk about why we're here."

"Of course," she says. "Please."

"The most obvious thing is that nobody has anything. Except for that *Globe* piece, which they let die. You saw that?"

"But why does *DROP* even care?"

He shrugs. "My boss thought we should dig around. She saw the *Globe* story, she needs stuff. Who knows? It's summer, nothing's happening. I do have a salary to legitimize." He snaps his gum. "I'll tell you what, her instincts were on the money. Quote-unquote."

Justin proceeds to recite facts, which Leela mostly knows already.

That a kid from Claymore, Nick Toussaint Jr., had shown up drunk in New Jersey several weeks earlier, with two dead bodies in the back of his car. Since then, he'd confessed to murder, saying that, back in Claymore, he'd killed a local doctor and his wife, the Ashburns, during a home invasion gone wrong. Grisly stuff. Consequently, due to the murders occurring in New Hampshire, not New Jersey, he'd been whisked back to the White Mountains, shoveled into custody while trial awaits, and as of yet there was no bail on offer, so in custody he sat.

"Did you know him from around town?" Justin asks. "The Toussaint kid? Or the Ashburns?"

"I don't," she says. Which is true. Though there are certain things she needs to keep secret, she reminds herself. When her natural instinct is to share what she knows.

"Anyway, so now we're talking a couple more months before anything really gets going. Maybe the fall. Wheels of justice turn slow, and so on. But that's under normal circumstances. Which, as of recently, are no longer normal."

"What do you mean?"

Justin pulls out his gum and sticks it to his napkin. "The kid started singing a different story. As of a week ago. That he didn't do it. Which isn't public yet, FYI."

"Wait a second." She's confused. "How do you know that?"

"Part of the job. Figure out which nipples to twist."

"Seriously?"

"I've got a leak in the defender's office. One of the support assistants likes bourbon. Sidebar, do you know anyone around here I could buy some weed from?"

"I don't think so."

"No yoga, no weed. What good are you?"

Their sandwiches arrive.

"The good thing is," says Justin, "everyone's still talking. I've got a follow-up scheduled tomorrow with the kid's girlfriend. She's involved up to the neck. I talked with her this afternoon. Check it out, sixteen years old. Not an idiot. Sort of Tomboy of the North."

"Back up a second," she says. "If the boy didn't do it, who did?"

"You remember that bumper sticker, KILL YOUR TELEVISION? I saw one today."

"Justin."

He laughs, scratches his face. Crumbs dot his tie. "I had to caution the girl. I was like, I'm recording this, you know that, right? Leela, you're not going to believe all the shit I've got."

"At least try me," she says. "I'm so lost."

"The kid says the sheriff did it. Killed the doctor and his wife."

"The sheriff? Why?"

"Exactly."

"No, why would the sheriff do it?"

"It turns out, the guy was molesting his daughter for years."

"Are you joking? Wait, who?" She feels instantly colder, and much more confused. "What does that have to do with anything?"

"Wait until you read my story. Here's what's up: our kid, this guy Nick, the one nabbed in Jersey, before any of that shit happened, he was dating this girl. Who's younger than him by some significant years. But they're in love, they've got big plans, mostly focused on the need to get the hell out of town. Anyway, through her, Nick finds out about this past abuse, on the sheriff's part. And it drives him mad."

"Because his girlfriend is the sheriff's daughter."

"Nails it! I always said you were smart."

"Thank you," she says formally, but it's from deep inside, a cover-up.

Justin doesn't notice. "So now our boy's one true love turns out to have been sexually molested all this time by Daddy. Nick flips out. Because she still lives at home. Evidently the abuse stopped at some point, a couple years ago, but still. Nick loves her, he'll do anything. Also, her mom's a basket case, in a mental asylum somewhere, and for what it's worth the boy's dad is also out of the picture, bad blood, plus his mom's a drunk. Families suck. Anyway, the point is that now Nick's feeling like The Man, but in a bad way. He has to do something. He needs to protect her, he needs advice. So what he does is telephone his doctor, right? Guy turns out to be a friend of the family, trusted adult or whatever, because the kid had a leg injury a while back and the doctor took care of him. Anyhow, so Nick goes over to the doctor's house. And the doctor hears the story."

"I'm so lost."

"There's more."

"Is this your story?"

"So the doctor is now informed. He's on the verge of figuring out what to do next, while the kid's still there, then *ding-dong*, guess who arrives at the doorstep."

"The sheriff? But how?"

"He'd been tailing the two of them for months, so says the girl."

"The girl, Emily," she says. "Who's the sheriff's daughter."

"Yeah. Hey, how'd you know her name?"

Oh shit.

"The girl? You said it."

"I did?"

"But I don't understand," she says quickly, "the girl told you all this, about her dad? The girl who was raped told you this?"

Justin looks at her oddly. "Is it 'raped'? 'Raped' sounds wrong."

"It sounds like rape to me."

"She told me, yeah. Totally stone-faced, ice-cold. She's in love with her boyfriend, she doesn't give a shit otherwise. Screw Daddy, basically."

"The father. The rapist cop."

"Sheriff rapist, right. In any case, who'd blame her? So, they're at the doctor's house, late at night, the doctor and Nick, when the sheriff shows up. There's a few words back and forth, again this is according to the boy's eyewitness, then the sheriff stabs the doctor in the gut."

"Oh god."

"And dude bleeds out. In his own foyer."

"That's horrible."

"It gets worse. Next he runs upstairs and kills the wife."

"The sheriff does?"

"Guess why. Not that we have a body camera for this."

"Because the wife might know the secret, too."

He gives her a silent round of applause.

"But it's unbelievable," Leela says. "I mean, this is my hometown."

"At which point," Justin continues, "our boy and the sheriff load the bodies into the kid's car, while the sheriff hands out instructions. First, ditch the bodies, get rid of them, though making sure any 'identifying characteristics' are gone. Meaning, smash their faces in with a shovel."

"No shit."

"Second, no one can find out. So the sheriff will hang back and clean up the mess, because he's an expert at such, being a cop, while the kid buries the bodies elsewhere. Again, this is according to the kid's revised testimony. And the sheriff's final instruction, the kid says, is that if the truth should in some way emerge about this shit, somehow blow back on him, he'll murder the kid's mom."

Leela is silent, trying to take it in, the enormous awfulness of it all.

Justin finishes his sandwich.

He adds, chuckling, "And that's just the start."

"Are you kidding?" She laughs nervously. "What else can there be?"

He wipes his mouth.

"Justin, come on."

"Read the piece, then we'll talk."

During their time working together, there'd been a moment when she almost walked out. A slow Friday, midafternoon. She'd stopped by his desk to ask, offhand, for career tips. She'd seen someone list something similar online. Like, what had he done to get where he was, that she could do for herself? "So you want the shortcut to my career?" he said. "Basically," she said, laughing. "Just tell me what mistakes you made, so I don't make them." She thought it was a reasonable question. But his face got all stony. "I get it," he said. "Because you shouldn't have to put up with crap. You feel like you should get fast-tracked to the top." She was about to protest, but she heard his temper rising, so she said nothing. Wrong decision. Justin abruptly stood up on his chair. "Can I have people's attention?" he announced to the entire newsroom, two dozen people. "All interns, anybody born between let's say 1982 and 2003, will you please remove your earbuds for a second?" Already Leela was cringing. Ready to jump out the window and hang glide away. "Allow me to reintroduce something, to any people of similar age to Leela here. You do not have the right to vampire-suck your elders. We get it, you want it all, you deserve it because you're specialer. That's all great. Except please wake up to the truth that every previous generation had the grace to suck up: that having a quote-unquote successful career means doing crap for a while. A lot of it. At an entry-level job, entry-level pay, while working below other people. For which you will get zero credit, and deserve none. So just deal, okay?" Justin sat down again. A few senior people laughed awkwardly. Mostly everyone stared around the room, wondering what had just happened, then turned back to their computers. "That might've been too much," he said to her quietly a second later, cooling down. She'd laughed, when really she wanted to die.

She waited five minutes, checking her phone, then went to the bath-room, where no one could see her, to hold her head with two hands to keep it from splitting apart. The following Monday, Justin apologized right away. He said he felt terrible, he shouldn't have singled her out. Which wasn't mea culpa, exactly, but after lunch he brought her a Thin Mint Frappuccino just the way she liked it, extra chocolate, no whip. She hadn't known he'd noticed.

Justin gestures for the check. "It's on me. On *DROP*, I should say."

She smiles, but his gesture only makes her feel more awkward. The gulf between them is bigger than she realized. Age. Expertise. Money. Never mind all the details to whatever story he's about to publish. A story she'd thought she had to herself, that she may have none of what-soever.

"You're still holding something back," she says randomly.

"I'm holding a ton back."

She sighs. "It's such a crazy story."

He stares at her. "I'm so soft. Okay, tomorrow, come with me."

"Where? When?"

"Eight a.m., Denny's. It's right down the street."

"I know where the Denny's is."

"I'm meeting the girl. For a follow-up. At the very least you'll get an introduction. Once my story's up, as far as I'm concerned it's all yours. At least until everybody else gets in town."

"Seriously? That would be great, Justin. I really appreciate it."

"No problem."

"So you think people will?"

"Will what?"

"Show up."

Justin stares at her for a moment, as if he'd misjudged her. He says, "This town is going to be overrun within a week."

■

White people. White culture. Memories of a mostly white childhood. The Whitehall quarry, perpetual hangout of local kids as white as snow. Antique off-white houses triumphed by oak trees, bark fading to flax. White pines. White mountains. White trucks with beige camper shells. Plus any and all Anglo-Saxon seagulls, Styrofoam cups in puddles, wishy-washy bodies on the sand. Seashell collections. Cream poured into coffee. Toddlers in bone-colored Synchilla. Not to mention all the Caucasian retirees who sit around town in folding chairs, with faces like so much yellowed lace.

Early the next morning, Leela drives around Claymore and sees the town with fresh eyes, New York eyes. It's surreal to be home but not *of* home anymore. The old houses, the barns, the clipped lawns that are disproportionately green compared to other colors in sight. It all now looks editorial, like a New England postcard, or is that just her?

Then the layers begin to flake away. By the ocean are portions of embankments where storms for years had cut away ground and carried off land. She drives by the dollar-beer bars near the ocean—the Harbor, Dave's Dockside—that seemed so dangerous when she was sixteen, and now they just look seedy. The Sundial's still standing, the site of her first real kiss, the summer before junior year.

She stops at a stoplight. Tourists cross the road. She parks in the public lot and walks down to the beach. On the way a skinny homeless kid tries to sell her weed, no matter the hour. His hands are tattooed with elephant heads. She turns him down. He whispers, "Bitch," then to his dog, "Gronk, *move*," and sidles on.

Low tide. She takes off her sneakers. She stands in the water until her ankles sting from cold. She smiles. She feels a tiny surge of trouble, but in a good way. Nerves she can use.

There's a story here, she knows it. And she's the perfect person to write it.

The day before, with Justin, she'd been careful not to give any noticeable indication that she could tell him one specific thing that she *did* know about the story: the fact that she'd already met Emily Portis, on the morning before their lunch. Thanks to a post she'd found during a late dumpster dive into social media: a girl at CHS had been mocking an "Emily" over some high school incident, then another kid pointed out that this Emily was the known girlfriend of the kid wanted for those murders. In reply, someone else said that such an Emily happened to work in a shop downtown, a fabric boutique. So Leela had stopped by on her way to the lunch with Justin. She'd had an idea of which store to try; in the same shopping plaza was a used-books store her father loved. She made sure to park on the other side of the lot. Inside the fabric shop were sewing machines, bolts of colored fabric, quilts, and there, behind the register: the girl in question, name-tagged Emily. Leela took a deep breath and introduced herself, explained who she was. She gave her one of the *Village Voice* business cards to establish legitimacy. The girl was forthcoming, noncommittal, obviously confused. She said she'd talked to one other reporter, a black guy in a tie, Justin something. Leela kept it brief, though she did explain her background, the fact that she, too, was from the area, had even gone to Claymore High. And so, if Emily ever wanted to chat, wanted a chance to tell her story, then perhaps a young woman from Claymore would better understand what a young woman from Claymore was going through.

Leela leaves the beach, drives to Denny's, the breakfast crowd of retirees. Justin and Emily are just sitting down when she arrives. "Thanks for meeting me again," Justin says to Emily as she joins them. "I have a few follow-up questions. I hope you don't mind, this is Leela, another journalist."

"I know," Emily says. "We met yesterday."

"That's right," Leela says. "Sorry I'm late."

"Wait a second, what?" says Justin. He looks at her, for her to explain. She's saved by the girl leaning across the table.

"I want to set the record straight," Emily says. "That's why I came."

"Well, yeah," Justin says, recovering, coolly. "That's why we're here."

Leela's impression from the day before, now confirmed in the restaurant, is that Emily Portis is basically an American Girl doll come to life. Outdoorsy, confident, attentive, though braced by watchfulness, with an edge of agitation and too much need behind her face. The girl's only sixteen, Leela remembers; it's easy to forget. She seems a lot older than her years.

"So I was hoping we could run over a few of the questions I asked you the other day," Justin says. "To see if you had any further thoughts."

"Okay."

"Some of these questions may get a little delicate."

"I understand."

Leela butts in, "Can I ask? Why are you talking to us?"

"Leela—"

"Like I told him," Emily says quickly. "I don't want any rumors out there. And he said," indicating Justin, "that this will help Nick's case."

"I said it might," Justin says. Glancing at Leela: *What the hell?*

"Well, I'll do anything," says Emily. "For the truth to come out."

"Do you think you've been misrepresented?" Leela asks.

"What do you mean?"

"In the press. I mean, have you been represented at all? You said you don't want any rumors out there."

The girl looks at Justin, then back at Leela, animated by her confusion.

"I just mean," Leela says, "have you seen something out there that's untrue?"

"But no one's asked me anything," the girl says rigidly. "Besides you guys. Do you mean like stuff on the internet? That's just gossip."

"If we can change tack," Justin says brusquely. "You said the pictures you took were meant for Nick."

"Of course. Why else would I take them?"

Leela looks at Justin quickly, trying to mask her confusion. *What pictures?*

"I understand," he says. "Again, I'm sorry, this is going to be a little tough. I spoke to a young man yesterday, Michael. I believe he goes by Jersey Mike."

The girl stops dead, staring. "How do you know about that?"

"From what he tells me, his story is pretty different. Which doesn't mean anything on the surface."

"He stole them," says Emily angrily. "I asked you, how do you even know about that?"

"I understand you're upset. Here's the thing," Justin says softly. "Mike says he didn't steal them. He denies stealing them. I spoke with him last night."

"That's crazy."

"I know, but it's what he said. So we have to look into it."

"But it's a lie. He's lying. You have to believe me."

"We do believe you," Leela says, but she barely gets it out before Justin adds, "He says he saw them just like anybody else has seen them."

"What 'anybody else'? That's not true."

"He says that you posted them, Emily. For attention. That you wanted them to be seen. I'm sorry, but that's what he said—it's right here in my notes. So I have to ask, for the record, do you have any comment on that?"

Leela has no idea what's being discussed, only that the girl in front of her is starting to crumble. She looks right and left for an exit, she fidgets in her seat. And either Justin doesn't notice, or he does and wants to push anyway, to some investigative end that Leela can't fathom.

"Emily," he says, "I can't imagine how hard this must be to hear."

"He stole them," the girl says. Her voice catches. People around the restaurant turn to watch. She shifts quickly in the vinyl booth, and her voice starts to rise. "Go ahead and ask anybody." She leans hard across the table. "Alex told me what happened. He saw them on her sister's computer and stole them and sent them out, that's how they got online."

"I'm sure we can trace who posted them," Leela says, without really knowing what she's talking about. "It shouldn't be that hard."

"Actually, it is hard," says Justin. "Leela, why don't you and I talk about this later?" He turns back to the girl. "We've got a request in for assistance. I haven't heard back yet but I'm sure we will soon. In the meantime—"

The girl says, "I'm going to go now."

"Emily, wait. I understand it's tough. But it's your word against his."

"I'm sixteen. *Sixteen.*"

Then she's gone, hurling herself toward the bathrooms.

"What was that?"

"You could have handled that better," she says.

"Honestly, you went around behind my back? After all I've done for you?"

Leela ignores him, gets up, finds the girl in the women's restroom. She's drying her cheeks, red and damp, with a paper towel.

"You said you wanted to be my friend."

"I'm so sorry. Justin and I don't even work together. We used to work in the same office, that's it."

"All of that is lies, what he said."

"I believe you."

Leela hands her a tissue packet from her bag.

The girl blows her nose.

"What's your name again?"

"Leela."

"I didn't post those photos."

"Of course you didn't. Why would you?"

■

It's been five years since she was eleven, the year she made Father a wreck, turned him into a cave animal who overslept and slouched around the house. It began on the night of her refusal, when she attacked him, when her feelings expanded like flammable gas. Once again, he'd lain down in her bed, the wrinkled sheets, for their Sunday games, and she'd been filled with the normal paralysis, fear, intense shame, and tolerance. But that night, she couldn't contain it anymore. The feeling surprised her: a full-on stop. He pulled her body onto his. She resisted. He pulled harder. She lunged like a bobcat—and sank her teeth into his arm. At the same time, a horrible fear split her in two. She felt a wild satisfaction, and she was full of guilt and regret and terror, plus an acute sense of betrayal, and badness. What a horrible girl she was! A wild animal.

But instead of killing her, he'd lurched backward and burst into tears, then tossed himself out, into the upstairs hallway, without a word.

Then came the period, several weeks, of dejected looks and disturbed atmosphere. A broken barn window. A coffee table overturned. Even Mother, in the house, in her stupor, seemed to notice something wrong. At the dinner table Emily was made to feel stupid, vain, and callous. He wanted to win the war, to hurt her, and of course he did. Though he didn't come near her at night ever again.

The next year, she turned twelve. Father was not only back at work, he was elected sheriff after his boss retired, and was constantly out of the house.

Emily drives home from the Denny's, eyes on fire. Fate locked forward, with her heart galloping alongside. The empty road is lined with sumacs, flowering red and sharp. There's a large rock on the seat beside her. She squeezes it in her hand. Every inch of muscle in her body clenches with conviction around how much she hates this town, everyone in it, everyone in the county, a twenty-mile radius, for everything they know about her, or think they know.

At a red light, she bashes the rock against the inside of the windshield until it makes a starburst.

Just the other day, a short round woman, dressed like a laundry pile, came into the store to buy yarn and said she wanted to know if she, Emily, and her boyfriend, were aware of the negative impact they'd had on the local economy.

The light changes. The truck roars. Her emotions darken with each passing driveway. Each driveway that leads to a house, inside of which is a computer, a phone, and inside every computer or phone were pictures of her, pictures stared at by someone she didn't know, someone she'd on no account want to know. But what Emily Portis wants never seems to matter.

Except on two counts.

Two staggering, amazing things.

The first: her father's in jail. It's almost impossible to contemplate. She's been dying to know more ever since she found out. The images stretch and twist in her mind. What he's saying and doing, how he looks, what he eats.

The second: Nick is free. His attorney got bail approved, somehow payment was made; no one knows by whom. Everything's mysterious, without explanation. But it doesn't matter. Suzanne had phoned, said that Emily should be the one to pick him up. She'd gone to the courthouse at the proper hour. The door opened slightly, at the top of the stairs. Suddenly there was Nick, wearing normal clothes as if nothing had happened. He looked up and down the block. He smiled when he saw her and his smile cut her to the heart. She ran, flung forward by need, defenseless and so happy, even a little hurt by the intensity of all the feelings.

For at least a week she'd feared the feelings wouldn't come back, physically. That she'd become too comfortable writing letters and not needing more. But then he kissed her. No one watched, no one cared. For a moment they were immersed. It felt as good as it ever had. She wanted it to last forever. They pulled back from each other, and the look in his eyes squashed all of her fears.

In the crazy depths of that moment, she'd vowed to care for nothing else ever again. Anything else in the world was just noise, like a television, and she could choose whether or not to watch it, and she chose not.

Before Denny's, she'd really thought everything was changed for the better.

■

A week before the sheriff was arrested, before the media shit hit the fan, everything that went wrong with Nick's mom started on the night that Martin drove her up to Maine, to the cheap motel, and the screen door on his cabin sprang off its hinges when she knocked.

She was wondering, Suzanne had said a moment later, through the empty doorway, if Martin wouldn't enjoy getting a drink. The screen door lay to the side like hurricane debris.

It would be a week of surprises. Not all of them bad.

"I don't drink," Martin said.

"Who cares? We'll order wine."

Tall and dark. Hair wet from a shower, messily put up. Black jeans. Blue top. Darkish lipstick, like raspberry juice.

"No wine either, I'm afraid."

"You know, you're a really bleak sort of guy."

"I can see why you'd think that."

He'd grabbed his jacket, followed her out into the evening. What else to do? It was dark, testily cold. His back ached from the drive. A fish restaurant was open across the street. Ragged old picnic tables, and a cozy bar inside the entrance. He caught himself in a window's reflection: craggy, beleaguered, with cheeks like pork chops. People inside were clinking beer bottles. He had an acidic ambivalence toward whatever happened next.

Nick's mother pulled out a stool and ordered herself a martini. Above their heads was a rack of harpoons. He stood instead of sitting, he asked for a large tonic with lemon. A TV played CNN. The newscaster had Lillian's hairstyle.

"So you think my son's guilty," Suzanne said.

"I wouldn't be here if I did."

"What if he is?"

Bitterness welled up inside him, staring at the television, the newscaster's hair.

"He's not."

"It would be ironic."

"Do you ever think that sort of thing's genetic?" she said darkly, after a pause.

"That's a weird thing to say."

"I'm a mother," she said. Swallowing nearly half her drink. "Mothers always know the truth."

His phone rang. The screen displayed a picture of his daughter, on a beach near Los Angeles. He'd been in the city for a conference. She was going through a bad breakup at the time. She got pulled over in the hills, doing seventy in a forty-five. He'd called in a favor to get the ticket bumped—but she didn't want his help. She said it was deserved, implying: *like so much else*. They'd argued old arguments. Little things became big things. Camille knew every little way to twist him around. He'd flown back east feeling like he'd done nothing whatsoever, and probably made things worse.

"Camille?"

"Dad. Is this a bad time?"

He hurried outside, mashing the phone against his ear.

"Of course not. Where are you?"

"I'm at home," she said. "So how's it going? Mom said there's been trouble with Lillian."

How did she know that? Lillian must have called his ex-wife. Had he known they were on speaking terms? He felt his mind shift into a different lane.

"You know, I don't really want to talk about that right now."

"I got your check. It's actually kind of the reason I'm calling."

"Are you in trouble?"

"Dad, you sound weird. Tell you what, I'll call you later."

"No. I mean, go ahead. Tell me."

"It's about Roger."

"Roger who?"

"Roger Federer." She laughed. "The guy I've been seeing for the past six months? We've talked about him, like, a dozen times."

"Honey, I'm sorry." He laughed. "It's been a long day."

"It's about his new film," she said. "So he just finished his latest script. It's great I mean, it's really good. So we're starting to reach out to people."

Roger, he remembered Roger. Roger the film school graduate, who wanted to tell the world's most difficult stories: Roger came back to him. There'd been the short film Camille had sent him, that he'd watched half of for her sake, about exploited prostitutes in Colombia. With, for his taste, too much emphasis on prostitutes, not enough on exploitation. Roger, he didn't like Roger.

"We don't want to do a Kickstarter or something hacky, we've already got some good partners on board. Honestly the story's *great*. It's a heist movie, do you know what that means? Like a bank robbery."

"I'm a cop," he said, smiling. "I know what a heist is."

"But here's the twist: The bank robbers are kids. They're orphans, they're refugees from Syria. So they're pulled along by this need to survive, right?"

"Okay."

"Anyway, we're reaching out to people who'd like to get in from page one."

"You're looking for money."

"Well, yeah," she said. "Think of it this way: here's a chance to invest in something meaningful. I mean, not only financially, with a decent return, depending how things go, but you also get to be involved in creating something."

"I get it."

"Dad, I don't want to twist your arm."

"How much are we talking?"

"For angel investors, it's like twenty. But I was thinking maybe more like two to five? I know it's an ask."

He'd laughed, and tried too late to keep it muffled, but couldn't help himself.

"Are you still there?" she said.

"Honey, I love you, I'm just processing," he said. "You know, I'm a cop. An ex-cop. Not a banker. Not a lawyer."

It was only two grand. But it was the principle that bothered him. Calling up out of the blue, never to connect. For "an ask."

"I'm totally springing this on you, I get it," she said. "Maybe if you were a consultant or something, on law enforcement stuff."

"It's a lot of money. Twenty thousand dollars."

"You're not listening."

"Even ten thousand. That's a lot of money."

"Dad, listen to me."

"You have to be realistic."

"You know what," she said a moment later, "forget it. I shouldn't have called."

"Now hold on."

"I'm going to let you go. We're good."

"Camille, please. Wait a second."

The line went dead.

He called back: no answer.

Thirty seconds later, back inside, Nick's mother asked who'd called. He grinned dismally at the floor, in a daze, but didn't answer. She said they should skip dinner, she could tell he was too preoccupied to stick around. They crossed the road in the dark. The wind cut through his jacket. At the motel, he watched her run up the drive, somehow jogging in heels. He called softly for her to wait, but she ran to her cabin, slammed the front door closed without a backward glance. Not even a good night. The daze kept him staring in the dark for a good thirty seconds.

His bedroom was bitterly cold. He ran a hot bath. All afternoon, he hadn't been able to escape a feeling: something bad was coming. He undressed and lay in the water. Maybe his relationship with his daughter was dead at last. All her life, he bought her every little toy, a car when she turned sixteen. When she was five, she once made him so angry, he'd grabbed her by the face, like he was about to shake her. Like her head was a grapefruit. It was the worst thing he ever did. The kind of thing his own father would have done. Except his father would have started to squeeze, not release her in terror.

For a couple months he'd seen a psychiatrist once a week. Then work got in the way, and his drinking.

He forced other thoughts from his mind. The void filled with Nick's mother. Her long neck, her lips. He put his wet hands over his eyes, pictured the bathroom door open. Steam drifted past her and out into the bedroom. Enough. He emptied the bath and pissed down the drain. Pulled on his pants, a shirt, a thin cotton sweater. And in the next moment, as he put on his shoes, Martin decided that he was done: no more marriage. He grabbed his phone and texted his wife's lawyer. Then shut off the phone and was on his way out to go buy a pint of ice cream at a gas station when the cabin's front door opened suddenly, minus the sigh of the screen door's hydraulic arm.

"Going somewhere?"

He laughed. "Ice cream. You want some?"

Suzanne smiled coldly and held it as if with effort. She closed the door and walked past him, lowered her long body into a plaid love seat. With a fresh varnish of lipstick, and a bottle of vodka in her hand.

He brought her a juice glass from the bathroom.

"Martin, let's talk."

"Oh, good."

"Sometimes," she said slowly, "you can have a dialogue even if only one person is talking."

He sat down on the side of the bed. "Tell me something. How come people say 'dialogue' these days when they really mean 'conversation'?"

She ignored him. "Here's what I was thinking, in my room. That there is no shortage of opportunities. For heartbreak in a mother's life."

She hiccupped and placed her hand over her mouth.

"Suzanne, what are we doing right now?"

"I just wanted to talk," she said. "You don't like to talk?"

"Not with someone who's drunk."

"I am drunk. It makes me perceptible."

"Perceptive."

She laughed and shut her eyes. He stared at her feet. Her feet were faultless. Perverts would pay good money to spoil them. Thirty seconds and she opened her eyes again, face all bright.

"You're patronizing," she said.

"Maybe you shouldn't drink so much."

"I worry that I have a drinking problem."

"You know who doesn't worry if they have a drinking problem?"

"People who don't have drinking problems. See? Patronizing."

"You're right," he said. "You are perceptive."

"But not you." She readjusted herself in the seat. She said, "You really should have made a move tonight."

"What?" he said, truly startled.

She stared around the room. Outside the windows, treetops swung in the wind and made the sky seem even blacker.

"Men are so stupid," she said. "You know, I used to really like sex. You could've had me for nothing."

Then she lifted an arm, sleeve raised, and her head tilted slightly so that a piece of hair fell into her face. Part of him wanted to fling her out the door. The rest wanted to throw her on the bed. Kiss her, undress her. A strong wind tossed the screen door loudly skittering across the parking lot. Suzanne stood up. She looked around the room with fresh eyes, with abhorrence. But he wasn't fast enough to see any of it, or he didn't want to, he was already up, in action, his hand grabbed her arm, he pulled her in. She let him. She touched his sweater and let the touch linger. He kissed her. She didn't kiss back.

"This room is hideous," she said quietly, when their lips parted. She grinned and closed her eyes at the same time, like every other drunk on the planet. He lay down in bed. Every inch of his body was sedate. Every ounce of his soul still felt reckless.

"You've got a wife," she said. "Where's she hiding?"

"She's in New Jersey."

"But something's wrong. You're here. Look at you. You'd fuck me in a minute."

She got up and sat lightly on an arm of the love seat.

God, he did want to fuck her.

"The wife's screwing around, isn't she?"

"Will you please go?"

"So she is. And you don't even get to drink. It's a crock, man. Look at you, you're not even protesting.

"You look like a dad," she added.

"I've got a daughter," he said softly.

"I'll bet she's great," she said, fully sincere, almost whispering out of some kind of respect. "I'll also bet she's not the daughter. Of the current Mrs. Krug."

"You should have been a cop."

"Allow me."

"Oh, please," he said, all cold now. "Go ahead."

She lay down next to him on the bed. They stared at the ceiling. "You're retired," she said quietly, sounding not quite drunk and not quite sober. "Newly retired. So that's done. We'll call that personal truth number one. Number two, the wife is sleeping with somebody else. So something's wrong with you, is what you're thinking. And it's true. You're not the guy. Number two. But you had your career, you used to be somebody. Then there's addiction, the drinking, the recovery. That's who you are now. Then you get hooked on my son. Not for some do-gooder bullshit. You needed distraction. From your own crap. It's Martin's hour of need. That's number three. So now you're here. Second chance. Make good on all you messed up. Except, push comes to shove, what are you? My son's in jail, and the one time something gets done around here is when he tells you what to do. So look at that: in the end? You're a chauffeur. You're useless. You're the messenger."

She got up to leave and crossed the room unsteadily. She caught herself on the doorjamb just as Martin was rustling his body off the comforter. She laughed, but it sounded stricken.

"I really would've fucked you," she said. "But not the way you wanted."

From the doorway he watched her walk back to her little cabin. He was turning back when he heard her heel snap. She fell so fast, she couldn't brace herself, she smacked her face on the cement outside her

229

cabin with a crunch that turned his stomach. Nose bleeding, mouth gushing blood. The last time he'd seen blood like that, it was from her son. She was bawling. He ran and pulled her up. He ripped off his sweater to blot the wounds. She tried to stand, but couldn't put weight on the ankle. It looked like her teeth had sliced through her bottom lip.

He shoved her into the car. The motel clerk came running, said there was a hospital downtown. Suzanne wanted to see her lip in the visor mirror, she'd pulled off the hand that was supposed to be holding the dressing in place. Blood ran off her chin. He crammed her hand back against her mouth, and she howled in pain.

They made the hospital in seven minutes. Green rooms, bright lights, the smell of tea, the smell of industrial disinfectant. Empty rows of seats in the waiting area like church on a Tuesday. Nurses in scrubs came out quickly, softened by the sight of blood. He let them mistake him for her husband to cut through the bullshit. Ninety minutes later, the intern who did the stitches pronounced Suzanne Toussaint very, very lucky. Her nose wasn't broken. The ankle was merely sprained. Her teeth had cut into her lip, but not through it. There would be scarring, but less than originally thought. Martin listened, nodding, the dutiful man. Suzanne meanwhile was half-comatose, drunk, woozy with agony. Her face was swollen, brown and purple beneath the gauze. Once they were alone Martin subsided into a plastic chair beside the bed. He held her hand for a few minutes. She squeezed it, but she'd long ago closed her eyes; it was probably just a twitch. Why would she have wanted to sleep with him? He got up and darkened the overhead light. The stench of the room was acrid. He opened the sliding window. It overlooked a concrete patio, a single nurse smoking a cigarette under an orange light. He waved to her unconsciously. Did the kiss with Suzanne mean something more than just a kiss? Did it matter? Do kisses mean anything when they're not shared? He felt confused, sad, and also slightly relieved. After all, when was the last time anyone said he was fuckable?

He unrolled an egg-crate mattress that one of the nurses had left him. His knobby vertebrae compressed the slender foam. Under his breath he sang a song that he used to sing to Camille when she was little. He remembered how she'd watch him sing, how her eyes would converge tiredly on his lips. And how wonderful it felt; what peace. To know that it was him singing, more than the song itself, that was responsible for lulling her to sleep—he'd never felt so valuable in his life.

Early the next morning, Suzanne was awake when Martin opened his eyes and found her watching him anxiously over the side of the bed, her face a bandaged mess.

"How are you feeling?" he'd said groggily.

He got up slowly. It would take at least a week for his spinal cord to forgive him. He took Suzanne's hand. Her face was badly swollen, much worse bruised. Creased by her muscles' response to being battered. She squeezed his hand. He made a feeble attempt at smiling. She took up a small dry-erase board and a magic marker.

DOCTOR VISITED. NO TALKING 72 HRS. SO EMBARRASSED.

"You look like shit," he said. "That's the good news."

ASSHOLE.

She wrote something else, in smaller letters. She stared intensely at him through sudden tears when she slotted the board in his grip. *FEEL HORRIBLE ABOUT LAST NIGHT. ESP. WHAT I SAID. SUCH A BITCH. SORRY.*

"Don't worry about it," he said. "It's all behind you."

She pleaded with her eyes. Even grinned, miserably. Then she wiped away the tears, and erased the board with a little blue rag.

I NEED A DRINK

"I know. I've been there."

I'M NOT JOKING

"No drink. This is the bottom."

PLEASE

"Listen to me. It's going to be rough. It'll feel like death's door. But you're a lot stronger than you think you are."

Her eyes were angry. Flammable. She turned away with a choking sob.

He held her hand until the tears quit and her shoulders relaxed. Then he made promises to be back as soon as possible, and on his way out he informed the nurses to watch for withdrawal symptoms, to make sure she didn't try to drink the mouthwash. From the hospital he drove straight back to Claymore. Pine trees stood out razor-edged against the blue sky. There were two voicemails on his phone, one from Lillian's lawyer. As soon as the guy started, he erased the message.

The second message: "Martin. Walter Dennis. How are you. Look, I was too hasty. Was it two weeks ago? The last thing you needed was some old prick telling you that you're confused. I want you to call an old friend of mine. She's terrific, she operates a group specifically for guys our age. I already told her a little about you. Just trust me, I'm going to give you the number, call her. You don't want to go through this alone."

■

"I took off. I panicked."

"You were scared."

"I was going crazy. I thought I was going to explode."

Because he and Emily had stayed in the dark as long as possible, as long as he could take, until it was too much and he'd needed to get out of that house, off the mountain, and do something. Otherwise he couldn't live with himself.

"All right," Martin said. "You panic, you leave. Then what?"

He couldn't just do nothing. Not after listening to everything she'd said.

"I went to the Ashburns," Nick said.

"Why?"

Because his thought had been, *Must do something.* An impulse like a character in a video game, bouncing up and down, only capable of doing one single thing.

"Dr. Ashburn was cool when my leg was messed up. I just needed to talk to somebody."

"What time did this happen?"

"I got something to drink first. So, like, ten, ten-thirty."

He remembered the night like it was yesterday. He'd never felt so crazed. His head had been full of everything she'd said, he couldn't just pretend he hadn't heard anything. He caught a buzz in the Ashburns' driveway, from a fifth he had in the glove compartment, he drank like Typically was challenging him to a duel. And afterward, his whole head was light, his body relaxed. He felt better. Any problems would be overcome.

"I got sick."

What the FUCK dude FUCK.

"What kind of sick?"

"I threw up. Out the window." All down the door, like a paint-can spill. "Then I went and rang the bell."

And someone called out, *Will you get it?* The wife opened the front door in a bathrobe, all surprised. *Hey, Mrs. Ashburn.* The wife said,

Nick, what are you doing here? He said, *Is Dr. Ashburn here?* Mrs. Ashburn said, *Of course. Is it an emergency?* He said, *Do you think I could speak to Dr. Ashburn, please?* The wife allowed him by, staring oblong, pausing halfway up the stairs when the doctor came up from the basement. The doctor sized things up fast. *I'll be there in a minute,* the doctor said, and the wife went upstairs, like it was no big deal to either of them, this showing up. And that actually had made him feel a little better. They went into the study. *Nick, what's this all about?* He'd been dreading the question. He tried repeating exactly what Emily said, but he screwed it up. The doctor said he got the gist. The doctor asked about Emily, wanting to know if she was okay. But he was still trying to explain at that point how he'd needed to do something, she'd been crying, after all, and he held her, listened, kissed her, did everything the way you should—if there even *was* a way you should—with his heart drumming full speed, but still it reached a point where having that type of stuff in his head, all those images crashing into each other—and the little room in her house was dead silent—he was all nerves, grossed-out, upset, so mad. Someone needed to do something. *You're absolutely right, Nick. And we are going to do something. But for the moment I need you to calm down.*

It was then that she spoke through the door.

"That who spoke through the door?" asked the cop.

Does anyone need anything? asked the wife. *Darling, I'll be right up,* the doctor said. *No, excuse me,* the wife said, *you're going to tell me right now what's going on.* So the doctor stepped out, returned after a minute. *Mrs. Ashburn is going to bed.* At this point his memory starts to get a little blurry. Something like five minutes of questions and answers exchanged. Yes, he believed Emily and her story. No, he didn't know if she'd told anyone else. No, he'd never met somebody who'd been through this kind of thing before, and no, Emily didn't mention any other children, of course he didn't think to ask. The doorbell rang. *Who the hell is that?* The doctor went out and answered. Emily's father's voice was heard before he was even around the corner. *I don't see why that's any of your business,* the doctor was saying. *His car is right outside,* the sheriff said. Which is when two things happened. First, the doctor began to tell the sheriff something, sort of aggro, a gloss of what Emily had said. Then the sheriff knocked the doctor down, *wham,* and the doctor's head hit the floor. Blood sprayed. The sheriff drew a knife, stabbed straight into the doctor's gut while Nick watched, standing there, not doing shit, staring at the blood soaking into the doctor's shirt. Next the sheriff yanked the knife up but it was stuck in the body. More blood. Then the knife was out again, stabbed again, then wrenched up further. The sheriff grunted, as if trying to yank an axe out from a stump, and showed his teeth. The doctor hacked up globs of blood. *Where's his wife?* the sheriff hissed. At the same time, above them, a female voice called down the stairs, *Nathan?* And while Nick stood hopelessly frozen, mouth dilated, all fear, piss in his boxers, the sheriff looked around the hallway, ripped the phone off the table and wrapped the cord around his hand, then ran up the stairs two at a time.

And he still couldn't move, his body rebelled, to everlasting shame. Listening, staring. He knew that his inaction was embarrassing and cowardly, even evil, complicit in what was happening. He heard scuffling, angry sounds, a yell upstairs. Now was the time to act, and instead he pissed himself again. His bones were locked in place. The sounds quit. And then and only then could he move again, run outside by order of his stomach and dry-heave over the bushes.

He didn't remember much after that except when the sheriff came back down and hissed at him and bossed him around. The air was cold. The air was full of frog sounds. He obeyed, exactly as told. *You do this or else*, the sheriff hissed, while they moved the bodies together. Because, from that point on, his task was to bury the bodies, *not in Claymore, not even in the state*, the sheriff ordered. And make them unrecognizable first. For the faces and teeth, use a shovel. The sheriff would stay behind to clean up the scene of the crime. *This is your mess, all of this, therefore it's your head if this shit ever comes out.*

For Nick was to understand that this was now his life, one and only existence, to make sure nothing ever got out. Because if anything went crooked and he didn't take the fall, *I'll kill your mother, just like I did those two. Without a second thought.*

And from there came the drive, tequila bottle, shovel, full night spent parked in a turnout one hour west, stars upon stars, then the early-morning drive into Massachusetts, freaking out, back up to New Hampshire, into Vermont, looking for a spot to dump the bodies, random exits, turnouts, drives down empty roads but nothing was ever right, and always the fear, shaking hands, piss bottle in the cup holder, awful headache that led to a few hours' bad sleep in a shopping-mall parking lot before the panic was unleashed, a security guard who smacked on the window with his flashlight—while two bodies lay still in the back of the car—and then the resumption of driving down through New York state, the misery of sunrise, truckers maybe looking down through their windows, also the fear generally of state troopers, the plan of no plan, awful freak-out around Emily and what might happen, until eventually his mind began to brown out and the drive became more flat and narrow, the direction of no direction and endless road, the guidance of tequila, traffic, sports radio on AM stations, musical lulls, and the time he fell asleep at the wheel, another freak-out, the Snickers bars, the slow drive through Connecticut, the refusal to stop until he needed gas, and the crossing of bridges, the thought of his mom, who'd be better off without him, tequila and his father, who arrived to escort him into the brake-light nightmare that was driving into New York City, unavoidable somehow, that he was forced by a sudden shift of highways into entering and got stuck in a slave anarchy of crosswalks, aggressive tension, traffic lights, the massive girth of buses, delivery trucks, angry cyclists, dazed office workers, pretzel carts being rolled into the street, hostile taxis honking and a hundred police cars every block and what sounded like five million people hungry for blood, at which point the despair became anger, became regret and fear and then more fear, more panic while stuck, until finally a soundless moment when the plan for Mexico became manifest, holy deliverance—he saw him and Emily follow the white beach around its arc, toward an orange sun, and she took his hand and slid hers inside, and the Pacific beckoned, and they'd never need to see anyone ever again and they didn't care— while he worked it out frantically on his phone, buried in standstill gridlock in a tunnel, and from those calculations came hope, drink, a smile, then the gray swamps of New Jersey appeared, to be endured, the smokestacks of New Jersey were there to be endured, and finally it became one long plow south—Mexico—amid gloomy night, rain clouds, total anguish, exhaustion, condition: hopeless, the fear that deformed to include not even his dad to keep him company but relentless remorse, blame in the rainy windshield, blame for his disgrace, with nobody inside the blame but him and a shovel, and in the panic that was dark and raw Nick realized his only company was a neon cowgirl with a mechanically swinging skirt, and finally, *finally*, in the outfield of his ultimate desperation, he had those six or seven seconds of letting go. Beyond power, beyond help, before the blazing crash, he could at last relax and slip down below the steering wheel, beneath the oncoming steel wave that would obliterate him, while everything thankfully came to an end.

•

It had been a long two days. The eventful journey with the kid's mom, the game-changing morning with her son. Only then, with the kid's confession revised, did Martin realize how tired he was. Outdoors, he took a bench on the old town square and held his head in two hands. Conceded to himself that he didn't truly know fact one about the criminal mind. And then he got out his phone to call Brenner and promptly activate any and all legal and procedural machinery available to their powers, now that he had Nick's revised testimony in hand.

Within an hour many phones rang. Emails skyrocketed. He met with Brenner. "God. Oh, god," she said, when he played her his recording of Nick's new version of events. The Tape of Revelation. She looked hard at the recorder while she listened. When it stopped, she stood up and stared at the wall, and asked three questions quietly.

First, if Nick wasn't out to deceive them again, how skeptical should they be?

Second, what causes might he possess to lie this time, and how could they work around them, build an argument for his innocence anyway?

Finally, and here she looked away from the window, straight into Martin's eyes, how'd the sheriff know to show up at the doctor's house?

But never mind for the moment, there was work to do: meetings to call at the Public Defender's Office, with Brenner's staff brainstorming next steps. Because justice was war, and humans love war. To the point that, in different offices that week, Martin's face reddened to purple as they shocked the wits out of clerks and officials. Who at first were disinclined to listen, who wore the same grave pride as their ancestors while attending a public hanging, but then gradually they acquired a different take.

First charge: a special plea to the prosecution. Brenner led the crusade, she even threw together a PowerPoint, outlining to the other side of the law—a crag-faced woman wearing an olive-green skirt suit and hose—exactly what Nick's new story said and why it should free him, how it fit the known evidence in ways, far more convincing ways than the prosecution had considered.

And when the prosecutor said, twenty-five minutes later, with a hint of wry reluctance, that the case still looked in her eyes to hang between an unreliable teenager's statement—a story he'd changed, she pointed out, for reasons unknown, maybe because he'd had time to consider the price of his actions?—and an officer of the law who also happened to be an elected public official—that's when Martin revealed their trump.

They'd found a cheap tracking beacon installed in Nick's Ford Explorer.

And they were one hundred percent certain, Brenner added softly, that a solid link would be established showing that the device had been put there by the sheriff, without a warrant, connected to software to be found on his department-issue laptop.

The previous evening, Martin had gone online, read installation manuals, then gotten a garage in the morning to throw the kid's truck up on a lift so he could take a look. And when he spotted and detached the damn thing, the thrill of satisfaction was one he hadn't felt in months. Strong enough so he could jettison every other theory he'd had about the case.

The prosecutor asked Martin to leave the room.

Brenner found him in the parking lot twenty minutes later, eating sunflower seeds.

"The good news is they're going to move on this fast," she said, more excited than he'd seen her before. "Obviously it'd be idiotic to go after the sheriff directly right now, though who knows, to be honest; people can be weird. They need to do two things: verify the story, then get as much info on the night, to fill in new unknowns. If it were up to me, I'd pull some kind of ruse inventory. Yank a ton of stuff so it doesn't look weird to grab his laptop, then see if they can make the tracking connection. If it works, that's huge. And if he's dumb enough to make that mistake, you look around his browsing history, for any image folders tucked away. I mean, just because the daughter got left alone, doesn't mean he lost desire for fucked-up shit. I don't know. Different direction, you get a court order under seal, grab all the info on his phone, see what adds up there. Or, what else?"

She took the sunflower seeds and poured herself a handful.

"I wouldn't be surprised if they don't want Nick released," she said, chewing. "They'll want to talk to Emily, any witnesses who won't ex-pose the investigation. So maybe they use him, wire him up, see if in private she'll corroborate."

"Do you think she's up to it?"

"That's the least of my concerns. I've got to file a detailed motion in the morning, I want to get bail reconsidered. We put down a big list of factors, see who else will put their names on the bond. From where I sit, it's actually got a decent shot at working."

"But if Nick's free," Martin said cautiously, "what about the mother's safety?"

"Ninety percent of the time, a prosecutor just goes direct. Full con-frontation. I mean, it'd be stupid, in my opinion, seeing how our guy is law enforcement. But like I said, you never know. I mean, look at the type of shit he thought he'd get away with."

Brenner smirked at the sky. Gray clouds, glossy sunlight cracking through. She said quietly, "Are we missing something? Are we being stupid?"

"I really hope not."

"Again, how come he knew to knock on the doctor's door?"

"Because of the beacon. The trace on the kid's car."

"That's just the means, that's the how. The 'why' wants to know, why would Portis intuit that the doctor's house wasn't just a routine visit? Where did his suspicion come from? How'd he know that Nick had gone there with the dirty?"

Martin stared at the ground. Agitated again. Haphazard again.

Brenner clenched his arm. "Let's be thankful for what we've got," she said. "Martin, I don't know everything you did, but this is a good day in the neighborhood."

They both smiled coldly, nodding like windup toys. In no part relieved of their apprehension.

∙

Day three of the Revelation, they caught an extremely lucky break: the Ashburns' neighbor made contact. The redhead had kept Martin's num-ber, she said she remembered that she'd seen a police car that night parked outside the Ashburns' house. But the weird thing wasn't that it was a patrol car—it was that the car was there two hours before the crime took place, supposedly, based on what she'd heard. And then the car was still there hours later. So why was it parked right outside the whole time?

They arrested the sheriff that afternoon. Martin made sure to be in the parking lot. The sheriff came out with officers on either side. No restraints, nothing visibly different about him. Hat in hand, hair brushed high, a stiff, pained gait, like he was walking on bunions. If the sheriff saw ex-Chief Krug on the sidewalk, he gave no reaction. But Martin didn't need a reaction.

Each night that week his duties included a drive up to Maine to hold Suzanne's hand, before he'd drive back to Claymore late. He helped her cry. He helped her stomach the emptiness of a life without booze. He found out she liked cheap drugstore lipstick, he'd bring her kitschy colors to try on in the mirror. He fed her progress on the case to give her something to think about, something to celebrate. Though not yet the truth about the sheriff's threat.

First thing Suzanne took to doing, whenever Martin walked in, was to compliment him on that evening's clothes. "You practically look local," she said the first time. And it was true. He'd gotten tired of asking his innkeepers to run his single load of laundry. So he'd gone to a shop in town, purchased new clothes, new walking shoes, a jacket made for fishing pressed on him by the saleswoman. It wasn't exactly Zegna, but everything fit.

The last commute to Maine, he retrieved Suzanne from the hospital. The sky was an orange and purple dome, trees along the highway were darkly green. Suzanne met him in the outpatient lobby, under an icy glare of blue lights. Her bruises had faded to yellows and browns. But with her bags, on her way out, she looked lost, fragile. Her blue jeans looked awkwardly too big. The first twenty minutes of the drive, he tried to be helpful. Talked about her son's case, asked how he could continue to be of help, if she had someone who could stay with her. He scanned the horizon for more to say but came up short. Suzanne was silent and watchful. She sat shotgun this time, leaned away from him, smoked out the window. She had on a thick wool cardigan she'd asked Martin to bring to her on a previous visit. He'd found it, as instructed, upstairs in the old house, in a closet. He'd been amazed by her and Nick's home, once he was further inside—so presentable and highborn in the living room, then one grim room after another, of disuse and mildew, silence and old age.

"I spoke to Nicky on the phone," she said, and brushed hair away from her face. "He says you got the asshole."

"We did."

"When were you going to tell me?"

"Tonight."

"So that means Nick's free to go?"

"Unfortunately not," Martin said. "For now Nick's still an accessory."

"That man threatened to kill me. Nicky told me."

Martin didn't say anything. It was now in the air, the fact that he hadn't told her. But she'd already moved on, more heated: "So why not? He didn't do it."

"It's complicated."

She laughed, quieter and quieter. "You think I've got a big hole in my head."

"We barely know who you are," Suzanne added a second later, more coldly. "But all of a sudden you're my son's confidant, you're my keeper. You're just our great white hope, aren't you?"

"All I want to do is get you back to town and take you to a meeting."

They'd discussed AA during his previous visits. Not to positive ends. Not once had they talked about their kiss in the motel.

"Fuck off with that crap."

"I'm telling you," he said, "you can do this."

"And I'm telling you to take your psychobabble shit and shove it."

He rolled down his window to clear the air. "That's bullshit actually," he said. She didn't take the bait. She smoked the rest of the drive, smoked as he watched her walk up the weathered steps to her old house under the dark green, giant trees.

Brenner telephoned an hour later with news. Nick's bail had been set, one hundred thousand dollars, ten percent down. More chains had been rattled, rattled harder. She was excited and proud. It was a win. Though ten thousand dollars wasn't the kind of money, Martin knew, that Nick had tucked away, or Suzanne for that matter.

Without a second thought, still on the phone, he thought about how he could withdraw that much at an ATM if needed.

■

The afternoon that Nick is released from jail, Martin lies on the floor of his hotel room, back massaged by tennis balls, shoes kicked to the corner. Job competently done, mission sufficiently accomplished, and now comes whatever's next—comes divorce, again, the need to split up old photographs, divide the furniture, find someone new to lie with at night. Isn't that how it works? So maybe, instead of running home, he should stay in New Hampshire a little while longer. Enjoy the beach. Eat healthy. He realizes he is powerfully hungry. He orders dinner over the phone, a feast: eggplant Parmesan, French fries, two slices of strawberry pie, a large Coke.

As soon as he puts down the phone, Brenner's question comes right back to bug him: Why did the sheriff visit the doctor's house that night?

Half an hour later, Demeke knocks on the door. The blond hair is gone, his head's freshly shaved, there's a red tint to what remains. Otherwise the same kid, weathered T-shirt, jeans.

"You changed your hair."

"You changed your order."

Demeke stares at the food as he sets down the tray. "This is a lot of saturated fat for a guy your age."

"What age is that?"

"Dude, you watch *Jeopardy!*"

In fact, they'd done this several times in the past three weeks, he and Demeke, watched *Jeopardy!* together. With Alex Trebek and his missing mustache. Martin would eat dinner while Demeke called out answers, sneakers scuffed and dirty, long legs hugged by his shrink-wrapped jeans, watchful and lethargic in the way of teenage boys.

Martin tucks into his food. "So what's new?"

"I hate my life," Demeke says.

"That sounds dumb."

The kid stretches his arms and folds back his fingers.

"I met someone," Demeke says. "He's a total jerk."

"You went on a date?"

"What?" The kid laughs, sniffs, and wipes his nose. "No. Forget it."

"How was he a jerk?"

"He hoped I was lighter-skinned. He said this, like, right after we hooked up."

"Sounds like an asshole."

"Exactly."

"Did you use protection?"

"Oh, wow." Demeke laughs, adds darkly, "There is no protection against assholes."

"I'll tell you what," says Martin. "I don't think I could handle being gay."

The kid sits up straight. "Who said I was gay?"

"What?"

"I didn't say I was gay."

"But this was a guy you were with."

"So?"

Martin stares at the television, completely confused. Like the pool he's been swimming around in turns out to be twice as big as he thought.

"Demeke, I apologize if I got it wrong, I didn't realize—"

The kid yawns and stretches his arm. There's a long silence, as if to give Martin time to recover from his gaffe. Which is fine by him.

"So I've been meaning to ask you," he says, still a little unsure where they stand. "What you're going to do next."

"Smoke weed. If you mean tonight."

"This fall. Are you going to college?"

The kid exhales loudly.

"I have an internship. In October. At a music production company in Boston. I'm taking a year off. My parents are so pissed."

"You should go to college."

"Yeah, thanks, I know."

He looks Demeke in the eye, doubtfully. The kid holds it openly, unafraid. And with the height, the hands, the knock knees, and despite the skin color, the sexuality, whatever he is, Martin is reminded of himself.

"Tell me something," he says. "How involved do you want your parents?"

"In what, my life?"

"Exactly."

"Like, not at all."

"You don't mean that."

"I mean, I don't know."

"If they weren't involved for a while, you'd be okay with that."

The kid laughs. "That's like my dream scenario."

"Because they're adults, they've got their own lives."

242

"Exactly. They've got shit to deal with. Let me handle my own."

"So in this scenario you're not angry. Or insulted. That what they need to do is more important to them than you. I just don't buy that, respectfully," he says. "You'd be upset. You'd feel rejected."

"Respectfully, I disagree," the kid says. "The sooner they leave me alone, the better."

"I don't think so," Martin says, laughing. But the laughter tears open a bit. Bleakness inside. Anger, cold fire. Commercial break. He uses the bathroom. The piss that dribbles out looks like juice from a gray lemon. What is he doing? He never would have believed it two months ago. He'd already called the bank, arranged the money for Nick's bail, to pay anonymously. Yet it only occurs to him now, with a sudden gobsmack—idiot of idiots—that the same amount of money, even half of it, could have gone to his daughter, for something she'd desired him to participate in. He hadn't put two and two together.

He comes back, sits heavily down on the bed and feels all of his years, and says angrily, "You need to go. I have to make a call."

"Whatever."

The kid clumsily grabs the tray, makes to leave, face vacant.

"So what do you want, huh? You want to forget about your parents? All they do is pay the rent, right?"

"Dude, you need to chill."

"I'm being serious. What do you want, Demeke?"

"Jesus, I'm so gone."

"You think you're so cool. I'll tell you something, it's a front. I've seen tough. That's not you. You're just ungrateful."

"Well why don't you go fuck yourself."

"Great. I'll do that."

The kid shifts away, tray in hand, then pauses, turning back, vividly eighteen, shell slipped and with an individuality, Martin sees, that he never had at that age, at any age.

"Like a year ago, there was this family staying, right? It was snowing out, a whiteout, we're all stuck. So we're playing this game. You pick a piece of paper out of a hat. You're trying to get your team to guess the clue. So it's the daughter's turn. She's like the little bunny rabbit they take care of. Except her brother's making fun of her, saying how stupid she is. And she can't get it, whatever's on the paper. She's pissed, so she points at me. 'Where he comes from.' As her clue. Now everyone's, like,

243

oh shit. All freaked out. So the girl's dad is like, you know, 'Oh, god, not Africa.' And then the mom's like, 'Baby, Africa's a continent. Do you mean Nigeria?' Then the brother says, all pissed, 'Mom, they said he's from Kenya.' You know, bless him. But the girl, she's clueless, she's flipping around the piece of paper. 'I meant from gorillas,' she says. 'It says gorilla.' And it does. 'Gorilla.' At which point, you know, we're all like, wow. She's totally sincere. And I'm the dumbest. I mean, I took AP Bio, everybody comes from monkeys, the girl's on point, even if the point's not the one she's trying—whatever. They're embarrassed. This isn't Tamir Rice or some shit. But my dad, he's so angry. Like he's going to kick them out. But he didn't yell. He came to my room later. We just hung out. We talked. I mean, I haven't made it easy on him. But you hear what I'm saying? So don't talk to me like I'm some little piece of shit. Because that shit's on you."

·

Nick's been out of jail for two days, they've had utter paradise for two days, when Alex explains the complete truth of her treachery, after Emily returns her phone call—because in her voicemail Alex was so overcome with hiccupping apology that she barely could make herself understood, through sobbing, to the best friend and soul sister whom she had so utterly betrayed, had never understood, who contained inside her this terrible history all along that Alex had never even detected—that on top of stoner dickface Jersey Mike seeing the pics, Emily's photographs, on Meg's laptop, as they all knew, it appeared that he'd gone back to them a few days later while Alex was taking a shower, and, being a complete and utterly heartless sex-crime-committing scumbag, whom Alex will never speak to again outside of the voodoo curses she plans to inscribe in her own blood on the backs of shaved rats before she jam-packs them up his asshole, Jersey Mike then decided to log into his email, attach some JPEGs off Meg's hard drive, and send them to a chick named Corrinne, a friend of his, a senior girl from school and a mighty Zeta, and everything *might* have stopped there, Alex points out mournfully, because Corrinne is actually a decent human being, at least an easily frightened one—she'd later told Alex that she texted Mike along the lines of *What are you doing you creep,* and *You know this is illegal,* but before Mike read her reply, he'd already emailed two shitheads on the hockey team, who emailed other shitheads on the hockey team, who emailed their shitty friends, and soon several of them were loading the files into digital vaults, posting images elsewhere, and now those images were everywhere, potentially, all of which completed a most heinous act of betrayal, that Alex had set in motion, that Alex is responsible for and will regret hugely forever, for which she'll never forgive herself.

Alex gathers her breath, but Emily hangs up before she can say another word.

She feels sick, flattened, and full of hate.

Nick vows he'll murder the kid that night.

■

Five days later, on the same day that Leela and Justin confront Emily Portis in the Claymore Denny's about nude photographs that have appeared online, the same day that, later on, Justin Johnson departs New Hampshire for New York City, with his story complete on his laptop but not yet published online, not yet news in its own right, Leela Mann does not sleep well in her roost.

All night long there are weird noises around the house. Waves of sulfur smells that punch through the window screen, source unknown, and wake her up and turn her stomach. In the morning she stares at her blotchy face in the bathroom mirror. She pinches her cheeks. Her face is doughy, bruised from not sleeping, weirdly yellow in spots. Who is she? What is she? There's no way she can do this job. Why should the Portis girl ever talk to her again? Definitely not for her credentials. A few articles, a shitty start to a shitty novel. What if Emily thought to look her up online? Even in the virtual world, she's basically profile-less, with few followers, no channel of her own, no wallpaper to say: *This is me.*

On a typical post, for pictures of his snowboard, Satnam got double the likes she'd ever received.

And still her ego demands greatness; it'll even stand for mediocrity. Anything but an unfurnished-rental suicide.

Somewhere nearby, within twenty miles of that room, her poor parents wake to yet another day of an uncertain future. And still don't know that their only daughter is staying nearby. Back in New York, two of her roommates always complained that they couldn't escape their families, that they weren't being allowed to grow up. She wrote an article around it, quoted both of them. And in the same story wrote about those sad young adults her age who were forced by economic reasons to move home, nestle back down in the pillowy parental bosom.

And then there was Leela Mann, who only wanted family at her own convenience, like a microwaved burrito.

The sun outside is a heat lamp. She drives not to the Claymore Starbucks, but to a shopping-center Dunkin' Donuts in Merrimack. At a corner table she sets up her laptop, phone, notebook. French leather jacket draped on the back of her chair, if only to feel officially in step with old rituals. Still feeling fearful, clueless, more than a thousand times a little unsure of herself. Which somehow enables her to text the girl.

> Hi this is Leela. Just wanted to say again I'm so sorry about Denny's. That guy Justin is a total jerk. I'm here to talk if you ever want. Apology face, flower, sunshine.

Then she revisits the plan she typed up the night before, after wasting a long hour looking up stuff with her phone, like, *How do you report a big story*, and *How to be a journalist*, and *What am I doing*. But she does have a plan. At least half of one, to confirm her journalism degree. First off, to visit CHS, her old school. Look through old yearbooks that she knows are stored in the library's stacks, to see if she can figure out more of the girl's social circles, find some friends online or in the phone book to interview. Hopefully by that time she'll have heard back from Emily and can further befriend her—and not, Leela confirms in her gut, just for the story. She actually likes the girl. Admires her strength, her rawness.

After that, she'll attempt to track down those photos Justin mentioned, of which so far she hasn't seen a trace, even within the CHS friend groups she's infiltrated online. Also find out if she can pester a stray teacher or school official into an interview. Mr. Fockers, her old calc teacher, maybe he taught Emily, too? Finally, for shoe leather's sake, as one of her college professors used to put it, she'll take a walk in the afternoon by the beach and look for teenagers to bother. Maybe even visit Whitehall, see if anyone young still hangs out up there.

For the moment, though, she nurses an immense coffee and stares at the laptop screen in a daze. It's the moment of transition, the step into the hologram. Whereby the slow motions of imagining herself as the writer she is not quite yet prepare her to open the proper files, type the proper keys. And at the same time, in the background—command-tab, command-R—she refreshes *DROP*'s website every minute, in case Justin's story should appear.

A voice says, "Can I get you a refill?"

An employee looms over her, materialized into place. Leela laughs. Dunkin' Donuts has table service now? "No thanks, I'm good." She strains to see his face, the guy's so tall.

"Holy shit," the guy says. "Leela?"

She jolts awake.

"Robbie," she says. Robbie Miller? "Hey."

He laughs. "It's Rob now. Holy crap, this is amazing. What are you doing here? I thought you were in New York?"

The fact that Robbie/Rob Miller not only remembers her name, but also attaches enough significance to her identity that he knows something of her life, post-CHS, what does it mean?

She says, lightly laughing, "I was. I mean, I am."

"Let me get you a refill, hold on."

He's back a minute later with another coffee.

"Seriously, what the hell are you doing here?"

"I'm here for work. How are you?"

"I heard you're a journalist. That's really cool."

"Thanks," she says, feeling weirdly nervous. The same way she would have been if Robbie had complimented her when she was seventeen. Mortifying! "So you work here?"

"My parents own the franchise. I'm taking classes at UNH. So who are you a journalist for?"

"*The Village Voice*. Most recently."

"And you're here about the murders?"

"You've heard about them?"

"Are you kidding?"

He laughs, looks at his shoes, stuffs his hands in his pockets. Hands that once strummed acoustic guitar onstage during talent shows. *Robbie Miller is nervous around me.* She sat behind him in English class, two years in a row. He used to write poems in her mind.

"You know, if it helps, my mom knows somebody," he says offhandedly, "who knows the kid's mother or something. She says he did it for the money."

247

"No kidding?"

"I can put you in touch with her, if that would help."

"That could be great."

"Hey, I don't know what you're doing, but I'm having people over on Friday. Do you want to come? You could make some connections, maybe someone can help you out with your story."

She laughs, but he's serious.

"I'd love that. That would be fun."

"Rad," he says, grinning. "I'll shoot you the address. You don't surf, do you?"

Robbie Miller surfs, of course he does.

"I don't, actually."

"No worries. Anyway, I'll let you get back to it."

He smiles and walks away, to help a pair of teenage girls who've just appeared at the counter, girls who probably know leggings aren't really pants but don't care, and why should they, with such bodies? Those white bodies that fill out in all the right ways? They look just like the girls she remembers from CHS, the Zetas, bodies that hers never resembled.

But are they invited to Rob's place to hang out?

If they knew she'd been invited, would they be jealous?

She hits refresh on her browser and puts on a stern frown to appear more serious, to conceal a smile. But now the *DROP* site has a new headline, "The Claymore Kids." And below the massive typeface and Justin Johnson's byline is a large, semi-blurred photograph of Emily Portis posing on a bed, innocent but sultry, mostly nude.

▪

OK so this will be the longest series of
texts I've sent in my life and it may ruin
my fingers but if so I deserve it because
EMILY I WAS SOOOOOOO WRONG

So stupid and so sorry I was totally
wrong please forgive me and take me
back and in the meantime I'll be over
here breathing deeply because I would
call you again and say all this over the

phone or just come over and say it to
your face but I'm worried you hate me
enough and I don't blame you at all and
fuck me forever literally FOREVER but
hopefully I can put into words all my
regret and you'll hate your so-called best
friend a little less

Basically I'm a self centered bitch and
you were so much completely in the
right. What I'm trying to say is I really
screwed up and I'm so sorry

Tonight I was taking a bathroom selfie
and then it all started to click. I swear
this will make sense but basically I
figured out that girls taking pics of
themselves? Are probably the BEST
thing that's come out of the internet.
Because how hard is it to be girls IRL
right when in actuality I hate my face
body hair THE BIRTHMARK clothes
everything But so does Meg and all her
friends that's just the way it goes. You
are what you eat and you're as good as
you're judged by somebody else
somebody who probably can get you
pregnant and then that's the way society
is going to be anyway BECAUSE
PENIS so grab your friends and vagina
blab etc FML crawl back into the
buttcrack of self hate. But actually I feel
kinda awesome taking photos of myself
and so what? At least I did. And it's not
like the whole world is my costar or that
bullshit but it makes me feel good about
myself and I feel confident, glittery eye
shadow and all and isn't that sort of cool

to feel good about myself and how I look
ANYWAYYYYYYYYY

But listen the point is YOU taught me
that. Even if I wasn't being a good
listener friend eventually it sank in and I
had to calm the hell down. Because this
isn't about me for once it's YOU Emily
my best friend in the whole universe the
most amazing strongest biggest
superhero survivor and I want to shout
out the window right now that you were
right!!!!!!!!!!

And no matter what happened those
pictures you took were basically pro level

GOD GIRL I admire you and love you
so much YASSSSSSS I want to put you
on the front of my car like a Mercedes
emblem. So fuck them fuck them ALL
and I'm so sorry I was part of Them for
a while. I can't take back what
happened but believe me I would
especially after what that shit prick
dickface has done

What I've done is not how a good friend
should treat you. Or any friend. You are
a warrior goddess, you deserve to be
happy and I want to be part of your
happy even though I don't deserve to be
but I'm on your side no matter what.
Really I love you so much and think
you're incredibly brave so does Meg and
if you'll have me back I will love you no
judgy and will do anything to help you
get through all this crap

Woman, I love you, and I am really
really sorry and I really want to be your
best friend again because you are my
one true love

∎

*Less than an hour's drive north of Boston, a New Hampshire fishing village
that was settled in 1671 has lately found itself, for all intents and purposes,
rocked 21st-century-style by the same forces of bloodshed, blackmail, and
incest that once spellbound the audiences of Euripides.*

*And in this tragedy, the following facts are not up for dispute. That there
are two persons dead, Dr. Nathan Ashburn, 69, and his wife, Violet Ashburn, 64, hailing from Claymore, NH, the village in question. The Ashburns, both native to town, were married for thirty-nine years. They loved
New Hampshire. They loved golf. They leave behind a daughter who grieves.
"Get out of my face," she told a reporter recently, from behind her front door.*

*Another fact: The deaths of the Ashburns were not accidents. Another:
The Ashburn home, surrounded by old trees in a modern cul-de-sac, is
now a macabre crime scene. And from the scene extends a ghost trail
south of rash, Anthropocene madness, which leads us to more facts, like the
one that a wild, freewheeling escape from the state was made this past
June by a young man driving a 1997 black Ford Explorer down I-95, fueled by Jose Cuervo, and during that drive the Ashburns' bodies were
transported via said Explorer across multiple state lines, over the course of
48-plus hours on cheap agave fumes; and what happens in said time, two-
plus days, is something that no one can detail to any satisfaction, regarding
why a young man would get drunk and gallivant around the byways of
New England with two corpses in his trunk.*

*Further fact: The young man in question crashed his SUV into a
12-foot-tall metal boot worn by a 107-foot cowgirl statue, a neon land-
mark on the New Jersey shore in the ocean-facing town of Eagle Mount—
which is kind of tangential, admittedly, but also sufficiently Jersey-weird
enough to include here.*

*But as to why the Ashburns' bodies washed up in New Jersey, six hours
south of Claymore, no one is entirely sure, and this is no less messed-up for
additionally being true . . .*

And after twelve thousand more words of Justin Johnson's uncontrolled
rococo prose, in which he repeatedly refers to Nick and Emily as

"the Claymore Kids," where even his egotism blushes purple, where any jargon box to do with "going viral" is checked in sentences that are illogically arranged yet nonetheless stocked with moralisms, psychologisms, and unveiled *Scarlet Letter* references, all the while exuding what a girlfriend of Leela's back at *The Village Voice* once characterized in a post as "the cologne-ad shitposting of the modern bro reporter"—and that's *not* to mention the article's inclusion of several photos of Emily Portis, as good as naked, that span the browser window, fuzzed and black-barred just enough to be safe for work but still plenty relatable and unambiguous—from there Leela switches over to Facebook, and voilà, it's Justin, available, green-lit to chat.

hey i just read it

> wow fast yeah went up 30 mins ago, so
> what'd you think?

I think you nailed every buzzword first
of all

> lmao

who decided to include the photos????

> lol why

wait WHAT

> why do you think

they weren't public

> uh-huh

not to the world they weren't

> DROP isn't the world despite what you
> hear

don't bullshit you know exactly what i
mean

        hold on brb

this will ruin her life

        sorry, phoner, gotta go in a sec. so what
        now?

JUSTIN

        yo! chill. melodramatic much? it's not
        like we slut-shamed her or whatever.

omg fUCK off

        1. news, 2. business, 3. grow up

not like this

        it's not like we shot the photos, you get
        that right? did you not pick up on any of
        the themes? i.e. tech-age irony of a girl
        who upskirts herself? of a victim of
        child abuse sending sexts? . . . thus illo
        is somewhat necessary, yeah?

no it's not. and give me a break please.
"themes"

        "Not exactly sext so much as
        anti-sext, or super-sext. Considered,
        cooled, even ironically inventive,
        ergo postmodern—an incredibly
        specific comment on these reductive
        times. Perhaps the girl's photos
        point a way forward, can gaslight the

American public's sex shame to change
the culture. So, if not the new phone
sex, perhaps such photos will be a balm
to revenge porn, even become the new
lover's note."

u really just quoted yourself
it's not like you were all that subtle

well maybe b/c the story's not about
child pornography it's about the fact
that sexting's not going away and no one
really wants it to, it's about the fact that
it's **the children who are the new
pornographers** now tell me that's not
a killer hook

what about legal

what about legal?
all vetted, no identifiers, first
amendment, news value, et al

but you don't own them

read the fine print

but still

look pls chill im out of nicorette

just saying

WHAT exactly

you want me to spell it out??

y pls

well inasmuch as you refrain from
saying this openly in the piece but
anyone who knows what the word
"infer" means will read between the
lines the pretty obvious fact that you
think the girl took those photos herself
and shared them at the same time that
her father was getting arrested and for
her this is some kind of Machiavellian
weirdo backwoods baller feminist power
move out of revenge for being locked
away with her rapist dad for all those
years AND OTHER RELATED
RIDICULOUS SHIT

        so you did read the article ;)

dude DID you get her permission or not

        look call me later when you've processed

you mean after my period

        lol

whatever i can't. bye forever.

        do yourself a favor, get over yourself

        leela did you at least like the story? i
        thought the "Katniss Prynne" thing was
        pretty sweet.

        allo leela?

        hey what's up?

        hey so did you like the piece?

One photo shows Emily smiling coyly, seated on a wooden floor, with up-tugged skirt and bare ass, while she playfully holds up her voluminous hair.

One finds her in dark stockings, squeezing her tits together, with the tip of her little pink tongue resting against her upper lip.

One picture has Emily pressing her pale breasts together again, between her arms, but this time with face and mouth alluring, eyelashes dark with mascara, knees spread, butt thrust backward.

One has her right arm held up, right hand tucked behind her head, other hand covering the right nipple, which has been lifted aloft by the raised arm, and her face is indifferent, but not closed, legs encased again in stockings but this time with her vagina and pubic hair shown, full familiar.

There's one that Justin singled out in his story, where Emily's smiling again, this time wearing a large headdress, with a loose feather seeming put to good use between her legs.

And still there are more of them, a succession, of different poses and looks, and all of them, Leela thinks, are on the whole pretty vanilla, even tasteful, softly erotic, and not much of a shock these days. They're definitely not pornography. But her own cheeks flush just looking at them, all trembling with an intimacy for precisely and only one other person—an excitement and tenderness it would be unfair to say that a sixteen-year-old can't feel, she thinks.

Clearly none of them are meant to be seen by her or anyone else.

But Justin didn't pick up on any of that.

Her face flushes again. Not just from the photos. Her heart sags, full of genuine sadness, fiery indignation. The start of big outrage. She can barely stand to have her own picture taken—how would she feel if similar images of her were in the public eye?

The amount of information that Justin had held back from her at lunch is beyond infuriating. If only because it makes her ignorance seem that much more noxious.

Leela shuts her laptop loudly in the Dunkin' Donuts. She's nervous. She's *mad*. She gathers her jacket and things and doesn't care if Rob Miller notices her rushing out with hurried steps, going to the parking lot without a word of goodbye, exiting into the sun-blown noon.

There's so much she hasn't done. So much she needs to do.

Her first thought is of the girl.

Hey dad. Got your message. First off thank you for the generous offer but Roger and I are going to pass at this stage. Not because it is too late or anything and not because the production can't use the money. In fact it definitely can but I'm still going to say no. The fact is that it looks like Roger and I are going to go our separate ways. He is just not dependable in ways I need and I am probably too dependent on him. Same old story, I get jealous and clingy, I already see me doing it. Know thyself, and I really don't like that about myself. And guess what, surprise, he drinks. But anyway I'm grateful that you reached out. Because it forced some important thinking on my part about what is true and what is false and I have reached a decision that I should have reached a long time ago but I really need you to hear it now. I want you to please stop sending me any further checks or financial support. I know that sounds weird and honestly it's been a huge help all these years and I'm grateful but I would like to move on. In a new direction. Also please do not call and do not respond to this text regarding this or anything else for the moment. I know that you care about me in your way, I really do, but please try to understand where I am coming from. I'm finally getting to a good place. It was bad for a while in ways you and mom don't know about and don't want to know about trust me but I don't want to go in any direction but forward from here on out. And to do that I need space around me. Empty space. For a long time that's what I absolutely didn't want. The truth is your absence when I was growing up is hardwired into my brain when I think about myself because yes you provided for us financially but you did not provide what I needed most. So I need you to stop providing for me now. I hope that makes sense. I am seeing a new therapist and she's really helping me make progress, she helps me understand a lot of my issues in a whole new light. She says I can't always expect to make my environment reflect what I need. I can't make people into what I need them to be. For example she pointed out that you did love me in a way but you had a disease, you have a disease, and it is the disease that got in the way of your love. I mean some Al-Anon groups I've been in there were kids

257

who were beaten, abandoned, they got kicked out, their parents died, they lost everything. So in a weird way I know I'm lucky. All you did was fall down on your face once in a while. But that's only when you were there for me to see you fall down. You weren't there. And I thought that was my fault, I thought you hated me, I wasn't good enough to deserve attention. Basically I learned that the truth was that I was unlovable, that I was in the way of you and mom ever being happy again. I know now it wasn't my fault. But that's what I thought for a long time. Now all of that's in the past. It must seem completely alien to you that I am putting all of this into a text message but believe me it's not a generational thing I really just don't have the strength to say any of this out loud, so please respect that and don't answer this message or call me. I don't know why I've been quiet for so long probably self-blame low self-esteem etc. but now I'm talking, it just needs to be via text. Dad, I release you from being active in my life. We have built a relationship in the past couple years that is thanks to your efforts, I recognize that and respect that, and you deserve credit. But I don't want pleasant I don't want polite. Most of all I want to be in control, I want to stop letting other people dictate the terms. Not that you do that completely but just trust me it's all part of the same problem. I'm not saying never and I'm not saying forever but I know in my heart it's right for now. I love you and thank you. But goodbye.

∎

Claymore meets August's record temperatures with a wide, gap-toothed smile. The month will be the hottest on record in New England since 1880, as media crews arrive with their luggage and production cases from New York and Los Angeles, from London and Berlin, and find themselves cooked on the Logan tarmac.

They're also swiftly aggravated when the county's hotels reach capacity. Rooms were long ago booked by motorcycle tourists, in town for a rally, and reporters find themselves pushed to rooms in towns like York and Shalks, as far away as North Berwick. Which doesn't stop the producers from bullying Claymore's front-desk clerks.

Radio journalists, normally genteel, lose their tempers. Some journalists, of a certain era, after years of rumbling across the battlefields of political primaries with expense accounts, turn especially crabby from being shoveled so far away from the story, sixty to ninety minutes in some cases, depending on traffic, depending on the bikers, and they end up demanding replacements.

All told, within a week of Justin Johnson's *DROP* article, the media number almost forty. News trucks, reporters, producers, silver-fox photographers, radio rookies with headphones around their necks. All looking for a story that their bosses heard about and want a piece of for themselves, whatever nibs may be found around the woods, the beaches, the suburban developments. Really anything new to do with "the Claymore Kids," those believed-to-be star-crossed teens, eyes aflame with young love, or what some are calling a mockery of love, a travesty of penitence, considering the dead bodies lying at their feet. And ultimately it won't cost their bosses much; the story will be hot for a week or two and they need something to fill the slots. The most important thing is, get the girl.

Starting August tenth, the press gathers each morning for impromptu briefings in a parking lot next to the county courthouse. They assemble under a white tent repurposed from the previous year's Coastline Artisans Fine Arts and Crafts Show, as the banner reads. Of the mass, a dozen are local TV. Twenty are from national networks, in four crews total. Then there are batteries from BBC and Deutsche Welle, who look like the odd fish out, cameramen in blue windbreakers with unfamiliar logos, female newscasters with reddish hair, in sleeveless sheaths.

And as the media and their entourage start to clog up the downtown with trucks and cars, they do one thing consistently: they apologize, especially when it appears like it'll get them something. Because they've done this before, and they've got budgets to spare, and they're humble if it suits you, Mr. or Ms. Claymore—because *you* are what matters. You count, finally, for once in your pitiable little life, and they are ready to pay attention to your opinion in its entirety, and not just listen, but listen ravenously, perchance to broadcast, publish, stream, and make historical fact.

All together, the media behave in the manner of a friend who plans to ask you for a loan tomorrow, but is prepared for the moment, all gentleness and encouragement, to say almost anything to gain your sympathy.

If you wear a Patriots hat, guess who does now, too?

And between the KISS-like roaring of motorcycle tourists and all the frothing of rumor, Claymore gains a heady atmosphere. The press mentality is siege warfare. The courthouse, the Portis farmhouse, the old Toussaint home downtown, all are fair play to be observed, researched, crawled around. High school teachers go on record, regret it later. Several loudmouths, afforded their fifteen seconds, find out that they can't help but stammer in the spotlight. Foolishness and spite get confused.

Of course, many outlets run stories without interviewing anyone, no boots on the ground. Paraphrasing, repurposing, republishing. And many of the journalists who are present do their best to impersonate other journalists they've known; and even the most ethical among them dream of articles that become movie deals. But there is still realness, guts, a slack tide of cub reporters in black-rimmed glasses. Four of whom, of Leela's generation, who don't mind car camping, who feel the stubborn calling, who have an inheritance to earn. Who pursue their crafts and speak earnestly, who take to calling the Claymore McDonald's their "HQ," what with the free Wi-Fi, the clean restrooms, the surfeit of electrical outlets.

In essence, the story that Leela Mann thought she'd have to herself quickly becomes communal property, just as Justin predicted. And her chance to make a name, get a job, afford something to eat other than ramen is rapidly diminishing.

∎

He is alone in jail, on the other side of the bars, and for the initial days Granville Portis discovers that he prefers it this way, with so little to bother him.

He is abstemious, refusing food. Alone with his relief and dull anger. But he is wise enough to expect no miracles.

He is visited, and the visitors presume to know his mind. Their questions and threats are laughable. He refuses any further visits.

By day two of his entrapment, all of the old sadnesses and jealousies and hurts rise in his heart, all of the injustice he's put up with. He reads the Bible, the way his father used to. And he makes a list of names who acted against him.

While asleep, he is awake, hungry, restless in his pain, rooted in his intestines. His bunions crave attention. He receives back his body, diarrhea, cramping. He's light-headed most of the time.

What his heart craves is nourishment.

He receives additional visitors, but says nothing to nobody. He studies the sweaty nacre of their faces, two-dimensional and flat.

He keeps his own counsel.

He will not allow them to make him the subject of their interests.

Then, on the third day, Granville Portis wakes to an unquenchable thirst.

■

It is a beautiful summer up on the mountain, and Nick's been out of jail for a week, and all he and Emily want is their privacy. But then the *DROP* story comes out, the *Los Angeles Times* story comes out, the StankTuna story goes online, and the phone begins to ring every ten or fifteen minutes, and the sound starts to make Emily anxiously unhappy, arousing emotions that are at odds with one another.

She doesn't mind the idea of someone calling her. She resents being unable to answer. But even when the phone's not ringing, she hears the sound in her head, like an alarm. So she hides her nerves, she's cheerful and optimistic, she's the girl whom Nick fell in love with originally and can depend upon, not one who breaks down over a telephone call.

They check caller ID each time anyway. Just in case it's Suzanne or Alex or Meg, maybe even Emily's mother's clinic. But nearly every number turns up as unknown ID.

They keep the curtains closed. Try to pretend the noise doesn't bother them, even when it's as if the whole house is ringing. Occasionally Nick's phone rings and he answers it automatically, until he has to stop doing that, too.

Before the ringing, before her name became public news, their days passed pleasantly, even joyfully. They didn't talk about the trial, her father, the crimes. If they could help it, they didn't even think about what had happened. They lugged her mattress down to the living room. It transformed the space, the bed nestled between the wood stove and the potted plants. To wake up together was even better than sex. They kissed and kissed, they burned through condoms, they poured out their feelings in the middle of the night. One morning, when Nick was still asleep, Emily went for a run in one of his T-shirts. She loved how it smelled just like him. The sweat on her arms and legs felt cool in the mist. The branches of the big trees swung in the same direction that she ran. She paused on a hillside to look down across the valley, and in a rush of feelings, which both turned her on more and also made her feel protective, even strong, she started thinking about all the things that she would do to him when she got back to the house, their house.

In the mornings they took long walks in the woods, her childhood kingdoms. Everything was suddenly reclaimed. They sat by the creek below the hunting camp. He skipped stones and talked about California. The crimes were far away, the deaths behind them. It was like there were no crimes, no Ashburns, while he talked about the different routes that they could drive. He'd been studying an atlas he'd found in the barn, squashed behind an old horse halter. It looked old enough to work for Lewis and Clark.

For meals, Emily took pride in her cooking. At dinnertime they lit candles, they ate on the floor. She liked watching him clean up. She enjoyed keeping them to a tight routine. She felt brand-new.

She wished time would stop.

One afternoon, there was a knock at the door. It was the Indian journalist, Leela, the woman who'd also gone to CHS. Yet another persecutory figure, as far as Emily was concerned. Though with four grocery bags at her feet.

It was the same day, Emily learned later, that the *DROP* story was electrifying the internet.

"Who is it?" Nick called from inside.

"It's all right," she said. She turned to Leela. "What do you want?"

"Nothing, actually." Leela gestured to the bags. "These are for you. I just thought you might not want to go to the store for a week or so."

"Why not?" she'd said angrily, on the verge of slamming the door. Who did this woman think she was?

Leela was unfazed.

"In case you're recognized," she said. "You're going to get recognized. People may give you a hard time." Then she sighed, as if actually pained by what she was saying. Later, it was the moment that made Emily start to like her. "There's people coming," Leela said. "Media people. Like me. More like that guy Justin you met. I don't know how to say this. They're going to get in your face. They're going to say things in front of you that sound insane."

Silence. Emily didn't know what to say. Leela stepped back off the porch, brooding over something. She looked up with a pained smile.

"If I were you, I'd put up a sign down at the end of the driveway, to remind people it's private property. That you're not talking. Otherwise they'll bother you nonstop."

A moment later Leela waved goodbye with another sad smile, and walked down to an old Subaru parked on the road.

And she was right: The attention became enormous. Even a little thrilling at first, in its own freaky way. Like an electrical storm crackling in the sky. Soon it was exasperating. Emily felt trapped in the house, stuck in ceaseless dread. Like a helicopter was parked above their heads, hovering loudly day and night. One evening, after fried eggs for dinner, the phone rang something like thirty times in a row. Nick was trying to read a magazine, one of her father's old *National Geographics*. He picked it up without a word and stomped upstairs, away from the ringing phone. She watched his boots between the railings, she felt a crimson panic in her cheeks. In the nest that afternoon, after sex, they'd taken a nap, but she hadn't been able to sleep, all she could think about was that night, as if out of obligation. The dead doctor. The doctor's dead wife. She'd wanted to erase everything that had happened, in both of their minds, but obviously she couldn't, not even in make-believe. The stories weren't hers to erase. Which brought her to a realization that she hated, but couldn't shake, about what a horrible sensation it is to feel all alone when the person you love is lying right next to you.

When Nick came down, fifteen minutes later, he found her on the couch talking on the phone about pattern making.

"Who is it?" he said.

"Some woman from a fashion magazine," she said, covering the mouthpiece.

Nick lunged for the wall and unplugged the cord. The line went dead.

"What the heck?"

"What?"

"Why did you do that?"

"What did we talk about?"

"Don't sound like that," she said. "It wasn't like that." She turned her chin into her shoulder, quickly regretful. Knowing exactly why he had reason to be angry, but still furious at his stupid, silly gesture.

"She was nice," she said.

"You think she's calling you up to discuss clothes."

"I didn't say that."

"Because you're a big fashion designer she wants to talk to."

"Don't be a jerk. She said she wanted to hear my story."

"They all want to 'hear your story.' So they can turn you into some messed-up girl for the five o'clock news."

"Don't yell at me. Obviously I know that."

"Then act like it."

At which point she'd felt so unpleasant, so loathsome, that when his voice escalated at the last second it shocked her with a jolt. Didn't he see her regret? If not, what else was he missing?

Somehow they had the sense to cool down in separate rooms.

Emily wakes to the sound of airy silence. Nick's still asleep in the nest, curled up on his side. She stares at the side of his face, the blush in his ears. Months before, they'd told each other they were in love. The declaration had made so much sense at the time, so obedient to natural facts, there was little surprise for either of them, she'd thought. But maybe she had it wrong.

She likes to remember how, several times in the past week, she spied him rearranging objects around the house, as if it's his house. When he was still in jail, she'd spent a lot of time thinking about their first days, the sweetness, lots of kissing, the daring. But the memories are vague, they're even sore from overremembering. They'd both read the *DROP* story, the other stories. She yelled at the computer, she vowed never to go on the internet again. It left her feeling schizophrenic, truly crazy, reading about "herself," a girl she barely recognized. And at the same time she was crowded by so many feelings, it was like she was two people, the character and her.

In the afternoons Nick goes to the garage, or out to see his mother. The reporters on the road harass him with questions. Meanwhile, she has long hours to herself, to remember and worry, wander pointlessly around the rooms, peek out of the curtains and try to guess what happens next. Only occasionally does she think about her parents. More often, she thinks about the doctor, the doctor's wife, the allegation of Nick smashing the doctor's wife's face with a shovel; she can't bring herself to ask him about it.

She knows something is coming. Something bad.

The morning light out the windows is blue and gold. Nick starts to snore lightly. She goes to the bathroom and pauses by the hall mirror. Her heart stops. She sees pebbly eyes, her mother's cheeks, an ugly fat rabbit with beady eyes. Why would anyone ever be in love with *her*?

That week, she will become incredibly annoyed over little things that Nick does without noticing. The way he needs to be reminded five times to take out the garbage. The way he jiggles his leg when he sits. They'll start to fight in ways they haven't before. They fight twice one afternoon, big blowouts. Of course they also make up instantly, talk about the future. She's even surprised by how apologetic she becomes, lying next to him. All the time, she'll admire how he sticks to his vision for what comes next, the big move. Pronouncing how, as soon as the judicial trial clears, they'll resume their plans, though it may take a year, year and a half, he says. But that'll allow her to finish school, which is a good thing, he thinks, to prevent any legal complications regarding transferring, when the plan still is to go west and leave Claymore.

But on days when it's nice out and she's dying to go for a run, she stays inside. She reads old books. Two times, when Nick's home, just to make little tests—though she's not exactly sure why she needs to test him, but she does—she'll point out things that could go wrong with their plan, and he's up instantly, mad about it, accusing her of not believing in them anymore, in him anymore. And she's relieved. Though both times he grabs his phone and leaves the room instead of sitting down to talk it out. And both times she reflects that it's probably true, what he accuses her of in the heat of the moment: she has begun to feel doubts.

And with each hour that follows, she will notice how her old feelings, which had come through her pen so fluidly when she wrote those letters to him in jail, have begun to dim. And at night, in the mornings, when she lies awake and can't sleep, she tracks dreams across his face with dazed attention. The room glows red. He's obviously having nightmares, she'd do anything to make them stop. But when she asks what they're about, he doesn't tell her, he just leaves, gets in his car, and drives away. And so she starts to have dreams of her own, secret dreams, that she suspects aren't exactly the same as his.

■

Friday afternoon, Nick goes into town to have dinner with Suzanne. Emily stays behind, shivering in the living room. The old walls exude a chill, despite the heat. She stares at the walls, knowing other eyes on the other side are staring back, two dozen eyes over the hoods of parked cars.

The first car stopped on the day of the *LA Times* article, the same

day as the StankTuna posting, August eighth. Ten minutes later, someone knocked on the front door. Emily stared down from an upstairs
window. A man in slacks, white golf shirt. She'd dared him to look up,
but he didn't look, just turned around, got back in his car, and stayed in
his seat.

Two days later, there were two cars, two vans. Someone erected a
sun tent. By that point Nick had posted the signs like Leela suggested,
and the reporters knew better than to approach the house, but they still
remained and stared with vague patience, as though waiting for an
event foretold.

By Friday, the night Nick goes to meet his mom for dinner, it's more
or less an encampment. Emily looks out the window. The journalists
play cards. She plugs in the landline, just to test it. Like under a magic
spell, it rings two minutes later. A local number, not one she recognizes
but also not anonymous: someone named Fetterley.

"Is this Emily Portis?"

"Who's this?"

A man's voice, high-pitched. "Don't hang up."

"Who is this?"

"My name's Richard. Richard Fetterley. I'm a photographer. You can
search my name on the web, F-E-T-T-E-R-L-E-Y. I live in Foxborough."

"We're not talking to the media."

"Of course not," he says. "I'm sure you're not."

She waits a moment.

"Where's Foxborough?"

"It's in Massachusetts. It's where the Patriots play."

"What do you want?"

He sounds nervous, but in a nice way. Not sinister. Amateurish.

"I don't know how to say this. I was hoping to take your picture."

"We're not doing pictures," she says impatiently.

"I'm sorry, I'm really bad at this. I'm an artist. I want to make a portrait. Not for the media or anything. I'll pay you." He says, "I've never
done this sort of thing before."

"What kind of portrait?"

"It's for a series I'm doing. About real women who live here."

"We live in Claymore."

"I know. I mean, in New England. The media's making up a version
of you. Whatever version they like, that's what they put on the news.

But it's not you. It can't be you. You're a real person, with your own feelings, your own thoughts. That's the person I want to capture. Do you see what I'm saying?"

"How much will you pay," she says after a moment.

"A hundred dollars."

"A hundred dollars?"

"Two hundred dollars."

"Two hundred dollars."

'Two hundred and fifty. That's as high as I can go."

She sucks in her breath.

"I need to think about it."

"I understand. Look me up. It's Richard Fetterley, F-E-T-T-E-R-L-E-Y."

She finds the guy online. His website includes a photography portfolio. In a series called "New England Women," it's one photo after another, black-and-white, of women in lingerie, women in leather, women tied up with rope in unusual positions, with elaborate knots.

"He's a pervert," Nick says that night when she shows it to him. "Who does he think he is, calling you?"

"He's a good photographer."

"Are you crazy?"

Nick shuts off the screen.

"I was looking at that."

"Are you kidding me?"

"What's your problem?"

"What's my problem? Have you gone nuts?"

She watches while he crisscrosses the room nervously. She decides that nothing of what she sees in his face is really there.

She deliberately stops herself from thinking about Mrs. Ashburn.

"You're not going to talk," he says vehemently. "Not to that guy, not anybody."

"Says who?"

"I said."

"Now you're my father."

"Give me a break."

"I didn't say I wanted to do it."

"Of course you do."

She decides that none of this is awful, none of it is heartbreaking. She says quietly, "Why are you telling me what to do?"

"Someone should. Obviously you're enjoying the attention."

"That's a horrible thing to say."

"I'm sorry, okay? I'm sorry. This is making me insane. I don't even know who I'm talking to anymore."

"Where are you going?"

He walks out. She follows him to the front door. She watches as he struts to his car in the dark, pulling his limp alongside him. At the end of the drive, the media wakes, turns toward him. She runs back to the kitchen, to call 911 and report trespassers. But stops when the idea strikes her as so ludicrous, beyond mocking, too horrible to let stand, that she starts to laugh and remains there, until the telephone bleats in her ear.

■

An hour and a half after parking in Rob Miller's driveway, Leela is several beers into getting stupid at a pace that her liver is untrained to process, and she is doing this because there is too much happening of insignificance, too little to do with her story, too much discomfort and early-onset social anxiety disorder (SAD!) to process sober, and so to be drunk, just *drunk*, she must get there singularly fast.

"His house" turned out to be "his parents' house," a modern white box overlooking the northernmost stretch of Claymore beach. Where Rob still lived, high above the sand, above one of the more chichi neighborhoods in Claymore, in his own separate white box, aka "the garage," connected to the main house by a breezeway, in what appeared to be an apartment. And the apartment, when Leela first approached, walking up the driveway, looked to be stuffed with two dozen people her age she didn't know, except for one woman she most definitely did know and recognized once she got close enough, an extremely pretty girl standing in the window. None other than Meg "the Body" Rosenthal.

When Leela was a first-year at CHS, Meg was a senior girl whom all the boys in school, as they prowled the grounds, whisper-called "the Body." And who seemed, through the window glass, to have come straight to Rob's bachelor quarters from the sea, roughly naked, with cutoffs for modesty to accompany her bikini top, but otherwise only in a bikini top, that was merely a suggestion of a bikini top. And the Body wasn't one that Leela could even hate properly. They'd been friends, sort of. After school, they belonged to an extracurricular women's studies group, a dozen girls who met once a week to discuss a reading, take occasional trips to help a political candidate knock on doors. And Meg was always nice, full stop. Maybe a little distant, self-involved, but rumors said that there'd been something messed up about her family? One of her parents had died, or both? Leela never worked up the guts to ask. The point was, Meg had been both friendly and ultra-hot, yet somehow unable to have the easiest time at school, with boys or in life.

"Leela," Rob exclaimed when he opened the door. Teeth white as snow. Hair like a catalog model. He offered her a double high-five. "You made it."

"You thought I wouldn't?" she said.

"And look at that, you brought wine. Little Miss Sophisticated."

Oh god.

"I don't even have a corkscrew. Hold on, my dad's really into wine, let me ask."

Through the doorway she smelled weed, saw people drinking beer from cans. And she'd brought sauvignon blanc. What was she, thirty-nine?

"Holy crap, Leela? How are you?"

Within microseconds the Body had cling-wrapped itself around her own. And soon Meg was holding her arm as she told her about Rob's parents' retractable staircase to the beach. This came after describing an earlier surf session with Rob, explaining that she, Meg, was new to surfing, but Rob was an amazing, patient instructor. "The stairs go right down the cliff. Then they retract. You pull this lever. So weirdos can't, like, walk up and rob the house. Talk about a good deal, right?"

"It sounds amazing," she confirmed.

"You should totally come out with us," Meg said, squeezing her hand. She hadn't asked her a single question. "We're going in the morning. You'll love it. God, it's so great to see you."

"Yeah, I don't think so."

"What?"

"I mean tomorrow. Surfing."

"So what are you even doing here? I mean, back in town."

"I'm visiting my parents."

"Awesome," said Meg. "Is it awesome?"

"It's so awesome," Leela said. "Will you excuse me a second?"

Back at Sandra's house, her little haven, getting ready had not been easy. Awful quickly, her Claymore story was turning to shit. She had almost nothing of value. She needed a lot more, fast. The quotes she'd obtained weren't interesting, the interviews hadn't led to much. Her old math teacher. Some kids on the beach. And of everyone else she'd contacted, a hundred percent of them had refused to participate after the *LA Times* story appeared. No matter that she was local, she was one of *them*.

More reporters arrived still. She'd barely slept three hours the previous night. Rapidly feeling her chances dwindling, her fate sliding out of grasp.

And so, in a glimmering moment of drunkenness, only ninety minutes after she arrived at Rob's garage apartment, she is on beer number four, a ridiculous number, trying to measure the circumference of the Body's left butt cheek from ten feet away. Thanks to four factors: (1) She'd talked to nearly everyone in the room and no one knew anything about the Claymore Kids that wasn't gossip or lies or facts she already had; (2) no one had any interesting connections to speak of; (3) four beers was about three and a half more beers than her usual number of beers; (4) drinking beer made her butt-cheek-crazy, it appears. In the same time, Rob had returned and fallen into deep conversation with the Body on a couch. So the two of them were hooking up. What a surprise. But who wouldn't hook up with either one of them, or both of their bodies at once? Leela smiles. It encourages a guy to introduce himself. His name is Tim. Tim starts off interesting. He's short and cute, he's a skydiving instructor. Has she ever been skydiving? "Why would I?" Leela says. Wondering, does he know anything? She feels him out about the murders. He's not interested. Somehow he finds his way to a monologue about how girls who wear lipstick are communicating an evolution of mating signals that date back to girl monkeys' red genitals, and doesn't she think so?

Which is when she decides it's time to call a car. Though she does briefly wonder about the shade of Meg Rosenthal's vulva.

"Leela, wait," Rob calls from across the room, when she's near the door. "Are you leaving?"

"Thank you so much for inviting me."

"We've barely had any time to hang. Are you okay to drive?"

She smiles.

"Come with me," says Rob. "There's something I want to show you."

She trails him down a set of wooden stairs, to a room off the breezeway connecting to the main house. A large study. Someone's office. He turns on lights that softly glow. The most prominent feature is a drafting table, lots of blueprints, file folders. She guesses one of the parents is an architect? Many bookcases, big windows. Outside it's pitch-black. Above the water is a thin shard of moon. The music from the party is barely audible. There's a plastic water bottle on a table. She opens it and gulps down half. In a minute she'll leave, get the hell to bed, sober up for tomorrow. Tomorrow will be different, she promises herself.

Rob suddenly comes in close. "Is that a tattoo? I love it." He touches the snowflake inside her wrist. "Hey, I've got a favor to ask."

"Okay."

He's holding her arm.

"I need your help."

On a shelf is a thick stack of printer paper, held together with rubber bands. He takes it down delicately.

"What's that?"

"Okay, I'm sure you get this all the time."

"I mean," she says, "not really."

Wondering what the hell is going on.

"I wrote a novel."

"I thought you wrote poetry," she says.

"What?"

"In high school. In English class. Never mind."

"Now I know I'm not a writer, I know that." He's downcast. Deadly serious. "But I really want to be. I have this urge."

"Okay," she says dully.

"I realize how stupid I sound. But it's like I have this thing inside, I need to get it out of me. Does that make sense?"

"It could be appendicitis."

The joke doesn't land. He looks pained. She can't stand how earnest he's become, and for some reason also weirdly keyed up, as if to confess something he'd been forced to hold back.

"I'm not really a writer," she says.

Rob only laughs.

"Nice try," he says. "You always had the talent. Everyone knew you'd make it. Listen, it would mean the world to me," he says, holding out the pages, his baby. "Be as tough as you want. I need to get better. I can take it, believe me. I want the hardest shot you've got."

She laughs lightly, and is now deeply uncomfortable. His self-deprecation, she notices, has an uneasy, aggressive edge.

"So is that a yes?"

"Maybe. I guess."

"Leela, you are the best."

She hears noise from the party, someone shouting happily. She reads the cover page: "The War on Men: A Novel. By Rob Miller." When she looks up, he's turning around, holding out a crystal glass and a pen.

"Since you're into wine," he says. "It's my dad's favorite Scotch."

"I think I've had enough to drink."

"It's peaty. Try the nose."

"The what?"

Then something dawns on her, from the glowing wattage of his expectancy, the Scotch, the fact that the pen cap is red.

"Did you want me to read this now?"

"Is that cool?" A second later he freezes. Distressed. "Oh shit."

"Oh. It's fine."

"Wait, I'm such an asshole. That's, like, so male privilege. I'm sorry."

He takes back the pages before she can resist. She feels bad, which is quickly compounded by the emotional hangover from her long day of disappointment. After all, who does she think she is? Rob Miller invited her to a party, he wanted to help her. Was it his fault that his friends came up empty?

"How about this," she says, "I'll give it a start."

"Are you sure?"

"It's fine, seriously," she says, and hopes she's not as drunk as she sounds. At the very least, it will give her time to sober up.

"Dude," he says, "you don't know how much this means to me."

He smiles and stares deep into her eyes. The way a boy does when he's about to kiss you. Maybe he *is* about to kiss her. Rob Miller? But he just called her dude—is that a problem? Is that a good problem?

Her seventeen-year-old self says in a deep voice: *Fuck it.*

She puts her hand on his arm.

He comes in closer.

The tension's unbearable, also wonderful.

"Here, I'll get you situated," Rob says, and pushes her down into a leather easy chair. Which she allows, and does enjoy after a drunken fashion. If only he'd keep pushing. He covers her legs with a wool blanket, like she's his grandmother, then hands her the pages, and shuts the door with a neighborly wave.

Well, shit.

She takes a gulp of Scotch, another one. Things could be worse. Did Robbie Miller not just call her talented and smart? *Everyone knew you'd make it.* Her chest warms. She smiles; she'll dine out on this for years. And she will read his manuscript with gratitude, drink his dad's whiskey, and make helpful notes in red ink.

Leela pulls up the blanket and peels off the cover page. From the get-go: wide margins, big font. He's using Garamond? There's an impressive copyright notification in the footer. She sighs and can't help but start, then can't help but continue, though more in the manner of rubbernecking than anything else. She'll need another glass of Scotch. If not the bottle.

It was a dark and lonely afternoon at Dunkin' Donuts. In fact, every afternoon at Dunkin' Donuts is rather orange and pink, all credit to an interior design think tank somewhere. But who said dark and lonely were specific hues? Welcome to my humble existence. I'm the manager. Do you desire cream with your coffee, you cunt?

■

Suzanne breathes out raspily, clears her throat, only ends up hacking up some gravel from her lungs. Does she hear a car in the drive? Ostensibly her son's come down from his girlfriend's mountain cave so the two of them can have dinner together, and he can help her with her computer. Also, ostensibly, she's not drinking anymore, perhaps even not smoking cigarettes, and isn't life a thrill. And in the morning she'll be picked up by a condescending ex-cop to attend a cult meeting in a church basement. Maybe she'll blow him off—she doesn't quite know yet. Or maybe she'll go through with the meeting and hit up the farmer's market after, take a yoga class and grab a smoothie with Stephanie Condren and compliment her tights.

But terrifically little of any of that remains in her mind, is relevant or even real, on the Friday night that her only child arrives for dinner, sits down in the living room, closes his eyes, and begins, unprompted, to relate the entire story of what happened those weeks ago, as he'd promised her he would do—it's as if he's not her son at all, but some strange young man who wandered in and picked up the police blotter—and for once she's able to keep her mouth shut, just cower, creep into the tunnel of her inner safest space and listen, absorb, accept without protest, as she actually hears him—but she's only able to do this with clenched fists, deliberate self-control, while she resists every inclination to interrupt, deny that which is surreal and unlikely, and also peculiarly terrifying for actually happening to her own son.

And by the end, after about fifteen minutes, it's quite unworkable to even start to address the hell that's just been described, or what happened since, or what happens tomorrow and what will occur in the days to come—whatever is the time frame of this endless crisis, in the wake of fear—so she goes out to the garage.

Ten minutes later, Nick finds his mother behind the steering wheel. The nose of the car points out the garage bay, faces the neighbors' dark houses, the sticky night, the scant brightness of two streetlamps and the neighborhood's glow. Several beer cans stand in a row across the dash. She's got her favorite sweater wrapped around her, his grandfather's ratty old cardigan. It looks like one of those blankets firefighters give people after car accidents.

"What are you doing in here?"

"I don't know."

Her eyes are red. He never knows what comes next, but this might be pushing it. He gets in shotgun. He notices that none of the beers are open.

"If Emily's mother is in a clinic, won't the state intervene?" she says. "Protective Services or whatnot?"

"Not if we don't tell anyone. Are you going to report us?"

"Of course not."

"How'd you find that out?"

"From the cop."

Probably the last thing he wants to do is be there. Her nose and face are all messed up, she still hasn't told him how. She did promise to tell him, if he'd explain how everything else had played out. The sort of shitty tit-for-tat that only his mom would consider part of a normal relationship.

"You know it's your turn," he says. "To tell me about your face."

"I know that. Thank you."

"So what are you waiting for?"

"Would you mind if I had a drink?"

"I thought you quit."

"I did."

"Whatever."

She could kiss him. She takes one down. She tries not to drink it too quickly. She sees herself in the mirror, her ruined face.

"I didn't want any of this to happen," she says.

"That's a messed-up thing to say."

"I mean it."

"What? What does that even mean?"

He stares dejectedly out the window. His eyes land on a scraggly tomato patch she grows by the corner of the garage each year, each year a half-assed effort.

"This is such bullshit," he says. "You don't change."

"I should have done better."

"And it's all about you, once again."

For the first time, if only briefly, he steps into the mind-set of his dad when he left. The relief he must have felt. But he can't go any further with it. More easily, more quickly, the short exercise makes him realize how humiliated his mother must have felt, probably still feels.

"Actually I don't think it's about me," she says. "You know, I don't think much of myself." She takes a deep breath, as if it's her final breath. Her heart climbs into her throat—no defenses left. "I know how I seem." Her voice buckles. "To you. Your friends. I barely get out of bed in the morning. What do I have left? I have a brain, what's left of it. My education. My memories. And I have you, Nicky, and not even that anymore."

"Mom—"

"Just don't let it be enough," she says angrily. "Not for you."

They sit in silence for a minute. The air's still hot from the day. She grimaces down and sideways.

"I'm a terrible mother."

He laughs. "You're not the best."

It's a joke but she doesn't answer. Then she laughs, she can't help it, and he laughs quickly, too. Soon the sound of the laughter's so loud it can be heard up and down the block.

.

Late that night, two in the morning, Martin drops the barbells on the floor, and they hit the ground with a refreshing crash. Still, he winces. There are dull pangs in his lower back, in his buttocks, even numbness. Probably he's pushed himself too hard. For the last couple days he ran five miles a day, between the beach and the road. And that evening he'd found himself drawn to the hotel's tiny exercise room in the attic, mostly because he couldn't sleep.

A few minutes later, the big innkeeper opens the door.

"Mr. Krug?"

What does he see? Another old man, grizzled and sweating, shorts and undershirt soaked.

"Sorry about the noise."

"There is a reason the sign's here."

The sign on the door says it's after hours, he's in violation of the rules.

"It's just," the innkeeper says gravely, "we have other guests. My family lives here, too."

"I understand. It won't happen again."

Sweat gets in his eyes. He looks up. The guy's still there. Demeke's dad.

"There's something we should talk about," the man says. With an undertone of antagonism.

"What is that?" Martin asks.

The guy closes the door.

"Moira Ashburn. The Ashburns' daughter."

"I know who she is."

"She's a friend of ours. Well, a friend of my wife. Gabriela saw her tonight for dinner."

"How's she holding up?"

The guy glares incredulously, quickly emotional. "Her family was murdered."

"I apologize. I meant it in all sincerity."

The innkeeper leans resignedly against the arm of the old treadmill. He and Martin are about the same size. Between them they take up nearly every inch of space in the room.

"She wasn't in a great place to begin with. When all this shit happened. To the degree that this is any of my business, granted."

There's a tiny porthole window that looks out over the dark sea.

"Well, it sounds like you've made it your business."

"She's having a hard time. Not just from your lot."

Martin can't help but laugh.

"She said we gave her a hard time?"

The innkeeper crouches by the treadmill and rubs his neck. "A lot of people don't know where this thing's going," he says. "Don't know and don't like it. The media's making us out like we're some kind of a hellhole. This is a small town. We like it quiet. Business isn't always great. People say the valley's cursed. Years ago, a lady almost set nearly the whole valley on fire. People honestly talk about that. There's been a lot of bad breaks. For too long. The recession did us bad. People don't know what's coming next. For a tourist town, all these journalists snooping around, this thing is the plague. Which obviously those kids didn't understand, that Emily girl."

"Let's leave the kids out of it."

"Now that's my point. You're not from around here, you don't get it. If you were from town . . ." He strokes his mustache, agitated about something. "My wife and I get a single bad review, we're up all night worrying about our mortgage. That's how things work now. Fine. But then these kids decide to screw around, take out their smartphones, take their clothes off."

"I appreciate—"

"Mr. Krug, people have things. That they want to protect. That they don't want other people to know about. That shouldn't be a privilege."

Martin pauses to try and air out the room. He looks out the window again, just to avoid seeing the guy in the mirrored wall.

"So as to avoid confusion," he says, and hears himself switch over to cop mode, "why don't you tell me what you're really saying, nice and simple."

"It's two in the morning."

"I'm aware of that."

"Maybe the problem is you don't listen good," the guy says, and straightens up. He rolls his neck and rakes his mustache with his fingers and steps a little closer. If they were anywhere else, not a tiny attic room full of exercise equipment, he'd need to consider it an aggressive play.

"Things were stable around here," the guy says. "People were happy."

"Are you holding me accountable for something?"

"I don't think I am."

"Tell me what your wife's friend wants."

"She wants justice. She feels like she's been harassed."

"It's a homicide investigation."

"Yeah, and she lost her parents."

"She didn't even like her parents."

The guy can't help but laugh, too shocked to reply. He makes to leave. He says under his breath, "Just leave us all alone."

Martin sits on the bench again. Something's wrong, he knows it. A barely noticeable shift in tone, but just enough to notice. Not for the first time he wonders if he got it all wrong somehow.

"There's something you're not telling me." The guy stops in the doorway. "It's about the girlfriend, Moira's girlfriend?"

The innkeeper twists the corner of his mouth a little. As if he's looking at the world's biggest idiot.

"You should be ashamed of yourself."

Martin smiles tightly.

"Fine. I'm ashamed of myself. Now what?"

•

At some point in the early hours, Leela wakes up in the darkest dark, the blackest night, absolutely freezing despite a blanket that suffocates her legs and torso. She's drunk. Ultra drunk. Her head's a swimming pool filled with electrified Jell-O. She really needs to pee.

All is silent. There's no moonlight left. This is not her living room in Madbury. What room is this? Did she hook up with somebody? On her chest and the floor are papers like fallen leaves. The manuscript, the party, Rob's party, his parents' house, his parents' office—she must have fallen asleep. Shit.

Her mouth tastes like the rodent apocalypse.

She lurches out of her wool tomb, stumbles around the room, tries to find the light switch but can't find the light switch because there is no light switch, so, hallway, and where's the bathroom? Must pee, then depart immediately, post-peeing. But first pee.

She lurches down the hallway, finds the bathroom door, opens the door, closes it behind her. No lock on the door? No light switch? Not even a motion sensor? Bladder *exploding*.

She tries to rip her jeans down but sways and stumbles, because her jeans are too tight and they bunch at the knee. Double shit! She tilts against the wall, falls over. Somehow gets herself back up to a squatting position over the toilet and wrenches her pants down to her ankles, along with her underwear. Finally: great relief and satisfaction. Until a headache of tidal proportions breaks through a distant seawall behind her eyeballs and begins to approach.

She must flee, but first a wave of terror: what if someone yanks open the unlocked door? She grips the doorknob and holds it, straining to finish, alive with fear only. She closes her eyes.

Twenty minutes later, she's awake. Must've nodded off? *Shit shit shit.* She reaches down to pull up her underwear. It's missing. What happened to her underwear? Where are her jeans? The dark's too dark, she can't see, she paws the ground. She can't even see her hands. Finally she feels them, her jeans, so screw it, no underwear, she yanks on her pants and stumbles out, down the hardwood floor in the hallway with one hand against the wall. Then she trips over something and falls with a *smack* that's the sound of her knee hitting something hard. So painful! Her knee is on fire. It feels sticky. Her head bongs with alarms. Are the alarms outside her head? Are they music, is everyone still partying? Is everyone gone? What time is it?

She's never been this drunk in her entire life.

Leela sees a chink of moonlight through an open door. Her arms are freezing. She follows the light on her hands and knees, until she crawls back into the big warm chair, pulls up the blanket, tells herself to set the alarm on her phone, set two alarms just in case, that way she'll be out of there before anyone else wakes up. She should definitely drink a ton of water. Is there any water? She can't bear the idea of leaving the chair, not when she's warm again. Her head is suffused with an aura of suffering, of tidal waves approaching that will hurt, and nausea. But if she sleeps, maybe they'll pass her by.

Three hours later, a man's voice: "Excuse me."

Louder, a second later: *"Excuse* me."

Leela cracks open her eyes. Sour light. Trippy pulses. Abysmal headache. She squashes her face into the cushion, to garlic-press the pain out through the back of her skull.

"Honey, I'm sorry," the voice says, "but if you don't mind."

"I'm sleeping," she blurts out. What is this bullshit? She will homicide this guy once her head quits splitting apart. What sort of rapist just breaks into your cabin and starts talking shit?

"I appreciate that," the voice says, a deep voice, slightly chuckling. "But I need my shorts."

The chuckle pulls her out of the abyss, gradually. She turns, rolling onto her side, and recognizes that her left knee burns for some reason. Like someone hit it with a hammer. She opens her eyes again. Bookshelves, file boxes. Is she not in Madbury? Did the chatty rapist kidnap her?

OH SHIT.

She rolls the rest of the way around and squints, which exacerbates the throbbing in her head. At the same time she feels cold air on her legs. Because there's no blanket. She looks down. Blanket's on the floor. She must've kicked it off. Her legs are bare for some reason, and one's bloody, scabbed darkly with dried blood.

The floor, also, has a trail of dried blood.

But where are her jeans?

A figure shifts, out of the light. A man looms over her, in a white undershirt and a blue bathrobe, with silver hair. She sees his face—it's Rob, but in his fifties.

"Sir, excuse me," says Leela, as formally as she can. "I think I'm hungover."

"And you might've bumped your knee," the man says gently. "Look, you can go back to sleep. I just need my work shorts. I have to be at a job site in ten minutes."

"I'm sorry to hear that," she says.

"But the shorts."

"What shorts?"

But her mind is too crippled by pain to figure out what he's complaining about. Her headache is the kind people use surgery to relieve. Still, she should go, let the man sort out his clothing problems. So she reaches down for her car keys and touches, and looks down, and finds canvas shorts—she's wearing canvas shorts covered in paint splatters.

She catapults herself to a standing position. The headache claims her on a visceral level. She almost collapses.

"Are you okay?" asks Mr. Miller.

"Excuse me," she whispers, and races out.

Doorway. Hallway. Dried blood on the floor. She's about to be sick. Where is the bathroom? First door: guest room. Second door: a closet full of linens, and on the floor are dark blue jeans that look just like hers. Which is weird? And underwear, that look like hers—that are hers. Plus a laundry hamper, with someone's T-shirt on top, that appears to be wet. And it takes only a brief sparkling moment to piece together a chain of events that should be beyond human understanding if it didn't ring so many bells, before she tears off the shorts, yanks on her jeans as fast as possible, feels her keys in one pocket, and stuffs her underwear into another. Grabs the T-shirt, balls it up—*this is not happening*—and tries to hide the shirt when she hustles back, ignores the blood, holds down the vomit, hands the man his shorts, the man who is Rob Miller's father, the shorts that are Mr. Miller's shorts, shorts that she must've grabbed from the floor of his family's linen closet, out of their laundry basket, thinking at four in the morning that his shorts were her jeans, thinking that the closet was a bathroom, after she'd squatted over his laundry hamper and pissed all over someone's T-shirt.

The pissy shirt that's in her hands.

The father who's now rolling his eyes.

Leela dashes away without a word, out the nearest door. Outdoors. Cold air. A sour yellow sun hangs above the ocean, surrounded by storm clouds. She stumbles down a perfectly mowed lawn toward her car, throws the balled-up shirt in the backseat, twists the key in the ignition. It turns over, thank god. The clock says 7:12. She reverses quickly down the driveway and heads for town.

She who pissed on their laundry, Rob Miller's laundry.

She who wore his dad's shorts to bed, nestled in his crappy novel.

She who bled up and down their hallway, and for the sake of what? Nothing had been gained, no connections made; her story was no further along. Ocean-smelling wind passes through the car and turns her stomach. She can't help but reconsider her future. In which the reconstitution of any sort of pride does not seem possible. Public life, ever again: impossible. She's going to be sick. She rolls down the window. Her stomach doesn't explode somehow. At a stoplight below the neighborhood, she laughs miserably: it's too *insane*. She wants to cry. The light changes. She turns away from the sun and heads west, toward mountains, toward Madbury.

And while turning she passes a dirty red sedan with a surfboard strapped to the roof. The car's driven by a beautiful young woman, a perfectly designed young woman. The kind of young woman possessed of a sort of physical beauty that's algorithmic, it's so precise, and goes beyond just appearances: it suggests who she is inside, someone good.

And to the woman's sideways expression, which contains hasty recognition and a quick smile, the start of "Hey, Leela," and then a look of bewilderment, even pain, she is stone-faced as her final measure of protection. Eyes forward. Mouth closed. Inwardly warping. A young woman with nothing left to protect, only the impulse to protect.

■

By late afternoon, when he's wearing nothing more than boxer shorts, with four Motrin in his bloodstream, Martin can't find a single comfortable position in order to use his laptop. The best he can do is perch the computer on his lap, in bed, with sweat dripping off his forehead, and from there he faces with a stupid expression on his face so many headlines like "Incest America" and "The Demise of the Great American Sweetheart." Idiotic websites, idiotic articles, in which "Emily Portis" becomes the starting point for all kinds of slow-witted sound and fury. Martin clicks and clicks, he can't stop clicking. How many publications can the internet contain? In videos, smug man after smug man addresses a camera. Martin can hardly listen to them. He can't believe that they exist. Everything, everywhere, focuses on the girl, though how exactly the nude pictures of her surfaced online still remains unknown, days later, though copies flourish for anyone who knows where to search, and people talk about that like it's somehow allowable in this day and age, no matter the girl being sixteen. He's full of rage.

That morning, Suzanne had refused to get out of his car. He'd picked her up at her house. She smelled drunk. At least he got her to agree to go. They rode to the meeting in silence. The church was on the town's center square, immense and gray. He'd parked. Lights were on in the basement. Nearly a dozen people stood around outside. Coffee drinkers, cigarette smokers, in casual catch-up. It was Martin's regular meeting in Claymore, of a mix typical to meetings anyplace. Upper-crust drunks. Bottom-rung drunks. The wholesome middle who'd lost custody of their kids.

"They look nice," Nick's mother said, as if surprised.

"They are," he said gently. "So are you."

He'd started to get out. She laughed. "I'm not going in there."

"Sure you are."

"You think I'm crazy? Half of those guys I went to high school with."

"I'll be there with you."

"If you think I'm going to join a cult, you're crazier than I thought."

For fifteen minutes he coaxed, he listened. It only made things worse. "Who the hell do you think you are anyway? You kissed me, and now we're here?" She piled it on, eventually shouting, "Who gave you the right to play god anyway? You're such an asshole."

People heard the noise, stared for a second, looked away. It had happened a thousand times before, to each of them.

Nick's mom finally said icily, "Why do you get to make me feel this way?" Then wouldn't say anything else or budge. So he drove her home. Parked in the driveway. She slammed the door. He watched her go up the drive. For some reason he thought of Lillian and her doctor. For the first time, it didn't bother him as much as it had. He actually wondered if they were happy.

He drove back to the meeting. He caught the eye of a couple people, they nodded or gestured. They all went inside.

In the glow of his laptop, Martin picks up his phone. He needs to help the girl. He calls the number in the book, for Portis. The number's been disconnected. In Brenner's files is an email address. He composes a note, pecking at his keyboard.

Hi Emily. My name is Martin Krug. We met previously . . .

He sends the message. Then in his inbox finds a reply to a message he'd sent the day before. Attached are the call logs to Dr. Ashburn's house for the week of the murders. He quickly scrolls. He stops. Double-checks the times. He makes notes on a sheet of paper.

Twenty minutes later comes a text message, unrelated, from Lillian's lawyer, requesting that Martin call him immediately, to arrange for a face-to-face as soon as possible.

But at that moment Martin's in the shower and doesn't hear the beep.

That evening, at dusk, two seagulls picket a wooden fence. He hops in his car and speeds out of town, up the road into the mountains. It really is pretty, the higher the road climbs. Like a postcard of virgin new world. The light falls away behind him, the houses become fewer and fewer. Then a car comes flying down the middle of the road. Martin hits the horn and swerves, nearly jams into a ditch.

Two motorcycles fly by, side by side. Headlights that he mistook for a single vehicle, an illusion of two sources.

Another five minutes and there's half a dozen cars parked along the road. He slows and parks. Trudges his heavy legs up a ditch toward the media encampment. Sun tent. Several folding chairs. Nearly a dozen people, and someone's running a halogen lamp off a generator. Could be a refugee site, could be a tailgate party. The Portis house sits two hundred yards uphill from the road. Old and dark, with a steep sloping roof, and two small wood and stone outbuildings, plus a barn that's brown and black, as if covered in mold. The field's fortressed by cords of firewood and a tractor. There's a basketball hoop, a snowplow blade, a beat-up truck parked in the dirt drive, pointed uphill. Forest on either side canvases up the mountainside. A single light's on upstairs in the house, otherwise the structures are as dark as the sky.

On the road is a mailbox with several handwritten signs stored inside plastic bags. *Private Property* and *No Trespassing* and *No Interviews* and *Go Away*.

"You should be ashamed of yourselves," Martin announces, to no one, as he gets closer to the media people. In return he only sees hooded eyes. He stops and plants his feet. "Why don't you all just go home?"

Two men pause a card game to observe him dully, from plaid folding chairs.

Martin says loudly, "She's done nothing wrong."

More heads turn.

"You don't know what the hell's going on," he shouts.

Someone says, "Get outta here."

"Why don't you get a life? Let them get on with theirs."

Another voice says, "Who the hell are you?"

He's about to answer. At the same time he's about to walk up the drive and offer to the girl to eject them properly. Then the light in the Portis house shuts off. A few of them turn to notice, Martin included.

"Wait a second, you're that cop. From New Jersey. Can I get an interview?"

■

"Who's this?"

"Nick, it's Martin Krug. Don't hang up."

"What do you want?"

"I just have a question. The night at the Ashburns. When everything happened. Did you hear the phone ring?"

"What?"

"I got the call logs. There was a phone call. Right when everything went down. You didn't mention it."

"I don't know what you're talking about."

"So you didn't hear the phone ring? Or maybe Dr. Ashburn excused himself, when you were in the study together. The number that called the house, Nick, it was Emily's dad. It's his phone number."

"What are you talking about?"

"Just wait. Do you or do you not remember the phone ringing?"

"Look, I would've said something."

"Just hold on. Listen to me. I'm trying to help you. I need you to tell me, okay? Because, if not, potentially we're back to square one. There's something missing, I can feel it, around this call. So if there's something you're not telling me, I need you to tell me."

"I gotta go."

"Nick, wait!"

•

Forty-five minutes later, back at the hotel, Martin bends down angrily in the dark to yank off his shoe when it happens: utter lockdown.

When every muscle, from the middle of his back down to his tailbone, tenses and clenches in unison, and he yells out and crashes to the floor.

The pain is like a fantasy, a dream. It doesn't seem real. His whole body is immobilized. It's almost impossible to breathe, like a big iron jacket just leapt out of the dark and wrapped itself around his body. Sweat breaks out on his face. It's never happened before. Complete deactivation, from the spine out. He clenches his eyes shut. The tension continues to spread. Agonizing pain. His chest seizes, his jaw clamps shut, he can barely make a sound. He'd almost feel awe if it were happening to someone else.

He manages to yell again.

A minute later, the kid, Demeke, "Holy shit. Are you okay?"

"My back," Martin says, through gritted teeth. He forces his eyes open. A night wind whips through the door. He can only see the walkway.

Tears leak from his eyes. A nearly unbearable rigidity clenches his spine, a deadness that's got him locked up to his neck vertebrae, searing hot and numbing cold at the same time.

"What happened?"

"My back. Went out."

"I'll get my dad."

"Just wait," he says, gasping, crying.

"Okay."

The kid calmly sits in a chair. Martin wants to laugh. Thank god for this kid—

And when that thought crosses his consciousness, some type of interior gate falls, like a great sigh, and all of his loneliness and sadness defy gravity, come flooding up his body at the same time as the pain from his back, and it's like there's a cannonball in his throat that comes roaring out—

"AHHHHHHHH!"

"Now I'm going."

"No." He says slowly, breath hissing, "I'm fine."

But every muscle cramps worse. Then words start to float up from his heart. Is he about to faint?

"My kid," he says, eyes blurring.

"What?"

Surprising himself: "My daughter."

"What's she got to do with it?"

Martin clutches the rug. He breathes through his mouth like a dying bear. The night is quiet. He's about to say he doesn't know, he can't explain it, but his mind knows better, it operates flawlessly within the warped body, so that in clusters of three or four stuttered words, panting, struggling out, he discovers at the same time as Demeke that it *is* his daughter—

"Who wants nothing—from me—

"I was lousy—a drunk—you have—no idea—

"She's grown—she doesn't want—anything to do—

"After what—

"Look at me—

"I'm a loser—I'm a *loser*—"

"You're not a loser," Demeke says.

But he's wrong. Even a wreck, Martin knows it. When all you want

286

from life is the impossible: the definition of a loser. He's lost his equilibrium. He's bawling, from the pain. Because if you abandon your kid, pick drinking over her childhood, then get sober down the road, you realize that that time is gone. You can't get it back. You're a loser to even dream.

"Then go tell her that," Demeke says.

"I have to—respect her space."

"That's bullshit. Just send her an email."

"She deserves—"

"Yeah, no shit."

A small chime rings: a text message. The kid's face illuminates while he stares at his screen. Martin's never been close enough to hear the sound of someone typing on a phone. It's like rain hitting glass, or no sound at all. He nods at the image of Demeke and his phone, and closes his eyes.

■

On Saturday afternoon the final line item is decided among the Sisterhood Triumvirate, that any monies resulting from the various financial transactions that will constitute the business of Emily Portis Media Day should be tucked away for Emily's higher education.

But before they get to that, they sit and establish all budding parameters to be monetized, using Meg's philosophical guidance and familiarity with e-commerce, Alex's practical advice, and any tips Emily has gleaned from quickly studying the wire-bound reading packet that was distributed in Meg's internet business class.

Said parameters depending on applicable interest and branded content, as to be issued in a press release that is Meg's domain, based on her working knowledge of online marketing, women's defiance of social censure, and how this stuff in the real world actually works.

"Just search for 'press release,'" Meg says. "You get a ton of examples."

The apartment is stuffy. Emily opens the living room windows. A hot summer wind blows through the room, warm and salty, and makes the hairs on her arms stand up. Meg and Alex are busy staring at Meg's laptop, bound together by a shared urgency, the emergency that is her. She's been aware of this all morning, and therefore isn't completely at home in her own body. It's like she's been floating above them, watching them talk.

Her first thought had been to fly out the door, when the meeting was proposed. Stupid, helpless, scared, she could be that girl so easily. But, to her own surprise, she wasn't, and she's not. And neither is the young woman they've discussed.

Emily takes a seat. Alex stands up a second later and starts to braid her hair, still in discussion with Meg, about auction rights. She feels Alex's hands tugging her hair, she feels decidedly calm. Ever since that morning, when the three of them started talking about this crazy plan, she feels better and better.

Meg lays out the criteria to be included during Media Day. Location, setting, wardrobe, potential props. What props? "Family house, family truck. It's also important to think about format," Meg says. Still photographs, film footage, film montage. Editorial or candid, interview or no interview. Certain subjects out-of-bounds, to be determined.

For interviews, group, private, and private with shared activity are all available, at different price tiers, with other assets offered upon inquiry. But no access, the statement makes plain, to be granted gratis, no exceptions.

Emily asks, "What does 'gratis' mean?"

"It means they don't have to pay anything," Meg says. "That's what we don't want. Neither do they; it would mean you're worth less. Basically you're going to be this week's eight-year-old who gets Botox."

"Are you sure this is how it's done?"

"Look at TMZ. It makes sense, doesn't it? News shows pay people all the time."

Alex kisses her on the head. "The important thing is that you're in charge," she says. "It's your story, you own it."

"Why should they profit off you?" says Meg. "And have you not get shit."

"Totally," Alex says.

"What are the 'other assets'?" asks Emily, pointing to a sheet that Meg printed out. She feels a little reluctant to know too many details, but also feels she must know them, must contribute now to prepare for her participation later.

"To be honest, I don't know yet, I just thought it would be good to have that in there," says Meg. "We want to leave all options open."

As of that morning, the world had begun to retilt to a more positive angle. It started when Alex had walked up from the road. Nick was out, she'd had the house to herself. Alex knocked on the old wooden door.

She wore the yellow dress that Emily made her so many months earlier. Sunglasses in her hand, eyeliner smudged, hair uncombed and ratty. She basically repeated her text messages out loud, she was apologetic, scared, upset about everything that had happened, most especially Mike and the leaked photos, but also her tantrum in her bedroom, and all the terrible stuff she'd seen about Emily and Nick in the news.

She felt horrible for her part, and Meg felt horrible for her part, and they'd do whatever they could to make amends.

"I'll try everything," Alex had said, "I'll do anything."

Emily grabbed her friend so hard she thought she'd break her. The chasm between them instantly closed.

"If this doesn't kill you, you're immortal," Alex said in her ear.

Someone on the road had started clicking photos. Two reporters with cameras stood by the fence rail like horses. Emily yanked her best friend into the house. Inside, Alex paused near the couch. They both stared at the messy nest of cushions and blankets on the floor, clothes strewn around, dishes with food on them, books and magazines and newspapers split open.

"You don't have to tell me. About your dad," Alex said cautiously. "But if you want to, I'm here."

"Okay," she'd said, standing stiff, agonizing. "Thanks."

But soon the clumsiness vanished. It was like nothing had come between them. They sat out back in the sunlight, out of view, facing the old barn and the woods. Birds chirped. The grass at their feet was strewn with lamb's-quarter weeds. It was as though the world had returned temporarily to whatever used to constitute normal, even better than normal. Alex told her funny stories from work. And during a brief spell of silence, she introduced Meg's big idea, about Media Day, while Emily listened. Her breath started speeding, her mind dragged behind. She was scared.

Alex took off her sneakers and kicked them away in the grass.

"You don't have to do it. It's just an idea."

"I want to do it," she said. "I want to."

But did she? She did. She did now.

They went from there to the Sisterhood to figure out details, with a couple of the media cars trailing after them like tiny fish. And by the end of the meeting, much was agreed upon, including roles. Plans called for Meg to be Emily's "handler," official representative and publicity agent, to protect her best interests, also in charge of driving her to appointments. Alex would handle communications, schedule, payments, anything that required a laptop. Once the statement was done, Meg would return to the press encampment at Emily's house and present it, and hope that any absent reporters would receive word from the others.

"Unless you think we should do it more officially," Meg says. "Like at the courthouse?"

"Hey, should we talk to Nick's lawyer about this?" Alex asks.

"No," Emily says suddenly. She rouses herself up and folds the quilt. "I don't want to."

"Are you sure?" says Alex.

"I don't know." Her voice clings to the silence. She goes into the kitchen and pours herself a glass of water. A peace comes over her; she knows her mind quite clearly. "Yes, I'm sure."

At the start of the conversation, the first thing decided among the three of them had been that Media Day sounded like a pretty good idea. Whatever happened, at least she'd be in charge. Oddly, she'd been thinking something similar, without knowing how to put it into words. The night before, when Nick was out, she'd called the photographer, the guy in Foxborough who telephoned. She told him that she'd accept his offer, but that it would need to be scheduled in light of other requests she'd received. She held her breath. There were no other requests, it just sounded good.

The guy sighed. He said he was disappointed. He said he wanted to back out. He said it needed to be an exclusive or nothing.

She said she was fine with nothing, and hung up. It was one of the most thrilling things she'd ever done.

Two minutes later, he called back, still interested. She upped the price. Four hundred dollars.

He said that was impossible. Who did she think she was?

Five hundred dollars, she said.

The photographer hung up.

She couldn't help but laugh.

He called back half an hour later.

∎

"I don't have to talk to you."

"I realize that," Martin says. "I just need a favor."

"You said you're sick."

"My back went out. I'm stuck in my hotel."

"What can I do for you, Martin?"

He'd found her phone number in his notes: "Sneakers," aka Jennifer Cruz, the girlfriend of the Ashburn daughter.

"It's about the case," he says. "You've seen the news."

"They put that asshole in jail. Your client must be happy."

"So I'm trying to tie up a loose end. I need your help."

He couldn't go back to Nick again. But he couldn't let it go either.

"I still have your word," she says. "About Moira."

"Solemn vow," he says.

For Jennifer, this had been his guarantee, that he'd promised weeks earlier, around the time that Nick's mother went into the hospital: that he'd go to his own funeral with her secret in his chest, the relationship he'd uncovered between her and the deceased doctor.

"Here's my question," he says. "And I'm sorry it's personal. What was your attraction to him?"

She asks darkly, "What do you mean?"

"You're young, you're beautiful. What made you choose him?"

She sighs. There's a long pause.

"Do you know anything about addiction?"

"Let's say I'm familiar."

"That's what I thought."

"Connect the dots for me."

"But we're done after this," she says after a pause. "If I do this. No more phone calls. No favors."

"Agreed. You'll never hear from me again."

"I had a crash," she says. "Five years ago. I was on a training ride, on my bike. I basically got run over by a soccer mom on her cell phone. Hit-and-run, never caught her. It was nasty. I broke my right femur. They put me on Vicodin for the pain. Anyway, I used to party a lot. Like, a lot. But that was years ago. It was behind me. Then comes Vicodin. Things got out of hand. I worked for a pediatrician at the time. She retired, she recommended me to Dr. Ashburn. A couple months go by, he catches me stealing a script, a prescription pad.

"I was putting my little sister through school," she says. "I couldn't lose this job."

"He offered you a deal."

"He offered me a deal." Her voice catches. "It lasted a month. I couldn't take it anymore. I quit, I got straight. My sister was the one who helped me. She wanted me to report the guy. I had, like, thirty days sober. So I went to the Sheriff's Department."

"You spoke to the sheriff?"

"He talked me out of it. He said I shouldn't 'go down that road.' What did I know? I'm not a lawyer. I was scared."

"And so now," Martin muses, "the sheriff had leverage on the doctor. Which maybe he applied, lightly. So the doctor knew where the power lay."

"What do you mean?"

"Forget it. Please go on."

"There's not much else. I met Moira, it was a total coincidence. We matched online. We got coffee. I figured out who she was. Honestly I sort of thought it would be a revenge fuck. Then within a week, what can I say, I was in love."

Her voice cracks.

"I have to tell her," she says shakily. "Don't I?"

"I don't know," Martin says.

A police officer lives off the unhappy—or is it just unique to him?

"Look, you've been a big help," he says.

"We're done then. Forever. We are, right?"

"Forever."

•

A "posse-up" rumor is the frothing buzz at Saturday's midmorning press conference. The going story says the vox populi of Claymore may not only wall itself off from further inquiry, but is considering an act of retail, a public sale of its story to a single outlet, come cash, come flash-bulbs. It's as though an atmospheric interruption took place sometime in the last few nights, a clash of weather systems and electricity and air pollutants, but none of the professional observers had noticed.

Saturday, ten a.m., the brethren of Leela Mann uniformly complain about how the *LA Times* article, the one that truly broke the story, had been too ground-razing to begin with, too scorching. Lips weren't just sealed shut but burned. Worse, the girl and boy still won't talk, even though everyone's sure the girl is being circled by management offers, book offers, tour deals, requests for event appearances.

Older reporters joke how, from across the country, you can hear the whumping of helicopters warming up in Beverly Hills, the sound of William Morris paratroopers zipping up their jumpsuits. Which still doesn't preclude a greater, ever-present menace to them all: what if they get snaked by social media?

Even the McDonald's band of young reporters starts to break up.

And so, aside from the regular bullshit, the press conference is just another sexless gang bang. Little useful information is shared. *Thanks for coming, bottled water near the restrooms.* Reporters snack from bags of bagels. Cameramen struggle to establish position. One guy smashes a lens and it's the only event of any significance to occur in twenty-four hours.

Afterward, the scrum breaks, parts around the TV people doing set-ups, and Leela heads for the CVS like it's an emergency. Because it *is* an emergency: to buy enough Rolaids and Gatorade to make her system stable.

Not better, not even good, just stable.

And on her way she passes the Angry Goat, the bar and grill where she ate lunch that day with Justin Johnson, where she ate dinner the night that she graduated high school. A guy with a light beard and an apron smokes a cigarette by the door. A Canadian flag bandanna is wrapped around his head. He stares at her darkly. He says loudly, "You're all scum."

She wants to agree but it would hurt too much.

That morning, at dawn, she'd driven straight to Madbury from Rob Miller's house while feeling about as low as she'd ever felt. Was sick twice, pre- and postshower, therefore she'd required a second shower. Somehow she made it to the courthouse, and felt like she was the biggest imposter yet to walk the planet.

She almost sent an email to Bryan James, telling him not to bother anymore.

During the press conference, she'd gotten a text from Sandra: her parents needed Leela out of the house by next week, they had tenants moving in.

Is it physiologically possible to have a panic attack on top of the worst hangover of your life?

At the CVS she buys a liter of Diet Coke, drinks half of it. Buys a lemon-lime Gatorade, drinks half of it. Tops it off with Rolaids, then fills the rest of the Diet Coke bottle with lemon-lime Gatorade and shakes it together. The day is hot and bright. She closes her eyes in the sunlight. Her bag makes noises. It may as well be her pulsating head. She pulls out her phone. Several texts from her mother flow through in free verse:

We got an offer on the house.

Significantly below asking price.

We took it.

At least it's something.

Please don't be mad.

We really don't need that from you presently.

Best not to call for a few days.

XO Mom.

Her heart thumps emptily in her chest.
Suddenly, full of drive, she gets back in the car.
But it's just the knowledge—really only a clumsy conviction, half dumbass stupidity and half bullish confidence, that she knows how misery works, and that things can't get worse, so why not—that propels her to back out of her parking space, pull out into the square and take Lincoln up to Foreside, Foreside to Thomas, Thomas to Old Farm Road—streets she remembers from childhood to streets she doesn't know, directed by a robotic woman's voice from her phone—before she parks outside an unfamiliar condo block, twenty minutes later.

The address was in an old email, Leduc's "Thousand Oaks Village." Where her parents had been forced to move. What she finds is a seventies Ewok village in the woods, thirty or forty condos painted earth colors. Fir Landing. Pine Corner. Ash Creek. Each cul-de-sac is a suspended slab of a dozen units, edged with ivy, with bubble skylights on every roof turned black from decades of sap drippings.

And her mother, her poor mother, with her bad knees and her arthri-
tis, is hunched over in front of a small garden patch. Leela parks the car.
The watering can catches her breath. It's one she remembers from when
she was little—dented, rusty, crimped inside the handle—when she
helped her mom in the garden. Her mother the disciplinarian, the stan-
dard keeper, the cautiously affectionate. Her mother looks more stooped
these days, less plump. Leela feels heat prick up and down her body.

And she herself is fifteen again, she's sixteen, she's twenty-four and
no wiser; eternally clumsy, eternally happy-go-unlucky, always and only
Leela Mann from Claymore, New Hampshire.

Then her father starts banging on a window. He looks straight at
her, staring so intensely it's like he's about to have a fit.

Her mother looks up from the garden, to see what the craziness is
about, just as she gets out of the car.

"Leela?"

"Hi, Mom."

"What are you doing here?"

"I meant to call."

"Did you not get my text messages?"

"Of course I did."

"Obviously now is not a good time."

As if a five-hour drive had been accomplished in the last twenty
minutes.

"I understand," she says, almost angrily.

"Then what?"

"I was in town, so I thought."

Her voice trails off. Her father disappears from the window. She
closes the distance with her mother, she's too tired and sick to do anything else.

"But what are you doing here?" her mother snaps defensively. "Is
something wrong with you?"

How long has it been? A year? A year and a half?

"I just thought I'd visit."

"You don't look good, you know," her mother says, involuntarily, and
pulls off her gardening gloves. Leela wants to hug her, but the words
make her hold back. Maybe she should just leave. Then her mother
bundles forward in a rush and clasps her thin hands around her waist
and throbs in her arms. "Have I missed you," whispers her mother with
an urgent plea, as if she's not sure if it's a statement or a question. Which

provokes a reaction, Leela's hangover melts, and she's undone by the absurdity of the situation, and her mother cries, too, her mother who always sounds like a hiccupping dog when she cries.

And while they're standing there together, until both of them are chuckling, and they have to wipe the corners of their eyes, Leela sees her father appear in the front door, and she's intensely ashamed that she's surprised, like a disgraceful idiot, to see his face radiate with so much joy.

.

The writing's on the wall, literally: the front windows of the New Balance shop in Claymore feature a word-balloon tornado of adrenalized hashtags, like #HUSTLER #BABY #GETSOME #GOTSOME #GOTQUICK? #FINDYOURQUICK #QUICKITANDHITIT #QUICKITORQUIT #YOUCANJUSTQUITCOMPLAINING.

The New Balance store is her mother's idea, her genius mother. The night before, they'd eaten dinner off their laps in the sitting room, like guests at a wake. The furniture of her childhood was crammed in awkwardly around them. Her father was frequently at a loss for words. Still bald, still bespectacled, but also thoroughly confounded, so pleased was he to have her in his house again. And Leela could not have been much more happily enveloped. She didn't mention her credit card debt. They didn't talk about the condo. No one mentioned her brother, Satnam, except to talk around him, to agree that medical marijuana seemed a joke, scientifically, if it was being sold in the form of candy bars.

But she did confess that she'd been laid off. They switched right into parental mode—troubled, sympathetic, pragmatic, evidently grateful to resume their familiar roles. Did she need money? Did she want to move home? Her father even made a joke about how the two of them could pool resources, drive each other to job interviews.

She told them about the possible opening at the Magazine, why she was in New Hampshire in the first place, to write a story about the Claymore Kids.

"It's a real tragedy," her mother said. "I feel for this girl."

"I think it is a complete insult to my intelligence," her father said, getting up. "People forget, we are at war still. In Afghanistan. In Syria. Instead I have to listen to nonsense about these children."

"Your daughter is attempting to add to that nonsense," her mother said drily.

"Well, not really," Leela tried.

"Of course not. Leela is different. She is a real journalist."

"Your father, in his holy wisdom," her mother said, "decided to submit an application for a position at MSNBC."

"Do not even start with that."

"Where one applies, so I'm told, by writing unsolicited letters full of nonsense."

"Leela, I had a letter published in the newspaper last week."

"Please. He did not."

"Yes I did."

"The co-op newsletter doesn't count."

"Of course it does. She's always trying to drag me down!"

"You'd have your daughter working in Guantánamo if it were up to you."

"If it would mean getting that place shut down, then yes!"

Her bed was an inflatable mattress in a back room. An hour after dinner, Leela had said good night, prepared herself a cup of tea, and listened to her parents squabble happily over the dishes. Being around them gave her a renewed sense of confidence. In her room, she got out her laptop, sat against the wall, resumed her latest project: trying to track down the Ashburns' daughter, Moira.

The day before, she'd found an address in an old White Pages. It was for a condo in Leduc. She'd knocked on the door: no response. And there'd been no answer to three calls she'd made to a mobile number she found online in a profile; no reaction to a note she'd left at a veterinary clinic where Moira Ashburn was listed among the staff on the clinic's website; no reply to a note she'd slipped under the Leduc condo's door.

But then, from the sagging air-bed, within twenty minutes she turned up gold: a months-old photo album with public visibility. In which the Ashburns' daughter appeared to have a girlfriend. According to the photos, they went hiking a lot, and tended to kiss on mountain summits.

Something was remarkable about that, but she couldn't pin down what. She made a note to herself to review the photos again in the morning.

At breakfast, her mother mentioned that she needed to go buy new sneakers, she planned to drive over to the New Balance outlet if Leela wanted to come along—which made Leela smack down her oatmeal spoon, run and grab her computer.

The girlfriend, in all the pictures, in a variety of Day-Glo outfits, always wore head-to-toe New Balance gear, all of it brand-spanking-new.

So, a New Balance employee. It's a start. Even if the company employed over a hundred people in Claymore, it was worth a shot to join her mother to the outlet. Nothing. So she dropped her mom at home, went alone to the retail store afterward. She figures she'll try the factory next, see if she can sneak past reception. But then, through the store's display there she is, #baby, to all appearances #hustling: Moira Ashburn's girlfriend through the window, the one from the photos.

Deep breath and Leela's out the door.

"Hi, excuse me?"

"Can I help you?"

She grabs a sneaker at random. "Do you have this in a seven?"

"We should," the woman says. "Do you want me to grab anything else?"

"No, that's it."

It's definitely the same woman as in the pictures, but even tinier, more muscular.

She returns two minutes later, with two boxes.

"We have the seven, but I thought we might try a half-size up, just in case. This model tends to fit a little small."

Leela removes her Converse, thrusts in her feet.

The woman instructs her to jog down a track in a hallway.

"How do they feel?"

"They feel great."

It's true. And if only she had $120 to spend on new sneakers.

"Awesome." The woman smiles brightly when she returns. "They look really good on you. That's not the main thing, but it's a plus."

"Can I ask you a question? It's Jennifer, right?"

It says so on her name tag. Honestly, what right does she have to invade this woman's life?

"Do we know each other?"

"I'm Leela."

"Hi, Leela," she says guardedly.

"I should have said before, I'm a journalist. I'm up here doing a story about the Ashburn case."

The woman looks around, as if for someone else.

"What do you want?"

"I'm actually from Claymore, originally. My parents live down the street. Do you think I could take you out for coffee sometime? I just want to ask you a couple questions."

The woman stares at her, not listening to a single word. She says accusingly, "Are you with Martin?"

"Who's Martin?"

"Martin Krug. This is such bullshit."

"I honestly don't know who that is."

"I don't know what you think you're doing here—"

"Wait, I don't know what you're talking about. I found a picture of you and the Ashburns' daughter online, you were hiking together. I just want to ask you a couple questions."

The woman stares hard. Leela can't help but look away. After a couple more seconds, it's clear to both of them who's won.

The woman says quietly, "I don't give a shit what you want." She picks up the shoes and adds, "I'll just take these to the counter."

"Sure," Leela says reluctantly. "Thank you."

Five minutes later, she has new shoes on her credit card.

■

I dont know who you are but pparently you kno w me or my son because somehow your comments appear in my "newsfeed". So I guess that means you can say whatever you want. You don't know the HALF of it. We have rights. We are not your sidesohw. Why not all of you, or maybe the only one to think that you try, there is a real person out there that reads this. This is supposed to be a community well imagine this was a child of yours. Two people were killed. Lives arebeing RUINED. You think you're my neighbors?? And that's how talk to each other neighbors noawadays ????

■

The Sheriff's Department doesn't have any Martin Krugs, the receptionist says, but she suggests that Leela try the Public Defender's Office, where a touchy young man says that, yes, they've had a Martin Krug consulting recently, from New Jersey.

Which enables some simple math on her part.

"Isn't he the one who found the kid in the first place?"

"You must watch the news," the guy says sarcastically.

"What's the best way I can reach him?"

"I can't give out that type of information."

Ten minutes later, she's called six motels: no luck. She tries the first listing under Claymore's bed-and-breakfasts.

"He's not in at the moment," a man says after the second ring. "May I take a message?"

"Do you know when to expect him back?"

"May I ask who's calling?"

Half an hour later, Leela parks in front of the hotel, down near the beach. In her lifetime she's probably driven by it a dozen times, but never really noticed the sign, the iron water pump, the American flag with only a dozen-plus stars.

A teenager sweeps the walk, in a T-shirt and shorts, shower sandals with black socks, plugged into his smartphone.

"Excuse me."

The kid looks up. Doesn't say anything.

"I'm looking for Martin Krug."

"Yeah?"

"I like your nose ring."

"Do I look like I work here?"

"You have a broom."

"This is my house," he says loudly.

"Well, the sign says it's a hotel."

The boy pulls out his earbuds.

"What do you want him for?"

Before she can answer the kid drops the broom, slumps down on the porch swing, starts to watch something on his phone.

"I'm Leela," she says. "I'm a journalist."

"Cool."

"Can I sit with you?"

The boy doesn't say no.

She remembers how mostly horrible life is prior to nineteen.

"It must be interesting," she says, sitting down. "Living in a hotel."

"You're in town about the murders."

"That's right."

"It's fucked-up. Like truly."

"Totally."

"You realize those photos are bullshit, right?"

"You know about the photos?"

The boy gives her a nutty look.

"Emily and I used to run track. What people are saying about her is disgusting."

"I actually went to CHS."

"No shit?"

"Six years ago. What's your name?"

"Demeke."

"I'm Leela. So why exactly," she says, "are the pictures bullshit?"

He doesn't say anything for a moment. "Trust me, if you knew her, you'd know that girl would never put stuff like that online."

"That's a good point."

"She's a total weirdo, don't get me wrong. I mean, she's nice, she's just not that type of person."

"Can you tell me more?"

∎

So Leela Mann packs up all her crap, again, sweeps out Sandra's family's little house, and moves her stuff to Leduc, one of a billion kids moving back in with their parents. And during the drive, she tells herself that it's only temporary, until the story's done. Plus her parents want her there, she loves her mom's cooking. And now she's building what starts to feel, knock on wood, like a solid lead.

With the bed-and-breakfast kid's guidance, she's able to track down the boy interviewed in Justin's story, the hockey player, a kid named Michael. The one who accused Emily Portis of posting her own photographs on the web. The same young man who Emily says stole her pictures in the first place.

He works at an ice cream shop on the strip. The shop windows are full of chocolate, candy in plastic cages. The window frames are trimmed with roses and jasmine. The door jingles when Leela walks in. A boy behind the counter chats up two girls. He's got one of those sweep hairdos, like a college quarterback, and exudes fatigue and overconfidence, as if he's too important in the world to be awake.

The girls are lanky and barefoot, in tank tops and cutoffs. They hover around the register like sand midges.

Within a minute, the boy denies that he has anything to do with the photographs, and this is before she's even asked him a single question, only announced her occupation. He also denies he's even seen them, he wouldn't need to, he's not that type of guy.

301

"Besides, why would I?"

"Would you what?" asks Leela.

"Put them up on Snapchat or whatever."

"Who said anything about Snapchat?"

"Nice try," says one of the girls. "Everyone knows it was."

Leela ignores her.

"Maybe you thought it would be funny. Maybe one of your buddies on the hockey team told you to pass it around."

"Even if he did?" says the other girl. "It's not like he's the one who took the photographs. That's who you should be looking for. That's pornography."

"It's sick," says the first.

"So you've seen the photos. What did you think?" she says, turning on the girls.

They don't say anything.

"You're right: it is pornography. Did you know that sending pornography like that to somebody else, over the internet, is a federal crime?"

"Yeah, we know that."

"In this case it's referred to as sexual exploitation of a minor," she says, while she looks at the boy. "People go to prison for this kind of thing. You're a sex offender. You're on a public registry for life."

The previous evening, on a hunch, she'd emailed Matteo, her ex-boyfriend from college. He'd since gone through law school, he was a clerk in Delaware. He said that although distribution of child porn was a federal crime, there were so many cases, so few case workers, prosecutors didn't automatically go full tilt unless a certain threshold of images was met. Especially in the case of sexts or what seemed like sexts. It was the realpolitik of child porn today—but she didn't need to share all of that just yet.

"It's still a total slut thing to do," says the first girl.

"Exactly," says the second. "It's so desperate."

The boy laughs. The girls giggle.

"So are you guys friends with this girl?" Leela asks.

"No way."

"She's the kind of person who thinks she's better than everybody else."

"And you can quote us on that," the first girl says, and the two of them start to laugh.

"Hey," the boy says, "why don't you write a story about my band?"

Enough. Leela ignores the boy, turns all her focus on the first girl, says she *will* quote her on that, and what is her full name? The girl stumbles, caught off-guard. The other says her parents told her not to talk to the media. The air cools. A few tourists in shorts and golf shirts enter, the door behind them jingles. The boy says loudly he's not even supposed to be talking to people like her, she needs to leave or he'll call the manager.

Leela expresses her gratitude and dangles her business card over the counter.

"Anytime you want to talk," she says.

And on her way out she turns off the record function on the audio app on her phone.

Outside, in the midday heat, she frowns to herself. She texts the boy at the bed-and-breakfast from her car. He writes back immediately: the person she should really talk to is Emily's BFF, Alex Rosenthal. He doesn't have her number, but he can get it.

Rosenthal, as in Meg Rosenthal?

Lol wha?

In the late afternoon, she drives back to her parents' condo to take a nap. The house is quiet. Both of them are out. The fact that the Body, Meg Rosenthal, may be her next stepping-stone is met with relief and aggravation. She's about to fall asleep facedown on the couch when she gets a text.

Hey Leela what's up. Lol so I don't know what happened the other night but my dad says he found you wearing his work shorts???? That is SICK I totally need to hear all about it, let's get a beer. Also I really want to get your thoughts about my book. Just in case you didn't finish I've got a pdf, I'll email you in a sec. I can also drop one off if you prefer a print-out haha. I don't need your edits written, we can just meet up. Btw I meant to ask do you have a literary agent? Looking forward! Rob

After twenty or thirty shutter clicks, Emily shuts her eyes and takes a deep breath. She's full of irritation. She's been uncomfortable the whole time. She wants to wake up in another world, make the delirious moment go away. But when she opens her eyes, the man is still there, waiting, staring impatiently.

"Can we continue now, please?" he says, with a heavy German accent, and an undertone of crabby irritation.

Click, click, click.

People watch from the sidewalk, gaping from a distance. She goes along, drops her chin to her shoulder the way he asks and looks slightly to the side, at the sporting goods store across the street.

Click, click, click.

The night before, she dreamed of Nick. It made her whole body warm, like her circulatory system was smiling. She'd woken up so happy, she reached out for him. He was gone. A note on his pillow said his boss wanted him in early.

She'd planned to tell him that morning about Media Day, the thought had filled her with nervous fear. She took his early departure for a sign, that it was okay to let him know later.

The German newspaper is the first booking. The photographer's an older man, with a white mustache and camouflage shorts. He arrived with a young woman, also German. He takes a few more pictures, stops, mutters bitterly to himself, then walks in a small circle with his neck cranked back, as if watching something in the sky.

The initial idea had been a portrait with the courthouse for backdrop. Five hundred bucks, Meg negotiated, one outfit, one setting.

Cars drive around the square. Some drivers gawk.

"This is not working," the photographer announces in English.

"What's not working," Meg says.

He ignores her. "What about the idea you were having," he says to his companion. Until that moment she'd been silent, standing five feet from Emily, holding a collapsible silver disk to reflect the light.

"What other idea?" asks Meg loudly.

The woman and the photographer step away. Meg stands with her arms crossed, annoyed. The woman comes back to confer with Meg, and the two of them step away. Emily watches the whole thing. She wants to ask loudly if anyone plans to consult her, ever.

Meg jogs over. She says in a rush under her breath, "They want to do a shot in a bathing suit."

"A bathing suit? Like at the beach?"

"Yeah, no. They want to do it here. Against a tree or something. Or in the grass."

She feels like a child, like someone's toy.

"I don't get it."

"Oh, come on. Think about it." Meg exhales, looks away. "I told them it could only be a one-piece."

"We're in a park. I'm not putting on a bathing suit."

"It's five hundred bucks."

"I know that."

"No. Another five hundred bucks."

"Really?"

Meg sighs, irritated, nothing coy.

"But that's a thousand bucks."

"Maybe it's a German thing. What's your size?"

"I want one thousand two hundred," Emily says. She stares at the mountain above town. "I want twelve hundred bucks."

Meg eyes her for a long moment, then smiles and jogs back to the German woman. They walk away and chat some more. From the distance, with a different kind of interest, the woman stares at Emily over Meg's shoulder. She knits something into her stare and doesn't look away. Emily doesn't look away either.

The woman barks something snappish to the photographer. He responds with a grunt, he doesn't even look up from his phone.

The woman walks briskly away toward the sporting goods store.

"You got your twelve hundred," Meg says.

While they wait, Meg runs down the schedule listed on her phone. Up next is an interview, on camera, with a Canadian true-crime program, to be filmed in a motel room near the beach. Then two interviews, forty-five minutes apiece, with journalists from American gossip magazines. Then lunch. After that, another photo shoot, maybe two, depending, then another interview, in a diner, then photographs at a barn dance that evening in Rinehart.

Plus there were foreign inquiries still being tended by Alex, but time zones made it difficult to lock appointments. Also, a *Lifetime* producer was interested in talking as soon as possible.

"And everyone's paying for this?" Emily whispers.

"Of course," Meg says, laughing, suddenly an old pro. "They don't care. That's what I figured out: it's not their money."

The German woman comes jogging, with a red one-piece, scalloped white ribbon along the top. Emily changes in the public restroom next to the gazebo. Inside is a brown-spotted mirror screwed to the cinder blocks. She brushes out her hair with her fingers. She looks like a flower someone just yanked out of a garden bed. Her legs look like vanilla ice cream cones. What will Nick think when he finds out? Meg calls for her to hurry up. She stuffs her jeans and T-shirt in the shopping bag from the store and walks out slowly.

The photographer is next to her before she even has a chance to think. His instructions come with a different tone, more commanding, faster. He compliments her, he says she looks "very beautiful," and now he wants her over there, doing this, then doing that. Her first reaction is to recoil, instant shame—except then it evaporates. *This was all her idea.* She understands exactly what he wants, what's happening. She does what he says, translated through the female assistant. She is to remove the shoes. She is to stand at the old tree, back to trunk, then grasp the trunk, lean forward, and step up on her toes so the feet arch.

He smiles, ducks back behind the camera, raises one of his hands— and in an extraordinary way that Emily can't explain, but that she senses down to her toes, she feels like she's the one who put him there, that she's the one positioning *him.*

"This is beautiful," the photographer says.

Click click click.

"Now more, more, please."

"So the chest is out," the woman says.

"Like this?" she says.

Next, stand more on the toes. Next, smile, look to the side. Next, direct the chest toward the lens. Emily smiles, she responds, it's just play, it's *her* play. Next, lie down on her side in the grass, knees together, legs slightly bent, one hand behind her head with her elbow pointing to the clouded sky—so it would appear that, if she hazards an interpretation, they've caught her out sunbathing on the lawn, in a little red bathing suit, the way American girls do.

And when she yawns, reaches back to fix her hair, she exposes her décolletage in the process.

Click click click.

A pair of older women in running outfits stop to watch the show. Kids near the gazebo pause, run over toward them, come close enough that the German woman shoos them away. All eyeballs on her, her public display, her public disorder. But Emily doesn't recognize them, none of them. She's sure they know her name, or can guess, and have opinions of what she's doing, and she doesn't care, she *must* not care. She sucks in her stomach *and* their foggy gazes and tries to push all that tension straight into the camera lens. A satisfied flush rises in her face when she remembers Alex's advice from a text she received that morning, when she and Meg had left in the car.

Say what you want and do what you
want and most importantly JUST DO
YOU. And if any biotch has a problem
we'll feel bad for her later that it bothers
her so much

The photographer gets closer to the ground.

"That's good, your smile," he says, so only she can hear him. He raises the camera to his eye. "Now, please, more of the chest?"

■

And that's how it is. Nick keeps himself occupied all day, feels his days are full enough as things stand, between work, keeping his head down, attending to Suzanne's needs when asked, or when not asked but the need is obvious, such as a night he finds her passed out in front of the computer and decides to change her passwords on certain internet forums, to prevent any further drunken posting. But overall he does a first-rate impression of someone who's so busy he doesn't have a moment to think. Though he thinks a lot. Worries constantly. Endures the vivid dreaming. Sometimes his throat closes and he gets choked up, feeling fooled despite whatever hard look's on his face.

The fact is he doesn't like Emily's struggle with him lately, or with herself. Because that's what it is. When she tries to talk them out of reality, sway him away from thinking about what's really happening, or pretend nothing's happened at all.

As far as he's concerned, days start bad and get worse. *Unpredictably.*

So he stays as busy as possible, otherwise his mind gets way too raw. He'll see the Ashburns' faces in his dreams like they're wallpaper in his skull. He thinks sometimes, *So this is what it's like to be insane.*

But then sometimes with Emily it's randomly better. Like with sex. One night, he's up at the house, her family's old house, and nearly everything he proposes doing she refuses. Movie, TV, reading. Stupid comments, stupid fights, they fight from room to room. But then they start to kiss, making out while also moving, and she puts his hands on her chest, uses his fingers to squeeze her own nipples, and soon he's naked, she's naked, hooking herself on top of him so she can rub herself into him, then turn around and keep doing the same thing, only backward—it makes him explode.

A couple times, she takes a nap, he stares at her face, and she looks like a total stranger to him at certain angles. Like some random girl he just met.

He doesn't have a clue what she's thinking half the time.

He tries not to provoke her. Sometimes she cooks, but mostly their meals are scavenged, microwaved, eaten on paper towels in front of the TV. He tells a joke, she snuggles into his body. It's not just good, it's great. And he feels for a moment like they're on equal footing. After a frustrating day, or a call with the lawyer, when he feels like he can't bear all the pressure for one more minute, it's amazing when they can just be like that, boyfriend and girlfriend, normal people. For whom anything seems possible. She lays her cheek on his shoulder. Donut sugar glitters on the surface of her lips.

He's gotten in the habit of thinking that what's worst about him is what needs her so badly: his lack of resolve when she has plenty. It's just the truth. Nick Toussaint Jr. comes up with big plans, then doesn't follow through: that'll be his life story.

He's not even conscious of the first time he wants to be with her forever, until it sits in his brain like simple fact.

But now he knows a new type of pain: what arrives when someone does or does not take out the garbage by a certain point, and this is pointed out to him as indicative of bigger things. Or something else too stupid to fight about. They fight as if nights were made for fighting. If only he had her on camera! So Emily could see every time she's being nuts, saying she did one thing when she did another. He feels lost half the time. Like he's lost himself somehow.

He remembers reading Hunter Thompson in his old bed, he can't believe he'd ever been so naive. Love is the worst. And lying? Lying's *essential*.

Sometimes they even fight about why they fight. It makes him want to yell at the ceiling. Her words fly in and bang around his head for hours. All worked up, he has to go for walks to keep from exploding. He trudges up the mountainside in the dark, kick-stepping mulch, and tries to outdistance the stress, the ghosts. He returns sweaty and wiped out. He takes a shower. He still can't sleep. He's not angry anymore, he's not scared, but he's something, he just doesn't have a name for it.

Then by the morning, while he's gone over every word they said twice, she barely remembers if or why they'd fought at all. It makes him furious all over again.

And the depressive qualities that were already in his soul begin to grow over what had always been essentially a cheerful disposition.

Tourists order pizza and insist he's late so they get the discount. Bikers give him dirty looks at the tire center. He's constantly on guard, and all the time wondering if they recognize him from the news. One night, during a fight, he says to Emily something like, "I can't be afraid of pissing you off all the time." And it's true. But all at once, all the anger he'd kept in check was about to come flooding out. He'd thrown away his life on this girl. It freaked him out: how much resentment was in his blood; it couldn't all be just about her. So he ran. Without a word, drove down the mountain, all the way to the beach. The water was black, the waves were silver. But the sight of it didn't do anything for him like it used to.

He couldn't stop thinking, *My life is insane*. And yet he was heartsick, still in love. Deep down, did she feel the same way about him anymore? He'd never met anyone like her. He never would again. They just needed to get out of town.

So he'd gone back to the house, planning to tell her they should leave in the morning, just drive, go anywhere, away from a situation that was stuck in lose-lose. But she was mad that he'd walked out and wouldn't talk to him.

The next morning, Nick wakes up early, nervous, climbs out of their mangy nest of old quilts in the living room. He glances at Emily's sleeping face in the yellow dark while he writes a note to say he's due at work. Which isn't true, but close enough.

He works the morning at the garage. His chin is dark and itchy. When was the last time he shaved? At lunch, he reports to the restaurant. First thing to do is turn a stack of flats into delivery boxes. He's halfway done when his phone rings. It's Brenner, the lawyer, saying that there's a new scandal in Claymore. She needs to know pronto, is he at all involved in what his girlfriend's been up to thus far that day.

"I don't know what you're talking about."

"When was the last time you saw her?"

"This morning."

"And she didn't tell you about her plans."

"I just said that."

"Seriously, Nick," the lawyer says, in an angry tenor, "you're saying she didn't share shit with you. No pillow talk or whatever."

She says something away from her phone, at someone in the office, then comes back and rips him a new one, tells him this was *not* agreed upon, *not* wise, not even well executed if it needed to be done for some reason. And how does Emily not see, she wants to know, that this Media Day stunt will only make things worse? The very thing to convince people that she disseminated those photos in the first place, that she's some sort of narcissistic lunatic?

He says nothing. He feels as alone as he's ever felt.

"This needs a couple things, ASAP," Brenner says.

"Like what."

"Control, to start," Brenner says coldly. "Curtailment as soon as possible. Nick, this looks bad for everybody, I'm betting your full parole. You need to get involved in this up to your neck."

"Yeah, okay," he says. And hangs up.

On his arm is a rash from the heat. He stands at the door, scratching his arm, and stares out at the busy street, the crowded boardwalk, the summer tourists in beach gear walking between narrow canopies of shade. Typically, his former friend, what's he doing at that moment? Typically hadn't reached out once since his arrest. No visit, not a word. Even after he got out, Nick had texted him multiple times, called him twice and left messages. Even stopped by the Angry Goat. It didn't make sense.

He walks down the sidewalk, around the palisade's thick bushes, up through the little public park where the burnouts sleep. The hell with Typically, the hell with them all. The sky's vastly blue. He should probably call Emily, but that's the last thing he wants to do. He hates the idea all the more for knowing it's what he *should* do. He ducks his head in the wind. The nylon banners rustle. If she's really doing what the lawyer says, maybe it's for travel money, maybe it's a good sign?

He stops, faces the choppy ocean, impulsively texts Typically.

WHERE R U

Then he ducks down a side street, under a tree of stringy branches. Walks another sun-flecked block, across a rough, grassy park, and finds himself at the front door of the Crow's Nest Inn. Realizing, with amazement, that he'd planned to go there all along.

A big man with a crew cut stands on the porch, hard as nails, with big white teeth. There's a trace of recognition in his face. Before Nick does anything, the guy says, "You're looking for Martin?"

"Yeah."

"Around to the left, the yellow door. He's leaving tonight."

"Where's he going?"

"Couldn't tell you. Ask him yourself."

Nick goes around the corner. The sunlight through the trees turns green. His knee hurts from all the walking. At the end of the little row beside the building is a view of the sea. He knocks on the door and it swings in, unlocked.

"Nick, what a surprise," the cop says. "Come on in."

The old man's shirt isn't buttoned. He's wearing canvas hiking shorts and around his middle what looks like an old-fashioned corset, but made from Velcro. On the bed is an open suitcase.

"Going somewhere?" Nick says suspiciously, looking around.

"In a manner of speaking."

The cop reaches his hand inside the corset to scratch himself, like a woman fixing her bra. Nick doesn't even know where to start.

"What is that thing?"

"A back brace. Take a seat. If you want," the cop says, awkwardly. As if they hadn't sat a dozen times facing each other. "I'm glad to see you. I was just thinking to myself, it's all going to work out for Nick. They'll drop the charges. You'll see."

The cop buttons up his shirt.

Nick sits on the end of the bed and says nothing for a moment. He's all the more uncomfortable for being in that room. "I meant to say thanks," he says morosely. "For what you did. I mean, what you've done."

"I should be the one thanking you."

"What?"

The cop sits stiffly next to him. His legs in the shorts look like barkless trees.

"How's your mother doing?"

"Drunk, probably."

"I tried to help her. I don't think she was ready."

"Yeah, well, thanks."

It is true he likes the cop, or trusts him. The guy never lied to him that he could tell. Suzanne had said as much, vaguely. Brenner said he'd put up the bail money. But why? And what did he want in return?

"So where are you going?" he asks.

"California."

"No shit."

"My daughter lives there. I'm trying to patch up some things."

Nick almost asks him how she got there, but it makes no sense.

"I want to go to California. When this is over." The rash on his arm burns. Nick scratches it away. "Look," he says impulsively, "could you give me some advice?"

"Of course. For what it's worth."

"It's Emily. She's doing all this stuff."

"What stuff?"

He fills the cop in on what the lawyer said, about the photographs, the interviews. Based on the guy's face, he wonders if he knows some of it already. How does everybody know everything before him?

"Let me ask you something, Nick," Martin says after a second. "What do you want? For yourself?"

"What does that mean?" he says angrily.

"I mean for you. For your future."

He doesn't know how to answer. The cop must sense that. He stands up and goes back to packing his clothes.

"Nick, let me walk you through a scenario," the cop says quietly, addressing his suitcase. "There's one or two things that remain unsaid. And I'm worried, if you don't deal with them, it's going to be worse in the long run."

"I don't know what you're talking about."

"That night. There was a phone call. It was the sheriff. He called the doctor while you were there." Nick starts to protest but the cop holds up a hand. "Don't worry. This is just a game. I can't prove a thing. Just hear me out. With the beacon, Emily's dad tracked you to the doctor's house. What you don't know, he's got leverage with the doctor, he's got power over him. It doesn't matter how, just trust me. The point is that if he wanted the doctor to tell him something, the doctor was going to tell him. So here's what happened, as far as I've pieced together. The phone rings. The doctor answers. Probably leaves you in the study to go pick it up in the kitchen. It's Emily's dad. He wants to know what you're doing there. Who knows why, but he's obsessed, he's following you. The doctor's gotta be surprised. And scared. Because how does this guy know? Now what I'm pretty sure happens next is that the doctor says something. About Emily. Something that alerts the sheriff as to what's going on. Whatever it is, the crucial thing is that it sounds off to *you*."

The cop turns, stares at him. Almost daring him to protest.

"I think you heard him. Maybe it's a warning. Regarding the information you've just shared, the sheriff's crimes. I think you overheard it, or just enough of it. Either way, you're enraged. Here's the one adult you thought you could trust, and he just betrayed you. You couldn't go to the authorities. The 'authority' is the guy who attacked his own daughter, the girl you love. Now the guy you turned to appears to be on the other side. So, maybe you confronted him. Maybe you got in a fight. Somehow the doctor hits the back of his head, we know from the autopsy. There's a contusion, a bruise. From the lab reports they're actually able to know it took place before the stabbings. Now, it didn't kill him, I got that confirmed, too. But that's what I'm getting at. Because once I figured this all out, and I'm not saying I got it even half-right—in fact, I don't want you to tell me if I'm right or not. But I realized, all this time, basically since the night we met, some part of you may think you were complicit in all of this. Going to the doctor's house. What you heard. Whatever happened between you and him. Kid, you've got enough to shoulder as it is. You didn't kill them, any of them. If you never listened to me before, then this is the one time. You didn't do this. He did. You understand?"

He doesn't say anything. Doesn't look up from his hands. The night is never far away. The phone rang. The doctor excused himself. *So what do you want me to do with him?* The total mind-fuck, the wild punch he threw. The cordless phone went clattering. And a second later Emily's dad was there, in the door, on the floor. *Is he dead?* He'd felt for a pulse, then pulled out the knife.

"He said he was going to kill my mom."

"I know."

He gets up to leave. He doesn't have to listen to this, on top of everything else. "Don't you think I thought about turning myself in? He's a cop. What was I supposed to do?"

"Nick, I'm sorry. Calm down."

His forehead hurts. His knee throbs. "And then I had to—"

"Nick, I know."

He clutches his knee and sits down hard on a bench.

"It's eating me up."

"I know. I'm sorry."

Martin sits down next to him and puts his big arm around him. Nick flinches, he can't help himself. After a minute the cop gets up and brings him a glass of water.

"You ask for my advice? Figure out what you want. For *you*. It's as simple as that. Just answer that one question."

■

Granville Portis is alone and he prefers it this way, for he is in control.

He refuses to eat, refuses legal counsel, refuses to be visited by medical professionals. He paces and seethes, thinks about everyone against him, about an entire society that never understood him.

He is visited nightly by his father, his father's haranguing and sermons.

He is visited by Marleen, their love affair.

He holds his pride intact. Still, he's attacked by stomach cramps, eaten alive from the inside out, shitting and groaning, made to perform scrounging ablutions with toilet paper every hour.

He does feel occasionally a transporting pleasure, of pure innocence, to remember what had once been. Then he thinks about the wife who became sick, who tricked him, whose blood turned traitor. And then the daughter who turned against him, who dishonored him, who gave up everything they had. Who'd been the one and only one who—

And the boy in the end to turn her against him finally, a Toussaint!

He hears his father's I-told-you-so, a haunting from beyond the grave.

He is the most misunderstood man.

He wakes up in the middle of the night in sweat-soaked sheets. He knows what he did, he accepts it, because the boy finally caved, to be expected from someone of his background—and yet Granville is still not understood, he is understood less. So he continues to refuse any food or advice from his minders, of whom he knows none, doesn't remember their names, doesn't answer their questions. He is glad they're so angry.

For he will not give his enemies any satisfaction, and he will be absolved, furthermore will heed no regret and will not waver.

The solitary man is different from what people think. He is believed to be of no consequence. In fact he is of the greatest consequence. He is like an eternal child, of the most tender sensitivities. And so he must learn to prefer his own company, forever misunderstood, cruelly outcast. But therefore he will never be alone, for he has himself.

And he understands, better than anyone, the significance and insignificance of his place in the greater order.

For whom vengeance is there to be claimed.

He has a plan.

■

First there's a song. It echoes in the barn like it's being played by a dozen fiddlers, but there's only one musician, a man onstage in a blue wool vest, with a caller to his left holding a microphone, a woman who tells the roomful of dancers what to do next. There's simply no escaping the call once you're in its grip. And even the most closed hearts open to contra's song, which happens once a month in Rinehart, twenty minutes north of Claymore, free to all, with do-si-do in the residual warmth of a summer day.

The dance takes place in an old barn. The room has that bland, updated rustic look, like an advertisement for Green Mountain Coffee. Other nights, the hall is available for rent, an immaculate piece of restored Yankee architecture that's useful for weddings and business seminars, with a stainless steel industrial kitchen, but also plank walls held together not by nails but wooden pegs, the way things once were built.

And on fourth Fridays, if nothing else is happening, the contra dance is happening.

Couples arrive in pairs or fours. Women with young families smile at one another and mouth things behind their husbands' backs. The single men, with long hair and Hawaiian shirts, hurry to find friends inside, find older women who remember them from previous dances and take pity. Some of the women arrive in drop-crotch pants. Some of the men wear Vibrams. Some people are so nervous they make fake phone calls to give themselves something to do.

There are plenty of teenagers, surprisingly, but that's because the county offers free pizza as a way to suck kids into something wholesome. Once the adults are finished, a DJ takes over, and until midnight he or she will play pop and rap and EDM. But the only way the kids are allowed in later is if they're there on the spot at six to get a ticket.

At dusk, the air is still hot. Mosquitoes circulate. Boys cling to the rails and measure up the girls, under the bored glances of mother types who know exactly what they're thinking. Other boys stick to the paved lot, the handicapped ramps where skateboarding is tolerated. And if occasionally one of them scores a case of beer, they vanish into the crabapple trees. The girls also huddle, but their groupings are more ordered, by proximity to the best views of the action inside, Zetas near the front, other cliques toward the cars.

And inside the barn, beneath limp cords of lights, the adults dance like busy brooms, in formal rotations that look practically Victorian.

Emily watches from the wall. Meg is buzzed before the dance even starts, her braids shine like gold. She has no problem asking guys if they want to dance. Several of whom look like they've seen her dance before. Emily's almost too tired to watch. Her feet hurt, her lungs hurt. She'd been looked at and questioned all day. The sky was darkly blue when Meg drove them away from their last appointment. She fell asleep. Fifteen minutes later, Meg had another big idea and nudged her awake.

"You need to treat yourself right," Meg said. "Now that you're rich."

They'd parked outside a JCPenney, in the old River Run mall. The lights were so bright, it could have been a baseball stadium. No one was around. Bats swung through the air. Meg pushed her through the big doors. She'd never shopped there before, never shopped before, period, not like this, where almost anything could be hers. Fifteen minutes later she'd picked out a dress, $249. She found it on one of the mannequins. It looked straight out of a magazine, a tiered dress with a round neck and darted bust. The construction looked so complicated, she just wanted to turn it inside out and see how it was made.

"Just once, for me, please?" Meg trailed her to the dressing room. "And please do not wear your jeans underneath."

The dress was off-white, slightly structured with a yielding feel, with a lace inset at the bodice and waistline. Meg didn't even have to ask: Emily wore it out of the store. The skirt lent a shape that felt connected to a dream, a different person. She caught sight of herself in a mirror, she almost didn't recognize herself. It filled her with a pleasure she'd never felt before.

The barn was their final appointment of the day. Walking in with Meg, her anxiety was almost numbing, then it disappeared. People didn't notice her, or didn't recognize her. Maybe it's the dress. Half an hour into arriving, she feels changed, enveloped in a warm feeling— a different sensation from the day so far. She hadn't minded the photographers, but the reporters made her uncomfortable. Less their questions than how they seemed: dishonest, mercenary. They gave off a weird lack of self-interest, as if their jobs were below them, as if they were the ones who deserved sympathy. Sweating in a motel room, unbuttoning wrinkled sleeves. "How about we talk about your childhood?"

The barn fills with adults, over a hundred. Lights dim. Alex arrives from the apartment. At that moment Meg twirls a little old man in logging boots.

"What is my sister doing?"

The music changes. Meg shoos the man away. "That was Howie," she says, "and we were dancing." The music starts up again, the adults start to move in fours. Women in skirts with scalloped trimmings, boots with tassels, little heeled sandals. Someone nearby drops a glass and there's a crash. Emily's heart skips a beat. By the far wall, she spots Jessie Baker, her freshman-year torturer, pointing at her, talking out of the side of her mouth to her friends, who turn and look.

"Emily, what are you wearing?" Alex asks her loudly, above the music.

"What?"

"That dress. It's amazing."

Meg shouts, "Emily, let's get a move on, you're keeping this guy waiting."

She'd almost forgotten: her final assignment. Along the side, ten feet down the wall, a man from a magazine stands under a wooden beam, with a pair of cameras slung over his shoulder.

"You're supposed to dance," Meg says. "With a man. Preferably an older man, god knows why, until he gets the shot. Then we get the hell out of here."

The photographer nods at her. She's seriously tired. People dance faster, their gazes turn toward her, placing her face.

"I don't want to," she says in a quiet voice.

"It's good money."

"I don't care."

She looks around for Nick. She'd texted him, he said he'd come.

"Really good money," Meg says. "Think of all the dresses you can buy."

"What is this for, anyway?" Alex asks. "*Ho-Down Monthly?*"

"*In Touch,*" Meg says. "Or *Us Weekly.* He says he'll pay up front, he can sell the photos later. Who cares? Emily, he only needs you dancing for one song."

"It's my decision," she announces firmly, but the music lifts in volume and no one hears her. There are more musicians now, a woman cradling an acoustic guitar, a boy plucking at a mandolin. The dancers twirl in synchronized patterns, everyone sweating, moving in tight circles, switching partners while matching hands.

"Tell you what," Meg shouts, "I'll grab Howie."

Half a minute later, Emily is led onto the floor by a sinewy old man with scratchy hands. They're surrounded by moving couples. It all seems so ridiculous. Even her legs are sweating, it's so hot. Why can't someone turn on a fan? The old man says he'll show her what to do, then he turns her like she's a doll, deeper into the crowd, and at the same time his eyes droop, out of bashfulness or embarrassment or politeness, she isn't sure, but she appreciates it and decides to make an effort. She tries to mimic everyone else. She fights back the bad feelings rising in her throat. But her feet are dead and graceless. Heat radiates off her chest. The dress is confining. A big fat man spins around next to her and bangs into her shoulder.

The little old man scurries her deeper into the masses. But she refuses his eyes when they lift, refuses any eyes watching. Her blood's hot. Her vision's blotchy. Even the walls are perspiring.

She doesn't acknowledge the photographer, though she sees the outline of his shoes, hears his cameras clacking while the old man pulls her in, puts his little rubber lips against her ear and asks her name. She says nothing. The satisfaction is not to answer. But her satisfaction feels eyes raking up and down her back. *Who does she think she is? Hasn't she done enough?* The caller onstage directs something new and Howie tries to hand her off to another man, and her satisfaction refuses, clutches the old man's hands, and makes him stop so that the two of them stand in place.

Suddenly everything is awkward. People try to dance around them, bump into them. The lights burn. Her sweat drips. The music races. She lets go of Howie's hands and runs away, slips through lines, ducks under arms. She can't breathe. Finally she reaches the edge, heads back toward Meg and Alex, while kids from school watch her, with faces like mirrors, throwing everything back, her panic, her present, her past. *Emily!* someone yells, then someone else says it even louder, in the same tone, *Emily!* Like the whole room is echoing, shrieking hysterically, *Emily!*

A hand grabs her shoulder.

Nick says, "What the hell are you doing?"

She looks at him with a start. It was Nick all along.

He pulls her away by the hand. "Didn't you hear me? I've been calling you. Let's get out of here."

They run away, out the barn, and don't look back.

■

@EPortisClaymore It's called battered women syndrome. Read up.

@EPortisClaymore id hit that

@EPortisClaymore a woman chooses to put up with abuse or not

@EPortisClaymore Hey girl wishing you peace and love and Christ's light

@EPortisClaymore close ur legs

@EPortisClaymore Hugs to you

@EPortisClaymore kill yourself oh wait did i hurt u show me ur tits

Down below the mountain, the town is dark and quiet. A flock of bats whips southward, blacker than the sky.

Their mothers are disappeared for all intents and purposes. Their fathers are virtually dead. They aren't interested in the past, they have no stake in the histories of their families or town. They have few people to rely on, none to care for, no one really whose obligations they must meet. Haven't they erred by seeking to please others? A shared weakness, an edge too thin, giving to others before attending to their own needs.

They have cash. They need to move. Hours of passion will stretch into love-filled years, but only if they're brave.

To yield at this point is to be pulled in two different directions.

Yielding even a little will crack them in half.

In the dark of her family's old house, across the endless wasteland of the internet, they read stories about themselves, watch videos of people who discuss their crimes, people who share opinions as though they're fact. Not a single account gets their story close to right. They can't stand much of it for long. No one mentions that they're in love. *They are in love.* Love of the kind that proves true love is real.

And the consequences of such love dying, they decide, are the worst possible consequences. They decide this late that evening, early the next morning, in the luminous darkness, when the simple truth is that he wants to be hers, and she wants to be his.

To survive, they must run.

But before they leave, Emily can't help but seize an impulse, grab her phone and send a text message, though really it's from both of them, to set the record straight.

SALAMANDRA: THE EMILY PORTIS STORY

Mount Washington is the tallest mountain in New England, 6,290 feet tall. The mountain stands farther north, going by latitude, than Toronto, Milwaukee, or San Francisco. Geologically, its makeup is mostly quartzite and mica schist, a bluntly pointed mound of rubble, shaped to earn its local nickname, the Hand. Some people say it looks like it's giving the finger to Massachusetts.

Historical documents explain that the first man on record to climb Mount Washington achieved the summit in 1621. Born in Boston, a son of Welsh immigrants, Aron Prichard mountaineered with the assistance of two American Indian guides, whose names were not recorded, except that they likely belonged to the Sequassen, a tribe native to the region.[1] The Sequassen called the mountain Sahkekapáwo and said it was a holy place. According to his account, Prichard's guides acted mainly as porters and balked from fear when he went for the summit. The allegation fit his plan. He'd pursued the climb to make a point, he wrote, that he wished the Sequassen to know that they were correct to be intimidated, and that they should also fear the white men as gods, men like himself whom he believed to be the humans closest to the all-powerful, with skin tone to match the peaks and clouds. After all, if holy strongholds could be breached

1. *The Domain of Mount Washington: Sequassen Peoples in the Presidential Range, 1500–2000*, Vol. 1 (2007).

safely by the white man, what hope had any red or brown men, bound to soil?[2]

Since that day, many thousands have reached the top under their own steam, people of myriad skin tones and passports.[3] In the same time period, over a hundred climbers have died.

Since 1943, the United States Alpine Research and Mountaineering Institute has kept a taxonomy of deaths, with an eye for detail. Fatalities are filed under categories such as "Fall on Ice," "High Winds," "Inadequate Equipment," "Inexperience," and "Exceeding Abilities."[4] Anecdotes describe ice climbers tumbling down gullies. Mountaineers die of exposure. Climbers fall down headwalls and "tomahawk" until their necks snap. Hikers lose their footing. Backcountry skiers, overrun by avalanches, choke to death in head-high snow, and are filed under "Asphyxiation."[5]

So no surprise, really, that a popular bumper sticker in the area reads THIS CAR CLIMBED MOUNT WASHINGTON.

Recently, a girl and a boy, New Hampshire natives, sixteen and twenty, hereafter called the Girl and the Boy, decided they wanted the sticker for themselves. A silly thing, just something to do, but in their case it was also a gesture of specific profundity. Also, they invited a journalist to come along. And this *should* be an oddity under normal

---

2. Prichard's actual death is less reverent. Nine years after his Washington summit, he was killed in a bar fight, having been accused—rightfully, says one of his sons, Nathaniel Prichard, in his own memoirs—of stealing and selling a prize horse of a wealthy neighbor, in order to make payment to another man to whom he owed gambling debts.

3. There's actually a sign above the tree line for any visiting Québécois: BIENVENUE A LA ZONE ALPINE DU MONT WASHINGTON.

4. The local rescue service, New Hampshire Volunteer Search and Rescue, has operated since 1949 out of North Conway, a village nearby. It responds to wilderness emergencies around the clock, and works in partnership with the United States Park Service's Winter Ranger team. A recent visit found the staff to be highly trained, expertly equipped, fit enough to be featured on a calendar of topless firemen. They even have a helicopter at their disposal. Still, one rescuer told this reporter, "All the high-tech gear in the world won't keep people from doing stupid shit."

5. A typical report, from 2006: "At 19:11 on February 21 USPS Winter Rangers were informed that a Skier, 25y/o male, had not returned from attempted climb / ski descent in Wilkens Ravine. When Skier signed the book at Pindell House, he communicated plans to ascend the North Gully. Beginning at 21:15, (2) rescue teams of (3) members canvassed access routes into Wilkens. Snow was precarious, with stability concerns. Therefore rescue teams did not actually reach avalanche terrain until the following morning. 08:20 Skier's body was discovered on top of debris. Skier was littered and transported to Pindell. In regards to snow stability, choosing another gully would have been a safer option."

circumstances; the two of them are not frequently in the company of journalists. But days are strange.

The Boy was only just released on bail, to await trial for two charges of homicide that may or may not stand. The father of the Girl, who happened to be the sheriff of their county, was also charged with murder, two murders; in fact, the same pair of killings that the Boy originally was accused of, before the sheriff's guilt began to seem more plausible to prosecutors, based on forensic evidence.

Furthermore, sexual matters were being discussed publicly, which involved the Boy, the Girl and the sheriff, and other parties. And so their hometown of Claymore, a small former fishing village[6] in southern New Hampshire, has lately been abuzz with rumor and allegation and gossip, and wasn't where they wanted to be. Instead, encircled by chaos, two young people decided to visit the tallest mountain in the state, the nearest, largest thing that would appear to be immovable, to have forever been the way it was.[7]

In the short lives of the Boy and Girl, during their brief romance and sudden infamy, the world had shown itself capable of rapid, uncontrollable transformation. But what if it had always been this way?

■

When the Boy and Girl invited a journalist—hereafter called the Journalist; to be explained later   to join them for a road trip, the plan was to blow out of town. They'd settled on driving north, just north; and when the Boy said this out loud, "north," the Girl determinedly nodded her head, hooked her fingers into his waistband, and he put his arm around her, protectively.

The Boy is under average height, with deep-set blue eyes and greasy dark hair that he tucks behind his ears. Sometimes, in front of the Journalist, when the Girl was absent, he complained about his current place

---

6. What's called contemporary Rust Belt, albeit more mariney: a harbor town struggling to survive in the backwash of departed industry. Think: the collapse of Newfoundland fisheries. Think: Gloucester, Mass. Think: embittered Marky Mark in *The Perfect Storm*, probably with a newfound opioid addiction, given the times and economy.

Even today people in Claymore persist in calling their harbor "the Mouth," because it's what their parents called it and their grandparents called it, before overfishing killed the stocks. Because from the Mouth were their own mouths fed, and into the Mouth were some ancestors lost.

7. They also needed to stay in state, to not break the rules of the Boy's release.

in life, his rotten luck. But he was also quick to smile, eager to please, always outgoing with strangers they met on the road.

The Girl is two inches taller and slender, with straight brown hair to the middle of her back and small brown eyes. Shy where the Boy is garrulous, pensive when he is humorous, somehow, time and again, she came across as both middle-aged and preteen.

But these are just one reporter's observations. This past summer, the Girl was portrayed in many ways, across all sorts of media around the world. But reports tended to suggest one thing to a point of cliché: that a young woman with her previous experiences was not merely teenager but mutant. That a girl of such "psychological scarring," an oft-repeated phrase, would determinably become, in due course, that most coveted archetype in our society: the Victim. Victim of violence at home. Victim of nurture, if not nature. A person engulfed by her upbringing, then unfolded by tragic events in public view.

A young woman, therefore, who lacked the agency to grasp her own story, to see herself for herself, and so her story, the Victim's story, needed to be told by others.

The Boy drove, the Girl rode shotgun, the Journalist rode middle-back. The truck belonged to the Girl's family, a 1997 Chevrolet 1500, brown and ramshackle, with red trim. By noon in mid-August, a hot sunny day, it was roaring up a state road, headed north, at which time the Journalist decided unwisely,[8] fifteen minutes into their trip together, to kick things off by paraphrasing the situation that the Girl now found herself in, with regard to how people saw her, both in town and in the media.[9]

The Girl responded, with hardness, "That's not all of it."

---

8. To be honest, it wasn't until then that the Journalist realized that, by doing just so, she was in effect behaving exactly how the Girl and Boy expected a typical journalist to behave in such a scenario, repeating what all the other journalists had done: telling the Girl who and what she was.

9. It should also be confessed that the Journalist was still pretty shocked and even a little weirded out that she'd been invited on this trip. Who does that? And yet, as explained to her on the telephone, she'd been picked from a pool of many writers who'd expressed interest in the Claymore Kids' story to be the single person granted access to write their official account—after which point the Boy and Girl planned to never again speak on record—all because, they said, the Journalist had befriended the Girl before anyone else, and seemed "real," not "bullshit." And perhaps also because, in full disclosure, the Journalist is originally from the same dingy hometown, Claymore, and even attended the same middling public high school as the Kids, though several years earlier, and was classmates with the older sister of the Girl's best friend.

The Boy said quietly, "This is stupid."

"We invited her. We both did," the Girl said, as if to confirm it for herself.

"Hey, check it out," the Boy said, reading a passing sign. "Mount Washington. A hundred miles."

■

Two days earlier, during a self-staged Media Day of her invention, the Girl's story was disseminated in a different fashion from the norm. As if to demonstrate her savviness, she auctioned off interview and image opportunities to those national and international media willing to bid for them.[10]

From which she and her appointed representatives—her best friend and her best friend's older sister—sold seven interviews, five photography sessions, plus two telephone interviews, with journalists in Japan and Brazil respectively, for a total of $21,675,[11] paid in cash or through online money transfers.

"I just wanted it all to end," she said. "It seemed like the only way."

In addition, she received supplementary offers that she did not accept, like round-trip travel to fly to Qatar, all expenses paid, to audition for an aspiring film director. Or a bid of two thousand dollars for a one-year option on the screen rights to her story, submitted by a production company in Los Angeles.

Also not interesting to the Girl: from the adult entertainment company Azuretory, the Brussels-based owner of video-streaming websites such as PornSwatch and Spanktoid, a bid of travel to the San Fernando Valley in California, plus accommodations, plus other compensation to be determined, for a modeling shoot, if not more.[12]

Among further unsolicited things, the Girl also had several scary encounters in public, and received through the internet and postal mail

10. This reporter offered no compensation for this story, and indeed can barely afford her own rent.

11. "The point was to own the story," the Girl explained when asked, sounding like she'd said this before, or had been coached to say it. "Yeah, like literally own it," her boyfriend chimed in, laughing uncomfortably.

12. Email verification was obtained for most offers. Also, not only was an Azuretory representative eager to speak on the telephone and confirm their offer, she then offered a commission if acceptance could be facilitated.

more than one marriage proposal, proposal of gang rape, pornographic image drawn in her likeness. Advertisements in her name, to sell carnal services, appeared on escort websites. Her Social Security number became public knowledge. Trolls opened social media accounts in her father's name, her mother's name; one was even quoted in a newspaper article, as though verified.

For a period of weeks this summer, New England Gothic was the new black. In cities and towns across the United States, the Girl and Boy[13] were famous. People believed they knew just how this story went,[14] all its shade. For example, they knew the Boy to be tethered to the state's justice system by a tamper-resistant monitor attached to his ankle. They knew him to be a young man from an old family, yet one who's virtually fatherless. Who dropped out of high school after a tragic snowmobile accident, and continues to live at home with a hard-drinking single mother—to the fulfillment of stereotypes everywhere regarding burnouts from the working class, though elevated to the ranks of hard-faded richie riches. In the same way, on the part of the Girl, she was believed to be many things, indistinctly, all at once. So, a sexpot. Abuse victim. Attention-seeking slut. A young woman who'd been isolated from modern society, like a lost tribe in the Amazon, until recent days when she'd been thrust into the hands of the twenty-first century

13. If it's not yet totally clear, or too obnoxious, the preference of the Journalist is to employ "Boy" and "Girl" in lieu of proper names. Partially because these are conventional titles in the romance genre—even if the pair is composed of a young man and a young woman, and they're a couple whose romance is anything but conventional, not exactly fairy-tale material as commonly understood—but also for respect for straightforward fact: people already know these names. *You* know their names. But such proper nouns can no longer be employed with accuracy, in relation to the persons who bear them, because to apply the names now, outside of court documents, is to guarantee imprecision, to dabble in myth. Is Oprah Winfrey really "Oprah Winfrey"? Is "Gisele Bündchen" the supermodel, or is she the tired wife to whom Thomas Brady, or "Tom Brady," wakes up? There's too much innuendo and scandal here, too much smoke, at least as of this writing, and it's this Journalist's stipulation that the young woman and man, the Girl and Boy, are simply not the persons believed to correspond to their names.

14. Still, even devotees won't know that the Girl, during the drive, would cite *Singin' in the Rain* as her favorite movie, and that her favorite scene from the movie was not, she said bluntly, the same one that everyone else likes, when Donald O'Connor does his slapstick routine, but instead the eponymous sequence, Gene Kelly tap dancing through a downpour, twirling while he smiles, smiles, smiles before a crabby patrolman gives him a look like he thinks Kelly is nuts. "He isn't crazy, that's what's crazy," the Girl said meaningfully. "He's just realized he's in love."

and all its ruthless merchants, where her purity hadn't only been spoiled, but exploited, sold into whoredom.

In addition, the public knew that her dad, until recently the elected sheriff of Claymore County, stood accused of murdering two people to protect a terrible secret: his rape of the Girl over many years. The same sheriff who, postmurdering, as the allegations hold, then roped in the Boy—wrong place, wrong time—and told him to do away with the bodies, bludgeon their faces to prevent easy identification and bury them outside the state, then assume blame if the crimes ever came to light. Otherwise, the sheriff threatened, he'd flat-out murder the Boy's mom.[15]

In an interview[16] for the German tabloid *Die Sonne*, a publication that boasts a circulation of three million, the Girl was asked how it felt to be a spokeswoman for victims of sexual abuse. How she'd come to decide, while demonstrating through her self-photographed sexuality,[17] that women indeed may refute abuses visited upon their bodies through their own sexual self-manifestations. To which she said, or is quoted as saying, "I don't know what that means. We just want to be left alone." And the rest of the article was not much more informative than that, which didn't seem to be of concern. Because it was accompanied by a photograph of the Girl in a one-piece bathing suit, posed next to a tree in the town square of Claymore—even though the closest beach is a half-mile away, and there's no swimming pool out of frame, no sunbathing area—with as much cleavage on view as is allowed in a family newspaper.[18]

Regarding this photograph, the first of many taken on Media Day, the Girl said the photographer art-directed the picture quite exactly, and she hadn't yet known to what degree she could control the situation.

---

15. The Girl's father, the sheriff, who'd recently been taken into police custody, twice refused requests from the Journalist to visit him in jail.

16. An interview for which the Girl said she was paid twelve hundred dollars for a thirty-minute conversation, plus photographs.

17. More on this in a moment.

18. The fact that her décolletage was so abundantly on view, indeed glimmering dewily in the picture, was because, the Girl explained, (1) the photographer had asked her to squeeze her boobs together with her arms; and (2) his assistant moistened the Girl's cleavage from a spray bottle. "Like she was watering a plant."

But on this point, the Journalist protested that, actually, hadn't she been in good and goddamn control of the situation? Hadn't she created the situation? She was being paid for the situation, at her request? If she wanted to be left alone, why convene Media Day in the first place?

To that, the Girl said nothing. Her face blushed angrily.

The Boy, driving, rattled his fingers on the wheel, and his eyes snapped left and right like windshield wipers.

For those who still don't know, the primary reason the Girl recently attracted so much attention—on top of her father's abuse, the arrests, the small-town homicides—was because, at nearly the same time that the sheriff was arrested, a series of photographs became known publicly on the internet, showing the Girl, often nude, in sexually suggestive poses. This people believed was a stunt of her own devising, that she commissioned the photos and spread them around to attract attention, for celebrity. Like so many sex-tape-style "scandals" of recent years. Whereas her claim is that she took the photos with a friend, as a private gift for the Boy while he was in jail, intended to be completely confidential, never for social media. But then, according to the Girl, another student[19] at Claymore High School, a boy, managed to steal the images, screen-grab them, distribute them, pass them to friends via his phone, other boys who went on to upload them to assorted data dumps online.

And still, the photos might not have reached an audience wider than zip codes near Claymore County if an article on the website of *DROP* hadn't republished them, applying concealment bars to cloak nudity; though let's be honest: the bars were not all that big. So buzz swarmed. And the original pictures were quickly found, reposted in corners of the web in full nudity, assembled into animations, featured in montages and performer pages on video websites catering to pornography for the general public.

All of this no matter that the age of the Girl, the girl in the photos, is sixteen.

Soon the farmhouse where she lived came to be under siege. Making

---

19. When approached, the kid denied this story, full stop. Though it's worth noting that on the same day that the truck of three (Boy, Girl, Journalist) departed for Mount Washington, the Office of the Attorney General of New Hampshire announced that it was launching a probe into theft and distribution, targeting the same boy. And when reached that afternoon for comment, the boy hung up the phone, then a lawyer returned the call on his behalf a day later, to protest his innocence and refuse participation in this article.

it difficult for the Girl and Boy to live normally, to nidificate in peace, to go on believing each morning that what was happening around them would end someday soon, that this was not their new, permanent existence.

During Media Day, for $750: A London photographer asked the Girl to lie in a mess of newspapers on a fur rug, in a skirt and crop top, while propped on one elbow, smiling, holding up a *Boston Globe* from that week. Headline: "Sheriff Portis Suspected as Slayer."

So not exactly Burt Reynolds in *Playgirl*. In fact something far more complicated, sinister, and wrong.

∎

Half an hour before Mount Washington, the Boy stopped at a gas station to use the restroom. Two motorcycles were parked outside, horse-sized and shiny black. The Journalist took the opportunity to talk to the customers inside, two men and two women, all four in Harley-Davidson vests and black T-shirts.

She asked them about the infamous photos, whether or not they'd heard of them, and then, yes or no, had they seen them?

The men both said they'd heard of the story, the Claymore Kids— referring to a nickname bestowed on them by the national media. Both also said they'd seen the photos.

"Someone sent me a link to them," one said.

The women in the store were sisters; they also happened to be the men's girlfriends. One had heard about the story on the TV news. The other was clueless. Neither had seen the photographs.

When asked if any of them had known that the girl was underage, one of the men said no. The other said, after blustery silence, "Someone should be locked up, is what should happen." He pleaded the difficulty of knowing the ages of any women online.

One of the women said, "She shouldn't have stuck them on the internet if she didn't want nobody to look at them."

None of the four would give their names.

∎

The village of North Conway, New Hampshire, with a year-round population of just over two thousand people, is considered a gateway to Mount Washington, with the top of the mountain being only about a thirty-minute drive from downtown.

The group decided to find rooms for the night; the summit would be saved for morning. The Girl walked inside a small motel, the Snowdrift. The Boy and Journalist stood outside. Above them, the motel sign was striated with color, against a matte dark sky. The Journalist inquired after the Boy's plans, by which she meant dinner. But he misunderstood and said the two of them had big plans, *big* plans, for their lives ahead, once his trial was finished. He elaborated quickly how they envisioned driving west, the sooner the better, and someday working in Hollywood together, in the movies, the Girl as a costume designer, the Boy in some unspecified occupation. "Probably as a production assistant to start."

From there he launched into a defensive, excited monologue, about how "everybody has to start somewhere," and "no path fits everybody." Besides, "the American dream's only a fantasy at this point," "to help rich people sleep at night," and "college is a joke these days," an open bar for rich kids. "Why not start sooner and get to work?"

When his girlfriend came out, she reported that the motel would suit their needs. The group took two rooms. The Journalist watched the couple walk away, holding hands, to explore town.

That evening, around ten o'clock, there was a knock on the Journalist's door. The Girl stood outside. "I want to talk to you," she said. "One-on-one."

She patrolled the small bedroom. She picked up the coverlet off the floor, folded it in half, and rested it on a chair. "I just want to talk," the Girl said firmly. Another silence. When she was asked what she wanted to talk about, she didn't say anything, just stared at the dark TV.

"I've been here before," she said.

"This motel?"

"Mount Washington. With my dad. So how do you get to do this?" the Girl asked. "Your job. Asking people questions."

The Girl closed the curtains in the window that overlooked the parking lot.

The Journalist said she'd gone to school for it, she worked at it.

"How did you find out about me?"

The Journalist said it was a big story.

"Yeah, I know." She didn't say anything else for a moment. "He raped me. When I was a kid. I don't remember a lot of it."

The Journalist said she was extremely sorry.

"He put his dick inside me. He liked to eat me out. Have you ever been raped?"

The Journalist shook her head.

"So you don't know what it's like. But you're going to write like you do. My mother didn't do anything about it."

The Journalist was about to ask about this, but was starting to cry.

"So honestly," the Girl said, "how can you do your job and live with yourself?"

The Journalist apologized for crying, apologized for her industry.

"But you think it's my fault," the Girl interrupted.

The Journalist denied this, but the Girl didn't believe her. "Of course you do." Her face was tight and pained, she was dog-tired. Both of them were. Neither seemed to know what would happen next.

"You think you understand what's going on," the Girl said quietly. "You're just like everybody else."

She stood up quickly and grabbed the back of the desk chair, as if reconsidering her plan. Then paused. Accepting something.

"I'll tell you everything you want to know, on one condition," she said. "You have to record it and then write it down just like I say, without changing it."

The Journalist inquired if, instead, she could put some of the Girl's statements into her own words? Otherwise it would be a monologue. The Girl agreed. A minute later, the Journalist had set up her phone on the room's tiny table and poured them both glasses of water. The Girl sat down. Then, after a brief awkward moment, she started to talk and didn't stop, aside from short pauses and bathroom breaks, for the next six hours.

■

Until Emily Portis was eleven, she was ready to accept nearly any responsibility. Country existence was hard, full of activity, particularly where she and her family lived, only eleven miles west of the ocean but nearly two thousand feet above sea level, perched on the side of a mountain.

And with elevation, with isolation, came responsibility. In the summertime, low bushes flowered with berries to be picked. The rocky soil gave up vegetables, but only with coaxing. In winter the snow could be four feet deep. Everyone needed to do their share; Emily absorbed this truth at a young age. Her family had lived on the land for multiple generations, and gradually she learned that the most important law in country life, to ensure survival, is acceptance—of everything that nature gives or takes away.

They lived in the lower ruffles of the Langley range. Decades earlier, a set of roads had been carved from the hillsides. Here and there stood buckled houses, feeble old barns, where once upon a time wagons had passed, busily coming and going. During her childhood there were few visitors, few strangers, only the woods teeming with invisible pretty things that sang to keep themselves company, or so it seemed to Emily when she was little.

She was an energetic, precocious child. She'd feel faint and press her hand to her forehead and collapse to the floor, like she'd seen in old movies. She ran around the house with a pressing sense of self-importance. Often she left rooms announcing, "I need to go now," before heading off to a next appointment. But she didn't mind chores, she liked them. Outdoors, she'd applaud to watch Mother[20] take something heavy and lift it high above her head. At the age of three, she was taught how to build a fire. She weeded the vegetable gardens while the family dog sniffed at her heels. "I liked feeling older," she said.

On summer mornings, before her father joined the police force, when he still worked as a contractor for hire, Emily would bring him his large mug of coffee, black with five sugars, and he'd pour some for her into a tiny cup, and they'd sit together on the porch while he told her about the history of her family, which had lived for many generations in that region. How, for example, up in the high field, under the branches of an old maple tree that once was struck by lightning and still bore the scars, there were three graves dug next to one another, no markers, containing three ancestors who had died in a terrible fire, Father said.

By and large it was just the three of them for company and conversation. Mother was big on the importance of conversation, stories, songs to sing.[21] On proper language, she was particularly strict. There were differences between "may" and "can," and other important things to

---

20. It was a strange facet of her childhood, she would see later, that for as long as she could remember, Emily had always called her father Father, her mother Mother, in mimicry of how they referred to themselves: Father does this, Mother does that.

21. Sometimes her mother sang to herself at night in the kitchen while putting the dishes away. Almost always it was the same song: "Down in a willow garden, my true love and I did meet, and while we were a-sitting discoursing, my true love dropped off to sleep."

know, such as when a young lady should say "please," "thank you," or "may I be excused?"

Only occasionally were there visitors, other children for Emily to play with. Mostly, she was alone with Mother and Pointer, a collie mix. In the summer of 2003, Mother was forced to kill Pointer. Emily was four years old as of that March. It was hot and muggy on the evening that Pointer suddenly turned up acting crazy. He'd killed something in the woods; he ran dizzily toward them across the meadow with froth on his lips.

"He went for us," Emily remembered her mother saying, out of fear, when Father got home that night. He'd quickly reached his boiling point, a look of rage beyond control; a look that meant the possibility of violence.[22] "He almost bit her," her mother had said loudly, into the face of her incensed husband, while she hid her daughter behind her legs, just in case.

That night they buried Pointer beneath the maple tree, under layers of brown silt that had washed down from the creek.

It was the first of two times in her life that Emily has seen her father cry.

For all of her childhood, love and duty were not very different things. There was sporadic violence, frequent beauty. Each fall Father hunted deer. He trekked down near where their woods blended into the national forest. A few times he let her join him, and she was proud and eager, so happy to be included. Father rarely got angry when he was hunting; plus she loved getting up in the dark, she loved the toasty quiet inside the truck when it was cold out, the sips of coffee he allowed her from his thermos cup, or a segment or two from the oranges[23] he carried. They stuck to old game trails. They never saw another person. "It was honestly the best thing to do in the whole world," she recalled, "at least that I could imagine at that age."[24]

---

22. Emily said she was spanked for punishment until she was ten, on occasion with a strap folded in half.

23. She hates orange now: orange flavoring, orange juice, orange candies, anything.

24. At home, Father skinned the animal from hooks in the woodshed. Emily would watch, force herself to be brave, the whole time holding her protests in her mouth, in case he might order her indoors. One early time out hunting she'd not been quiet, too excited; and she couldn't remember why, only that she'd said something too loudly and frightened away a prize buck; and Father had ripped down her pants and spanked her roughly as punishment, and then left her in the woods to find her own way home.

If Emily Portis belonged to the forest, growing up, it was because her father, the master outdoorsman, had showed her how. He had the ability to take the reality around them and make it magical with make-believe. When there were empty barns to explore, an abandoned hunting camp to lie down inside and imagine themselves king and queen, tickle each other across the old quilts he'd brought for their royal bedding.

One afternoon, she remembered, they found a salamander in the camp, black with orange spots.[25] Father said it was a species called the fire salamander, because it could set fires with its tail, so dangerous that even the forest elves stayed away.

And some nights, good nights, in the depth of a cold winter, Father would lie down at home after a long day's work and ask the forest elves to massage his back. Emily would run to another room, remove her socks, then come back and jump on top of him. He'd say, "The elves, the elves are here!" and Mother would laugh from her chair beside the woodstove, often sewing[26] clothes for the entire family.

They were truly an American family of old, homesteaders still alive, with little interest in television, the internet, or anything too tied to the grid. Occasionally the three of them watched old movies on a clunky VCR, but usually they made their own amusements, high above the glittering town.

And at the end of the night, before sleep, they would kiss delicate fairy kisses, Emily and Father, lips to lips; and Father and Mother would kiss with lips; and the daughter would kiss Mother on the lips, too.

And all these things, and more besides, the sky above and the valley below, constituted the life of Emily Portis before the months and years to come when her mother got sick, when her mother disappeared. Around April of 2006, Mother started to go away for weeks at a time, to seek neurological betterment at different treatment centers[27] around New

---

25. *Salamandra salamandra*, usually found in Europe. They don't, in fact, have the capability to set anything on fire, but they do defend themselves by exuding toxic secretions when grasped by a predator.

26. It was from her mother, Emily said, that she initially learned how to sew, to operate a sewing machine, to use freezer paper to make dress patterns.

27. These visits, which became biannual events, were endorsed by Father, Emily believed, primarily because they enabled those back in Claymore to have more private time together. To do things like candlepin bowling, an old favorite of her father's, or just stay at home.

England. And returned home barely improved. Eventually, she vanished within the old house itself, sequestered in a back room, before she was sent away completely. And Emily and her father were left alone.

■

The sickness that came to define the life of her mother was not interesting enough to Emily to warrant relating to this Journalist in detail.

She remembered an afternoon when Father was outside in the yard, repairing a chain saw. Mother was in the garden. Emily was in the kitchen. Heavy gray clouds hung over the valley. Her parents had been fighting, continuing an argument from the previous evening. Mother had stopped in the broccoli row. She was talking to herself, but her daughter couldn't make out what she was saying. Her mouth moved faster, her voice became louder. Soon she was shouting things at the sky. Father put down the chain saw. He slapped her so hard that she sat down heavily on the ground. Emily saw everything. She ran outside. Her father turned on her quickly. "Do *not* help her," he commanded. Fires banked in his eyes. While Mother looked at Emily with blushing anguish, that also seemed to verge on a kind of strange excitement, and called her by name.

"Don't," Father said to her. "You did this to yourself."

Naturally Emily rushed to her mother, but Father yanked her away by the arm, pulling so hard it felt like her shoulder had been dislocated. She shrieked, but he didn't let go.

"Come here, Emily," Mother urged. She froze. Her mother would not stop staring, she started grinning at her. There was a smell of frenzy in the air, like the day Pointer died. Mother smiled wider, her tone was colder. "I said come here. Right now."

Emily whispered "no" and squirmed away from her father's grasp.

"Of course you don't want to," her mother said. "Father is absolutely right. He's always right." At which point she brushed the dirt off her arms and walked into the house.

Beginning that afternoon, the garden overgrew. The illness that previously seemed like Mother's way of being, her tics and worry, began to flourish. Entire days she wouldn't get out of bed, then multiple days in a row. There were crying bouts, gloomy silences, mysterious absences, before she'd reappear around the house and fuss noisily, scold and grasp at her daughter, before she retreated into her room again.

No exhortations from Emily made any difference.[28] Doctors visited the house, to no avail. She'd find her mother in the middle of the barn, doing nothing, or weeping silently in the kitchen, leaned against the wall with the phone cord wrapped around her fingers.

There were discussions, family meetings, no more fairy kisses exchanged. Their previous existence was becoming more difficult to recall. Soon Father was on edge all the time, unpredictable, his temper flared unexpectedly. While Mother was consistently her new self, lethargic, refusing to engage, unwilling to speak to any of them. "She didn't even change her clothes anymore," Emily said.[29]

She remembered she sought out Father in the winter, one night while it snowed. He was chopping wood out by the barn. He sank the axe into the stump. "She's sick," he said, and clapped his leather gloves together. "We need to let her rest," he said. Emily thought about this for a moment before she asked, "Am I going to get sick?" Her father laughed. "You and I will be fine. The most important thing is we stick together."

■

One Sunday night in February, when Emily was eight years old, there were fireworks above the valley for no good reason. At that elevation, the explosions were directly in front of their front yard, red and blue like flowers in the sky.

She and Father watched from the door. It was so exciting. "I don't know why this is happening," Father said repeatedly.

And once the fireworks finished, they circulated back upstairs, to

28. One Sunday, after chores, she found Mother in her room and yelled, "Don't you love us anymore?" Instantly she felt so guilty that she burst into tears and threw herself into her mother's lap. "I don't expect you to understand," Mother said. "Of course I love you." Which didn't make any sense, all things considered, but Emily allowed herself to be held for a minute. But then her mom started making whimpering sounds like a cat, and Emily had to extricate herself.

29. One memory from a year later: Mother returned one night from town and brought in what appeared to be a rack of clothes in plastic bags. All sizes included, infant to teenager, pants and shorts and sweaters. Emily was going over her homework with Father. At first she was excited. So many bags! Mother beckoned her over, smiling, and told her to pick through the bounty. "None of these will fit," Emily said after a minute. "You got the wrong sizes." "Don't be dramatic," her mother said. "I know what size my own daughter wears." Father opened one of the bags and held up a pair of boy jeans, with cargo pockets. "These are for boys," he said quietly. "They're made for boys." Emily ran upstairs to her room before the shouting started.

the master bedroom, his bed, to resume going over the prior week's events, moments that had gone well and those that failed, so that Emily could improve herself. He'd say, "Do you recognize what you did wrong?" For example, one time she forgot to lock the back fence; five or six hens had wandered out and didn't come back. "How do you think that makes me feel, when you forget something that's so important to me?" he said. "It makes you sad," she said. "What kind of sad, do you think?" Occasionally she'd be bad and say things like, "Well how am *I* supposed to know?" Then he'd reprimand her, but he'd be chuckling a little, and would say something like, "Please don't talk so loudly. I want you to *think*."

From those years she remembered many exchanges along similar lines, when the two of them would lie in the bed on Sunday evenings in their pajamas, atop or under the quilts; conversations full of quizzes, coaxing, jokes, underpinned by moral lessons a girl needed to learn to grow up smart and strong. But they also played games, which always led eventually to the exercises that were intended to relax Father, where she helped to masturbate him, and eventually learned to masturbate him without any help, and on occasion he would "relax" her also, as he said, both with his hand and his mouth.

Whether her mother knew what was going on upstairs, Emily couldn't say for sure.

As a girl and young adolescent, there were moments from her life that stood out like hallucinations, acid trips, mirages of pain. In sixth grade, early October, one weekend she and Father climbed the first leg of Tuckerman Ravine on Mount Washington; the same mountain the Girl and Boy would visit years later. She was eleven. At the time, her mother had gone away for two weeks to a clinic in Cambridge. Father took her up to hike Mount Washington as another one of their outdoor adventures. At first Emily had feigned sickness. In the end she didn't have a choice. A mile from camp, a storm broke out. They ran the rest of the way. The rain fell in torrents. She remembered diving straight into her sleeping bag, starving and cold. But the dinner they'd planned was inedible without fire, and they lacked dry wood, and Father hadn't brought the stove. So they ate ketchup by the packet. They ate the donuts that were for breakfast. It was actually sort of fun. He was in his sleeping bag, too, when he started fantasizing about food. It was a game they used to play when she was little; he'd have these crazy ideas for made-up cheeseburgers. Gasoline burger. Dog-fart burger. Eventually she fell asleep, when it seemed like nothing would happen. When she woke up, the sun was out. He'd built a fire to dry their clothes. They roasted marshmallows for breakfast, packed their bags, and hiked back down to the truck.

But on the way down, her stomach started to cramp. A terrible feeling, Emily said, when she looks back and diagnoses what was probably a case of poisonous rejection—to realize, however unconsciously, that Father hadn't wanted to touch her the night before. That perhaps she wasn't wanted anymore in that way. Questions in her mind like, Who was she? What was she? Who would ever love her now?

Five minutes into the drive home, her breakfast had curdled. She threw up marshmallows all over the truck's front seat. And for the rest of the drive home she dove deeper into the immeasurable dark pools of her mind.

·

Also in sixth grade, Emily started running. She did "weirdly well" in her first 5K, placed first in her age group. It was an indoor track meet, a Sunday morning in February. The boldness of winning made her giddy. Her coach drove her home afterward and dropped her off a quarter mile below the house; the hill had more than a foot of unplowed new snow.

Twenty minutes later, by the mailbox, she found her father lying on his back, unconscious. He must have slipped in the snow and hit his head. Church bells rang in the valley. There was a smell of wood smoke. She stared into his face. He was still alive, breathing lightly. His hair was full of melting snow. She touched his cheek. The tip of his nose had turned yellow from the cold. It was a stressful year,[30] and the relaxation

---

30. That same year, Emily started curtailing what she ate. Eventually only a very specific list of foods was allowed. Strawberry Jell-O. Salted nuts. Rice cakes. Some candies. Lots of apples, lots of water, with ice and lemon. On her worst days she'd eat an entire box of ice-cream sandwiches, but would always need to cut each bar down to at least a dozen bite-sized pieces first, and actually she found that whole process more tedious than satisfying, so she didn't break bad very often.

Family dinnertimes, in the beginning, she made excuses: that she'd eaten already, after cross-country practice, or eaten a late lunch at school. Eventually she stopped making excuses and became difficult. She'd ask for bread, cut huge slices, not touch them. She made pyramids of butter slabs.

She'd figured out that, short of hospitalization, one thing Father could not do was make her eat. Though he'd say she couldn't get up until she ate her food. So he'd yell and

exercises had become more elaborate, with more serious tests of trust. The Mount Washington camping trip was an anomaly. More than ever, trust was vitally important. If he couldn't trust her, their entire world would come apart. Who'd pay for Mother's treatments? He liked to hold her between her legs during ejaculation. Beginning in the summer, he had started to penetrate her vaginally. He'd apologize profusely for it afterward, his lack of control, he was furious with himself. And each time he said it would never happen again—unless she wished. Afterward, back in her own bed, she'd lay coiled as tight as possible, and chew on her red knuckles, and dive down into her hatred, even through the floorboards to where her mother was downstairs, the woman she blamed.

Six months later, Emily ran in her first indoor track meet, and her coach drove her home, and she found her father collapsed in the snow. She had stared down into his pale face, thinking many things, then trudged up to the house to call an ambulance.

Their final Sunday evening together came that summer, the August before seventh grade. That Sunday, a cool night, just when he'd pulled her toward him by her hips, she decided she'd had enough, whipped around and bit him, truly sank her teeth deep into his arm. She drew blood. He recoiled and fell backward on the rug. He looked terrified, she remembers. He burst into tears. It was the second time, she said, that she'd seen him cry.

He never touched her again.

．

To appreciate the love story of Emily Portis and Nick Toussaint Jr., the reader must grasp the burning intensity of their love. On top of that, the Girl wants it understood that to know their love means the reader must accept, particularly in the twenty-first century, that it had come to include sexual intercourse and that this should be no big deal—no matter any federal or state laws about the difference in their ages, or

threaten, one time he pulled her hair. She'd pinch herself, until she started bleeding under her T-shirt. And sometimes she slipped, lost focus. But still she kept her lips shut and stayed in her seat. Then Father would *really* lose his temper, pound the table and bellow, demand pity and sympathy, threaten to knock her off her chair. Two nights she slept at the table, with a bowl of venison stew by her face. And every second, every second, was worth it. Because she knew she was winning, and she liked winning. And to the winner was awarded penalty, punishment, and control.

ridiculous ideas about her being "ruined" by her father's abuse. After nine months together, there was sex between them, and the sex was beautiful, uniquely; sex as an expression of something more than just intercourse, she suggested. After all, they loved each other profoundly, they expressed their love intimately; it was a love both physical and emotional, everything combined.

Because, in spite of her father and his crimes against her body and mind, Emily Portis was not a broken person, and she wanted this noted down in the plainest terms.

Over and over, during the night in the motel, she returned to the details of their first kiss, hers and Nick's. Lips together, the match of mouths. How the rough scrape of his chin had felt like an electric shock. She recalled the immediacy of his lips, and how, at the same moment of their first kiss, out of fear, her mind had run back quickly into the darkness of her imagination, her corral of hideous memories, her indestructible shame, and immediately thought the worst of the situation, that Nick despised her or tasted something disgusting on her breath, and he would tell everyone how she'd done everything wrong.

The kiss was shared on a beach. It was the autumn of her sophomore year at Claymore High School. Their first meeting had been a week earlier, by accident, a slight encounter in a local restaurant. But it had been followed by a written request from Nick to see her again. At the time, she was fifteen.[31] The day after the kiss, all day in school, she couldn't concentrate, she said. She repeated his name to herself under her breath. Things he'd said to her between kisses, no one had ever said to her before. But what if he was joking? She badly wanted his kiss again, but dared not hope. And she was sure he'd kidded around about

---

31. Until that day, said Emily, her life had been one long failure to feel love. She once wrote in her diary, "I want to be crazy in love. I have so much love I could give to someone." She had kept a diary most of her life. Entries were little things like the weather, animals, her feelings. Recently, she found a pair of old journals in her bedroom, from when she was seven or eight. "Clouds today. I got in trouble again with Mother. Because I pretended to be a princess from China and spilled all the milk when I was trying to finish my dance. I am sick and tired of being such a silly girl!"

The entries were irritating mainly, she recalled, for their tedious self-consciousness, their hopeless naïveté. Things like: "I can be so young and excited sometimes. I am not always a good girl. Father doesn't have to tell me, I know I can be stupid. I will try harder to be good, but it's so hard. But Father says he believes I can do it, and I am a very lucky girl that he loves me anyway."

She recounted this to the Journalist and laughed lightly, staring at the wall. "What a little idiot."

it by that point with his friends. By lunchtime she started to panic. All around the school she saw boys waiting for girls by their lockers, boys and girls holding hands. Would she ever have that? Then she ran into her best friend, Alexandra Rosenthal, between the last two periods. Alex had received a text message from Nick: "Hey u guys out at 3? need a ride?"

What had she been wearing that day? A decent hoodie, her favorite jeans. Had she eaten anything? Candy, chocolate milk. Her last class of the day was Western Civilization. Her heart was exploding by the time the bell rang. "It was almost too good, imagining that Nick had thought about me sometime that day. That he could be thinking about me at the same exact time that I was thinking about him." She sprinted out to the parking lot. There'd been a heat wave that week. She saw Nick's car and her stomach jumped up and down; she wondered if he would hear it. He got out slowly, wearing the same jacket, same jeans, same boots. How cute he looked! She was dying from the frantic hope that he liked how she looked, too. And he did.

For weeks to come, from that moment on, every minute she could outmaneuver her father was a moment to be shared with her new boyfriend, her first boyfriend. And if the moment was for some reason to be one spent out of his presence, it was a hellish ordeal. New nightmares rose from crippling doubt. Wondering if he'd lost interest, if he was kissing someone else. At first, she said, she could only interpret her emotions through fear. For his part, Nick goofed around all the time; he only expressed his feelings through jokes. But they got better at it. They talked about their thoughts. They kissed on public benches and held hands. She tried not to voice her terrors, like that he could be cheating on her, or he was about to dump her; twice she almost broke up with him, she was so convinced he wanted out. She just wanted to be good enough, pretty enough, smart enough. Most anything Nick said, even the stupidest things, she'd remember and archive, and write down in her diary to analyze for clues.[32]

The third time they kissed, his hands moved across her shirt. She'd known it was coming. Her body went electric, but her mind recoiled; she felt sick to her stomach. Then he lifted up her breasts in his hands. She turned away, she didn't know what she was feeling; she was chaos. A week later, they were kissing in the back of his car. She'd skipped

32. Like the time he said he liked her hair down? She hasn't worn her hair up a single day since.

cross-country practice. "At that point, I sort of didn't think I'd ever run again," she said. Thirty minutes into it, he lay on top of her, and she'd felt it pressed against her, his penis inside his jeans. Now she really felt nauseous, and started to panic; and she understood perfectly why she should not, if only for the sake of not scaring him, of being a good girl-friend, but she couldn't control herself; she had an urgent compulsion to leave. There was the pressure of his hand on her skin. The pressure of the air inside the car. She had to do anything she could to stop the situation from exploding, so for another ten minutes they rolled around, and she subtly discouraged him from doing anything more, without for one second letting him doubt her fondness for him. It was excruciating. And yet somehow he was soon content to drive her home, with just a kiss. She'd pulled it off.

Two days later, she made her move. The idea was to prevent him from making other moves first. They were in his bedroom. His mother was out. She took his penis in her mouth. It was obvious that he was genuinely shocked. In less than a minute, it was over. She went to the bathroom, returned, curled up next to him. She was so happy from re-lief, she offered to do it again. He laughed, turned her down, he was exhilarated; thanks to her. Then he asked where she'd learned how to do such a thing. And the room faded into other rooms. Smells into older smells. She got up, her whole body filled with an unidentified disgrace. She didn't know what to say. She asked to be driven home. He apolo-gized, with confusion. He said something like, "What just happened?"

"I need to go home now," she'd said, as carefully as she could, then went out to the front porch while he got dressed, so she couldn't do any more damage.

A week passed. She knew there was a good chance she'd lose him. She'd nearly destroyed the one thing in her life that gave her joy. Satur-day night, once more in his car, by the beach, she was determined to make up for it. She went down on him twice. She wanted to go for a third round, and that was the big mistake; she'd pressed her luck. Because then he said he wanted to make *her* happy and swung around on top, moving down, kissing her hips, her legs. She allowed him, figur-ing she'd budge him away in a moment.

In fact, what she remembered best from that night, what she'd en-joyed the most, had nothing to do with fooling around. It was listening to the wind off the ocean. Thinking about what other girls at school maybe were saying about her, now that she'd found a boyfriend. It was like she'd finally become one of the girls in the novels she read. Girls who had someone to love.

Then Nick licked her through her underwear. Her blood blackened. She pushed him off lightly, but he came back, pressing for more. She squirmed away, filled with exasperation, but he misinterpreted her hastiness for excitement, for coy feigning, he followed her and got his mouth between her legs. Her final effort was to control her breathing, or try to control it, while her blood boiled, her body folded, and her mind was inundated—and out with her breath went the rest of her control and she yelled, "Just don't."

A second later, Nick said, hushed, "What?"

She hated him then; she couldn't despise herself more. "I don't like it," she managed to say, louder than she wanted. "When you do that," she added, and chewed on her knuckles.

"You don't have to freak out about it," he said.

So she apologized repeatedly, but then he also started to apologize. She hated the sound of him apologizing. And just as quickly she felt an overpowering need to fix the problem, erase it, undo this one thing permanently with a much bigger event. She knew just how, if the courage could be found.

"Come here," she urged. "Do you have a condom?"

He laughed, he was so surprised; he quickly recovered. Ten minutes more and the deed was done. During the act, Emily addressed herself, as if from a distant lectern, and made herself promise the following: that in the future her body would have intercourse anytime he asked, however often, intercourse again and again, never mind as many blow jobs as he could handle in the afternoons, provided that all of it combined became enough to incinerate and make Nick forget that other act as best as possible.

Once, one month later, in the middle of sex,[33] he said repeatedly in her ear, "I love you," and it had pulled her down, back into her body, and she'd burst out crying. He'd never said it before. In that moment his

---

33. It did get easier, and not completely unpleasantly. Not that it ever became nice. But there'd be a moment during sex, nearly every time, when Nick finished, and the music became a quiet song, and he'd smile and look to her to smile, indicate that she'd enjoyed herself; and she always smiled, because she was enjoying herself, right then. Because that moment was heaven. That one moment, lying together. "It's more like sleeping together than anything else," she said. "Like little naps but really sleeping. You feel like one person." In that tiny moment, she said, she found escape.

voice was closer to her soul than even she was, she'd write in her diary. And so that became a pattern, too, saying the words during intercourse, until she requested him to stop, fearing the magic could die.

Sex does not define their love, it does not doom it or validate it. It's barely one-quarter or one-third of their connection, Emily says. But it's important, she wants it known, that soon the authority of the need for the other person became overpowering and obsessive, for both of them. They had sex all the time. Every kind of sex except that one kind. She got to decide how often and when. But they also spent many more hours doing all manner of other intimate things together. They held hands in public. They kissed in public. They didn't care what people thought. He started to call her "babe," which she loved, because she was proud of what it meant, that she was his, and vice versa.

●

But briefly, to go back to their first kiss, after that night on the beach, when Emily returned home, her mother accosted her as she came through the door.[34] Something about how Father was out, there'd been a big traffic accident in another county, Emily needed to sit down immediately for a serious talk.

Instead she'd flown up the stairs. She'd never kissed anyone before, never been kissed. It came with an electrifying sense of accomplishment. Was she in love? Did it happen that quickly? Then a new thought occurred to her, preying on her insecurity. What if the kiss had been a prank? After all, who'd want to kiss her?

And her impulsive bigheartedness, her rickety emotions, had just succumbed to this unhappy new reality when Mother rapped on her bedroom door and barged in, panting like a frightened animal, announcing, "Where's that suitcase you had, the blue one?"

Emily snapped at her mother to leave, but only got a hiss for a reply, that she should be quiet and hurry up, they didn't have much time. A moment later, Mother sat down on the bed. She was wrung out by whatever mania had brought her up the stairs.

"I spoke to one of my doctors," she said quietly, adjusting her glasses. "He says we can stay with him. While we get on our feet."

Emily asked what she was talking about.

---

34. A week later, Mother left for a treatment center outside Camden, Maine. Emily hasn't seen her since.

Her mother ignored her. One hand picked up a dirty sweatshirt off the floor. "We're going to need more money than I thought," she said. "It's going to take a lot of money. If you're not willing to put in the work, then I need to know now." She added a moment later, "This room is disgusting."

It was too much.

"What are you even talking about?" she snapped.

"We're leaving. You and me. We're leaving *him*."

Emily was thunderstruck, furious. All she could think about was what had taken place on the beach an hour earlier with Nick. Now her mother wanted to ruin everything, when she'd ruined so much besides.

What if she didn't want to leave, she asked.

"Don't be ridiculous. Just hurry up and pack."

"I don't want to."

"Of course you do."

They'd stood apart for a moment, staring at each other. Her mother laughed, and her laughter bounced off the walls. Emily remembered feeling shocked; she hadn't heard her mother laugh in years. But the face around the laughter was blank, a glaring vehemence.

A second later, her mother walked out into the hallway. "Your room is a pigsty," she called from the stairs. "Clean it up. Tonight. I don't want this blowing back on me."[35]

■

The first person she ever told about her father's abuse was her boyfriend. She badly regrets telling him. Especially considering, Emily pointed out, all the suffering that took place afterward, including the murders of Dr. and Mrs. Ashburn. She considers their deaths to be her fault. Her secret should have stayed hidden.

For a long time she'd vowed to tell no one; save them the embarrass-

---

35. A similar event, from a few months earlier: In the middle of the night, her mother pushed open her bedroom door and crawled into bed with her, as had happened on many nights before. Frail body in sweatpants and a pilled fleece top.

"We're going to do it," Mother said. "I'm just waiting for confirmation." Almost hissing. "I'm so relieved. Don't you see? It's finally happening." When Emily didn't answer, her mother filled in, "Honey, I just need a little more time, but it's all worked out."

She remembers the densest blackness, the choking air, the oppressive sorority of the smell of her mother's conditioner. "Please go away," Emily had said. "Now, Emily," her mother said. "Get out!" she'd shouted, and shoved her mom off the bed. And her mother hit the floor, ponytail swinging, but returned like a tiger on the back of its catch. Until the manic drive subsided a few minutes later and she shuffled dry-eyed back to her room downstairs.

ment. She never wrote about it in her diary. But her vow was broken unconsciously one night with Nick. They'd just had sex. Out of nowhere, as he woke up from a brief nap, she thought about telling him—then suddenly she was telling him. "I just started. I had no idea what I was going to say. I couldn't stop." She'd stared at a wall while she described the various types of intercourse her father had forced on her; the way he smelled; his congratulations the first time she had an orgasm. She took Nick right up to the night when she'd bitten his arm.

One topic she didn't tell Nick about, but would like included in this story, in case this article is read by any young girls who go through the same thing, was her own sense of rejection that night, revolting as it was. The unaccountable shame she felt for refusing her attacker, for attacking him back. "It's stupid," she said, "but I had this feeling, like, I was the one who should be punished. I'd attacked him. I was a horrible person. I'd ruined everything."

At which point Emily Portis abruptly stopped her account. The Journalist turned off her phone. It was nearly five in the morning. The Journalist opened the door to let in some air. In a couple of hours, the three of them planned to drive up a mountain. The Girl, Emily, looked exhausted, like a teenager who hadn't gotten enough sleep in weeks. A long silence passed before she said anything more.

In a steady tone, she said, "So we have an agreement."

The Journalist nodded.

"I want you to know," Emily said, "I'm never going to talk to you again."

■

Because the month was August, the day was a Thursday, and the weather was nice, even at seven-thirty in the morning there was a line of cars, trucks, and SUVs waiting to climb the Mount Washington Auto Road, to wind their way up eight miles[36] under the kitschy radiance of a summer sun.

After the entrance fee was paid, the Boy, the Girl, and the Journalist began the climb. As promised, the Girl did not speak again to the Journalist. The Boy settled on National Public Radio, a program featuring

---

36. A sign read ATTENTION: THE MOUNT WASHINGTON AUTO ROAD IS A STEEP, NARROW MOUNTAIN ROAD WITHOUT GUARDRAILS. IF YOU HAVE A FEAR OF HEIGHTS, YOU MAY NOT APPRECIATE THIS DRIVING EXPERIENCE.

German opera—which seemed fitting, given the alpine surroundings, the green mountain, the chalet hotels visible below.

The mountain was basically bald. If it weren't for the fog and clouds that swept in, the view might have been spectacular, all the way out to the coastline. There were football fields of alpine grass, lichen growing over rocks, long stretches dotted by cairns. In spots the mountain looked practically volcanic.

At the top was a gift shop, cafeteria, a lookout tower, scientific structures, weather-measuring devices. For some reason the air buzzed with bees. They lighted on people's windbreakers, on light-colored cars; and the noise of all their buzzing was prevalent despite the wind.[37]

Then more fog started to appear, cold and damp. The sound of the bees faded. At the top of the mountain, a sign read THE HIGHEST WIND EVER OBSERVED BY MAN WAS RECORDED HERE. The Boy pointed it out to the Journalist as they walked past. He was visibly excited as he wondered aloud what it would be like to live on such a mountain. Then he asked what had happened to his girlfriend; he hadn't seen her in a couple of minutes; he worried that she was lost in the fog. The Journalist said she'd seen her heading back toward the truck.

"I don't know what you're going to do with your story," he said a moment later. "Do you think you have enough to write about?" The Journalist said she thought so. Heavy clouds filled the sky. The weather was beginning to deteriorate. The Boy stared gravely. "You asked me what my plans are. I thought about it again this morning. I want her to be happy. That's what I want."

Ten minutes later the three of them were about to leave when the Boy realized he'd forgotten to buy the bumper sticker, THIS CAR CLIMBED MOUNT WASHINGTON. He climbed back up the hill toward the shop, hobbled by his limp. While they waited, his girlfriend was asked what she thought of the mountaintop. She said nothing; she had no expression on her face whatsoever. Dry lightning sparked far away. Her boyfriend returned a few minutes later. He suggested that they get going, but first put the sticker on the bumper. His girlfriend told him that sounded great, that he should do it, though quickly, she wanted to go. He countered, smiling, "You do it. It's your truck. You've earned it."

---

37. When a bee climbed up her yellow scarf, the Journalist remembered a tidbit that her father once taught her, that bees always crawl up, never down.

GIRL ZERO

On the drive home, her body grows colder, as though every cell is filled with dust, dust from the moon. She thinks about opening the door, tumbling out, a mannequin flipping down the road, head over heels at sixty miles an hour. Like the time she was high on mushrooms for the first time with Alex and almost jumped out of the car.

Only now she may really go through with it and there won't be any blood to see, just dust.

And through her overwrought melancholy, Emily gazes out the window. She does feel intensely sad, she's overwhelmed by it, her mind studies it as rapidly as it can. Trees rush by, a hymn of trees. It's as if she's reached a point of misery that it's actually an achievement, to reach the end of ends, to know unhappiness so well her soul commiserates with all the suffering they pass, the stained trailers, the dogs on chains, until she takes on *their* suffering and wants to cry for all the pain still to be found here and elsewhere, around the globe, from racism, climate change, the fate of nations—

And then she's done.

What an annoying teenager she's become. She's tired of such things, tired of thinking or feeling such things, just done with feeling shitty.

She's sick of feeling like there's something wrong with her all the time.

That morning, she'd gone back and lain down next to Nick in the motel bed, but she couldn't sleep. She was annoyed by him sleeping so easily, lightly snoring, ignorant of all she'd told the journalist. An orange sun had started to rise outside the window. She slipped out of the room. The village was drowsy. The small streets were empty, they'd been rinsed by rain overnight, everything was quiet and cool. A green cottage on a corner had its lights on. A sign in a window had a glowing aura around it, BAKERY. She realized how hungry she was. A bearded man inside cheerfully said good morning. He sold her a warm croissant off a tray. She sat on the curb outside and ate the whole thing, her eyes cast down dreamily. Then a young woman went by jogging, with a big brown dog, and she also wished her good morning, as if Emily were just another adult in the world. As if some disaster had happened, and Emily and the woman and the baker were among the few still alive, and each could decide what to do next with their lives, they could do anything.

And when Alex tells her, the moment that Emily and Nick return home, after dropping off Leela, that all the media had decamped once the Sisterhood convinced them that the Mount Washington expedition was the only time that Emily Portis would go on record ever again—*and they'd all missed out*—she thinks little of it, almost nothing. She smiles, gets down from the truck, doesn't say much more than "That's great, thank you."

And though she can tell that Alex and Meg, their welcoming committee, are disappointed not to get bigger thanks, bigger congratulations, she's just not up for it at that moment. She feels weak at the deepest levels. She goes inside. Five minutes later, Alex and Meg leave with a promise to Nick to check in the next day, and she can tell by Alex's look up at the window, at the last second, that she's concerned. Perhaps she's right to be concerned. She watches Nick walk down to check the mailbox, she watches him remove the handmade signs and feels a dull anger in her heart. She should telephone her mom at the clinic—but that's also not what she wants to do. Even though she's not at all sure what she wants to do.

So she goes out and sits on the porch, in the sun, in one of the old rocking chairs, and stares across the valley, and thinks.

And feels really old and really young at the same time.

An hour later, frogs chirp in the trees. Nick comes out of the house with two sandwiches. She looks up at him, from the vantage point of her sensitive mood. He's about to say something, to announce a plan, when his phone beeps three times, three texts. "You've gotta be kidding me," he says a second later. The muscles in his face tighten angrily. She listens to his fingers tap furiously on the screen. Then more messages arrive, it's like an alarm bell going off. But she doesn't ask what's the matter. She takes a deep breath and feels some of her strength return. Whereas normally she's overstuffed with impulses—combustible, contradictory—suddenly there's only a single feeling in her body at that moment, one thought in her mind, and it makes her smile.

■

Hey dude sorry for radio silence just got
back into town let's hang

Hey u there?

U in town?

WTF????

Dude I know completely so sorry my
bad. Cindy's brother got sick really sick
we had to go Boston for observation 2
weeks. Dude I'm so sorry. I heard ur out
let's hang

FUCK U!!!!!!!!!!!!!!!!!

I'm sorry I suck so hard

I'm a terrible friend obviously

I'm really really sorry let's hang

Dude look I was freaked out and
honestly I wanted to see u then Cindy
needed me for this thing and then I
don't know it was all too big to get my
head around

I figured you'd reach out if u needed
something

Dude come on

FUCK OFF

Hey I'm sorry I really am I know I talk
all kinds of shit then what do I

This is so fucked please I'M SORRY.

I didn't know what to do and then days
went by. So yeah I was scared it was a
total whiteout my part I TOTALLY get
why ur angry

I'm the shittiest shtty friend I hate me
too let me make it up to u. I want to
make things right

Hey I just tried calling u still there?

Honestly dude I'm so sorry I'll say it to
your face

I'm trying to do right if u want to get a
beer it's my trembling

Fucking autocorrect It's "my trembling"

FUCK

MY TREAT obviously

Please Nick I'm sorry

.

"Our view, Mr. Portis, is the same as when we all sat here last week. And that view will not change. We need you to understand, that should we be required to apply for court orders, we will apply for those orders. We are not asking you for authorization, for you to choose. We really want to be clear about that fact. We've got everything we need right here, it's all taken care of already.

"Sir, as you're aware, by this point you have lost fourteen pounds of body weight. Now, with hindsight, you might think no one is paying attention. We are paying attention. We have done this before. There is going to be a metallic taste in your mouth, that's what hunger tastes like. That's starvation.

"Don't think we aren't doing everything we can to understand—anticipate, in fact—the choices that you're making.

"So if we apply for the order, to start NST, nutrition-support therapy, and we demonstrate meeting the requirements to apply for the obtainment of that order, then we're going to get it. That means we come back, this time we'll have six or seven personnel. And do everything by the book. Believe me, we've read the book.

"To start, we're going to push a tube up your nose. The tube's plastic, but it is not as soft as it should be. It's rough. It's going to get pushed up there, then all the way right down into your stomach. You'll feel an intense burning sensation. Also, a feeling like you're drowning, that's how it's described, as something pretty near unadulterated misery. You'll vomit several times, we'll need to get past that point, because that's only the gag reflex. That's just the start. Each time we drip something down, that same reflex is going to activate, and it's going to happen again and again and again.

"Sir, do you understand what I'm saying?

"Nod if you understand what I'm saying to you, Mr. Portis.

"You can guess that I don't know how to operate a sheriff's department. No way. All that complexity, in this day and so on. But this procedure, this I know how to do. Take what's needed to manage consent decree. This isn't Gitmo. This isn't even California. The rules are clear. So what you need to understand is the role that you're in here, okay, as opposed to your previous role, and then you also need to appreciate the role that we're in. Sir, understand that our role is being that of caregivers. We are not here to hurt you. We're here to help you, according to your wishes. As to how you prefer to be helped. Nod once if you understand me.

"I'm not going to beat around the bush, Sheriff. Your case is too serious. We respect your decision, and we are treating it with respect. That's what this is, respecting your life.

"Then here we go. Rule of thumb, we're able to obtain the order to commence once the prisoner loses fifteen percent of current body weight. From this morning's weigh-in, that's an additional eleven and a half pounds in your case. According to our estimations, based on your size and weight loss thus far, at the going rate you're going to lose that amount in about one week. One week. So, we have to begin motions to request the court order now. This afternoon. Again, we very much do not want to do this, you have to understand that. We really need you to hear us on that point. I mean, it would bring us tears of relief, okay, to see this escalation averted. Because the law requires us to be in compliance, as your guardian and monitors, do you understand? To keep you alive. That's our responsibility. It's the law. Imagine you were diabetic and you quit taking your insulin. We'd administer that insulin no matter what. Because it's our duty to make sure our actions reflect your body's wishes, which are the wishes of your health, you understand?

"Mr. Portis, I'm getting through to you, I can tell. I'm glad to see that. Because there's something in your face right now, tells me we've come to a place of understanding. If that's right, just say yes or no.

"Just say yes or no.

"We're all trying here, it's pretty clear, our best to cooperate. But it's extremely important that you tell us anything you think we should know. Right now.

"Mr. Portis, please.

"Hey, personally I respect your right to remain silent. I get it. And it is your right. I'd hate to think that we're being insensitive about that situation. But your physical body is state property at this point. You see where I'm coming from? Now there are arguments about public safety I'm willing to indulge, and compliance, and so forth. I'll fudge and say, our understanding of alienation, the notice you've been given, may be different from what you believe you see, okay. But there is oversight going on. And we will see this through.

"I can see how we might seem to you, sir. But I'm encouraging you, right now, to please consider the consequences. We're talking lost teeth. Damage to the liver, gall bladder, other organs. We've been over this now, what, three times in the last week? It will go forward. As of today. And your silence will qualify as an informed decision, that's why I'm here right now, informing you. Because you will not be allowed to starve yourself any further.

"It really is an unfortunate case. Just so we're crystal clear, as of today, you, sir, Granville Portis, are granting the state of New Hampshire, the New Hampshire Department of Corrections, the team I've assembled here behind me, the chance to intubate you whenever we feel like it. Meaning we will stick a tube down your esophagus at any moment we see fit, to keep you alive. And it's going to hurt like nothing you've ever experienced. Like hell poured down your throat.

"There's still time. To stop this. One word, none of this has to take place.

"Sir, forget everything. Have you heard a single word I said in the last ten minutes?

"You find this funny.

"You're honestly laughing at me right now. Sir, you find this funny?"

▪

Suzanne doesn't know where to find her missing husband, Nicky's father, Nick Sr., only that she must find him and won't rest until he's found—because he's somewhere nearby, back in Claymore, she believes, and must be hunted down, so she goes in and out of old haunts, the back-alley entrances, but no one else has seen him, he's a ghost, he's long gone, not for years, and that's only when they recognize the name as the older one, the *père*, not the kid in the news.

Second shitty bar, the Harbor, she orders a drink, sips carefully, to avoid attention in the sawdust-tinged dark. But what difference will that make, really. She's got the nose splint, she needs to wear it the rest of the week—Hannibal Lecter's sister, there she is, in split mirrors, the bars' entrance to absolution: woman deformed, and still consumed with impatience—and among all the men in the room, none are Nick. They don't see her anyway, they wouldn't if she did naked splits on the bar. Some asshole plays "Fly Like an Eagle" on the jukebox—it's enough to launch her off her stool, to another bar, Dave's Dockside—and again no Nick, just another glass.

She checks her father's watch and winds it. She's missing students—well, let them knock, for once let them not get what they want. She tries a fourth bar, good old Goat, no sign of her husband there, either. And when someone's got the taste to play Etta James, she takes it as a sign, she's earned a pick-me-up, she asks too loudly, "Who put on Etta

James?" The bartender says, "Who put on what?" Who cares what time it is? She puts in her order, she grins too tightly, she empties the glass when it arrives and asks for one more—the bartender's looking at her as if she's got straw in her hair—the hell is he looking at? A jumbo fisherman's sweater over leggings, she should be boiling but can't sweat a drop. He toddles away. How hard is it to make vodka rocks? While she's swinging, weakly, from one emotional chandelier to the next, with *premeditation*, motherfucker.

And fuck that fucking cop, she has a job to do.

Oh, but she's low on cash, she drops a five-dollar bill on a twenty-dollar tab, she takes off out a side door—but where's her bag? She runs back for her bag, and may they all rot in peace.

That morning, during a lesson, she'd pulled back a curtain and spotted a car parked on the street, a rusty green sedan. Another stalker? More media? A photographer to chronicle her busted face? A man was inside, she couldn't see more. Hands on the wheel. Engine running. Then old Mrs. Hodges, squawking neighbor, came jotting down the sidewalk with her pushcart, and after she peered into the windshield of the strange car, she waved.

The man waved back.

But it wasn't until the car pulled away a moment later, peeling out, that Suzanne leapt up and staggered to the door.

How was it possible? How was she not prepared?

The one thing Nick did consistently, all the years she knew him, was peel out—on Main Street, at the mall, in the driveway they shared.

She'd imagined the moment so many times. Promised herself she'd let him have it, put him in a coma, be so hot the second he arrived he'd realize his flabbergasting error, never mind what he'd done to their son, to them. But wasn't it so like Nick to find a way around her.

She pilots her car around the corner and parks in front of her husband's old church, kisses the handicap signpost with her bumper. The same church her parents attended, her grandparents—they probably built the damn thing. Her husband loved to go to church, to unburden himself. She remembers he used to pick at his elbow whenever he felt insecure. Do men possess such a capacity to notice? See something in a woman, and never not see it again? She climbs out. A statue of the Virgin stands next to the front stairs. Suzanne crosses the cream-colored annex. All pews empty, flowerpots empty. Hanging over the altar is a large wooden cross—but no resurrected husband, no husband who won't stay buried. An old woman in an apron cuts flowers. A large chalice, beaded silver, lies next to her hands on a bed of rags. Suzanne works her way to a middle pew, sits and rests her weary feet.

"Excuse me," she says impulsively. The woman doesn't look up. "Excuse me?" The woman sticks a finger in her ear to adjust something, a white earbud; she's listening to headphones while doing flowers for Christ. Suzanne laughs and sinks deeper into her sweater, feels drunk, feels good, and thinks of her marriage with at least a little pride, because did she not survive? Did she not suffer? Hadn't she met her man's needs?

Had not the act of losing herself been enough loss for one marriage?

At the same moment the old words begin to bubble up in her mind, unbidden, and become words on her lips—*Take, eat, this is my body, do this in remembrance of me*—her brain is basically only a shoe box anyway, full of old feelings, quotations. Nick used to say that what the two of them had in common was that they were promise deferred. She hates him. *Will she ever be free? Will she be happy?* The questions are absurd— so much is wrong. She stares at the candle smoke and thinks, what got burned out of me is the capacity to forgive men of their bullshit.

And that makes her give thanks instead, for Nicky, her one good thing—who is much more than man, he's her son—whom she'd tried to nourish for so long despite her failings, despite her many horrible traits. She'd say to him *Take, eat, this is my body, which is given for you.* And then she'd take the wine and give it to him, saying *Drink, do this in re- membrance of me, for the remission of sins, the resurrection of the body.* And together they would say, *We will beseech the father to be gone from us forever, no longer will we desire him, for he is bullshit, and for our sacrifices we will give each other thanks and praise.*

Her eyes swim. Her broken nose hurts. At the altar, the old woman turns around, sees her, startles, disappears with clopped steps through a concealed wood door.

Alone, Suzanne lowers herself down into the pew. She lifts her long insect legs and rests her aging body, her aching body. In a life where love struggled to reach her, she is merely temporary. How many lives has she led by this point anyway? But she's not forever-lasting—it's her son who is forever. She screws her eyes shut against scalding tears. She won't be another screaming female. And whoever that man was on the street, he's gone, dead and buried. And now she is alone again to make mistakes.

What a terrible mother she's been. What a terrible drunk she's been.

What a terrible mother she *is*, what a terrible drunk she *is*.

Then an appalling sense of shame hits her with a jolt, and Suzanne Toussaint sits upright.

She's been dreaming.

■

The airport may as well belong to an island nation in the seventies. There's not even a passageway to connect the airplane to the terminal. Is there a terminal? The plane de-boards on the runway. Martin receives the pilot's goodbye, presses one hand to his lower back, covers his eyes with the other against the blinding sun.

Burbank, California. The air's hot enough to singe his eyebrows. Even the tips of his ears feel hot. Beyond the asphalt, in the distance, brown mountains wall off what appears to be endless flat land. The mountains are hard to make out in the wavy air.

There is a terminal, it turns out, just not much of one. It's not much cooler inside. He uses the bathroom, takes a stall, diligently finagles his way out of the back brace. Nine hours on airplanes may not have been the best idea.

In the concourse everybody's smiling, the carpets are frayed. The airport feels like a nondescript sports bar. There's a massive caricature of Bob Hope, taller than he is. When did Bob Hope die? It pleases Martin to think that he's probably among fewer than a hundred people in the airport who know who Bob Hope was.

And somewhere nearby lives his daughter. Inside his briefcase are directions to a shopping plaza, a sushi restaurant. They'd communicated several times when he was still back east. At first she didn't answer. He'd regretted taking Demeke's advice. Yet he kept taking it, he explained that he had listened, he understood her wishes, but he'd undergone a crisis of sorts. He went on to explain nearly everything that had happened in New Jersey, in New Hampshire, message after message, eventually voicemail, email. It took him three hours to get it all out, to expose everything, stuff he already felt was on full display to the world, so why not his daughter?

It feels like I'm trying to fill in a puzzle. I don't know what the puzzle will look like. I just know that you're a big part of it, or I want you to be.

At the very least, he finished, in the final note, he wanted to meet her for dinner. Afterward he'd fly home. She could pick the restaurant, location, day on the calendar. Everything was up to her. Love, Dad. Miss you, Dad. Regret terribly, more than she'd ever know, all his past mistakes, Dad.

Then he waited. Waited more. Of course his back spasmed again. Two and a half days, with a fistful of doctor bills, he was unable to untangle himself, and was left to stare out the window. He'd thought about calling the stripper for another spine-walking session. The harder painkillers, he refused, but he ate ibuprofen like it was candy. He lay in the bed thinking of everything he'd say to Camille in person, if only he could say it.

On the third afternoon, his phone vibrated on the side table.

You want to see me. For dinner

> Yes.

You'll fly all the way out here.

> Yes.

That's stupid

> No it's not.

And then you'll fly home, the next morning or whatever.

> I'll fly home the same night, I just want to see you.

We're getting sushi.

> Sushi sounds great.

You hate sushi

> I'm not coming for the sushi.

Lol

The baggage claim area turns out to be open-air, open to the sky. Only in California. He laughs with a tight throat. Up ahead stretches a colonnade of Rose Bowl flags. He goes looking for a taxi stand. The sunlight's intense. And the old Urge hits him, out of nowhere, to grab a quickie to steady his nerves.

His phone rings. He answers without looking.

"I want to talk."

Lillian.

"This isn't a good time."

"I want to talk," she says. "You haven't been exactly forthcoming."

In the days before he left New Hampshire, her lawyer had badgered him with messages. They wanted to set up a meeting in Eagle Mount, as soon as possible. He'd never answered. He wasn't ready. He didn't want to have an answer. He didn't want to be ready.

"It's your dime."

"That doesn't even make sense anymore. Martin, I'm sorry."

"I'm sorry."

"We were so unhappy."

"I was happy, actually," he says; he can't help himself. "Or something. Anyway, that's behind us now."

"We had issues," she says. "Individually and as a couple. I thought I had a handle on it. The ups and downs with my career. Getting older. All my struggles with my self-esteem. You know what I'm talking about."

"You did sleep with someone else."

"I became paranoid," she says, sounding plagued. "I can't explain it. I know you think I'm self-centered. Try to believe me: I thought I was going crazy. I hated depending on you."

"On me?" He laughs. "Your salary's double what I made."

"For anything. I'd been independent so long. I was depressed. I was scared." She pauses. He hears the sincerity in her voice; he can't help but be moved. God, he's not over her. He can't be.

"Honestly," she says. "I was convinced you were going to leave me at some point."

"Now that's bullshit."

Though he hears that it's not.

"I felt helpless," she says. "So I needed to make you feel even more helpless."

"It's fine. I get it."

"I know how this all must sound. What I've put you through, no one deserves that. How are you?"

"How am I?" He laughs again. The main problem with marriage is that it requires two people. But who wants to be alone? The thought makes him smile. To even exist as an older adult, as a human past fifty-five, is the most childish thing in the world. "I'm good," he says. "I'm good."

"What's that noise behind you? Where are you?"

A taxi pulls up to the curb. He signals to the driver. An old guy with dyed black hair gets out and pops the trunk. Martin turns away, stares into the airport, so many people finding rides, finding loved ones.

"I can't change what I did," she says. "I can't forgive myself."

"You'll come around," he says, but regrets it.

"Please don't make this into a joke."

"Lillian, I need to go."

"Neither of us are quitters. Martin, what do you want? Do you want us anymore?"

"What I want is to have this discussion tomorrow," he says. "I'll call you tomorrow, I promise. I'm in California right now."

"California? But why?"

"I'll call you tomorrow," he says. "I need to go."

The cabdriver takes his bag out of his hand. The sunlight is endless. It reminds him that he's thirsty. By the curb is a newsstand. He buys two bottles of water and drinks one straight down. He tosses the bottle away. Next to the recycling bin is a blue federal mailbox. He smiles, perches his briefcase on his knee, withdraws an envelope, drops it down the chute.

■

The Claymore County Courthouse houses the Sheriff's Department, the County Commissioner's Office, the court itself, the Claymore Historical Association, and the Public Defender's Office. It's easy to get lost, though by now Nick knows where to go whenever Brenner wants to meet. One of the assistants escorts him to a conference room, but he knows the way, knows there's a minifridge by the dry-erase board that's stocked with bottled water and Coke and iced teas.

The assistant says Brenner will be there soon. He stands at the window, watches cars leisurely swing around the square. His nerves are twisted. He can't keep still. Good news on the horizon, supposedly, she'd said. She called to let him know that all of the evidence under secondary investigation was squaring to his story, exoneration was all but guaranteed. He should be tremendously happy, she'd said.

That same morning, Emily had gone back to work. He should be happy about that, too, but she was different since they'd returned from the road trip. He couldn't pin it down. Like there was a gap between them now, something new, across which he can't quite reach. One second she's normal, says all the right things, and he's happy. But then she's quiet, disengaged. Like she no longer wants him around. New silences. New looks. He feels more alone when he's around her than when he's not. It's messed-up.

The night before, he'd had a big idea about the two of them doing a picnic on the beach that weekend. Figuring maybe he hadn't been romantic enough the way she liked, like guys in the movies. So he laid out the proposal: he'd pack a backpack, take a blanket, get the beach umbrella from Suzanne's garage.

She didn't even look up from the book she was reading to say that it would be pointless, too conspicuous, being in public together like that in a crowd.

"All that stuff's over," he'd said.

"No it's not. Of course it's not."

Two months ago, she would have jumped at the idea.

He said, "You've changed."

"What are you talking about?"

Then she yawned. It wasn't even a fake yawn. He couldn't help but start arguing; she knew precisely how to get under his skin. Two minutes more, suddenly he was going on about being loyal, not playing games—everything dire, extremely serious. He had a true flush of anger, it impelled him to raise his voice, but she let him rant, which made it worse, because he knew he was ranting! And when he was done, all she said was that she was tired, she was going to bed. She went upstairs calmly and softly closed her bedroom door. As if he hadn't said a word. As if it was a compulsory task to tolerate his presence. Like he was her mom or something. So he was pissed all over again.

Forty minutes later, he still savored the injury. Though he'd managed to consider that maybe he was in the wrong. After all, *he* was the one picking fights. Maybe he was the one who'd changed. He'd become needy like a girl, like Typically once said. He turned off the lights and lay down in the empty nest of blankets on the floor. A tightness gripped his chest. Did she love him anymore? Did *he* love her? Maybe the problem was twofold: maybe she had changed, and as a result he'd become desperate. Because he wanted her to feel the way she used to feel, the way he still felt. Feelings that maybe she no longer shared.

Then she was gone when he woke up. His phone woke him: of all things, his mother texted him. She was in a parking lot, outside an Alcoholics Anonymous meeting, just wanted to see if Nick was up, if he wanted to catch a movie that night, dinner, her treat.

A second later, another message:

Going in wish me luck

Another:

If my breath smells like Kool Aid later
you'll know why

He wrote back:

You can do it

She replied:

Thank you xo

An hour later:

Well that was bullshit

From the courthouse window, he watches the cars go around and around. A green car pulls out of the current, takes a parking space in front of the courthouse. A man gets out.

Nick stares. Stares harder.

Brenner opens the door behind him.

"Nick, buddy, how are you?"

"My dad," he stammers. "My dad."

"What are you talking about?"

"That's my dad."

The man he's pointing to is actually staring up at their building. But doesn't see Nick. He walks up the sidewalk slowly, as if unsure of where to go, up the stairs into the county sheriff's office.

"That's your father?"

He can't believe it. He's absolutely sure of it.

"You need to go down for me."

And every feeling he'd buried comes clawing up out of the dirt. Every time he felt haunted. Every time he was in a crowd, thought he'd spotted the back of his head.

"And do what?"

"Please. Just find out why he's here."

"Okay. Give me a minute."

Did he really see him? Was it him? Impossible. He doesn't recognize the car anyway. And yet, when the man had taken more than two steps, it was him, every inch. His mind races with everything he's wanted to say. What flushes through his body is terror.

His lawyer comes back into the room looking annoyed.

"You're not going to believe this."

"What?"

"You were right. It's him."

"Shit."

"He's looking for 'the media,' evidently. He asked for the press liaison, at the sheriff's office. He's in her office right now."

"Why? Why would he do that?"

"Nick."

"Tell me."

Brenner says slowly, "What he told the girl, after identifying himself as your father, is that he's interested in finding out how a person goes about selling his story. To the media."

Nick sits down and drops his head in his hands.

She says, "I don't know how long he's going to be in there. In case you want to go down. You could talk to him. I'll show you where he is. If you want."

"Jesus."

Then his body, his mind, become a single, rippling wish.

"Fine," he says a second later. "Let's go."

■

368

Eight days after her return to Claymore, three days into awkwardly hanging around her parents' condo with nothing to do but worry, Leela prevents herself from pinging Bryan James—ex-colleague, current lifeline, by chance a bridge to an ideal future—for some type of reply to the email that she sent him with a draft attached of her big story.

The trip to Mount Washington had been a shock. No sooner had Emily texted than Leela was riding in the truck, formulating questions on the fly. With no idea what she was doing. Barely had time to put on deodorant. *Get a grip*. Totally thoughtless, defenseless, nervous, unprepared. Then, when Emily came to her room that night, it was most definitely a matter of improvisation. The task was to keep her talking, muffle her own shock while guiding Emily into stories, when there was nothing that she wouldn't discuss.

But on the night they returned, after a long, lovely nap, Leela had sat in her makeshift room, on the air mattress, and plugged in her headphones, and quickly figured out that Emily's loquaciousness would be merely her second-biggest problem.

The whole ride back from the mountain, she'd kept her excitement hidden. When all she could think about was that she'd really gotten it: a scoop. The story that everyone wanted—was hers! So turning the material into an article would go beautifully, of course.

Quickly, that evening, she realized she was an insane person.

First, the material, she had too much material. Hours and hours, nearly seven hours of teenage talk. Endless stuff about cross-country meets, fashion interests, report-card worry, the friendship with Meg Rosenthal's little sister. It took her most of the night and the next morning just to transcribe the whole thing.

But her biggest problem wasn't the material. It was that, in a mountain of information, she didn't know what to use.

So the next day she did everything else on her to-do list instead. Research, reporting, burning the rubber off her new sneakers. She needed to build context: Emily Portis as teammate, student, employee. Nick Toussaint Jr. as mechanic, pizza deliveryman, drinking buddy. She got some good stuff, though almost everybody she talked to said they weren't talking to anyone, they were done.

But that night, after a quick dinner of her mother's baked chicken, she sat on the condo's back patio and read her transcription, and when she was done she kicked the railing posts from exasperation.

"I can't do this," she loudly told the trees.

A minute later, her father quietly opened the sliding door. She felt fifteen. Maybe twelve. He sat down next to her on a piece of plastic lawn furniture. Pine trees surrounded them, towering above.

"Sorry for yelling."

"What's the problem?"

"It's nothing."

"There's obviously a problem."

Her parents knew. The moment she'd returned, she told them about the trip. She'd explained with a satisfied smile how the story would write itself.

"I've got too much material," she said quietly, addressing her feet. "I don't know where to start."

"Well, what's the story?"

"What?"

"What's the story? Tell it to me."

"It's the girl, the road trip. All the stuff that she told me. So everything her dad did, and about her mom being sick. I need to fit in the murders and the crimes. But it's also about Nick and their relationship, and then you go back to the murders—"

"Leela, what's the story?"

"Why do you keep saying that?"

"What's the story?!"

"Why are you shouting at me?" she said. "I don't know!"

He got up gingerly.

She apologized.

"I don't know about these things," he said. "But it seems to me, if you figure out what the story is, then at least you know what it's not."

He went back inside.

And it wasn't until about eleven-thirty, after her parents were asleep, both snoring, that her father's comment came back to haunt her. She was lying on her back on the air mattress. What's the story, Leela? And there appeared the simplest answer, right in front of her nose: her promise. Her pledge to tell her story, Emily's story, as Emily saw it, all of it, all at once.

So that's what she'd do.

She didn't sleep, she outlined, she tiptoed to the kitchen and made coffee. Two days later, she had a draft. She printed it out at the public library, read it in her car. It wasn't too awful, too tragic. Probably too thinky-thinky? Way too DFW, obviously, and what did "nidificate" even mean? Since when did she use so many semicolons, what style was she aping?

But something felt right. Natural to the source. She'd tried to render the stories in a way that rang true, not transcription. Not merely a representation, but something more. And she kind of thought she did.

After her second reread, her brain blinked: Game Over. It was all so much crap. The pivots weren't even believable, the structure was obviously a ripoff. Every word was bullshit, hack bullshit. She was about to delete all and go drink Bloody Marys until Armageddon. Instead, she went for a run. Returned, showered, edited, and revised. Then did it again. She found the guts to share a copy with her dad, who'd already offered at least ten times to be her proofreader. And only when he returned with a grin, his glasses folded in one hand, did she manage to feel okay.

He even suggested the Burt Reynolds reference, which she'd needed to image-search on the web to even get.

By draft six, day five, at least it wasn't worth dying over. She emailed her draft to Bryan, explaining that it was as yet unfinished, *mucho* to be done still, but maybe there was something there, some *there* there. And she'd appreciate his feedback.

Now it's Friday. Three days since she pressed send. The Battle of Gettysburg took three days, fifty thousand dead. How long does Bryan need to read a couple pages? How many times had he jerked off in that span of time? Fifty-one thousand?

She's about to email him when a different email arrives, a different penis.

Hey Leela, just wanted to check in. How'd the read go??? Just come by the store. I can't wait to talk! Honestly I think the book can really use a Woman's perspective, know what I mean? Looking forward! Rob

She'd forgotten all about Rob Miller and his great donut novel. Karma is hell. Then again, what else does she have to do? Maybe giving Rob proper feedback will be cosmic payment paid forward to the critique she wants from Bryan. She grabs her laptop, opens the file. Reads the first pages again, then keeps going. It's the story of a not-so-secret misogynist in his twenties, who manages a Dunkin' Donuts franchise that his parents own in small-town New England. Hobbies? Surfing and guitar. But he speaks like he's Ichabod Crane's grammar master, and he can't meet women because he's too ugly, his face is lopsided, one of his eyes is oversized, semiprotruding.

She puts down her laptop. Basically it's Rob's life story, except the narrator's unattractive, and with an unaccounted-for wont for Middle English. And he hates women. Does Rob hate women? She can't help herself, she returns to the manuscript but skips to the end, skims the last three pages—wherein the police respond to an emergency call at Dunkin' Donuts, only to find the front doors locked. They peer through the windows: it's a lynching. Four girls, customers who'd ostensibly rejected the narrator's attempts at seduction, hang from nooses tied to the ceiling. At which moment the narrator, hanging himself, is gasping out a conclusion: "'I was afeared of offending you, sweet girls. Of upsetting what is politically correct with my wonton desires. So fearful that I never showed you my true self. Sometimes, to be a man in this world, it takes a little rope.'"

She closes the file, deletes his email, feels grossed-out and sticky, even sad.

That afternoon, Leela and her mother take a hike in a nearby state park and both complain about their knees. That night she watches a documentary about Civil War medical procedures after dinner with her dad. Everyone goes to bed by nine. Her phone waits in the bedroom. When she finally checks it, two messages wait.

The first is a text from Bryan, suggesting a meet-up, midtown Manhattan, no mention of her story, just the news that he's already at the bar, he's been there all day and wants to see her, come through.

The second message is an email, from a domain that makes her heart skip a beat, from the Magazine, Bryan's boss, who wonders if Leela can meet for coffee, as early as tomorrow, if she's free.

■

"Yo, Leela. Are you in the bar?"
    "I'm in New Hampshire."
    "What?"
    "New Hampshire."
    "No shit. So, what, no cocktails?"
    "Bryan, are you drunk right now?"

372

"Absolutely."

"Is it a holiday?"

"What do you mean?"

"You sound like you've been drinking all day."

"I got canned. Two days ago. I've been drinking for *two days*."

Wait, what?

"Are you serious? Bryan, I'm so sorry."

"It's super messed-up."

"What happened?"

"What happened is that old-ass companies are too fucking PC. So what's up with you? Holy shit, you're in Vermont."

"New Hampshire."

"That's what I meant. Honestly, though . . ."

She wants to reach through the phone, shake him into sobriety, into whatever moment preceded the moment he did something stupid and got fired. What did he do? What did he do to her? What if everything she's done has been for nothing?

"Bryan, seriously, what happened?"

"Dude, no. Let's talk about your article. That's so messed up, that you took my advice."

"Is it?"

"Hold on, let me grab it. I've got it with me." In the background she hears country music. "Leela, I'm not drunk."

"Yes you are."

"So honestly, it's not that bad. Sorry, I should lead with compliments."

"If you say so."

"Here's the deal. I can totally picture this chick. Emily whatever. Which is great. Like, everything she went through, how a girl *feels*. I think getting that whole female point of view through, that's rad."

"Thanks. That's good to hear."

"In terms of what's next, you've got two problems. We're not getting the bigger picture. The gestalt. Beyond the gender thing. That's number one."

"The gender thing?"

"There's the chick, clearly. But you have to ask yourself, like, who cares? Incest, child abuse, we've seen it. Borderline cliché. Homicide: we've seen it. The whole angle about kids-use-the-internet-omg, that's so played out. I'm just spitballing, but you should try thinking more outside the box. I mean, it's true crime, so what would Didion do, right? Hey, what would Cary Fukunaga do? Go *Serial* the shit out of it. Or try a media piece, or do historical. Like, a history of moral panic stretching back to Babylon."

"So you think the girl's story is not the story."

"People want blood. Editors want blood. The chick, the daddy banging, that's background. Human interest is boring. This is a murder story, so where's the blood?"

She doesn't say anything. She doesn't even know how to begin.

"Now dude," he says, "don't get all defensive."

"I'm not being defensive."

"Hold on, I'm stepping out to go smoke." A moment later: "So here's the main thing," he says. "Like, I just don't think this story sounds like you. Leela Mann. I mean, come on, footnotes?"

All she wants to do is hang up. Go outside and double-check that the sky is not falling.

"So, just so I'm clear," she says. "Barring the 'girl from a girl's perspective' stuff, you're saying (a) I chose the wrong story to tell, and (b) the way I told it is also wrong."

"Hold up, I didn't catch that. Can you say that again?"

"Bryan, I should go."

"Dude, don't freak out. I typed up my notes, I'll send them. I'm so wasted. Forget all this shit. You've got the start of something great, I know it. It just needs to, like, find itself. You know what I mean? Like anybody does. I'll email you."

■

Two days later, Leela waits across the street from a coffee shop in downtown Manhattan, early by thirty-five minutes, after a night of next to no sleep. The light changes. She trots across West Broadway, birdstepping in pumps that give her blisters. What if the editor's superearly, waiting in the window, witnessing her awkwardness?

Inside, she relaxes, slightly. The editor is not there, as far as she can tell. She stands at a metal counter by the window and sips an iced coffee. She's in her only suit. Her little station wagon is parked on a block in Queens. She'd arranged to crash the previous night on a college friend's couch. When she left New Hampshire, her father had tried to give her money. She refused him. Then she stopped for gas before getting on the highway and found the tank full; one of her parents must've snuck out to fill it. What had she ever done to deserve them?

For a moment, thinking about her parents takes her stress away. Then a short woman is suddenly at her elbow. "Leela? I'm Lian." She leads her to the rearmost booth. Midforties. Chinese-American? Taiwanese? Bright expression, short hair, buttoned black cardigan. No obvious adornments except for a silver cuff on her left ear, with a chain looping to a piercing, a small silver hoop. So, straight-up business, but subtly goth. Leela wants to be her, instantly.

"I'm really glad this worked out," Lian says.

"I appreciate you taking the time to meet with me."

"It's my pleasure."

"Well, thank you," Leela says.

"You seem nervous," Lian says a moment later. She smiles slightly, as if forced. Is it a test? Leela laughs nervously.

"I'm a little nervous."

"We're just having coffee."

"I understand."

"What I mean is," says Lian, "think of this as a conversation. Like you'd have with a friend."

"Sure, of course."

Now she's supremely nervous.

"So, I went over your résumé. I spoke to your references. Everything is looking positive. This morning is more about getting to know each other, if that makes sense?"

"Totally."

Totally? Could she sound dumber?

"Why don't you tell me a little about yourself? Where you're from, that sort of thing."

A coffee grinder growls in the background. Leela smiles tightly and starts—and proceeds to ramble for ten minutes. Mostly talking about her parents for some reason. Lian keeps nodding, encouraging, tersely smiling, or is it a weird frown? Should she have stopped by now? The voice in her head drowns out the words coming out of her mouth, so she can barely hear herself. Should she be talking about more professional stuff? Is everything ruined already?

She stops abruptly when she hears herself start talking about her brother's business plans.

Lian smiles tersely again. She explains about the job—five minutes—

then asks pointed questions about *The Village Voice*, her recent projects and responsibilities—fifteen minutes—then she reaches into her bag and pulls out two copies of the Magazine's latest issue.

"These are for you."

"Oh, that's okay," Leela says automatically. "I already read it."

"Really?"

"I read it on the day it arrives. It's an old habit."

Lian laughs. "How about this: Break it down for me. As much as you remember. What you liked, what worked for you, what didn't work. How you would've done something differently, if you were the editor. That kind of thing."

The café is suddenly empty. Her palms are sweating. She wipes them on her legs. *It must be a trick question.* Weirdly enough, it's the same game she and some of her friends played in college, when her infatuation began.

Twenty-five minutes later, even the Gopnik Sinusoid has been explained—the sine wave that Matteo once pinpointed, to account for the amount of wordplay in an Adam Gopnik article in relation to the subject's proximity to his personal life—and the woman across from her seems slightly approving, not completely weirded out, and Leela wonders if she has reason to feel optimistic.

"Your friend Bryan was let go recently," Lian says.

Or maybe not.

"I heard that. He's not exactly a friend."

"Really? He definitely sang your praises."

"That's nice," Leela says guardedly. "We used to work together, that's all." Is this the right thing to say? Does she sound unloyal? After they spoke on the phone, she'd gone through Bryan's notes. Thirty percent of them had been of some value, the rest she junked. On the biggest points, he was wrong, she was sure of it: Emily Portis *was* the story, at least the story that she felt obliged to tell. But she'd still spent the rest of the night rewriting, revising again just the night before, as well as that morning. Then she'd printed out a fresh version at a copy shop and shoved it in her bag, just in case.

"We do have another candidate for the job," Lian was saying. "It's really just a matter at this point of who's the right fit."

Her throat tightens.

"Of course."

"Bryan did mention that you were working on a story. About those murders up in New Hampshire. The town where you're from, in fact, is that right?"

"Yeah. I was up there reporting."

"And you wrote something?"

"I have a copy with me, actually."

"Can I read it?"

She's caught off guard. Her voice squeaks: "Really?"

Lian laughs. "Yes. Really."

She reaches down for her bag. She's choking. She's drowning.

The pages in her hand weigh a hundred pounds.

∎

"Is this Leela?"

"Who's this?"

"Leela, it's Lian. Do you have a minute?"

"Of course. I'm just doing some editing."

Total lie. It's been six hours since their coffee meeting, and she's outside in Queens, on a brick stoop, watching makeup tutorials on her phone to keep herself from thinking about Lian reading her story.

"So I just read your story."

"Oh. Great."

"I think you nailed it."

"What?"

What?

"What you were trying to achieve, I think it's all here. It's rough, obviously. But I thought there were some interesting portions. I have to say, I expected to get a media story, or a true-crime piece, so I was glad to read a profile."

"That's definitely what I was going for."

It is now, at least.

"Well, you had unique access. And the girl comes through, so that's good. To the piece overall, are you interested in my thoughts? I should warn you, I'm not a softie."

"No, yes, absolutely. Please."

Lian exhales lightly. "So I didn't mind the footnotes, but didn't love them. In any case, we'd never run something like that, it's just not our thing. Overall, the mountain metaphor was a little too on the nose, I'd lose that. Also, do teenagers really have so much going on upstairs? Or in their romantic relationships? I didn't at that age, but that could just be me. Anyway, I'd revisit the characterization; you don't want to over-invest. What I think needs the most work here is what's missing. I don't want to second-guess your reporting, but there's too much here that's anecdotal, if not mawkish. The whole confessional sequence, I mean, I don't even know where to start. Probably we'd cut it, but does the scaffolding elsewhere fall apart? Then all the 'Girl' and 'Boy' references, let's be honest: it's a gimmick. It just looks coy. Also, there was too much sex by half. Why are you in the story but not completely, you know what I mean? I guess the good news is that you've got all this material to work with, so you can cut a lot without losing muscle."

There's a long silence. Leela doesn't know whether to rage or cry.

A second ago, hadn't she "nailed it"?

"Lian, thank you anyway," she manages.

"You know, you should read 'Landing From the Sky,' Adrian Nicole LeBlanc. It'll give you an example of something to shoot for. I can give you a couple other directions to consider, if you like."

"Sure," she says. "That would be great."

"I meant what I said earlier. You found a story and an interesting way to tell it; you found a shape that fits. That's not easy. What I liked best about this piece has nothing to do with the narrative. You showed tenacity. To go after something and put it together. Down the road, who knows? Maybe a version will find its way to the website. But let's wait and see."

A bunch of kids run by on the street. Someone nearby is cooking onions. She's about to bite a fingernail off, but something tells her to snap to attention.

"I'm sorry?"

"I'm putting you forward for the job."

WHAT?

"But why?"

Lian laughs. "You're hilarious. Leela, this is a tough gig. There's a lot of pressure. There's plenty of competition, old habits, all the problems of a big institution. I need someone steady, day in, day out. What I don't need is a freelancer who turns around perfect profile articles in a week. That's not the kind of stuff we run anyway. Do you understand?"

"I think so."

"I'll send you an email tonight, we'll get the scheduling started."

"But this is amazing," Leela says quietly.

"You need to sit down with human resources, and there are people I want you to meet. You still need to interview with my boss; this is by no means a done deal."

"Lian, I can't even begin to tell you."

"One thing. Your friend, Bryan."

"We worked together."

"Do you know why he was let go?"

"No."

"They caught him jerking off at his desk. I mean, this is a hard enough business. And I don't like to fire anyone for reasons other than competence. He actually was good at his job. But stupid. You see what I'm saying?"

"I think so."

"You seem to me highly competent. Please also be smart."

"I will be. I mean, I am. I promise."

"We'll talk soon. Goodbye."

The connection goes dead. Leela stares at the phone. And does nothing more to express her exploding joy than to call her parents.

.

The house is empty. The sky's all clouds. A bird starts to sing, and the song is boxed by the *whuff* of a car driving fast up the mountain.

Emily snaps her eyes open and feels a really strong need, but for what isn't clear. She gets up and moves at a snail's pace from room to room, while the house slowly brightens. She goes into the dining room and stares at family pictures on the walls, framed portraits of grandfathers and great-grandfathers. The house is not hers anymore. She almost doesn't recognize the rooms. She feels like her life's sliding away from her, out from under her feet. Weirdly, she's not totally uncomfortable with the sensation. She stands in the yard. The gatherings of houses down in the valley look like pens of little animals gone to sleep. She imagines floating above them, on the wind, drifting slowly out of the state.

But it's not until around eleven that she puts her longing into words, what's been nagging her for days, the need that floats in her brain. And against great reluctance, she decides to do one of the things she promised herself she'd never do, not in this lifetime, without being begged.

The drive will take about three hours. The weather's unusually chilly. Emily tries the truck's heater, but it's broken. All she's got is her cross-country windbreaker and a T-shirt. The sun remains stubbornly behind the clouds the whole way. Still she feels an incredible sense of purpose, almost happiness. The single-mindedness of traveling, of being in charge. She counts signs and houses, red cars, green cars. She counts the number of songs a radio station will play in a row without commercials. She catches herself wondering what became of Leela, the journalist. She wants not to care but can't help it. She'd been so energized that night. The same feeling of being in charge, unafraid, almost no longer human, just force.

The truck loudly charges north and east. After two hours, the drive is now the longest Emily's ever driven, never mind gone so far alone. She checks her phone: nothing. At that moment Nick's at work. He worked the previous night, too. Alex and Meg had come over while he was out, the three of them talked into the night about the future.

She double-checks the directions she printed out.

When Emily arrives, the clinic is nothing like she imagined. No green meadows, no old buildings, no working farm. For no reason, she'd expected to find dozens of women in robes, hair tied up, happily working outdoors, hanging laundry, while they sang songs together. Instead it's like a nursing home, brown and yellow, sandwiched between a shopping development and woods. The sky's low and gray. She no longer feels so sure of herself. The blind yearning's gone. She pulls the truck slowly around a cul-de-sac. Vines crawl along a low brick wall. An old man watches her. He's got tubing up his nose, he doesn't move a muscle, he could be dead.

She keeps driving and avoids eye contact. She pulls back out into the road, then turns into the shopping complex next door, humping a rear wheel over the protruding curb when she takes the turn too hard.

She parks in front of an antiques shop. She wants to leave. A sign in the window says STORE CLOSING. For a long time she sits, squeezing her legs. She'd been mistaken, stupid to feel encouraged. How dumb can she be? Without looking, she counts the number of heater vents in the dashboard. She counts backward from twenty, and when she gets to zero she'll go. Then at seven the sun breaks through the clouds. She gets out and walks slowly around in circles in the sunlight to warm up. People must think she's a lunatic. Her stomach's raw. Her thoughts are still dark, competing with each other to collapse her spirits, reviewing everything said and done, covering years. What does she want? She gets in the truck again, locks the door. The light bounces off the glass and gets in her eyes, off the tiny starburst she made that time with the rock. She wonders . . .

Out of the truck bed she grabs a crowbar. No one's around. Without another thought she whacks the windshield. On the second try it cracks with a muffled booming sound. Two more times and it shatters with a smash, first into big pieces, then tiny shards.

She laughs out loud from shock.

Then she takes off her jacket. Yielding to an irresistible urge. She whacks the windshield from both sides, until it's totally gone. In the front of a store, a middle-aged man ducks down to peer out, to understand what's going on. Emily rings the crowbar around the window frame. Tiny diamonds spray across the hood and the dashboard and the front seat.

There was a night, early days, with her mother, when they'd gone for a winter hike and the snow was like diamonds. It's one of her favorite memories. She'll never forget it. Early December, after a two-day storm. Father thought they were crazy to go out. They'd put on boots and snow pants, wandered down the hill and out to the main road. They slipped through the dark, throwing snow, singing to themselves. Her mom came over at one point and hugged her. They stood there looking around at the quilted fields, all white. The valley below them was quiet, and it was just the two of them, forever, standing there while the world stood still.

She goes around to the back of the truck and sits in the bed. Her arms are hot and tired from swinging the crowbar. The exertion cleared her mind, the doubt, the anguish. *You're fine. You can do this.* Next to the shopping complex there's a culvert full of scrappy young trees, followed by a small hill. She stares for a moment, then gets down from the truck, walks over and climbs the hill, sidling her way up through the underbrush. It takes her ten minutes. From the top she's high enough above the treatment center that she can see down through a pair of skylights, into what looks like a recreation room. Small figures in a landscape. People who wave their arms up and down in a funny dance. It's mesmerizing, until her mind interrupts when she recognizes a woman and feels a pang in her heart. Raising one hand, lowering another. Swinging her arms like everyone else, moving at a speed almost too slow to describe as motion, as something other than robotic.

Emily hurries down the other side of the hill. Sweating, filled with nervousness. The old man is gone. Inside the front doors is a lobby, a desk, a tall potted houseplant with Mardi Gras beads strung in its branches. No one there, just a bell and a small sign, PLEASE RING FOR ASSISTANCE.

And though the tiny lobby's walled with frosted glass, she can see straight into other rooms. The room where the dancers face away from her, in sweatpants, T-shirts. A few people in the main room see her and stare at her presence, muscles tensed. She's never felt so alone. At that moment the dancers lean backward, hands raised, one hand facing out like a stop sign, the other hand beckoning, as if to fan the air. She wants to run. Instead, she taps the bell.

The sound is shattering. Half the dancers turn to look. Her mother turns. Recognition. Her face cracks in several places. She looks around as if searching for permission from someone, then hurries into the lobby.

"What are you doing here?"

"I don't know," Emily says. "I don't know."

"Let's go to my room."

Her mom pulls her away by the hand, then fear seizes her into stopping.

"Is he here?"

"It's just me," Emily says. Her chest tightens. Her heart caves.

"Where is he? I swear to god—"

"Mom, I promise, he's not here."

"I'm not going home," her mother stutters, her voice cracking into harmony. "Am I going home?"

"Not if you don't want to."

But she can't do it any longer. She found what she woke up craving. She breaks, completely, and her mother's face softens in recognition. She wraps her arms around Emily and holds her up in place.

∎

Dear Nick,

I am writing to you from an airplane, so this envelope will likely have a California postmark, where I'm visiting my daughter, as we spoke about. From there I'll return to New Jersey, most likely, and resume my normal life, so if you ever want to reach me you can do so at the address that I left with Ms. Brenner.

The reason I'm writing is because I want to say that I know as well as anybody that nothing's been easy for you lately. Everything gets turned inside out during a crime and a trial and people's emotions can get intense, as you well know. People react under pressure in ways you don't expect. You figure out who your real friends are, as the saying goes. So, I want you to know that I'm one of those friends.

Nick, I hope you heard me say that you are in no way responsible for what happened to the Ashburns. One man committed those crimes, no one else, and now he's gone, as I imagine you know by now, so you should strive to put this all behind you.

Also, I guess one of the reasons I'm writing is because I formed a sort of connection with you, which I would consider to be a friendship, even if it's only on my part. I can be sometimes a pretty emotional person, and I don't know if that's a good or bad thing, it's just how I'm wired. But I do feel compelled by some recent events in my life to share this bond with you and what I think it means, because I haven't ever been good about sharing those feelings when I should.

I guess in a way I see myself in you. I bet that sounds strange. But it's another reason why I'm writing. There were moments in our time together when I saw looks on your face that were looks I recognized from the mirror, to be honest. Which made me empathize with your situation. I probably would have done many of the same things you did had I been in your position, at your age.

As I said, by now you'll likely be aware of the news regarding Emily's father. I only heard last night. Considering the level of security I saw in their office, I can't say I am shocked he got away with it. In any case, I don't know if you'll ever have the closure you seek, but I'll just say that if at some point you can find something to pity or forgive about him, then believe me it will help you let go of all the pain sooner than later. Even if that sounds crazy or offensive considering everything that has happened.

Nick, you are a good and honorable person. Not a lot has been easy for you. The conversation we had in my hotel room, trust that I will keep my side of the bargain. And if I can ever provide any assistance going forward, please reach out.

Oddly enough an idea occurred to me on the airplane this afternoon, which you'll probably think is nuts, but if you ever think about a "career" I'd suggest that you consider law enforcement. You probably didn't see that coming, did you? There's bad news out there about police officers, and *there are different kinds of cops, and we have problems, big problems. But you'd be surprised how many men and women who uphold the law started out being familiar with its other side. Anyway, we always need all the good guys we can get, and it's not boring to say the least. So I thought it might appeal to you.*

Whatever you choose to do next with your life, and whether or not I hear from you ever again, please know that you've got a friend in an old man, and I wish you lots of happiness and good luck and all the best for your future.

You have my admiration.

Sincerely yours,

Martin Krug

■

Nick extracts the mail from the mailbox and reenters the living room. Suzanne's asleep on the couch. An hour earlier he'd picked her up from an AA meeting, number five in three days. She was jittery, upset, and angry. She smoked the whole drive. Then as soon as she got inside the house, her nerves wore out, exhaustion kicked in, and she fell asleep on the couch.

He dumps the mail pile on the piano. Mostly it's junk-mail flyers, two bills demanding payment. A clothing catalog slides off the piano and out tumbles an envelope addressed to him in square block letters. No return address. Postmark: Burbank, California. He's breaking the seal when his phone rings.

"I need to see you," Emily says urgently.

"Where are you?"

"I'm at Little Horse."

"What's going on?"

"I just need to see you. Can you come?"

"Are you okay?"

"It's not like that, I promise."

He drops the envelope and heads out the door. It's gotta be her dad. They haven't spoken about it yet. She must have been among the first to hear, but in how much detail? Brenner had told him over the phone that morning, how the sheriff had gotten ahold of a plastic bag and tied it off with a piece of bed fitting. Dead when they found him. There was more: images found on his laptop, downloaded from websites known to the police, that catered to pedophiles. Nick didn't know how to feel about it beyond sickened. He's glad the guy's dead. But for Emily it had to be way more complicated. He'd called her when he heard. She hadn't answered. They hadn't spoken all day.

By the time he reaches the beach, he's sweating. The distant water's flat. The parking lot's empty except for somebody's abandoned trailer, and then her, standing beside her truck. Which is missing the windshield for some reason.

He already hates the look on her face.

She climbs into the Explorer. She's dressed just like the girl who smiled at him in a restaurant, back in the day. But something's wrong. She's been crying. Instantly, he knows what's going to happen next.

"I really don't want to do this," she says.

"What is it?"

He was right. He pulls away, stunned.

"I'm so sorry," she says calmly.

"You're breaking up with me."

She doesn't respond. His heart thumps.

"You are. Holy shit."

"I'm leaving town," she says.

"What?"

"This weekend."

"What?!"

"I'm so sorry."

"Wait a second. That's bullshit. What does that even mean?"

"I'm going with Alex and Meg," she says. "To Oregon."

"To Oregon?"

He laughs, it's too crazy. What the hell is happening?

"You're kidding right now. This is all some practical joke."

"Nick, I'm sorry."

"You're serious. I can't believe this."

"Look at us. Look what happened to us. It destroyed everything," she says. "You know that."

He says, hysterically, "I went to jail for you."

She gasps.

"What did you say?"

He clutches his forehead. "What is happening right now? What are you even talking about? Why are you doing this to us?"

"I can't stay," she says after a long silence. "I can't be around this place."

"Which includes me."

"That's not what I meant."

"What about our plans? How come I'm not included? Did you think to talk to me about any of this?"

He can't bear to make eye contact with her. The ocean's calm through the windshield, endlessly murmuring.

"I'm a hundred percent serious," he says. "About us."

"What about the trial? What about your mom?"

"Forget my mom. What about your mom?"

"She's staying in Maine. I talked to a lawyer."

He bursts out laughing. "Whose lawyer? My lawyer?"

"The insurance company's taking care of it. So she can stay."

His body is rigid with anger, to hear how much she's thought out. It means the end is certain. Maybe she met somebody else, another guy. He can't get his mind to slow down.

"You know what? This is *his* fault, okay? Even now your dad's messing with us."

She won't even look at him. She tricked him, she changed when he wasn't looking. He's about to say, *You can't do this to me.* Except it hits him: she can.

"I'm making a choice," she says.

"You're not even making sense. You should hear yourself," he says hurriedly. He starts the car, puts the gear into reverse. "Let's get out of here."

"Nick," she says, "turn off the car."

After a second, he does.

"I'm so sorry," she says.

"I can fix this. I can fix this. Just tell me what I did."

"You didn't do anything."

"I hate this so much."

"I know, I love you."

"Then why are you doing this?" He gags, he's almost sick. She reaches across the console to clutch him. All his angry pride wants to do is kick her out and feed the flames, but he lets her lie there across his back.

And his body won't allow him to do anything but stay hunched over like that for another five minutes. Sinking deeper and deeper into memories while she talks, he talks, they cry together. She finally goes, he's obliged to acknowledge. With no signs of encouragement. The sound of the door when she closes it echoes sharply, penetrates all the way down to where he lies crooked at the bottom of his consciousness.

Later, late in the evening, in the house he shares with his mother, Nick Toussaint Jr. will glimpse at himself in the bathroom mirror and think in so many words, *The mind has needs you can't even begin to guess.* When he'd been sitting there, with all that pain, still his mind wouldn't do a single thing except be paralyzed, remembering. He was back in the hospital with his leg again, with the pain, when he couldn't run away from the retrospections. She'd said she loved him, she gave him the poignant certainty he craved. And they're still breaking up, damn their feelings. It will take years before he understands how two such facts can coexist. Instead they bear him deeply into his memory on two tracks, an empty mining cart tumbling down into a mine shaft, picking up speed.

For the moment, that night, for weeks and months to come, he will consider and reconsider every hope, every happiness fixed in his mind, all the ways she influenced and encouraged him and everything that he loved about her, that he lost. But first he needs to sit there and burn, miserable, sweaty, and cold.

■

Dear Nick,

I'm writing from my new room. From my bedroom window I look into the yard behind our building. In the morning it was gray and chilly and the same for the afternoon. People say it's like that here a lot but it's actually been sunny for the past week. There's a chicken coop I can see, it belongs to the people who live downstairs. They're pretty snobby actually. Meg says they think we're on welfare.

There are four big gray trees, and a yard full of weeds, and an old metal fence between us and the neighbor. We live in the northwest part of the city. I don't know the city yet so I'm not sure where we are compared to everything else. I don't know if you know this, but Portland is on a river. The city's really big. It's pretty different from Claymore. There are so many people first of all. And it's so noisy sometimes, too, all the cars and buses and the people. There's a whole house of college kids who live two doors down the street and play in a band. They practice at night and we can hear them in the kitchen. Alex already said hi to the girl who plays drums.

Alex loves college. They're letting her live off campus. It's a special exemption. We still don't see her a lot. Mostly it's just me and Meg unpacking stuff and trying to get settled in the apartment. I didn't bring much, mostly clothes. Registering for school has been really tough. Because of what happened they're sort of letting me go through it slowly. Meg's handling all of the paperwork. She does all the phone calls for the New Hampshire stuff. She said she wants me to start seeing a therapist. She's changed a lot, you'd be surprised. We talk about pretty much everything. I think she thinks of me as some kind of half sister, half daughter. She took me out for lunch yesterday. We went out for pizza. It was across the street from the biggest bookstore I've ever seen. Honestly I don't mind how Meg's acting, I kind of like it. I'm glad to be taken care of, I guess.

There are so many people, so many different people. I'm really nervous about starting in a new school. Meeting new people and all of them knowing whatever they think they know about me. The last six months already feel like a blur. Isn't that weird? Is it true for you, too? Sometimes I wish I could be a robot who was built yesterday and just start out brand-new. Actually I'm thinking pretty strongly of not going to school at all. I want to see if I can be homeschooled. That was Meg's idea. We got a book from the bookstore about it. Can you picture her as a teacher? She's thinking about going back to school, to get her teaching certificate. She's been dancing in a club to make money, but she's cutting back on her hours.

God you must be so bored by now. I'm sure you're not reading this letter anyway. You probably threw it away without even opening the envelope. I wouldn't blame you. I'd do the same thing in your position. Nick, I think about you all the time. About you and us and about everything that happened. I wake up thinking about it. I have nightmares. I worry sometimes I'm damaged forever, do you know what I mean? I tell myself I'm not. Maybe I should see someone, I don't know.

By the way I got an email yesterday from Leela, the reporter. She got a job at a magazine in New York. She said she tried to write an article about us, but they didn't like it. I guess I'm glad about that. I just want the past to be the past.

None of that's why I'm writing you right now. I'm writing because for weeks I've been thinking about us. One thing I told Meg yesterday is that you were the first person I ever really loved, <u>that I got to love</u>. Not the way I love Meg or Alex, or how I feel about my mom. With you I wasn't a friend, I wasn't a kid. I got to be myself. And you gave me that.

All my life I've felt things so much more intensely than I can put into words. When we were together, all those feelings got channeled into one thing. It was almost too intense. It probably was, with everything else going on. Something had to break. The last time we saw each other, I was already gone, I wasn't there at all. I couldn't be anything to you anymore, not like we were, does that make sense? I hope so.

I guess I've started to feel like I'm returning to myself. We'll see how I am in a couple months, or who I am. Listen to me ramble on. You're such an amazing person, Nick, an amazing boy, an amazing man. You're going to do incredible things with your life. If you write back to me, I'd love to hear from you, how you're doing, how Suzanne is doing. I just want you to know that no matter everything else, I still love you, I'll probably always love you. Loving you made me a person for the first time in my life.

I'm scared now, I'm really scared. But I'm less fragile than I used to be.

Whoever I am, whoever I'm becoming, a lot of that is thanks to a gift you gave me. And I'm thankful for that. Forever and ever.

Love,

Emily

ACKNOWLEDGMENTS

I am grateful to many people for their assistance with this book. In particular, in alphabetical order, Nikkitha Bakshani, Nora Barlow, Maya Binyam, Nic Brown, "Laurence" Bonaparte, Anthony Doerr, Leah Finnegan, Roxane Gay, Amelia Gray, Jamie Knowles, Joshua Knowles, Sean McDonald, PJ Mark, Sherri Murrell, the OCSC Writers Association, Daniel Riley, Nozlee Samadzadeh, Andrew Schopler, Marya Spence, Leslie Stetter, Andrew Winders, and Andrew Womack.

This book was written in many places over the course of six years. For their great support I thank the MacDowell Colony, the Norway Historical Society, the Legruder Foundation, and the Miami Writers Institute. Thanks also to my students (especially Cruickshank and Jones), and those who talked to me under more anonymous circumstances, particularly the Emilys, Leelas, and Martins of this world. Much appreciation also goes to Sarita Varma and everyone at Farrar, Straus and Giroux.

Most of all, for everything, Rachel Knowles.